Intimate
Betrayal

Dear Reader,

Thank you for picking up *Intimate Betrayal.* This sexy, suspenseful novel was the first of three of my novels to be made into a TV movie. The lead roles were portrayed by actors Monica Calhoun and Khalil Kain, who brought the characters Reese Delaware and Maxwell Knight to life. The heat between these lovers sizzles from their very first meeting. It's one of the reasons I'm so glad that Harlequin has reissued *Intimate Betrayal,* so that even more readers can enjoy this sexy couple.

If this is your second time reading this novel *or* if it's the first, I hope you love each and every twist and turn, and be sure to keep a glass of cold water nearby!

Happy reading,

Donna

Intimate *Betrayal*

DONNA HILL

ARABESQUE®

Recycling programs
for this product may
not exist in your area.

INTIMATE BETRAYAL

ISBN-13: 978-0-373-53442-5

First published by Kensington Publishing Corp in 1997

Copyright © 2011 by Donna Hill

www.kimanipress.com

Printed in U.S.A.

To all my wonderful readers who have faithfully kept me in print for 21 years! You all are awesome.

Donna

Prologue

Methodically, he paced the spacious confines of his posh mid-town Manhattan office, as stealthily as a caged black panther. His movements were smooth, controlled, precise—as was every aspect of his life.

One large hand was hidden in the pocket of his imported navy blue slacks, the other absently caressing the silken hairs of his ebony mustache.

On the surface, it appeared that Maxwell Knight was simply contemplating another brilliant computer innovation. That was on the surface. Beneath the inscrutable facade, turmoil and a sense of his life spinning out of control built steadily within him, growing in intensity.

His usually smooth, bronze-toned brow was furrowed in a maze of concentration. The last half hour of verbal volleyball with his Board of Directors had his sharply honed six-foot-three-inch frame coiled with tension—ready to spring at the slightest provocation.

He turned toward the floor-to-ceiling window, the expanse of the New York skyline spread out before him. From the ninety-fifth floor, Maxwell usually felt on top of the world, able to conquer anything or anyone. This unprecedented sense of futility over his own destiny filled him with an emotion he could not grasp.

At thirty-three, he had accomplished what many only dreamed of—read about—wished for. The existence of M.K. Enterprises—his self-named corporation—and his wizardry with computer programming had catapulted him into the limelight, the one place he had no desire to be. He guarded his privacy with a voracious tenacity. If anyone wanted to know about the M.K. behind M.K. Enterprises, they could read about it in the company's annual report, he felt. There was no reason to interview him. No reason to delve into his life— open doors that were best kept closed. But his development of the computer chip that was touted to revolutionize the speed of computer processing had set off a series of events that were no longer stoppable.

The Board had voted unanimously to take the company public, and he had agreed. But in order to make M.K.'s entry into the stock market an unquestionable success, they had also voted—against his wishes—to give the public what they'd craved for more than five years, an in-depth interview with Maxwell Knight, boy wonder.

His firm, smooth jaw clenched as he drew a deep contemplative breath. Something other than notoriety prompted the actions of the Board. They'd never given a damn in the past whether or not the company made headlines. These months prior to their launch into the market were crucial and best kept secret. Now was not the time to have some reporter following him around. If word leaked out, there would be hell to pay. Turning away from the window, his dark, almond-shaped eyes that curved slightly upward at the tips—the single trait that hinted at his mixed heritage—gazed upon the magazine he'd tossed on his desk.

Looking at it now, his misgivings, no matter how irrational, ignited anew. Phillip Hart, the publisher of *Visions Magazine,* had hounded him for months to give them the exclusive rights to an interview. Until today, Maxwell had been able to deny him.

The face of Barack Obama stared back at him from the cover. Yes, it was true that *Visions* had a stellar reputation in the industry. It was also true that it staked that reputation on getting beyond the surface of its subjects. Some of the biggest names in the journalism industry had written for *Visions*. That wasn't the issue for Maxwell. The issue was, he wasn't sure he wanted to find out what they might uncover.

Chicago

Reese Delaware was the type of woman who could charm a zebra right out of its stripes. Her powers of persuasion bordered on being lethal in a totally seductive way. She knew it and used her charm, wit and feminine wiles as easily as she breathed. Today was no exception. She was determined to convince the bull-headed editor of *Visions Magazine* that she could handle the interview of a lifetime even if it turned into another two hours of tug-of-war.

Many before her had tried and failed to get an exclusive with Maxwell Knight. Reese had no delusions of being among that group.

"Mr. Hart," Reese crooned in her distinctly throaty voice, tipped with southern charm. "If I say I can do something—I can." She gave him a long, slow look from startling amber eyes. Inwardly, she smiled as she watched the flush of crimson rise from his neck and mottle his face. She recrossed her long milk-chocolate legs.

Phillip Hart cleared his throat. He'd bumped heads with hundreds of hungry journalists over the years. He had yet to meet one who could compare with Reese Delaware. There was something that drove her, almost possessed her, to squeeze out every imaginable detail in a story. He'd already made up his mind to give her this assignment, but he couldn't resist the opportunity to see her use her "skills" to convince him.

"How soon can you be ready to leave for New York?" he asked in monotone, struggling to quell his rising libido.

"As soon as I can pack," she replied with a calm shrug that belied the rush of adrenaline that pumped through her veins.

Phillip leaned back in his overstuffed leather chair and peered at her from beneath puffy eyelids. He pursed his thin pink lips. "You may just be the person to get this job done right, Ms. Delaware." He threaded his fingers together. "You have sixty days to get this interview completed and on my desk, with pictures and quotes from the man himself and any and everybody who knows him," he added, pointing a stubby, cigarette-stained finger at her.

Reese felt like leaping out of her seat and throwing her arms around Phillip Hart's fat neck. However, she remained outwardly nonplussed, as if the whole discussion couldn't have gone any differently.

"You'll have your story, Mr. Hart," she said, that slow smile easing across her mouth. "And it'll be the best piece of work you've ever read."

Chapter 1

Maxwell sat behind his desk, his fingers steepled in front of him, his heavily lashed eyes almost closed as he spoke to his secretary, Carmen Valez.

"Have the office managers in the Los Angeles office and in Tokyo be prepared for our arrival," he instructed in his characteristically soft-spoken modulation.

His heavy baritone tended to sound threatening even in the most innocent of circumstances, Carmen recalled, thinking back to the early years of working with Maxwell. Over the years, he'd trained himself to speak in calm, measured tones, in a pitch so sensual and alluring that his voice seemed to compel the listener to draw closer and do his bidding. It bordered on hypnotic. But just as it could be a soothing balm, it could be as crushing as the blows he'd mastered as a ninth-degree black belt. Carmen was always grateful that his wrath had never been directed at her.

She'd been with Maxwell since he opened the doors of

M.K. Enterprises, five years earlier. They'd worked side by side every day for those five years, and sometimes she felt she knew him no better today than she did when she walked in the door. Whatever Maxwell thought or felt about anything that wasn't job related, he kept to himself. It was rare that he allowed the man inside to show through. She felt privileged to have been the recipient of his inner thoughts on those rare occasions. That didn't make him unpleasant to work with. On the contrary, he was probably one of the most charming and certainly the most gorgeous man she'd ever worked for. But he never let anyone get beyond the invisible wall he'd erected around himself. She felt sorry for the poor soul assigned to write the article about the enigmatic Maxwell Knight.

"When should I expect the reporter, Maxwell?"

For a fraction of a second, a shadow seemed to pass across his exotic bronzed features. "The Board received a fax this morning stating that a Reese Delaware would be arriving this afternoon," he replied in a turned-off tone.

"Should I make flight arrangements for Mr. Delaware as well, since you'll be traveling together?"

"I'm sure Mr. Delaware can make his own arrangements. But should he need some assistance, see what you can do."

"No problem." She gazed at him and his eyes met hers. "It's going to be fine," she said softly. "Don't worry so much."

He waved off her well-meant sentiment. "You know how I feel about this whole business, Carmen. This reporter is going to be a royal pain in the ass, and I'm the one stuck with having to squire him around." He clenched his jaw in frustration. "Reporters have been the bane of my existence for as long as I can remember. I prefer to stay as far away from those vultures as possible."

Carmen pressed her lips together to suppress a smile. "At least try to be pleasant."

Maxwell grumbled something unintelligible deep in his throat.

"Anything else?"

"If you would just check and make sure that the house in San Diego is taken care of and fully stocked, I'd appreciate that. And make whatever accommodations are necessary for the trip to Tokyo."

"I'll take care of it right away, and then I'm off to lunch." Carmen rose to leave.

Slowly Maxwell lowered his hands and placed them on the table, the first time he'd moved since Carmen entered the room. He smiled. "Thank you, Carmen. I don't know what I'd do without you."

"Neither do I," she teased, closing the door gently behind her.

Pushing away from the desk, Maxwell stood. What was he so concerned about? he chastised himself. The reporter was interested in how a seemingly ordinary kid from Maryland had become the leading computer expert in the world, beating out the Microsoft giant by mere months in the development of the ultra-fast processing chip. He was the first black to reach the heights that he'd achieved in the industry. As a result, he continued to be a prime target for newshounds who wanted the "inside story." What made Maxwell Knight tick?

He sighed, resigning himself to the fact that there wasn't much he could do about the situation. However, he would not allow access to his private life. He would control the direction of the interview.

He recrossed the highly polished wood floors and around the partition to where his drafting table rested. Slipping out of his taupe jacket, he hung it on the back of the chair and sat down, rolling up one sleeve and then the other. He slid the magnifying lens over the grids on the paper and began to work. Within moments he was immersed in what he loved best, developing computer chip circuits.

The persistent buzzing on his intercom finally jarred him away from his work. Frowning, he checked his watch. "Damn." He'd been sitting at his desk for three hours straight. In one smooth motion, he hopped down from the stool and reached for the phone that hung on the wall behind him.

"Yes, Carmen."

"Ah, the reporter from *Visions Magazine* is here." Carmen looked across to where Reese Delaware sat.

Maxwell clenched his jaw and drew a deep breath. "Send him in," he bit out, snatching his finger away from the intercom button.

"But it's not a…" Carmen's response was lost on him. She turned toward Reese, her smile wavering as she shrugged in apology. "He's really quite nice," she offered.

Reese picked up her heavy briefcase and crossed the space that separated her from Carmen. She stood in front of Carmen's desk. Reese's right eyebrow rose speculatively. "He thinks I'm a man," she stated more than asked, just the barest hint of amusement lacing her husky voice.

Carmen looked up at the striking woman, a tone of conspiracy in her response, "It appears so."

Reese's mouth curved into a grin. "May I go inside now?"

"Of course." Carmen stood up. "Follow me, Ms. Delaware. Mr. Knight's office is right down this corridor. I'm Carmen Valez, executive assistant in charge of East Coast operations and Mr. Knight's personal assistant. My desk is back there also, I'm just covering for lunch." They proceeded down the hall until they reached twin glass doors. Carmen placed her palm on the scanner and the doors slid open. Reese's eyes widened in awe. She'd only seen that done on television and in the movies.

She dutifully followed Carmen down the acoustically sound-treated, semi-hushed hall. Futuristic offices and security cubicles to the left and right were closed off from the hallway traffic by huge Plexiglas panels. Behind these smoke-tinted panels, high-tech equipment, most of which she couldn't even give a name to, occupied much of the space, expelling information to white-coated technicians and to others who looked no different from the video-game junkies who haunted the arcades.

What a group of nerds, she mused. She wondered if the mysterious Maxwell Knight was half as uninteresting.

Carmen stopped at the security panel and repeated the previous process. Upon entering the next corridor they turned left and Reese was instantly aware of the change in decor. There were no more glass walls. Heavy wood doors with gold-plated name tags had taken their place. Here was the suite of executive offices that ran M.K. Enterprises. "We call this the Black Forest because of all this oak," jibed Carmen.

She slowed, then stopped in front of an intricately carved door. She tapped once and turned the knob. Stepping aside she opened the door for Reese to enter.

Maxwell wasn't rude by nature, but this whole interview business had put him in a foul mood. He hadn't put on his jacket and didn't even bother to look up from his drafting table when the door opened.

"Have a seat, I'll be with you in a minute," he said with all the civility he could summon.

Reese's eyes swept across the room to locate the southern preacher's voice that seemed to emanate from the depths of a gospel standard.

Maxwell's heightened senses, ever alert, caught the subtle, yet potent whiff of her African Musk body oil before she'd stepped completely across the threshold. Every muscle in his body tensed, as if sensing imminent danger.

He came from around the dividing wall and their worlds collided. Reese Delaware was not a man by any means. The reality slammed against his invisible wall, causing tiny fissures in the structure.

Reese stepped farther into the room, noting the infinitesimal look of surprise that widened the irises of his unusual eyes. *This was no nerd.* She used her warm, slow smile as a beacon, allowing it to cut a path directly to his outstretched hand.

"Reese Delaware," she announced in a tone that seemed to stroke the tightened muscles of his body.

Husky, throaty, smoky, sultry. Her voice was all that and more. No. This definitely would not work.

"Ms. Delaware," he responded, his body virtually vibrating from the pressure of her slender hand in his. She was the first to pull away.

"I'm sorry you came all this way for nothing." He paused to gauge her reaction, and much to his chagrin he saw nothing.

She shot him a steady look from behind luminous amber eyes that seemed to whisper, "come to me."

He cleared his throat, his own hot stare meeting hers. "I'm sure that everything there is to know about my company can be gleaned from our annual reports."

Reese placed her briefcase at her feet, looked up at him from beneath heavy black lashes, then took a seat opposite his desk. With a deliberance that bordered on an "X" rating, she crossed her long legs. Her short, canary yellow skirt barely hit her mid-thigh. Max tore his gaze away.

"Let's get right to the point," she began, her low voice threading its way through his bloodstream. "You don't want me here. You know it and I know it. I don't have a problem with that, because I have a job to do, one which I take just as seriously as I'm sure you take yours. I intend to get my job done,' she added, emphasizing each word with an almost musical cadence. "So—" she exhaled a long breath "—we can do this the easy way or we can do it the ugly way." She flashed him a brilliant "Colgate" smile.

Damnit, he liked her. When was the last time that anyone, least of all a woman, told him just where to get off? However, these shaky emotions could be his undoing—and that couldn't happen. *Think with the head on top of your neck, buddy,* he warned himself.

"And not to belabor the subject," she continued, "but I'm not the least bit interested in your company, Mr. Knight." She paused for effect. "I'm interested in *you.*"

Maxwell gave her a long, hard look. "Humph," he chuckled. "You seem pretty sure of yourself, Ms. Delaware."

"Call me Reese, since we'll be working so closely together. And yes, I am very sure of myself. I have to be in this business—*Max.*" She saw the nerve jump beneath his right eye and mentally ticked off a point for herself. She couldn't afford to let her guard down for a minute. If he got the slightest inclination that he could railroad her, or intimidate her, this whole trip would be for nothing, just as he'd said. She had no intention of returning the ten-thousand-dollar advance. The money had been a lifesaver. Had it not been for the windfall, she'd probably be looking for someplace else to live. At least her apartment was secure for the time being. If only the other holes in her life could be filled as easily.

Maxwell turned away from her, took a seat behind his desk and proceeded to review the stack of documents in front of him. He didn't bother to look up when he next spoke. "I hope, *Reese,* that you're as talented at making yourself invisible as you claim you are at your job." He signed a document, put it to the side and continued, "I don't want to be hovered over, interrupted when I'm designing, or followed to the men's room."

She bit down on the inside of her lip to keep from laughing.

Suddenly he looked up, and she was assaulted once again by the allure of his eyes. She swallowed, cocked a brow and met his gaze head on.

"I was informed," he continued in that voice that could make a good girl do wicked things, "by the Board that you'd be with me for the next two months."

"I have that long to complete my story and hand it in," she corrected. "I'm sure I'll finish before then so that we can get out of each other's way as soon as possible."

The tiny corner of his mouth lifted, indicating the bare beginnings of a smile. "I hope you have your passport in order. After leaving the Los Angeles offices, I'll be heading to Tokyo."

"I'm aware of that. I was given your itinerary. Actually, I'm looking forward to the next six weeks." She smiled that slow, burning smile again and he felt his insides begin to smolder.

Maxwell stood and shoved his hands into his pants pockets, partly in dismissal, but mostly because he didn't know how his body would react if he touched her again.

Her eyes challenged his. She straightened her shoulders. "What time do you come in?"

Even a simple question sounded suggestive coming out of that mouth of hers, Maxwell thought, annoyed.

"I'm in the office by eight."

"Then I guess that's when we'll see each other again." She bent to retrieve her briefcase. "It was a pleasure to finally meet you Max. I'm sure we'll get along just fine."

"Take the elevator directly to your right," Maxwell

instructed, ignoring the pseudo-friendly overture. "Security on board will see you out."

Without another word, she turned and strolled out of the office, her hips swaying to a slow, erotic beat that only she could hear.

Alone now in his office, Maxwell could hear the rapid beating of his heart, feel the throb that pulsed between his muscular thighs, smell the scent of her that had settled over him like morning dew. This isn't going to work, he realized, and the sooner that was understood the better. Maxwell strode across the room, slung his hand into his pants pockets and stood in front of the window. He'd find out how much her advance was and write a check to whomever. The quicker Reese Delaware was out of his way and his life, the better for everyone.

For several seconds, unobserved, Reese stood on the opposite side of Maxwell's door, concentrating on breathing and getting her legs to stop trembling. Briefly she shut her eyes, and took a deep, calming breath.

That was more than just animal magnetism in there, Reese realized as she pushed the button for the elevator. Whatever thing that connected them and virtually lit up the room with electricity was something so powerful, it frightened her with its force.

Sure, she'd been turned on by men before and relished the thrill of watching them when she played "the game." This was no game—and whatever it was, she couldn't let it interfere with what she'd come to do. She would not. Getting at the truth was what drove her. It was what woke her up in the morning. If she couldn't find it or have it in her own life—she'd be damned if she wouldn't uncover it in everyone else's.

The elevator slowly descended. Reese exited and strolled

out into the sprawling complex of the Plaza. For now, she would put thoughts of Maxwell Knight aside. She'd deal with him tomorrow. What she needed was a good night's sleep so that she'd be sharp enough to duel with him toe to toe.

But sleep was not to come. For the first time in three years, the nightmares began again.

Chapter 2

The following morning, Reese took special care in preparing for what she knew would be a day of confrontation.

She'd barely slept two hours the entire night. She'd tossed, turned, leaped up in a sweat, dozed and began the process again.

Her hands were shaking when she attempted to stroke her lashes with mascara. "Must be those five cups of coffee you drank in less than an hour," she muttered to her reflection, attempting to smile.

Pressing her lips together, she shut her eyes and hung her head, bracing herself with her palms against the cool white porcelain sink. Her head pounded.

It had been three years since she'd had the nightmares. The headaches had all but disappeared. She no longer had to take the prescription medication for the pain; over-the-counter painkillers worked just fine. Until last night. The pain had gotten so intense, she'd had to call her physician in Chicago to phone in a prescription to the all-night drugstore.

She tasted salt in the corner of her mouth. She opened her eyes to see the tears slide slowly down her cheeks. "Not again," she whispered. "Please not again."

Maxwell knotted his silk tie and clipped it to his blue pin-striped shirt with a gold clasp bearing his initials: MJK. He took a final look in the mirror, his reflection bringing to the forefront his mixed ancestry. He peered a bit closer and brushed his finger across his left eyebrow where a martial arts mishap had left its mark.

He breathed heavily and shrugged into his jacket. The look of the corporate executive never suited him, but he also realized that it was all part of the facade. Although he always felt more comfortable in jeans, sneakers, and a sweatshirt, he'd always done what was necessary to fit in. Thinking that perhaps by doing so, he'd avoid the extra looks, the questions that had dogged him most of his life.

Maxwell was never ashamed of his mixed Japanese and African-American heritage. For the most part, his exotic looks acted as a magnet, drawing people to him. It was the questions, raised eyebrows, and murmurs of feigned understanding that bugged him the most. He couldn't answer the questions about his natural mother. He never knew her. According to James Knight, his father, his mother Suki had been killed in Japan shortly after his birth. James had married his stepmother, Claudia, some months later. And since Maxwell could not answer the questions about his Japanese mother, he'd created a picture of her to assuage the missing link of his life.

Over time, he'd gradually built up a wall around himself, keeping people and questions at bay. Yet there was a part of him that believed there was more to the story than his father cared to divulge.

He shook his head, scattering his ruminating. Now was not the time to indulge in things he could not change. So he continued to walk the line between being black and being Japanese, hoping that one day the two worlds would somehow meld into one.

Leaving his bedroom, he collected his keys and briefcase and walked out into the warm, early summer morning to face his day and the probing of Reese Delaware, a day he'd spent years trying to avoid.

Reese was already seated in the reception area when he got off the elevator. She was so engrossed in typing something onto her laptop computer, she didn't even look up, apparently unaware of his arrival. For a moment, he was glad to see her in her bright lime green linen suit. She wore her hair differently, he noted. Her shoulder-length tresses were pulled away from her face and neck and piled on top of her head in a tumble of jet black curls.

Then, just as quickly as the moment of joy had filled him, it was replaced with the realization that her only purpose was to dig into his life. His smooth brow creased into a frown. Loudly, he cleared his throat. Her head snapped up. Their eyes connected and the charge popped back and forth between them.

"Good morning. Glad to see you're an early riser," he greeted. He turned abruptly and strode down the hall to his office, his gait smooth and measured.

Reese took an exasperated breath and snapped her laptop shut. Collecting her things from the seat next to her, she rose and followed him down the corridor to his office. "Why did you come in through the peon entrance? You do have a private elevator," Reese queried in a taunting note, quickening her pace.

Maxwell pressed his palm on the scanner and stepped

beyond the opened doors. "I'm in the habit of taking a quick run through of my facilities before I settle in for the day, if you must know, Ms. Delaware," he grumbled in a caustic tone. He opened the door to his office.

"I have a very full day today, Ms. Delaware."

"Are we back to formalities so soon?" she retorted, closing the door behind her.

He turned toward her, and his heart slammed hard against his chest. "Habit," he offered, knowing that his real reason was the threat of intimacy. Calling her by her first name personalized her, softened her, took her from being a prying journalist to a breathtaking woman. A situation he had no intention of indulging.

Reese shrugged. "Suit yourself, Max." Meandering across the room, she took real note of her milieu. Maxwell Knight surrounded himself with an eclectic blend of Asian and African art.

His desk was of black lacquer, embossed with intricate jade and gold carvings along its edges. To the far left was a low wooden table surrounded by four pillows covered in brilliant African prints of oranges, golds and bronzes. Above the arrangement, hanging on the wall were two frightening looking swords, with black and gold handles and blades crafted from the finest steel. They glistened menacingly in the sunlight. On the opposite wall, beyond the partition that housed his drafting table, was an enormous wall unit of black lacquer and glass that encased an array of hand-carved statues and artifacts, including a set of African counting sticks. And then there was the bookcase that contained volume upon volume of every imaginable type of literature. Yes, Maxwell Knight was a very interesting man indeed, but it would take all of her skills and whatever else she needed to crack through the veneer he'd painted over himself.

"What's on our agenda?" She took a seat, and pulled a notepad from her briefcase.

"I have a meeting with the R & D techs—the Research and Development technicians," he corrected, noting the puzzled look on her exquisite face, "at ten."

"Will you be discussing the computer chip?"

"Yes, it's part of the meeting," he answered tersely, avoiding her steady amber gaze.

Reese nodded and made a note. "Will it be a problem if I bring a tape recorder into the meeting?"

Maxwell's head snapped in her direction. "I don't recall inviting you, nor do I recall your asking to attend."

"Consider it asked," she tossed back, glaring at him.

"Fine," he conceded on a growl deep in his throat. "But tape recording is out of the question and if I ask you to leave the room, I expect that you will—without a problem."

She flashed a coy smile. "Do I appear to be the type of woman to cause problems?" Languorously she crossed her long legs.

Yes, his mind screamed, and you know it. "I really wouldn't know that, Ms. Delaware, now would I?"

"Well, Max, we'll just have to find out, now won't we? In the meantime," she continued, not giving him a chance to recover, "I'd like to get started with some background information." She leaned down and reached into her bag to retrieve her recorder, and in doing so, gave Max a brief glimpse of the half-moons that strained against the fabric of her V-cut jacket.

He clenched his jaw and turned away.

Reese straightened and placed the recorder on the desk that separated them. Leaning slightly forward, she depressed the record button.

"I always find it best if the subjects ignore the machine and just talk as thoughts come to them." She took a breath.

"Why don't we start from the present and work our way backward. I think I'd like to open the story with the excitement surrounding your development of the computer chip and its impact in the marketplace. From there, we can delve into the man that made it all happen."

While she spoke, Maxwell was transfixed. Suddenly, he viewed her as the seasoned professional that she purported herself to be. She was poised, articulate and direct. Gone was the femme fatale who used her charm to keep men nipping at her heels. She knew when to play and when not to. He liked that.

With less reluctance than he'd anticipated, Maxwell took his seat behind his desk, leaned back, and waited, crossing his arms over his taut belly.

"How soon will the chip be ready for the consumer?" she began. "And how will it all come about?"

In measured tones, Maxwell laid out the future plans for the company he'd built from scratch. "In less than six months, M.K. Enterprises will be put in direct competition with the computer giants that have dominated the computer-chip industry for decades. The speed and software adaptability of the chip will revamp everything we understand computers to be today. We are braced at the threshold of an exciting new era…"

As Reese listened to Maxwell talk in that mesmerizing voice, it was the first time she saw him actually animated. The cool control, almost imperceptible movements were gone. He spoke with his hands, his eyes, his body. The excitement and pride rang through the melodic timbre of his rich baritone. He exuded a raw energy that was contagious. She became entranced, captivated by the magic of his dream.

While he talked and looked into her eyes, he believed, if only for the moment, that she was listening to him, interested in him as a man and not just someone from whom something could be gained. For his entire life, women were with him because of his looks, schoolmates hung around because of his brains, business associates befriended him because of what it could do for them by association. In the dojo he was simply feared for his mastery of the arts. He didn't want her to know him. Intimacy only brought him pain. His experience with Victoria Davenport proved that.

The sound of the recorder shutting off broke the spell.

Reese blinked several times as if awakening from a dream. Maxwell cleared his throat and slowly brought his hands up to steeple in front of his mouth. Reese watched the subtle transformation, almost as if someone else had replaced the man she was so briefly introduced to. She was more intrigued than ever.

"I need to get ready for my meeting," he said. "Would you like something to eat or drink in the meantime? I could have Carmen get something for you, if you're hungry."

Was that a hint of gentle concern she heard in his voice, or was she only hoping? "I think I've had my fill of coffee for the day," she said with a forced smile, recalling her sleepless night. "But some orange juice would be great if you have it."

"You didn't sleep well," he stated, surprising her with his astute observation. "And you have the beginnings of a headache."

"What makes you say that?" She watched him rise from his seat and come around to stand behind her.

He placed the balls of his thumbs at her temple and slowly began to rotate them, emitting just the slightest bit of pressure. She almost gasped out loud when the heat of his touch burned through the pain, stripping it away.

"Just relax," he crooned. "Close your eyes. This will only take a moment," he added in a hypnotic cadence. He shut his eyes when a piece of his wall crumbled at his feet.

The sensations that rippled through her sent rivers of soothing warmth floating through her body. Unable to resist, her eyes slid closed of their own volition. Inch by inch she felt her body relax, unwind and purr with delight.

He knew he should have never touched her. He should not have come close enough to inhale the fresh scent of her hair, absorb the sensual aroma of her femininity. It was a mistake, but he couldn't stop himself.

"You have magic in those hands," she said dreamily. She reached up behind her and clasped his hands in hers.

He pulled his hands from her grasp as if burned and stepped abruptly back.

Reese turned halfway in her seat to look back at him. His nostrils flared as if he struggled to breathe. Yet he barely moved.

"I…I feel much better." Her eyes roamed over him, searching for a clue to what he was feeling. "Thank you," she whispered. "How did you know?" she asked again, her gaze following him as he busied himself at the wall unit.

Maxwell bent down and opened the bottom cabinet to reveal a mini refrigerator. He took out a glass pitcher filled with what appeared to be fresh-squeezed orange juice. He then took a glass and filled it.

"It's in the eyes," he said finally, crossing the room in a steady fluid motion. "And that little crease between your brows." He looked down into her upturned face.

Reese opened her mouth to refute him, but couldn't—it was true. "Thank you—for the juice and the massage," she muttered pulling all the stops to regain her composure.

"I've got to be going. Feel free to sit here for a moment. Carmen can show you to the conference room when I'm ready." He needed to get away—now.

"I'd prefer to go with you, if you don't mind."

"Actually I do," he replied, comfortably reverting to the

man that could not be reached. "There are a few sensitive items I need to go over with the team." He gave her a long, unwavering look. "I'd prefer if you'd wait as I asked. I'll buzz Carmen and let her know when you can come in." His tone was clear. There would be no compromise.

She swallowed the last of the juice. "Fine.' She stood to leave, preferring to wait with Carmen, perhaps ask her a few questions about Mr. Knight. "If it's not too much of a bother, I'd rather wait near Carmen's desk. It's suddenly very chilly in here."

"Suit yourself."

Reese snatched up her belongings, flung the door open, and sashayed down the hall, giving Maxwell a good look at her long legs and swaying hips.

Maxwell sat at the head of the conference table and tried to concentrate on what Glen Hargrove, his chief technician, was saying. But his thoughts kept shifting back to Reese, the way she looked, smelled, felt beneath his fingertips.

Without trying, Reese Delaware had somehow made him feel again. A sensation that he'd long ago denied himself—out of reach of any woman. Victoria had taught him an invaluable lesson, one that he would never forget. Sure there'd been plenty of women who'd kept him warm at night since her betrayal, but they'd only warmed his body, never his heart.

"…so what do you think we should do, Max?" Glen was asking.

Maxwell shifted his gaze in Glen's direction. "Check the production tapes at the plant. Perhaps the tapes will show who's screwing up. If that's not it, then it's temperature and air quality. You'll have to get the bio team out there to check it out."

Glen nodded and took quick notes. He wanted to chuckle. He and Max had worked together since college. He knew

Max like a book. There was no way he was actually paying attention to what was being said—at least on the surface. Yet he was still able to answer his question without missing a beat.

"Why don't you guys take a five-minute break," Maxwell said, checking his watch. "When we reconvene we'll be joined by a Ms. Delaware." He cleared his throat. "She's the journalist from *Visions Magazine* who's been assigned to do a major article on the company. She may want to talk with some of you."

A unified groan rose from the group of ten technicians. Maxwell knew that his team was single-focused when they walked through the doors of M.K. Enterprises. The slightest deviation from their routine and they became the surliest group of people on the face of the planet. He chuckled silently. Reese Delaware was certainly a deviation.

"Your cooperation is appreciated," he continued. "See you in five."

"So, what's the deal with this Delaware woman? What's she like?" Glen asked, sidling up next to Maxwell.

He shuffled through some notes on the table and shrugged. "She's a journalist. And you know how I feel about them." He clenched his jaw.

Glen looked at his friend from the corner of his eye. "How long is she going to be hanging around?"

Maxwell took a long breath and exhaled. "She's been assigned to dog my tracks at all of our sites, interview me and anyone who knows me."

Glen's thick, brown eyebrows rose. "You agreed to that?"

Maxwell slanted his dark eyes toward Glen. "You know better than that. I got backed into a corner by the Board. They voted for it."

"Hey listen, before you know it, it'll be over and she'll be out of your hair—ancient history."

"Yeah, that's the day I'm living for," he joked, with a half smile.

"That's a pretty interesting group you have there," Reese commented as she and Maxwell left the conference room.

"They're the best in the business," he snapped, automatically taking her comment as a criticism. He picked up his pace. Her scent was getting to him. He couldn't think clearly with her so close. *She* was getting to him. Just as she'd gotten to his crew. They were like putty in her hands. It was comical the way they practically fell over each other to get her attention. She wound them around her pretty little finger like rubber bands. The realization rattled him.

"I didn't mean anything negative. I think they're phenomenal. They're all so young and brilliant. And obviously dedicated to you," she added.

He heard the ring of sincerity in her voice and it startled him. He gave her a curious look. The idea that his staff was dedicated to anything other than doing a first-class job never entered his mind. He always attributed their zeal to the love of their work.

He frowned. "Your writer's instinct must be off, Ms. Delaware," he stated in dismissal. He opened the door of his office and stood aside to let her pass. She looked up at him as she eased by, her warm amber eyes skimming across his face like a stone over water.

A tiny chip from the wall crumbled and fell between them.

Reese and Maxwell spent every day together, practically glued at the hip. The staff of M.K. Enterprises seemed to welcome her as one of them. They more than answered her questions and many volunteered to be interviewed just to be in her company. Reese Delaware had the ability to charm everyone she met. Even him. She was the first face he saw when he arrived and the last one before he left at night. As much as he hated to admit it, he had begun to look forward to seeing her every day. He even grudgingly enjoyed her myriad of questions.

"This has been a very enlightening two weeks," Reese said, stretching her long, lean body like a contented cat. "I've gotten a pretty good picture of who you are as the businessman through your staff and watching you interact with them." She waited for a reaction and got none, so she went in for the dig. "It's amazing how they can find so many decent things to say about you, Max." She strutted back and forth across the room, one arm crossed beneath her breasts, the other hand twirling a loose tendril of hair. "That's the most curious thing about this whole process," she added airily. "I'm really looking forward to the trip on Sunday. I can't wait to see what the California contingent has to say about the irreproachable Maxwell Knight."

Maxwell didn't look up from the paperwork strewn about his desk.

Slowly Reese crossed the room, bracing her palms on the desktop.

Still he refused to look up.

Feeling especially mischievous, she flicked a pencil across the desk, finally capturing his attention.

"What is it, Ms. Delaware?" he asked, his heart racing as their gazes connected.

Reese leaned closer, so close she could count the silken lashes rimming those incredible eyes. "I will not be ignored," she parodied in a great Glenn Close imitation from the movie classic, *Fatal Attraction*.

Whatever resistance Maxwell had left came tumbling

down. It started out as a chuckle, then slowly built in strength and volume to a full-fledged raucous laugh.

Reese, caught up in the moment, joined in with her own throaty laughter, enchanted by the sparkle in his eyes, the velvet timbre of his voice. She propped her hip on his desk.

"We needed that," she said, catching her breath.

Maxwell nodded in agreement. "I think you're right," he chuckled.

"You have a wonderful laugh," she uttered in a husky whisper. "You should do it more often."

The metamorphosis was slow but clear. The light gradually dimmed in his dark eyes. Maxwell straightened up in his seat. "Carmen has your airline ticket. Don't forget to pick it up before you leave." He cleared his throat. "If you need a car to take you to the airport in the morning, please inform Carmen on your way out." He returned his attention to the papers on his desk. But suddenly the words and diagrams were all a blur. The rational part of him wished she'd leave. The thoroughly male part of him wished she'd come closer.

Reese would not be dissuaded. "I haven't seen anything of the city since I arrived," she hedged. "Why don't you be the gentleman I know you can be and take me out? Give me the twenty-five-cent tour before we leave for California."

"I beg your pardon?"

"You can be a gentleman, can't you?" she taunted, bracing her hips with her fists in a defiant stance. "You have to eat, so why do it alone?"

"What makes you think I'll be eating alone?"

Her mouth curved up in a grin. "Writer's instinct?" Her cocked eyebrow punctuated her point.

Maxwell pushed away from his desk and stood up. "I think you need to sharpen up on your writer's instinct, Ms. Delaware." He paused then looked at her from beneath dark curly lashes. "But I wouldn't want you to go back to Chicago believing all the negative things you've heard about New Yorkers."

She watched him as he crossed the room and retrieved his jacket from the rack. A tiny tingle of anticipation rippled in her stomach. This is just the beginning, Mr. Knight, she mused. I'll get on the other side of that wall no matter what it takes. And you're gonna have a good time while I'm getting there.

Chapter 3

"Do you come here often?" Reese asked, taking a bite from a succulent piece of batter-dipped fried chicken.

"No. Actually, this is the first time. But I've heard a lot of the staff talk about Sylvia's. They've always had good things to say about the food."

"Believe me, it's almost good enough to have me make the trip from Chicago." She grinned. "The atmosphere is great. It's so cozy and personal."

"Hmm."

Reese took a sip of her chardonnay. "Where do you go? I mean—when you go out...on a date?"

"Getting a bit personal, aren't we?"

She gave him that slow, Mona Lisa smile that made his mouth water. "It's after hours, Boss Man," she teased. "Time to lighten up and 'Let It Flow,' as Toni Braxton would say."

Maxwell flashed her a look as cool as the chinks of ice that floated in his glass. He leaned across the table, his voice descending to an intimate low. "Is that right, Ms. Delaware?"

A rush of heat surged through her body. Her heart began to race. She lifted the crystal flute to her lips. Her eyebrows arched. "Very right, Mr. Knight."

"Will there be anything else, folks?" the waitress asked, successfully breaking their tenuous connection.

Maxwell's steamy stare never left Reese's face when he asked, "Would you like something else?"

"What I want I can't get here," she said, the seductive timbre of her voice winding its way through his heated bloodstream.

"No. Thank you. You can bring the check," he finally responded off-handedly.

His dark, haunting eyes glided over her smooth features of milk chocolate, scorching her from the inside out. "Do you have any idea what you're toying with?"

Slowly her tongue darted out and she licked her lips. "Why don't you tell me."

The corner of his mouth curled upward. "I'm not an easy man. I have no intention of building a relationship. I'm not looking for one, and I'm not interested in anyone that is. Still interested?"

"You only *think* you're not interested." She lifted the glass to her dampened lips and smiled. "Your problem is, you haven't found the right woman."

"And who might that woman be?"

"That's for you to discover."

Maxwell eased up out of his seat and came around behind Reese, helping her to her feet. Their bodies brushed. Maxwell inhaled from between clenched teeth when he felt the slight shiver run through her.

"When you play with fire, Ms. Delaware, you're liable to get burned."

She turned to face him and found herself breast to chest, belly to belly. To the casual observer, they appeared to be stepping into a mating dance, they were so close. Heat wafted around them.

"Let the games being," she breathed on a husky laugh.

The ride back downtown from 128th Street in Harlem was conducted in a soothing silence, save for the smooth sounds of the local jazz station, pumping from the speakers of the gray Infiniti Q24.

Maxwell drove with the sunroof open, letting the cool summer's night air lower his body temperature. From the corner of his eye, he looked at Reese. His large hands tightened around the wheel.

She was totally relaxed. Her head was arched slightly back against the headrest, exposing her long, chocolate neck. Her amber eyes were closed, giving her an illusion of innocence. He could almost laugh at that thought. A lot of things could be associated with Reese Delaware, but innocence was not one of them. She exuded a near lethal dose of sexuality every time she breathed. He couldn't remember being so aware of a woman before.

He felt his resistance to her slowly peel away. But he couldn't let that happen. Reese was interested in one thing and one thing alone—getting her story, and she'd do whatever was necessary to get it. *Even sleep with him?* The sudden thought rattled him. He'd been used enough to further people's careers. He'd be damned if he'd be an easy mark again.

Maxwell turned away and poured all of his attention into getting her back to her hotel and out of his car. He continued down Seventh Avenue, tunneling all of his thoughts on the stop-and-go traffic. He was so absorbed that at first he believed the soft moans he heard were coming from the radio, until they rose to a strangled cry.

Checking traffic, he veered sharply to his right, and pulled over at the first available space. Reese was thrashing her head back and forth and moaning as if she were in extreme agony.

"Oh, dear God, make it stop," she groaned. "Make it stop."

"Reese." His voice came to her like a gentle breeze in the midst of a storm. He reached out and touched her face. Her eyes flew open. Slowly she began to focus.

"It's your head again, isn't it?"

She could barely speak, but to nod in response would set off the jackhammers in her head again. "Yes. I…need to… take something…the pain. It's in my room."

"Shh. Don't try to talk. We'll be there in a few minutes. Just try to relax."

Maxwell eased the car away from the curb and jetted into the flow of traffic at the first break. He maneuvered around cars, trucks, buses and yellow cabs, all the while uttering soothing words of comfort. His deep hypnotic voice acted as a balm to her throbbing head.

"As soon as I get you inside, we'll take care of that pain. Breathe deeply in through your nose, and out through your mouth. The added pull of oxygen will help." He glanced in her direction, pleased to see that she was following his instructions. "Do you swim?"

"As…often as I can," she answered weakly, too exhausted to worry about where that question had come from.

"The Bahamas have some of the most beautiful beaches I've ever seen," he said in a slow, melodic tone. "The water is crystal clear. You can almost see the bottom. The waves are so gentle, they're like a warm caress."

Reese succumbed to the melody of his voice, allowing her mind and body to become infused with the tranquil images he'd created.

Maxwell watched her slowly begin to relax. The tension lines between her brow began to ease just as they pulled up to the hotel.

Miraculously, Maxwell found a parking space and came around to help her out. He slipped his arm around her waist and she instinctively leaned into him, letting him bear her weight.

Before they'd taken two steps, Maxwell swept her up into his arms and pushed through the revolving door. Without protest, Reese curled against him, savoring the comfort of his strength, the power of his nearness. She rested her head on his shoulder.

For a mere second, Maxwell shut his eyes and inhaled the scent of her hair, experienced the fragile delicateness of her lush body. He grew hard with desire and desperately wanted to lean downward and kiss her pain away.

"Just a few more minutes," he whispered in her ear. "Where is your room key?"

"In my purse."

Without losing his balance or her, he slipped her purse from her shoulder and fished out her key. He tightened his hold on her and pressed the button for the elevator.

"Where's your medication?" he asked as soon as they were inside the suite and he had her settled on the couch.

"It's in the medicine…cabinet," she stammered, shutting her eyes and leaning her head against the cushions of the couch.

Maxwell returned moments later with the medication and a concerned frown.

"Percodan. This is powerful stuff." He looked down at her and she squinted up at him to bring him into focus. "How long have you been taking it?"

"I haven't had to take anything but over-the-counter

painkillers for the past three years. But the pain got so intense since I've been here, I had to call my doctor in Chicago to call in a prescription."

Maxwell walked over to the lamp that sat on the end table near the couch and turned the light off. He crossed the room and turned on the stereo, reducing the volume to a mellow level. Stepping up behind her, he placed his thumbs at her temples and slowly applied a rotating pressure.

"Just close your eyes and relax," he coaxed. "You don't need that medicine," he continued in a lulling voice. "We can get rid of your pain together."

"But…"

"Shh. Trust me, Reese," he whispered.

"That's the second time you called me Reese tonight," she whispered over the pain. "I'm wearing you down," she added languidly.

Maxwell looked down into her exquisite face. He smiled.

"Magic fingers," she hummed deep in her throat. "Magic."

Reese awoke sometime after 1:00 a.m. to find herself alone in the semi-darkened suite with a quilt covering her. The faint aroma of Maxwell's distinctive scent lingered in the air. A slow smile tugged at her mouth. As much as Max tried to be the tough, unapproachable ice man there was an innate gentleness about him that warmed her as no man had been able to do before. His elusiveness was an aphrodisiac, a challenge that she couldn't resist. To hell with getting burned.

During the two weeks they'd spent together, she'd witnessed the gradual, if not grudging, change in him. But there was so much about him that she didn't understand. What was it that made him so distant at times, so leery of reporters, so unwilling to show the human side of himself?

All of her instincts told her that Maxwell Knight had so

much more to offer the right woman. And instinct also told her that she was that woman. Getting him to realize and accept that was going to be a lot tougher than getting her story. She stood, stretching her long body.

She'd never given up before, even when the doctors had given up on her. Even when she fought to overcome the nightmares, the loss of her family and her memory, she'd never given up.

She wanted Maxwell Knight. And she wouldn't give up until she had him—totally.

Chapter 4

Religiously, every Saturday morning for the past fifteen years, Maxwell went to the dojo, either in the role of the *Sahbamin*—teacher—or to work out. His class of eight-year-olds were not due to arrive for two hours.

When he arrived, the only other person present was his best friend, Chris Lewis. He was glad to see his buddy, who'd just returned from a martial arts tournament. He needed to talk.

Maxwell stowed his small duffel bag in his locker and changed into his *gui*. Shortly, he joined Chris in the small room where they meditated before each session.

Chris and Maxwell bowed toward each other and silently took their places on the straw mats. The peaceful atmosphere of the dojo was what Maxwell needed. His spirit was in disarray. He couldn't seem to focus or center his energy. And he'd been that way since Reese Delaware steamrolled into his life.

How was he going to be able to accomplish all that needed to be done in the next month when images of Reese haunted his every thought?

"You're not here today, brother," Chris said as they left the prayer room. "What's up?"

Maxwell walked out onto the practice floor, trying to form the words to explain to his friend.

As graceful as a gazelle, Maxwell moved through his warm-up paces of *Tai Kwon Do,* the only martial art accepted in Olympic competition. The intricate combinations of kicks and punches were a marvel to watch and difficult to master.

"Remember I told you about the Board's decision to allow a full-fledged article to be written about me and the company?"

"Yeah, I remember, and I had to listen to you bitch and moan about it for weeks." He chuckled. "So...what happened?"

Maxwell took a deep breath and on the exhale lashed out his right leg, cutting sharply through the air. He glanced briefly at Chris from the corner of his eye. "She's here."

Chris's eyes widened. "She?"

A quirky smile played around the corners of Maxwell's mouth. "Yeah, she."

"Well don't stop there. I take it *she's* the reason why you're performing like an amateur instead of a master teacher," he said, observing Maxwell's uncharacteristically choppy moves.

Maxwell dropped his hands to his sides and unclenched his fists. He crossed the huge room and took a seat on the wooden bench. Chris joined him.

"She...she has my head all messed up," Maxwell confessed,

avoiding Chris's questioning looks. He braced his forearms on his muscled thighs and leaned forward.

"She must really be something if she can raise *your* blood pressure. I've never known you to give a woman any more of your time than was absolutely necessary," he chuckled.

Maxwell laughed, then slowly sobered. "She's not like anyone I've ever met before," he said, a slight frown creasing his brow. "Every time I'm round her my hormones go on a rampage."

"Sounds like you need to just get it on and get it out of your system," Chris hedged, trying to goad his brother-friend into confessing what was really bothering him.

"It's not about sex, man. I mean, that's part of it," he added, feeling the throb of excitement just thinking about the possibilities. "But it's more than that." He shook his head in confusion, trying to find the words. "There's this…connection that I feel when I'm with her. She's exciting, intelligent, fun. She has this way of making me take a real look at myself. She's not afraid to challenge me."

"She sounds like a powerful lady." He patted Maxwell on the back. "Just the medicine you need, my brother. So what's the problem?"

"The same problem I always have. I just can't let go. How do I know if she's really interested in me, or just wants my story?"

"You won't until you put yourself out there and find out. Listen, I know you've been burned—bad. Victoria Davenport was a first-class bitch. I know that your Moms and Pops left a lot to be desired as parents. But there comes a time when you have to dust yourself off and try again."

Maxwell stood up. "Easier said than done."

"Give her a chance, man. Forget the fact that she's a reporter. And go with what you feel."

"I'll think about it."

Chris rose and joined his friend in the center of the floor. "That's your problem, my brother. You think too much."

Maxwell laughed.

"So, what's this wonder woman's name?"

"Reese," he said wistfully. "Reese Delaware."

Reese sat curled up on the couch, all traces of her headache from the previous night completely gone. She sipped a cup of herbal tea, while keying in the beginnings of her article on her laptop.

Maxwell Knight was definitely the most intriguing man she'd ever met. There were so many layers to his personality, but for some reason, he only chose to display one. She put the portable computer aside and got up. Crossing the small living area, she went to the window.

She wrapped her arms around her waist and sighed. Max was a man with a past, a part of him that he wished to keep hidden from the world. In that respect, they were totally dissimilar. For the past fifteen years, she'd tried desperately to remove the veil that shrouded her life, and had failed.

She turned away from the New York skyline. She was getting too close to this story. She was losing her objectivity. That was totally unlike her.

That was probably the reason for the sudden return of the headaches and the nightmares. She was becoming too involved with her subject.

She couldn't let that happen. This assignment was the chance of a lifetime—an opportunity that every journalist salivates for.

Reese smiled in resignation. Unfortunately, it was too late. What she was beginning to feel for Maxwell Knight had absolutely nothing to do with her job. But everything to do with her being a woman who wanted a man as much as she wanted to breathe.

The ringing phone pulled her rudely away from her reverie.

"Hello?"

"Good morning. I was calling to see how you were feeling."

The pulse began to pound in her ears, and the little butterflies went berserk in her tummy.

"I'm feeling fabulous, Max. Thanks to you."

"Did you sleep well?"

Not as well as I could have if you'd stayed, she wanted to say. "Very well. And you?"

"Let's bypass the small talk," he said suddenly, needing to take the plunge. "Are you dressed?"

"For what?" she teased, and his thoughts went out of order.

"For company. I want to come—over," he uttered, his comment full of innuendo. "Then I thought I'd take you around the city before we leave in the morning."

Her spirits soared. She was grinning so hard her jaw began to ache. "I'll be here," she said, her voice full of invitation.

"And *I'll* be there, shortly."

"Where are we going?" Reese questioned, settling herself in the car.

"For the twenty-five-cent tour, of course."

She laughed. "Very funny. But seriously, where?"

"That's what's wrong with all you reporter types," he teased, "just can't be satisfied without knowing every single detail." He pushed out a prolonged sigh. "If you must know, I thought I'd take you to the Top of the Sixes for lunch. Then down to Soho. There's an art gallery opening that I wanted to see." He turned to look at her. "I hope you like art," he stated more than asked.

"Let's put it this way, I know what I like when I see it. That's the extent of my knowledge of art." She chuckled.

He smiled when he realized he'd discovered a new level of admiration for her honesty.

"I can guarantee that you'll love this guy's work."

"I'll take your word for it."

For several moments they rode in companionable silence, until Reese spoke.

"What changed your mind?" she asked softly.

"About what?" he hedged.

"About me. What earth-shattering event made you want to spend your Saturday with me, the woman you love to hate?"

"I think your instincts are off again."

"You mean you don't hate me?" she taunted.

He slanted her a look. "It's not you." He paused to gauge his words. "It's what you represent."

Reese digested what he'd said. "What is it that you have against journalists?" she asked, struggling to maintain a lid on her temper.

His jaw clenched. "They tend not to have any conscience, for starters." The pain of remembrance laced his heavy voice, making it vibrate with emotion. "They have no qualms about intruding on a person's life and turning it upside down."

"I see. And you feel I'm no different from the nefarious 'they,'" she tossed out, fighting to disguise her hurt behind a wall of anger.

"Are you? Aren't you here to get 'your story' no matter what it takes?"

"Yes I'm here to get a story Max, because it's my job. Just because you've had a bad experience with reporters doesn't give you the right to paint me with the same black brush."

Maxwell spun the wheel, turning the car on two wheels,

causing traffic to swerve around them. The high-pitched squealing sound of the tires reminded Reese of pigs being led to the slaughterhouse. He jerked the car to a screeching halt.

He turned on her, his dark eyes blazing. "The right!" he boomed, his heavy voice reverberating in the small space. "I have every right. This is my life we're talking about, and you want a piece of it. Just like all the others. What makes you any different?"

Her sense of injustice made her want to fight back, to tell him what a bull-headed, stubborn fool he was being. But instinct told her that Max's outrage went much deeper. She reached out and touched his arm. "What happened to you, Max?" she asked so gently the words wrapped around his battered heart and cushioned it.

He looked down at the hand that held him, so long and slender. His gaze trailed up her arm to rest on her face and at eyes that beheld him with such compassion he was stunned by the impact. His eyes swam over her face, heating her.

Her grip tightened and he felt her warmth slowly spread through him.

He leaned closer. She held her breath, longing for what she knew was to come.

Maxwell reached out and stroked her face. His thumb traced the outline of her full, rich mouth. Her eyes slid shut as a tremor of delight tripped through her.

"Reese," he exhaled on a hot breath. Her eyes slowly opened and met his uncertain gaze.

"Don't be afraid," she uttered in a husky whisper. She closed the space between them. Her free hand reached out and ran across his hair of onyx silk. She caressed the smooth bronze jaw, the eyes of ebony that curved upward in invitation.

He turned his head to kiss her palm, then the tender inside of her wrist.

His kisses were hot, searing her, teasing her, sailing up her arm—short-circuiting her heart. She longed to pull him into her arms, to have him bury what had hurt him deep within her warmth. But she understood that for it to be right, it had to come from him. She would wait, even as her body trembled with a need that defied explanation.

Maxwell eased back, still holding her hand in his. Reese's eyes implored him to let go.

There was so much he wanted to say—needed to say. A part of him longed to share his deepest thoughts with this woman—share a part of himself with her—but he couldn't. Not anymore.

All he needed a woman for was to ease his physical needs. That's where his connection with them began and ended, he reminded himself. He would not allow Reese Delaware to change that fact.

"We'd better get going." He spoke so calmly, a casual listener wouldn't have the slightest clue as to what had almost transpired.

Reese, who gave just as good as she got, smiled her slow easy smile and said, "You're right. I was wondering why we stopped." If he wanted to act as if nothing happened, then as far as she was concerned nothing did, she fumed.

Maxwell checked his signals and pulled out into traffic. He forced his thoughts to clear. This was a mistake. He should have never offered to take her out. From today until the minute she left, he'd keep things between them strictly professional. It was obvious that she didn't give a damn one way or the other which way things went with them. Good. The hell with her. It was a damned good thing that Carmen would be traveling with them. At least he could palm Reese off on Carmen and not have to be bothered.

* * *

"Thank you for a wonderful day," Reese said brightly as they pulled up in front of the hotel. Even though Max had been relatively quiet for the better part of the day, she did enjoy herself. He'd been the perfect gentleman and they'd shared a few good laughs and created some wonderful memories. She swallowed. Her heart was beating so fast she thought it would explode. She wanted him to come upstairs, but she knew he wouldn't.

"A car will be here to pick you up at 9:00 a.m. We have a ten o'clock flight," he said, sidestepping her comment. As much as he was reluctant to admit it, he'd enjoyed every minute of their day together.

"I know." Reese leaned over the seat to retrieve her purse from the back. "It was so generous of you to get me a first-class ticket," she added, missing the look of stunned disbelief that momentarily carved his face into a mask of incredulity. She turned briefly toward him. "Well, good night. I'll see you in the morning."

He pressed a button on the driver's-side panel and released the lock. "Good night." His tone was as tense as he felt. He kept his gaze straight ahead, knowing that if he looked at her now, the night would be long from over.

Reese rolled her eyes in annoyance. Without another word, she alighted from the car, and pushing through the revolving doors, disappeared among the guests in the ornate lobby of the Hilton, never once looking back.

Maxwell roared off from the spot on the Avenue of the Americas. One of these days, he was actually going to strangle Carmen.

Maxwell tossed and turned in his sleep the entire night. Visions of Reese nestled in his arms tormented him with longing. How in the world would he be able to get through the next few weeks when his feelings for her were spiraling out of control?

He wished that he had it in him to let go. But after Victoria, he'd promised himself he'd never allow his heart to guide him again. Victoria Davenport was the first woman he'd begun to open himself up to, and even now, two years later, the pain of her betrayal could still flare raw and ragged.

When he'd first met Victoria at an engineering conference in Washington, D.C., he was instantly captivated. She was the fascinating combination of beauty and brains. What enchanted him the most was that she was the first woman who didn't trip all over herself trying to get his attention.

Finally, unable to stand her pointed rebuff a moment longer, he'd maneuvered his way around the throngs of people in the dining hall and introduced himself.

"Can I refresh your drink, Ms….?" Maxwell asked, easing up next to her.

Victoria turned cool, green eyes on him. "Don't tell me you came from clear across the room just to get me a drink?" she taunted, her smile a sweet invitation. "I truly thought chivalry was dead," she added, her soft Southern drawl like music to his ears.

He leaned against the bar. His eyes rolled up and down her slender frame. "Let me guess. You've been watching me just as hard as I've been watching you."

Her finely arched brows rose in feigned surprise. "What would make you think that?" She tried to sound indignant, but failed.

"How else would you know that I was way on the other side of the room?"

Victoria tossed back her head and laughed outright, her strawberry blond tresses skimming her bare shoulders. "Just for that, I'm going to tell you my name, you're going to tell me yours, and we're going to get to know each other. There's nothing I like better than a man who speaks his mind."

Maxwell joined in her laughter, enchanted by its musical quality. And they did get to know each other. They had tons of things in common both being computer engineers, she for the government and he in private practice.

For the next eighteen months, Maxwell made his home between D.C., where Victoria lived, and New York. During those months, Maxwell quickly learned that Victoria was the type of woman who lived on the edge, challenging everything and everyone. Her looks gave her entrée into the black world as easily as the white, and she played whatever role suited her at the moment.

"I was fortunate to be born with a choice," Victoria said to him one night after making love.

"We all have choices," Maxwell said, folding his hands beneath his head and staring up at the stuccoed ceiling.

She smiled, the kind of sly smile that compels you to want to know more.

"When I'm with you, I can let down my hair and go back to my roots. When I'm outside of 'our little circle' of friends and associates, I cross the line to my other world."

For several moments, Maxwell simply stared at her, too flabbergasted to speak.

"Don't look so shocked, darling. How many times in your life have you wished—prayed—that you could cross over into the Japanese world and be accepted, and at your whim return to the black world and not miss a beat? The only difference between you and me, is that I can."

The truth of her statement slammed him in the gut. For all of his thirty years, he had been on the fence of life, so to speak, trying to discover where he fit. Listening to her now, brought to bear his reality.

On all of the forms and applications he'd ever had to fill

out, he always checked "other." Other what? he'd always wanted to know. Yet he'd learned to live with it, at least on the surface.

What he couldn't accept was Victoria's cavalier attitude about her ethnicity. With effort, he managed to put her indiscretion aside. He convinced himself that he was falling in love with her, that what she did when she wasn't with him didn't affect him. That was the beginning.

It was several months after that revelation that they'd had a terrible argument. Maxwell was miserable without her. He'd decided to drive down to D.C. for the weekend and surprise her. That was the end.

He knew she always worked late on Friday, so he'd planned to beat her to the apartment and have dinner waiting—his way of making things up to her and telling her how sorry he was.

When he arrived at the apartment they shared, he thought he was alone until he heard noises coming from the back. Surprised, Maxwell put down his packages and headed for the back bedroom.

"Vicki, I didn't expect you…" He pushed open the bedroom door, and for a split second he couldn't focus. Victoria in all of her peaches-and-cream splendor was astride her boss, her head tossed back as the throes of climax gripped them both. Neither of them heard him enter or leave. They never spoke to or saw each other again.

The question that always nagged at him was: what role was she playing that afternoon with her white lover? And why had she chosen Max? What role had he played in the eighteen months of their relationship? He was soon to find out, when the *Washington Post* ran the story about Victoria Davenport and the innovative new computer program she'd developed that gave PC users unlimited access to the Internet—and enhanced processing speed—the very same program he'd been working on for months. When the press got wind of their relationship, they made his life pure hell for months.

His breakup with Victoria reconfirmed his mistrust, rekindled his belief that no one was as they appeared, and the shell around him had grown tight once again.

Until Reese.

Chapter 5

Reese was bone tired when her aunt Celeste phoned her at 7:00 a.m. Her night had been haunted by those faceless phantoms that had plagued her life for the past fifteen years.

Had she had these dreams—these nightmares—before that time? she wondered, letting the cool water sluice across her body. If she had, she couldn't remember. Just as she could remember nothing prior to that fateful day when her life was irrevocably changed.

Shadows, images, screeching tires and screams were all that she could recall. But something had led to it. Something or someone that she could not remember. And all of the hypnosis, therapy, and drugs had not brought her memory back. The first fifteen years of her life were nothing more than a black abyss.

Wrapping the thick, standard white hotel towel around her dripping milk-chocolate body, she thought about how guilty she had felt for so many years. Guilty that she'd survived, and could not remember anything about her mother or father, who had perished.

And whenever her guilt began to ebb, aunt Celeste would find a way to resurrect it, making her feel that she'd betrayed her family because she could not remember them, as she had moments ago.

Reese had assumed the early-morning phone call was her hotel wake-up call. Her heart thundered with trepidation when she heard her aunt's voice reach out to her across the wires.

"Aunt Celeste, how are you?"

"I'm fine," she answered in a tight voice. "But how would you know that, you don't remember to call."

Reese squeezed her eyes shut and took a long, calming breath.

"Aunt Celeste, I called you before I left Chicago. I gave you the number of the hotel here in New York."

"That was nearly two weeks ago," she accused. "I'm your only living relative. I'd think you'd treat me with more regard."

"Aunt Celeste, please," she whispered, feeling again like the lost, confused child she'd been for so many years. "Not today. I'm trying to get ready for my trip to Los Angeles."

"Humph. What you need to do is settle down and find yourself a husband—start a family instead of traipsing across the country digging into other people's lives when you can only claim half of your own!"

Reese felt the pain of her words as strongly as if she'd been smacked. "You still blame me. After all these years, you still blame me, as if my lack of memory is somehow responsible for everything and intended to hurt you. Well I can't help that I survived, Aunt Celeste. I'm me, Reese Delaware—or at least what there is of me. And I won't apologize for my existence anymore."

"Reese!"

"Goodbye, Aunt Celeste. I'll call you when I reach Los Angeles." She hung up the phone before her aunt could respond.

Sitting on the edge of the bed, Reese shielded her face with her hands, the weight of her pain seeping through her fingers to trickle down her cheeks.

"Why can't I remember?" she cried. "Why?"

"Victoria, you have a call on line one," the engineer who sat to her left said, tapping Victoria gently on the shoulder.

Victoria turned toward Cliff and nodded her thanks. Removing her headset, she took one quick look at the lighted board in front of her, sparkling with colored lights that detailed the circuitry she was working on. Satisfied for the moment, she pushed away from the digital panel.

At the young age of twenty-eight she was head of the engineering division for the Air Force, an unprecedented position. It was her sole responsibility to oversee every aspect of computer assembly and sign off on everything that left her department.

She'd worked damned hard to get to where she was. She'd done some things that made her skin crawl, but she'd survived. Her only regret was losing Max. She'd tried for months to get him to talk to her, but he'd refused. Eventually she'd given up and began to pick up the pieces of her life and move on. But she'd never forgotten the one man who'd almost made her do the right thing.

She depressed the flashing red button on the console. "Davenport," she said curtly, eager to get back to her design.

"Vicky, dear, I'm so sorry to bother you at work, but I had the most awful conversation with that witch, Reese."

Victoria twisted her mouth in annoyance. The last

person she wanted to hear about was her half sister, Reese Delaware.

"What happened now, Aunt Celeste?"

Victoria returned to her desk. Breathing hard, she just stared at the electronic board.

"Vic, are you alright?" Cliff asked, snatching off his headset. "You look pale."

Victoria shook her head. "No. I mean, yes—I'm fine. But I think I'll take the rest of the day off. Something came up." Quickly she shut down her sector, collected her belongings, and rushed out of the lab.

Driving more by instinct than from paying attention, Victoria took the Fourteenth Street Bridge out of D.C. into the suburbs to Arlington, Virginia.

"Dammit!" she railed, slamming her palms against the steering wheel. What were the chances of your ex-lover and a sister you've never met getting together? The irony of the situation was not lost on her. Reese had always wound up with everything—the family, the home, the security. She, on the other hand, was the big family secret. And now Reese would be spending the next six weeks with Max. Would she wind up with him, too?

An hour later Reese was still reeling from the conversation with her aunt when the phone rang again. With great reluctance, she answered.

"Hello?"

"Hey, girl, it's Lynnette."

Reese's smile lit up the room. A call from her homegirl was just the medicine she needed. She felt as if a weight had been lifted off of her chest.

"Lynnette, you couldn't have called at a better time."

"Sounds like you've been talking to the wicked witch of the east again," Lynnette teased.

Reese laughed out loud at the vision. However, her aunt could be more closely pegged as Glenda from the North. Celeste Winston was, on the surface, a stunning woman of fifty-two. Her exquisite peaches-and-cream face was smooth and unlined, haloed by sparkling auburn hair. She was in excellent shape, went to the hairdresser once per week, and spent her well-earned money as a private-duty nurse for the Air Force, on designer clothes. On the surface, Celeste had it all, but underneath she was a lonely, bitter woman who'd never married. And she seemed to take pleasure in venting her frustrations on the niece she'd been forced to raise.

"On target as usual. But I don't want to talk about her. There's not enough time in the world. What's happening at the magazine?"

"Hart is still busting my chops and as pig-headed as ever. I'm working my tail off as usual."

They both laughed. "But what I want to know is what's up with you? How is Mr. Wonderful Mystery Man up close and personal?"

"He's all that and more," Reese admitted on a wistful note.

"Mmm, sounds serious. Talk to me."

Reese sighed and sat down on the edge of the bed. She crossed her bare legs at the knee. "At first I was all about getting the story of my career, no matter what I had to do to get it. Literally. When we first met, I went into my bag and pulled out all of my tricks." She chuckled mirthlessly and shook her head. "But the more I'm with him, the more I want to be with him. It's no longer just the story I want, Lynn. It's him. And I know I'm really stretching the lines of ethics, but girl, I can't help myself. When we're together rockets go off. It's so intense, sometimes I feel like I can't breathe."

"Wow—!" Lynnette exhaled. "He must be something. In the ten years that I've known you, you've never talked about a man like this. What are you going to do about it? And secondly, how in the world are going to stay objective if you have to keep changing your panties whenever he's in the same air space?"

They both burst into another fit of raucous laughter visualizing Lynnette's ribald analogy.

"Girl, you are too crazy," Reese uttered, choking down the last of her chuckles.

"That's why we've been friends for so long. You're the sultry, sexy one who winds their way under a man's skin. I, on the other hand, just jump right in and say what's on my mind. Consequences be damned!"

"You're right about that one," she said.

Reese and Lynnette had met while undergrads at Howard University during a speech communication seminar. They clicked almost immediately and were roommates for the balance of their stay at Howard. After graduation, they both decided to take the plunge and move to Chicago. With their backgrounds and personal savvy, they both landed jobs almost immediately. Although Lynnette worked for *Visions* as a full-time staff writer, Reese preferred to freelance for a variety of newspapers and magazines. It didn't allow for a stable financial existence, but it gave her the opportunity to come and go as she pleased. Plus, she never got stuck having to write stories she had no interest in. She picked what she wanted.

"What time is your flight?" Lynnette asked, cutting into Reese's musings.

Reese yawned and checked the clock. "A car should be picking me up in about twenty minutes. Our flight leaves at ten o'clock."

"How long are you going to be on the coast? I have some

vacation days due to me. I might be able to pop out there and maybe I can squeeze in an interview with Quincy if I plan it right."

Reese let out a whoop of delight. "That would be fabulous. We're scheduled to be out there for about two weeks. Then it's on to Tokyo. Oh please come. I could use a friend," she pleaded in her best little girl voice.

"Ooh, girl, you know I hate it when you whine," she joked.

"So you'll come?"

"Of course. Any excuse to get out of the windy city. I'll get myself together and work out the details with Hart and I'll be there. Give me all of your hotel information."

Reese quickly rattled off her hotel name, along with her flight information. "I'll call you tonight once I get settled, and you can tell me if you were able to work things out."

"You know I'll be able to work things out. I have no intention of taking *maybe* for an answer. As a matter of fact, I'm packing as we speak."

"Can't wait," Reese said. "But listen, I've got to run. The last thing I need at the moment is to be late for my ride."

"No problem. I'll talk with you tonight. Have a safe trip."

"Thanks. Bye."

Reese hurried around the suite checking that she hadn't forgotten anything. She breezed by the bedroom mirror then back peddled and stopped. She gazed at her reflection and smiled, once again filled with her old self-confidence. In her throaty alto voice, she belted out the last line of the R&B classic "And I'm Telling You," by Jennifer Holiday. "I don't wanna be fre-e-e. I'm stay—in' and you're gonna love me! Yeah." She winked and hurried out of the suite.

When she reached the lobby, she was pleasantly surprised to see Carmen waiting.

"Carmen," she greeted, giving the older woman a quick peck on the cheek. "I didn't expect to see you. I thought you were just sending a car."

"The car is waiting. I just thought it would be nice if we rode together to the airport."

"I think so, too," Reese said with a smile, threading her arm through Carmen's. "What about Max—I mean, Mr. Knight?"

"He always drives his own car to the airport." She pushed through the revolving door and out into the balmy morning. "He hates being at the mercy of someone else," she tossed over her shoulder with a wink and a smile.

The double entendre was not lost on Reese.

He knew he was early and that there was plenty of time before boarding. That wasn't the point. Maxwell paced the waiting area, checking his watch every few minutes. He was edgy. His nerves felt like they were about to snap. The lack of sleep, haunted by dreams of Reese, compounded by the unexpected phone call from Victoria Davenport, had him ready to crush the first person who crossed him.

After nearly two years of complete silence, she calls out of the blue. Why? And why now? She said she'd been thinking about him a lot lately and had been too afraid to contact him for fear of rejection again. She'd said she'd heard through the grapevine about the chip development and she wanted to congratulate him. She, too, was planning on being in Los Angeles within the week, and wondered if he would be in town. If so maybe they could get together—just for a drink— for old time's sake.

Maxwell frowned and checked his watch again, retracing his path across the sparkling tile floor. Victoria, he'd learned the hard way, was not a woman who did anything without a damned good reason. If she wanted to see him again, she had one, and he was pretty certain her reason had nothing to do with congratulations or unrequited love.

He checked his watch, then compared it to the huge clock that hung above the reservationist's station. "Where is she?" he fumed between clenched teeth.

"Looking for someone?" Reese asked, easing up behind him to practically whisper in his ear.

He spun around and when his eyes landed on her smiling face, his stomach coiled into a knot of need. "Where in the devil have you been?" he growled in greeting. "Or don't you realize we have a flight to catch?" He turned away and strode toward the departure gate.

"This trip is going to be longer than I thought," she muttered to Carmen, who hid a smile behind her hand. Both women followed in comical military fashion behind the unsuspecting Maxwell Knight.

Maxwell's morning for stress was anything but over. Carmen had purposely seated them together. His intention was to sleep on the flight. But the heavenly scent of Reese's body oil invaded his senses, her every movement sent waves of longing zinging through his veins.

"Max…"

"Reese…"

They both looked at each other, speaking in unison.

Maxwell's stern countenance wavered and he smiled. "You first."

Reese took a breath, briefly looked down at her hands and then into the depth of his magnificent ebony eyes. "I don't want to intrude on your life, Max. I want you to know that. And I don't want you to think that I don't have a conscience. Over the next few weeks, we're going to be spending a lot of time together. I'm going to be asking you questions you're not going to want to answer. But we can get past all of that." Her eyes raced across the flawless honey-dipped face. "There's something much more than just interviewer-interviewee going on between us." Her husky voice lowered until it felt like a pulse beating in his body. "If I'm wrong, I want you to tell me—now."

Interminable minutes seemed to tick away before he spoke.

"I wish I could tell you how wrong you are—that your instincts are off." His large hand reached out and stroked the worry from her forehead. He clenched his jaw, the war of doubt still putting up a good fight. "But I can't," he finally said.

Reese let out a long-held shaky breath. She pressed her lips together and clasped his hand within hers. "I swear to you, Max, you won't regret it," she whispered.

He grinned like a young boy. "That remains to be seen, Ms. Delaware. But with Carmen behind the scenes orchestrating things, I never stood a chance."

She looked at him with wide-eyed innocence. "Carmen?"

"You must have guessed by now that Carmen thinks she's my mother. And as my mother, she must tend to my happiness—whatever she decides that may be." He chuckled. "I'm quite sure she made certain me and you would be sitting together on this flight, while she sat back there," he added, hitching his thumb over his left shoulder.

Reese twisted in her seat and looked over the heads behind her. She spotted Carmen peeking at her from above the top of a magazine. Reese grinned and Carmen gave her a thumbs-up sign.

"Has Carmen always had a penchant for organizing your personal life?" Reese questioned, settling down into her seat.

"She tries damned hard." He chortled. "Most of the time she's right."

"Do you generally take her advice?"

For a brief moment a dark shadow seemed to pass across his features. Carmen had warned him about Victoria early in their relationship. He hadn't listened. "For the most part."

Reese quickly sensed that there was more to the clipped statement, but would not press the point. There were so many things about Maxwell Knight that she wanted to discover, but her writer's instinct and her female intuition reminded her it would be a very difficult road indeed.

James Knight climbed the stairs to the attic of his two-story home. After receiving a large cash compensation from the military during his service, he'd had the house built. It was the house he'd tried to raise his son, Max, in. Instead, it was the house that he'd watched his life and his marriage crumble in. Beautiful on the outside with a wide front enclosed porch reminiscent of the plantations of the south, whitewashed with tall stately pillars and a perfectly manicured front and back lawn.

His wife, Claudia, had spent innumerable hours finding just the right fabric, piece of furniture, work of art. The house on Pinecroft Court was a palace, but it was never a home. She'd tried—Lord knows she'd tried, but there was always a shadow that hovered between them. It was there waiting for him when he'd returned from Japan.

Pushing open the attic door, he pulled a key from his pants pocket, crossed the small crawl space, and used the key to open an old footlocker.

From within he pulled out a gray metal box filled with yellowed paper, photographs, and signed documents.

James's warm brown eyes clouded over. For more than

fifteen years, what had been done had remained sealed away in his attic and in the "eyes only" files of the military.

But governments change. Policy and administrations change. His son was being interviewed by one of the most renowned publications in the country. Everything would slowly begin to unravel. He knew it as sure as he knew it would rain by the aches in his knees.

He pulled out a faded picture of a beautiful young geisha, Sukihara—Suki, whom he'd loved like no other. How different would his life have been if he'd remained in Tokyo...?

Tokyo, April 1960

The month of April is one of the busiest times in the geisha quarters. In the evenings, the teahouses and restaurants where the geishas—or artistic persons—entertain, are crowded with guests from surrounding cities who have journeyed to Tokyo for the cherry blossoms and the geisha dance festival.

It was late one April evening when James and his army buddy Larry Templeton, who'd been stationed in Tokyo for two months, decided to venture out and see what all the mystery was surrounding the geishas. Since being stationed in Tokyo, they had seen no more than their barracks and their immediate area. They felt totally isolated. Not only was there the language and cultural barriers to deal with, they were the only two black men they'd seen since their arrival. They started off with two strikes against them; they were the American military in a foreign country and they were black—the lowest men on the totem pole no matter where they went.

"Whaddaya want to do tonight?" Larry asked, lacing up his regulation boots.

James chuckled in his deep robust voice. "How many

choices do we have, man? It's not like we're the most welcomed folks in town."

"I guess you're right. But it's Friday. We have the whole weekend off. There ought to be something."

James shrugged his wide shoulders. His dark brown eyes slowly lit up. "How about checking out one of those teahouses I've always heard about?"

"Hey, why not? How do we get there?"

James sat down on the edge of his single bed and pulled out a slim map from the drawer.

"From what I've been hearing the really good ones are in Kyoto." He unfolded the map and spread it out on the bed. Both young men hovered over the finely drawn lines. James stuck out his index finger and traced a path.

"It's a good half-hour drive," Larry said, straightening up.

"You have something better to do?"

"Very funny. Let's go while the night is still young."

They drove for nearly an hour.

"You sure you know where you're going?" Larry taunted.

"It can't be too much farther. As a matter of fact, good buddy, there's the Kamo River now. I do believe we have arrived." James grinned and pointed to the elaborate structure that was pinpointed by brightly lit lanterns, the only illumination for miles around—giving the entire scene a picture postcard feel.

"Hot damn," Larry exclaimed. "I'm finally gonna meet me a real-life geisha. Wait till I tell the boys back home." He slapped his thigh and hopped out of the jeep.

When James and Larry entered the teahouse, it was like nothing they'd anticipated. Although they received cold or indifferent looks from the Japanese and white men who were ensconced in various locations of the establishment, it was the role of the geisha to welcome and entertain every man who crossed the threshold. And they did—from singing and dancing to pouring their sake.

All of the preconceived notions about geishas being no more than high-priced prostitutes were soon erased. These were pampered, talented, beautiful, sexy women, who because of the Japanese culture, were a necessary way of life. Wives, on the other hand, were subdued, obedient, and anything but sexy. They were everything that a geisha was not.

James slowly relaxed and began to truly enjoy the performances and the pampering, but his breath stopped in his chest when a young, beautiful girl, dressed in an elaborate costume of brilliant red and gold, took center stage. Her name was Sukihara, the petite, exotic nymph who'd changed his life.

Far off, James heard the ringing of the phone. With reluctance be returned the photos to the box and placed the box back in the footlocker.

Quickly he ran down the short flight of steps and answered the phone that sat in the foyer of the top floor.

Returning from her part-time job at the local library, and unaware that her husband was at home, Claudia picked up the extension on the ground floor. When she heard her husband's voice she intended to hang up until she heard the voice of the caller.

"Hello?"

"Colonel Knight?"

"Yes, speaking."

"This is Major General Murphy at Chevy Chase Air Force Base."

James's heart began to race with dread. He'd been expecting this call and hating its inevitability.

"What can I do for you, sir?"

"We've arranged to have a car pick you up at your home tomorrow morning at 0800 hours."

"Yes, sir."

"I hope this won't pose a problem for you."

"No, sir. Of course not."

"Good. See you then, Colonel." He broke the connection.

James Knight had spent forty years of his life in the Special Forces unit of the Air Force. Taking orders without question was second nature. Slowly he replaced the receiver. Taking orders was the reason his life had never been his own, the reason that haunted him every day of his life for the past fifteen years—the reason why his son must never discover what those orders had commanded him to do.

Claudia clutched the phone to her breasts and squeezed her eyes shut. When would they ever leave them alone? For fifteen years, they'd lived under the thumb of that demon from hell—Murphy. They'd never let James live in peace even after all that he'd done in their name. The military had stolen his spirit and Sukihara had stolen his heart.

Chapter 6

"After we check into the hotel, I need to head over to the office," Maxwell announced, as they moved through Los Angeles International Airport.

Reese and Carmen doubled their steps to keep up with his brisk, long-legged strides.

"I'll be going with you," Reese stated. "So I'll need a few minutes to freshen up."

Maxwell looked at her over his shoulder. He wanted to say that she looked fabulous just the way she was. Her raven mane was twisted into a fuss-free French roll, and her statuesque form was coated in a teal suit of micro-silk with a skirt that hit her just above those gorgeous knees. His eyes snaked down to those luscious legs that were shadowed by a sheer pair of black hose. Briefly he wondered if she wore pantyhose or real stockings with garter belts. In any event, there was no way she looked like she'd been on a plane for six hours.

"If you think it's necessary—to freshen up," he qualified. "But I don't have time to wait around all afternoon."

Reese and Carmen exchanged glances. "I'll be sure not to keep you waiting—too long," Reese coed sweetly.

Once inside her hotel room, Reese was suitably impressed. This room outdid the Hilton by light years. The living area looked out onto rows of swaying palms and gentle breezes. The thick ecru carpet was so deep it tickled her ankles when she walked. She crossed the room and twisted the gold knob of the door.

Her breath caught in her throat. A huge canopy bed of eggshell white demanded her immediate attention. Along the canopy's posters, white diaphanous fabric was dramatically draped. She smiled. Maxwell Knight certainly knew how to do things with panache.

Reese quickly tucked her suitcase and garment bag in the walk-in closet. She'd unpack later. She unzipped her garment bag and retrieved a pale peach suit of clinging rayon and silk. From another zippered compartment she took out a matching pair of low-heeled sandals. In record time, she'd changed clothes, repaired her minimal makeup, and tucked in some stray strands of hair.

Satisfied with her transformation, she grabbed her purse and briefcase and headed out of the suite. As soon as she stepped off of the elevator, she spotted the unmistakable figure of Maxwell pacing among the lobby crowd. For a moment, a rush of electricity whizzed through her, and she stood still as an Egyptian statue. To watch him, unobserved, was to see raw energy barely contained beneath bone and sinew. What would it be like to unleash that energy, to see it reach its apex? How would she ever find the words to convey to the reader what was almost mystical, something that had to be experienced—not explained—especially now when her emotions were beginning to cloud her judgment?

It was as if he sensed her presence, like a jungle cat becoming aware of a predator. He turned, not his whole body, just his head and looked straight at her with those incredible eyes.

The sudden contact caused Reese's heart to slam mercilessly in her chest. There was no mistake. What she saw in his eyes was pure, unadulterated hunger.

The current that snapped back and forth between them was broken when Carmen approached Maxwell and tapped him on the shoulder.

"The car is out front," she said.

Maxwell tore his gaze away from Reese and she was finally freed from the magnetic hold of his eyes.

Putting on her best smile, she approached the duo. "I hope I didn't keep you waiting too long."

The hot coals of his eyes raked over her, and it took all she had not to tremble.

"Not at all. I just came down myself."

Reese couldn't have been more stunned if he'd smacked her. Where were the cutting remarks, the sarcasm?

Maxwell sat opposite Reese and Carmen in the limousine. "Did you talk with the housekeeper, Carmen?"

"Yes. Everything is in order. You can have your things sent over whenever you're ready."

"Great. Thanks. If you could take care of that for me while Ms. Delaware and I are at the office, I'd appreciate it."

"No problem."

Curiously, Reese looked from one to the other waiting for someone to clue her in on what was going on. No one did. So she did what came naturally. She asked.

"Is there some reason why you're not staying at the hotel, Max?"

"Yes, there is." One reason is because I don't know how I'd be able to resist sneaking into your room each night, he thought. But instead he said, "I always promised myself that if I had to be away from home for long periods of time I'd have someplace I could call my own. I'm sure you'll be quite comfortable at the hotel," he added, seeming to want to assure her that the hotel was above reproach.

How interesting, she mused and made a mental note to explore that little revelation at a later date. "I'd love to see it before we leave."

Maxwell cleared his throat. "I'll make sure that you do," he returned, his simple statement full of innuendo.

Where the New York office was charged with an unmistakable energy, the L.A. contingent epitomized California cool. The techs ambled, never rushed, down the corridors. Everyone smiled and looked as though they were headed to the beach instead of one of the fastest growing engineering companies on both coasts.

As they made their way around the winding maze of cubicles and labs, in and out of security checkpoints, it seemed that every staff member found a way to gain Maxwell's attention. Everyone seemed thoroughly pleased that he'd returned.

"Max, good to have you back," enthused a fiftyish-looking engineer who stopped Maxwell just outside of his office.

Maxwell actually beamed with warmth, Reese noticed, as the two men embraced in a hearty bear hug. Maxwell turned to face Carmen and Reese with his arm draped across the man's shoulders.

This brief moment hinted at a dimension of his personality

that he very infrequently allowed to be revealed, Reese realized, as another corner of her heart softened.

"I'd like to introduce you to Reese Delaware. Ms. Delaware is the journalist from *Visions Magazine*."

At least he didn't call me a reporter.

"Ms. Delaware, this is Raymond St. John, the man who runs things in my absence—and when I'm here," he added, his laughter rumbling from deep in his chest.

Raymond stretched out his large hand to Reese, which she shook. "It's a pleasure to meet you, Ms. Delaware. Don't let ole Max give you a hard time," he added in a faint accent that she couldn't quite place. It was a melodic cross between Caribbean and Southern. She made another mental note and picked up the conversation.

"He just gets a little itchy and cranky around reporters. But he really is a right nice sorta fella," he chuckled, miming an exaggerated drawl.

"That remains to be seen," Reese teased, giving Raymond the benefit of her best smile.

"You just keep working on him," he offered in a stage whisper. "Get Carmen's help," he added, winking at Carmen. "She's the only one who can keep him in line."

"The way the two of you are talking, you're acting like I'm not even here," Maxwell shot in, pretending offense.

"I guess that's my cue," Raymond said. "Pleasure to meet you, Ms. Delaware. If you need anything, my office is right down the hall."

"Thank you. I appreciate that and please call me Reese."

"I sure will. As long as you call me R.J."

"Done."

Raymond moved down the hallway and disappeared around the corner.

"Are the two of you about ready?" Maxwell snapped in a

low rumble, annoyed by the innocent flirting between R.J. and Reese. He opened the door and stepped inside.

Carmen and Reese shared a curious look and crossed the threshold.

Reese's feet were on fire by the time Maxwell finished his tour of the tri-level facility. She'd lost count of the rooms, offices and various labs, not to mention the basement, and subbasement where all of the computer chips and electronic tapes were fabricated. No wonder everyone she ran into, no matter how fashionably they were dressed, wore sneakers.

What unnerved her the most was that Maxwell seemed to draw some sort of macabre pleasure at seeing her gritting her teeth from the ache in her toes. What happened to the man who all but admitted that something was happening between them?

"That about covers everything," he announced, when they returned to his office three hours later. He turned to her with what she'd swear was a look of mock concern. "I hope the tour wasn't too tiring. You do look a bit exhausted. Tokyo will be even more grueling. There are three different locations that I've selected, spread out across the provinces." He smiled a cat-like grin. "I hope you're up to it."

"I appreciated your concern," she replied in a tone strung as tight as the skin across a drum. "But there's no reason for it. So you don't have to pretend to care one way or the other."

"Whatever you may think of me, I'm not insensitive," he said in a voice so soft she felt herself drawing closer to be sure she'd heard correctly.

Sensing a moment of vulnerability, Reese took a deep breath and decided to take a chance. Purposefully she crossed the room and sat in a chair opposite his desk. She looked up at him.

"Then why do you treat me as though I was some awful

thing that has been dropped in your midst one minute and then act like you want to rip my clothes off the next? I know being followed around isn't easy. I know having someone ask questions about you from every Bubba, Buck, and Betty that knows you isn't always pleasant. But for the most part, a person in your position would kill for an opportunity like this. What is it that bothers you so much? Is it me?"

Maxwell looked at her for a long moment, seeing hurt, outrage and genuine concern brimming in her amber eyes.

"Are you hungry?" he asked in that same alluring tone, as if he hadn't heard a word she'd said. "I'm starved, and I know a wonderful restaurant where we can relax and talk."

She opened her mouth to toss out a sarcastic retort, but when she saw the gentle look in his eyes, she changed her mind. "Sounds perfect."

They rode for more than a half hour in silence. The only sounds were the soft notes of music coming from the incredible stereo system of Maxwell's black-on-black Corvette—his West Coast mode of transport.

He drove with a single-mindedness, intense—just as he appeared in every area of his life. A sudden, hot flush flooded Reese when she contemplated the thought of what he would be like as a lover. Would he be just as focused and controlled—just as relentless, consuming everything around him and giving little in return? Or was that the one aspect of the inscrutable Maxwell Knight that became unleashed?

She was so involved in her erotic meanderings that she didn't realize they'd stopped until Maxwell was at her side with the door open.

He leaned slightly forward and extended his hand. "We're here."

She looked up at him and her breath stuck in her throat when she saw the undeniable look of hunger dance in his exotic eyes. Almost as if afraid of being burned, she cautiously placed her hand in his.

The restaurant he'd selected was a half mile from the beach. From the vantage point of their table by the window, Reese could see the shoreline being stroked by the gentle lapping of the waves. Just off the horizon, the setting sun cast a brilliant orange glow across the shimmering water.

For several moments, Reese stared at the tranquil scene absorbing its beauty, allowing the moment to fill her with an inner peace.

While in profile, Maxwell seized the moment to enjoy watching Reese, unobserved, and felt the steady stirring within him. As much as he tried to deny it, Reese Delaware was getting under his skin and damnit, he wanted to keep her there. She embodied all of the qualities he'd want in his woman: brains, wit, confidence, honesty, beauty, and sexy as all hell. But he'd been burned before and wasn't sure if he could handle it again. What if he opened up to her, really opened up, and she spilled his deepest thoughts and dreams onto paper. His father had nearly been destroyed by a news-hungry journalist, and then they came after him when Victoria turned on him. It had taken months and a crack public-relations firm to cool the heels of the reporters.

He sighed in silence. He didn't get to where he was by not taking risks. And there was no question that Reese posed risks he probably could never conceive of.

As if aware of his close scrutiny, Reese turned her gaze in his direction and without preamble asked, "What are you thinking about, Max, right this minute?" She leaned forward as if his answer held the wisdom of the universe. Her eyes were transfixed on his face.

"I was wondering if I should take a chance—Reese." He, too, leaned closer until only the small glass centerpiece that held a scented candle separated them. He looked at her over the flickering flame. "I have every reason to be wary of you. My gut instinct tells me that I should give you the bare minimum and send you on your way."

"But," she whispered.

His chuckle was soft, deprecating. "But—" he smiled "—what I'm beginning to feel about you is telling me otherwise."

Reese grinned seductively. "Are you saying that you're having feelings for me Mr. Knight?" She ran her pearl-polished nail across his knuckle.

Maxwell laughed outright, shaking his head while he enclosed her hand in his. "Reese, any man would be a fool not to fall all over himself trying to find out what makes you tick." His voice descended another octave, and he stared into her questioning gaze. "And I don't consider myself to be anybody's fool."

Reese continued to look at him even as she raised his hand and brushed her moist lips across his knuckles. "Why don't we start from here, today," she said in her throaty voice, "to get to know each other and save the interviewing for the office." Her eyes were the wind racing across his face. "There are so many things I want to know about you—and believe me, they have nothing to do with my job." She grinned wickedly.

Maxwell's smile matched hers. "Things like what?" he challenged.

Reese opened her mouth to respond, when a shadow and the scent of Chanel No. 5 floated across their table. They both looked up simultaneously. Reese was instantly alert to the mixture of shock, anger, and something she couldn't place on Maxwell's face.

"Victoria," he said, his voice laden with memories.

The striking woman moved closer, her startling green eyes zeroing in on Maxwell. She reached for him, her long, slender hand the color of suntanned porcelain, clasped his, the one that had moments ago held Reese's.

"It's so good to see you again, Max." Her voice was light, almost musical in its quality, Reese noted with annoyance. Who was this woman and why in the devil did she have to show up now?

Victoria bent, daintily at the knee until she was eye-level with Maxwell. "How long will you be in town?"

He ignored her question, knowing that he'd answered it when they'd spoken on the phone. He eased his hand from her grasp and indicated Reese.

"Reese Delaware, this is Victoria Davenport." Reese spotted the telltale tightening of his jaw.

Slowly Victoria rose and Reese had the unsettling sensation that she knew this woman with the silky strawberry blond hair and green eyes. A dull pounding began in her temple. She winced.

Victoria summoned all of her self-control to quell the rage that bubbled to the surface like hot lava. So this was her. In the flesh. Her half sister. She swallowed her pride, and recalled her promise to her mother on her deathbed. Her smile never reached her uncanny eyes. "Nice to meet you. How did you two meet?" she asked in a sugar-based voice.

Maxwell leaned back in his seat. "Ms. Delaware is a journalist from *Visions Magazine*."

"Oh, yes," she said brightly. "I believe you did mention that on the phone."

Inwardly Reese cringed. So they'd spoken on the phone—recently. "Where are you from?" Reese queried, in her get-on-the-good-side interviewer's voice. "That's definitely not a California accent I hear." Her smile was full of encouragement, laced with venom.

Victoria tossed her mid-back-length hair over her shoulder

with a toss of her head—an affectation that Maxwell, at one time, thought was sexy. Now it annoyed him.

Victoria's smile was slow in coming. "Norfolk, Virginia. And you?"

"I grew up in Arlington, Virginia," Reese said slowly, as though searching for her thoughts.

Victoria felt a tightness in her chest. Her heart began to race. They'd practically been neighbors—all those years, she thought, the blood boiling in her veins with a surge of jealousy. "What a small world." She forced a smile.

Maxwell watched the exchange with growing interest. The two women were like night and day in personality and in looks. Reese with her dark beauty and Victoria with her lighter than air looks. How curious, he mused, that he had been, and now was, attracted to such opposites.

"Well," Victoria said on a long breath. "I must be going. I have some business clients waiting for me. Nice meeting you, Reese." She turned her attention toward Maxwell. "And I hope we can…get together before you head off to Tokyo."

"I don't see where I'll have time." He hesitated. "But maybe I'll give you a call."

She dug in her purse, pulled out a business card and jotted down a number. She handed the card to Maxwell. "Try," she softly urged. "That's the number where I'll be staying." She nodded in Reese's direction and glided away.

"So how long were you two involved?" Reese boldly asked.

"It's not anything I care to discuss," he replied succinctly, shutting down any further discussion on the subject of Victoria Davenport.

But even though Victoria was no longer in their midst, they were unable to recapture that brief moment of intimacy.

They ate their meal of steamed mussels and garnished

spaghetti in relative silence, punctuated by brief comments about the city of Los Angeles and places they'd traveled.

"I always envisioned Japan as an extremely exotic and mystical place," Reese said, as Maxwell drove toward the hotel.

He chuckled. "A lot of that is pure hype. For the most part, it's just like any other bustling metropolis, only more crowded."

"Humph. A lot of fun you are," she scoffed. "You've completely ruined my fantasy."

Maxwell sobered and slanted his eyes in her direction. "Seems like a few things got ruined tonight."

"We did seem to get sidetracked. But it isn't anything that can't be fixed." She turned in her seat to face his profile and waited.

Maxwell cut the engine of the Corvette. For a split second before he turned to her, he pursed his lips as if debating the inevitable. Catlike he turned toward her, his dark exotic eyes skimming across her face. His gaze seemed to hold her breath captive in her chest, and she began to feel the drumming of her pulse in her ears.

By infinitesimal degrees he leaned closer, his eyes never leaving her face. Just as his mouth was a whisper away from her, Reese's eyes fluttered closed in anticipation.

In a heady whisper, he commanded, "Look at me."

Reese slowly opened her eyes and was instantly drawn downward into the twin pools of midnight. His lips captured hers, his mouth hot, hard and moist. Unbidden, a sigh rose from deep in her throat when his tongue ran across her parted lips, before conquering the depths of her waiting mouth.

Fingers of steel clasped her head, pulling her closer, deeper into the kiss, while Reese clung to his shirt as if afraid of drowning in the tidal wave of the coupling.

A moan tore from Maxwell's throat as he pulled slowly

away. Gingerly he rested his forehead against hers and closed his eyes. He hadn't expected a simple kiss to affect him the way Reese's kisses did. Each time that his lips met hers, he lost another part of himself. He felt consumed by the roar in his heart. It would be so easy to let himself go with this woman—to give himself up to her and make her his.

Reese tenderly caressed the hard line of his jaw. She felt shaken, and lightheaded. Certainly she'd been kissed before more times than she could count. But never before had she experienced the awesomeness of a simple kiss. Max had transported her to a place she'd never been and her body, on fire, was screaming for more of the sweet torture.

Maxwell inhaled deeply then spoke in one long breath. "I think you ought to be getting upstairs. We have a busy day tomorrow," he added softly.

"Max, I…"

His dark eyes swirled, reflecting the raging storm that brewed in his spirit. But his voice masked the turmoil within. "It's really late Reese. I'll have a car pick you up at seven forty-five," he continued, now all business.

She'd never felt so humiliated. But she'd never give him the satisfaction of seeing her break down. "You're right. And I did want to get some writing done before I went to bed." She turned away from him and flipped the lock on the door. "Good night, Max, and thank you for a lovely evening."

Before he had a chance to respond, she was out of the car and pushing through the revolving doors of the hotel.

Maxwell pressed his head against the steering column. "You idiot," he bellowed, slamming his fists against the dashboard.

Reese walked blindly through the lobby, propelled by instinct. Each step she took she fought down the tears that

scorched her eyes. She would not cry, she vowed. The headache
that had begun at the restaurant built to a crescendo.

By the time she reached her room, she was weak with the
pain. Stumbling to the bathroom, she snatched her medication
from the cabinet. Downing two tablets without benefit of
water, she virtually crawled out of the bathroom to her bed.

Collapsing on top of the quilts, she squeezed her eyes shut
against the torrent of pain, and then the nightmares bloomed
with terrifying might.

Chapter 7

James Knight sat erect, waiting to be called in by his superiors. He knew what the questions would be. He was prepared.

"Colonel Knight."

James looked up, then stood at attention.

"The general will see you now."

James followed the secretary down the long corridor to the main conference room. Nothing good ever came out of meetings in this room, he reflected morosely. He'd attended enough of them to know.

Moments later, James was sequestered in the conference room full of secret service and high-ranking military staffers. He recognized several of the faces as Special Forces personnel as well.

"I'll get right to the point of this meeting Colonel Knight," General Murphy began. "It's been brought to our attention that your son," he paused and glanced at his notes, "Maxwell, is being interviewed by *Visions Magazine*."

"Yes, sir, he is."

General Murphy closed the folder and stared at James over the top of his glasses. "How much does he know, Colonel? And what are the chances of this reporter digging far enough back to uncover your activities?"

James cleared his throat and straightened in his seat. "My son knows absolutely nothing about what went on that morning, sir. He was only seventeen years old. As for the reporter, sir, I can't say what he or she will find out."

General Murphy pursed his lips, then clasped his hands in front of him. "That, unfortunately, is not good enough, Colonel Knight. We cannot allow even the slightest hint of wrongdoing to be linked to the military."

"I understand that, General. I…"

"No. I don't think you do understand, Colonel. We have a situation here. It's up to you to ensure that your son in no way points this reporter in our direction. Are you aware that the reporter is Hamilton Delaware's daughter?"

"Yes, sir." He swallowed back the memories. "She hasn't remembered anything, sir, or we would have known."

Murphy waved away his comment. "Do what you must, and we will do the same. Keep me posted." The general looked down at the files on the table. "You're dismissed, Colonel."

James stood at attention and saluted, turned on his heels and strode out. His son was in danger, he realized, the panic building with every step he took down the long, winding corridor. The general's message was shrouded, but clear. General Murphy would do whatever was necessary to cover the activities under his command. He'd done it once. He'd do it again and again. The Special Forces unit of the Air Force, of which James was still a part, would not be implicated, even if Murphy had to remove everyone with any knowledge of what they'd done.

James returned home feeling as if ten years had been added to his age. He knew what he had to do. Closing the door behind him, he walked into the kitchen, picked up the phone, and dialed his best friend Larry Templeton.

Victoria paced the carpeted living area of her hotel room. It was pure chance that she'd run into Max last night. Her intention was to arrive unannounced at his office. The fact that he'd taken Reese to what had once been their favorite restaurant in L.A. only fueled her anger. She only had three days in L.A. There was no way she could justify her absence from Washington any longer than that. She'd used her business contacts as an excuse for the trip, insisting that she'd be able to get the software manufacturers to mass-produce the new program she'd developed. She knew she had to go back with something. But her mind was on anything but business.

Whether Maxwell took her back or not, she would not sit idly by and let Reese get her privileged little claws into him. She faced herself in the mirror. She'd have to think of something.

Celeste awoke with the sun as she had for most of her adult life. She sat up in her queen-size bed, then sighed heavily. There was no reason to rush. She had nowhere to go and no one to rush to.

Until a year ago, she'd been a practicing RN doing private duty for the Air Force, until her growing illness made even that impossible. At least the money she still received helped. Two thousand dollars arrived in her account like clockwork. It's funny how twisted life becomes, she lamented. Twenty-eight years ago, she'd been paid to keep a secret. She'd felt outrage, humiliation. But she took it to survive. Thirteen years later, the stakes increased and the secret took on devastating proportions. She'd lived well, but lonely as a result. Now, once again, it was her means of survival.

She turned toward her nightstand to the framed photo of Hamilton Delaware, her one and only love.

With effort she pushed herself up from the bed. "Things could have been so different if you'd only given us a chance. My sister never loved you the way I did. Damn you Hamilton Delaware," she railed, hot tears of regret streaming down her smooth face of cinnamon. "Damn you for all you've done and God help me, I still love you."

She slipped to her knees and buried her face in the sheets of her bed, her body shaken by the force of her sobs.

The shrill ringing of the phone jarred Reese out of her troubled sleep. For several moments, she thought the sound was only part of the never-ending nightmare that had tortured her throughout the night.

The phone rang again. This time she opened her eyes but quickly shut them against the onslaught of the brilliant sun. With one hand over her eyes, she groped for the phone with the other.

"H-ello?"

"Hey, girl. It's me Lynnette. I'm at O'Hare on the next flight to L.A. I should be arriving at 5:00 p.m. your time."

"O-kay," she mumbled, struggling to get her thoughts to focus.

"Reese," Lynnette said, suddenly alert to Reese's disoriented tone. "What's wrong? Are you sick? I tried calling you all evening."

"No," she mumbled. "Really, I'm fine."

"Don't lie to me, Reese. It's the headaches again, isn't it? Tell me."

"Yes," she cried, burying her face in her hands. "And I don't know why. I was fine—until—I left Chicago."

"Something is triggering them. We need to just figure out what it is. What about the nightmares?" She held her breath.

"Those, too," she admitted in a ragged voice.

"Hang in there, girl. I'll see you in a few hours."

"Thank you, Lynn."

"It's gonna be cool. Gotta go, they're calling my flight." Lynnette hung up and dashed across the terminal, all the while thinking of her friend who was more like her sister. Growing up as teens, Lynnette had watched in fear, shock, and hurt when Reese would literally collapse under the force of the pain in her head. She'd spent nights with her when out of the blue, Reese would toss and turn, scream unintelligible sounds and practically leap from the bed, eyes wide and unseeing in a cold sweat. Yet she could remember nothing of the dreams.

Lynnette fastened her seatbelt and leaned back. It had been three years since the nightmares had stopped completely. The headaches were manageable. Lynnette closed her eyes. Why now? she wondered.

Chapter 8

Reese finally managed to get out of bed and make it to the bathroom. With great effort, she peeled her damp gown from her weary body.

Reaching for the faucets, she turned on the water full blast and stepped into the pounding shower.

Twenty minutes later she emerged from the bathroom, wrapped in a thick terry-cloth robe. She checked the clock on the nightstand. 10:30. She should have… "Oh, my God… the car…"

Walking as quickly as her wobbly legs would allow, she sat on the bed and dialed the front desk.

"Yes, Ms. Delaware. A driver was here for you this morning. We rang your room, but received no answer. When you didn't come down by eight-fifteen he left."

"I see. Thank you." Reese squeezed her eyes shut in frustration. "Now what am I going to do? Knowing Max he'll probably assume I'm having a tantrum about last night," she grumbled aloud. "Arrogant bastard."

She got up from the bed and began to pace, energy slowly winding its way through her body. "He had a helluva nerve kissing me like that and then acting as if nothing happened. He must take me for…"

The doorbell rang interrupting her diatribe. She stomped across the room fueled by her outrage and flung open the door.

"I got worried when the driver arrived without you."

Reese's stomach did a quick somersault while her brain scrambled for organization. "M-ax-well." At that precise moment, with him standing in front of her, looking for all the world as if he'd just stepped off the cover of *Ebony Man Magazine,* she had a difficult time trying to remember why she'd been so pissed-off only minutes ago.

"How's the headache?"

Briefly she frowned in confusion. "How did you…?"

"I could see the beginnings last night." He paused. "I should have stayed to make sure you were alright. I'm sorry."

His apology tugged on her heart. "There's no need to apologize. I didn't realize it was that obvious," she said softly.

He slipped his hands in the pockets of his cream-colored linen slacks in an effort to keep from reaching out and touching her. His dreams had been filled with her; in front of him, at his side, beneath him. When he finally tore himself away from his erotic dreams, he knew he had to see her.

Maxwell angled his chin in the direction of the interior of the suite. "May I come in?" His dark eyes swept over her and his voice reached down to the bottom of her soul. "I'll only stay as long as you want me to. I promise."

A surge of heat engulfed her, while her heart roared so

loudly she swore it would burst. "Sure." She stepped aside and tugged on the belt of her robe. "Come on in."

Maxwell followed her into the suite, the scent of her freshly bathed body leaving a sensual trail for him to follow.

"Make yourself comfortable," she suggested, stopping in front of the couch. "I'll just be a few minutes." Quickly she disappeared into the bedroom.

"What in the devil am I going to put on?" she mumbled, frantically tearing through her wardrobe. Finally she decided on a lemon-yellow tank top and lime green cotton slacks, with a pair of espadrilles that matched her top. She slipped a slinky gold belt through the loops of her slacks and pushed tiny gold studs through her ears.

A look in the mirror caused her to gasp in horror. Her hair was a wreck, hanging limply around her shoulders from the steam of the shower. She pulled a stiff brush through her hair and quickly twisted it into a neat French roll.

"Not bad," she nodded to her reflection. Then across her lips she added the barest hint of cinnamon lip gloss, and stroked her lashes with jet black mascara.

"You go, girl," she said, smiling. Taking a fortifying breath, she reentered the living area.

Maxwell stood up the moment she entered and his heart seemed to shift in his chest. *She was so lovely.*

"Hope I didn't take too long." She made her way across the room, but stopped several feet away from him.

Maxwell crossed the remaining space that separated them. He gave her one long heated look that set her body aglow, and without further waiting swiftly took her into his arms, crushing her against his pulsing body.

His mouth, hungry for the taste of her again, took her lips, briefly savoring their sweetness before dipping into the hot core of her mouth.

Reese wrapped her arms around his hard, lean body,

eager to feel the strength of him as he surged against her. She suckled his tongue, committing its texture to memory, allowing it to awaken every nerve ending in her body.

An unstoppable need to know her filled him with the force of a monsoon, building in ferocity. His hands began a slow dance along her back, compelling her to arch closer—tighter. Downward his hands trailed, stroking her round hips, pulling the heart of her desire against the heat of his.

He moaned her name as he pulled away from her lips, only to run his tongue along the tender cords of her neck. Reese trembled and cried out his name, tossing her head back to give him full access.

"I want you, Reese. Here and now. I won't deny that anymore. But that would be too easy," he groaned in her ear. He took a step back, looked into her eyes and stroked her face with his fingertip. "You deserve more than just a mating game." He took a breath. "And I don't know if I'm capable of giving more than that. Not anymore."

He set her away from him and turned his back to her.

"Max," she whispered, trembling from the aftermath of his loving. She reached out to touch his stiff shoulder. "Please don't turn away from me. Talk to me—please."

He expelled a short, hollow laugh. "Reese, I wouldn't know where to begin."

She came around to stand in front of him. "How about if I start first," she offered.

Maxwell looked into her eyes, expecting some insignificant piece of information. But nothing could have prepared him for her revelation.

Chapter 9

Maxwell stared at Reese for several long moments, attempting to digest what she'd said.

"Pretty unbelievable, huh?"

Maxwell's eyebrows rose then lowered in silent response. "How could you not remember anything before the accident?" he asked, his voice heavy with bewilderment.

Reese slowly shook her head. "I've been to every doctor, neurosurgeon, psychologist and psychiatrist worth their shingle. The general consensus is that there's nothing physically wrong with me. The headaches and the nightmares are all a manifestation of my intentional attempt to suppress my memory."

"That's what the doctors told you?" he sputtered in disbelief.

Reese nodded. "That's the only explanation any of them could offer. The trauma of the accident was so severe that I've completely erased it and my entire life leading up to it."

Maxwell leaned slightly forward, bracing his arms on his thighs. "You have no memory of the first fifteen years of your life?" he asked in astonished wonder.

"None," she said in a tone of resignation.

Maxwell heaved a sigh. "This is just incredible." He got up to kneel in front of where she sat. "How do you deal with it?" he asked with such absolute sincerity it tore at her heart.

"Day by day," she answered softly. "Just day by day."

He reached out, letting the tip of his index finger trail along the contours of her face. Then gently he asked, "Do you want to remember, Reese—really want to remember?"

Briefly she shut her eyes. "At times, especially when the pain and the nightmares are so bad that I just wish I would die. Then, when things are good, I don't want to know. If what happened was that horrible, maybe it's best I never remember."

"That can't be better, Reese. And the only way to rid yourself of the pain and the nightmares is to rid yourself of the fear of remembering."

"Yes, doc," she teased, chucking him under the chin in an attempt to lighten the somber mood. She popped up from her seat and slowly began to pace. Then she suddenly turned toward him. "What's most disturbing, at the moment, is that the headaches and the nightmares started again…when I met you."

Maxwell's dark eyes widened. "Let me get this straight. You started having these reoccurrences after we met?"

"Yes. At first I thought it was the stress of the trip. But the headaches started getting worse, like I told you. I had to begin taking the prescription medicine again. And then the nightmares." She shut her eyes and wrapped her arms around her waist as a tremor shimmied through her. "I hadn't suffered from those in close to three years."

An unnatural sense of foreboding settled in the pit of

Maxwell's belly. There was a reason for everything, he rationalized. But what could the reason be for him to be the catalyst that triggered her ordeal?

"How do you feel right now, right at this moment?"

"Right now I feel fine. The pain is gone and I can't remember my dreams."

"Good. Come on. Let's go." He grabbed her hand and pulled her toward the door.

"Where?" she cried doubling her step to keep up with him.

"Just get your purse, or whatever, and let's go. What you need is a little R&R. And I have just the place."

"But what about work?" she giggled, caught up in the moment.

"What about it?" he grinned over his shoulder.

Maxwell pressed the button for the sunroof of the car, turned up the music, and sped off.

"Now are you going to tell me where we're going?"

He turned to her and smiled. "Just relax," he said, patting her folded hands. "I guarantee you're going to love it."

Reese pouted but held her tongue. When was the last time she'd done anything spontaneously? Too long, she concluded. The only way she'd been able to manage her life, such as it was, was to organize and compartmentalize every aspect of it. That ritual seemed to give some validity to her existence, as if documenting her every move would eradicate the possibility that she'd ever forget anything again.

"Do you keep a journal?" Maxwell asked out of the blue, almost as if he'd just taken a short hop through her thoughts.

Reese turned to him. Her right eyebrow arched. "Why did you ask me that?"

"It just seems like you would. Keeping notes, a diary or

journal is a good way to record your thoughts. I would think that your…situation is a basis for you being a journalist as well. Always searching for the truth, uncovering information." He glanced at her. "So, do you?"

"Yes, Sherlock," she retorted, mystified by his astuteness. "As a matter of fact, I do."

"Did you keep a diary before—the accident?"

Sadly she shook her head. "I only wish that I had." Then she chuckled halfheartedly. "Even if I did, I wouldn't remember where I'd put it."

"That's unfortunate, but it's just so amazing to me how you've managed to cope all of these years. What about school? How did you function?"

"That's one of the curious things of this whole illness. After I came out of the coma, I was able to function relatively normally. I knew how to read, write, dress—everything. I hadn't forgotten any of it. But my life, my family, friends, places I'd been, things I'd heard or seen were gone as if they'd never existed."

Maxwell frowned and his admiration for Reese Delaware grew. She was a phenomenal woman. And to look at her and be in her presence, one would never suspect all that she'd endured. She was a survivor, strong and determined, like the great Sphinx of Egypt. But beneath the tough, got-it-together exterior was a very vulnerable woman who needed—and quite possibly needed more than he would ever be able to give. The thought saddened him.

They'd been on the road for more than two hours, driving in comfortable silence punctuated by brief comments about the magnificent scenery or the balmy air.

By degrees, Reese felt her entire self uncoil and relax as she gave in to the calming sensations that filled her spirit. She took in her surroundings and noticed that they turned onto the exit marked San Diego. Well, at least she had an idea what town they were headed for.

"We're almost there," Maxwell announced.

"Almost where?"

"You'll see." He grinned.

It was close to a half hour later when Maxwell turned onto a long sandy drive. Up ahead sat an architect's dream. The stunning structure was a model of glass, chrome, and wood. Even from where she sat, she could see the entire interior of the two-story home, with winding staircases and timeless furnishings.

He pulled into the underground garage and cut the engine. "Come on. Let me show you around."

Reese followed him around the rambling abode, awestruck. Words to describe the hideaway palace escaped her.

Every room on the second level opened to a deck where the beach was clearly visible. And as much as she hated to cook, she could easily change her tune if she had a kitchen like Max's. Light streamed in from every angle, dancing off of the chrome and aluminum fixtures and utensils. The center island was a work of art in black and white marble that matched the gleaming tile floors.

"Kick off your shoes and make yourself at home," he instructed. "Today is your day. If you feel like dancing," he said giving her a low bow, "we have—" he pressed a button in the wall "—music." The silky, sexy voice of Marvin Gaye's "Distant Lover" floated through the air. "If you feel like swimming, the heated pool is below." He indicated a door that led to the basement. He grinned mischievously as he watched the expression of childlike wonder skip across her face. "Should you care to immerse yourself in a jettison of aquatic relief, the Jacuzzi is upstairs."

Reese beamed in delight. "This is like taking a trip to Disney World. What about if I'm hungry?" she tossed out.

"The kitchen, madame, is thataway. I'm sure it's fully stocked and everything you could want is in there. Carmen is always good about taking care of those details."

Reese blew out a long breath, put her hands on her waist, and looked all around like a tourist on their first trip to the big city. "This place is absolutely fantastic," she said finally. She turned to find Maxwell leaning casually against the archway. "But when do you get the chance to enjoy it?"

"Not often enough," he admitted, folding his arms in front of him. "But I try to get down here at least every two to three months."

Reese nodded. She wanted to ask him how many women he'd shared the glass wonderland with. She wanted to ask him if this was all part of the seduction. And she did.

"How often do you bring company to this little den of delights?"

The corner of Maxwell's mouth quirked upward in a grin. "Do you really want to know?" he taunted.

"I wouldn't have asked if I didn't," she said, raising her chin in challenge.

"Not as often as I'd like," he said being intentionally evasive.

"Seems like I've heard that somewhere before."

Maxwell pushed away from the door, crossed the short space and stepped right up to her, forcing her to look up into his eyes. His voice dropped to a rumbling whisper. "Let's just say your question has been asked and answered." His dark gaze did a slow waltz across her face. "The important thing is you're here—right now. Anything or anyone before you, before now, doesn't matter. So don't let it."

He was so close, Reese could feel the heat from his body reach out and wrap around her. Her heart was racing and for a moment she couldn't breathe. Suddenly he turned away and the spell was broken.

"I'm going upstairs for a minute," he said over his shoulder. "Enjoy yourself in the meantime."

Reese watched him bound up the stairs. She shook her head in frustration. She just couldn't figure him out. One minute he was cool and distant, the next he acted as if he'd strip her bare with the slightest provocation.

She crossed the sunken living room and walked around the redwood table that dominated the center of the room. The hardwood floors, all the color of sand, gleamed as the rays of the sun bounced off of them.

Soft music drifted through the rooms from speakers built strategically into the walls. Reese opened the sliding glass doors and stepped out onto the enclosed deck. She inhaled deeply of the sea-washed air, invigorating herself. Where was all of the California smog she'd heard about? From her vantage point, she could see for miles in every direction. She thought she spotted a car nestled in the shrubs just beyond the perimeter of the house. But there was no reason for...

"Enjoying the view?"

Reese jumped at the sudden sound of his voice so close to her ear. She hadn't heard his approach.

"You should make some noise and let a person know you're around," she said, annoyed at having been caught unaware.

"Sorry," he chuckled. "Old habit."

"What kind of habit—scaring people to death?"

Maxwell hung his head and grinned. "Not exactly," he said, looking up.

If she didn't know better she'd swear his eyes were twinkling. "What exactly does that mean?"

He could see the beginning of a smile teasing the corners of her mouth and knew that he was on safer ground. He slid his hands into the pockets of his slacks. "Well I've studied martial arts for a little over twenty years," he began. "It stresses the importance of harnessing your energy to make your movements one with the environment. When you can accomplish that, you can virtually move from space to space without disturbance."

That would certainly account for his uncanny ability to sit for long periods of time without seeming to move a muscle, she realized. "Like a ninja or something," she offered trying to make a correlation to something familiar.

Maxwell chuckled and shook his head. "Yeah, something like that," he teased.

Reese impatiently folded her arms beneath her breasts. "Don't patronize me," she said in a huff. Her eyes narrowed daring him to challenge her.

He held up his palms in a fending off position. "Sorry," he apologized with what he felt was just the right amount of sincerity to appease her. She still rolled her eyes.

"Can I interest you in something to eat—to make amends?"

One side of her mouth inched upward as she struggled to keep from smiling. "That's a start."

Maxwell turned and stepped through the opening in the sliding door. Reese was on his heels beaming like a Cheshire cat.

Reese sat on one side of the island on a bar stool with her feet wrapped around the rungs watching Maxwell work wonders in the kitchen. Within minutes, mouthwatering aromas permeated the air.

"Smells good," Reese said, skepticism underscoring her husky voice.

"I'm sure you'll be quite pleased, Ms. Delaware," was his pointed reply. He refused to rise to the bait.

She had no intention of letting him off that easy. "So— what are we having?"

"Chef's surprise."

She tossed her head back and laughed. "I can see the headlines now," she spouted, theatrically spreading her hands through the air. "World-famous journalist, Reese Delaware, found poisoned in the posh home of computer wizard, Maxwell Knight."

"Very funny," he grumbled good-naturedly. "I'll have you know that I've been cooking since my preteen years. Since my father was in the military, we traveled a great deal." He paused to sprinkle some hand-chopped condiments onto the sizzling wok. "With my stepmother working, I learned how to cook as well as pick up some of the native recipes."

"What did your father do?"

"Military intelligence," he scoffed. "Some high-level stuff he never wanted to talk about."

"Hmm." Reese let that bit of information sink in. "What about your mother? You mentioned stepmother."

Maxwell shrugged. "I never knew my birth mother. My father met her when he was stationed in Japan." He looked down at his handiwork and stirred. "I always felt that it was a part of me that was missing. I never even saw a picture of her." He chuckled softly and continued as if speaking to himself. "I grew up with these fantasies about her, as if my thoughts could somehow make her real. My father never wanted to discuss her other than to say that she'd died shortly after my birth. I guess that's why I was so adamant about capturing and understanding that aspect of my heritage. I did my graduate work in Tokyo, learned the language, tried to assimilate into their society." He sighed. "But it didn't work. I never felt that I fit in."

The underlying pain in his voice touched her so deeply she could almost feel his loneliness. "But what about your stepmother?" she asked gently.

"She was there," he commented in a monotone. "We never really had a relationship. I always sensed that she resented me for some reason. And I could never understand why." He hesitated before speaking again. "I tried to get to know her, be a good son, but nothing made much of a difference."

"It's strange," she began slowly, "but we have a lot in common. Even though you had parents, they were lost to you, just as my parents are lost to me." She sighed, casting aside the melancholy. "Where are some of the places you've been?" she asked, wanting to change the subject.

"All over Japan." He briskly stirred the contents in the wok, then turned off the jet. "Parts of Europe, Africa, South America, and the Philippines." He shrugged nonchalantly.

"Is that the reason why it's so important for you to have a place to call home when you travel?"

He turned to look at her, curiosity and a deeper sense of awareness swam in his eyes. "That's part of it," he answered softly and turned back to his work, spooning the food onto a platter. Maxwell took a deep breath and let out an inaudible sigh. He struggled to keep from smiling. Just talking to her like a person and expressing his feelings about something so personal to him, actually felt good. It didn't hurt like he thought it would. She seemed to be able to read him and gauge his feelings. Maybe it was the journalist in her. But a part of him knew better. Reese was a naturally caring and compassionate woman. He wanted to trust her. He wanted to let go and be all that he could be—and he wanted it with her.

He felt the air stir around him and knew before turning that she had descended from her perch and was approaching him. He waited until he was certain she stood directly behind him before he spun around and pulled her belly to belly against him.

A gasp of surprise burst from her startled lips. Maxwell's grin was slow and sensual. His eyes darkened and the sun pouring into the kitchen bounced off of them making the orbs sparkle with mystery.

His voice started deep down in his chest. "You shouldn't sneak up on a person," he taunted, as he lowered his head to brush his lips against her neck. "I'll have to teach you how to become—" he planted a trail of hot kisses along her neck "—one with your environment." His fingers pressed into her supple flesh, searing her with his mark.

Breathless, she couldn't respond. Her eyes fluttered closed when the heat of his nearness entered her body, igniting her.

Maxwell let his tongue wander along the sensitive cord of her neck, suckling the muscle until Reese moaned and trembled with growing arousal. His hands slowly explored the curves of her body as his mind envisioned the lusciousness of her hips, the fullness of her breasts, the arch of her incredible legs as they would be, devoid of clothing—with her wearing no more than the mystical scent of her body oil.

Reese moaned, unabashed when the heat of his succulent mouth finally claimed hers. She felt her heart slam against her chest and the blood rush to her center when the pads of his thumbs stroked the undersides of her breasts. She swayed against him, needing him to be nearer, daring him to come closer.

"Reese," he uttered milliseconds before his heat-seeking tongue delved into the depths of her mouth. His fingers splayed and he used them like combs to thread through her hair, loosening it to fan around her, the pins holding it in place spiraling to the floor. Maxwell eased her toward the island until her lush bottom grazed the edge. He lifted her until she sat and he stepped between her parted thighs, his steely erection throbbing against her feminine heat.

Her mind was spinning. She couldn't think and didn't want

to. It all felt too good. "Yesss," she hissed between her teeth when his hands slid beneath her top to cup her bare breasts.

"Hmm, so sweet," he whispered. "I'm going to taste you Reese," he whispered, gently squeezing the firm mounds, his thumbs flicking across the dark almond nipples. He pushed the lemon-yellow top upward, inch by inch revealing the silken milk chocolate skin until her breasts jutted out to him, demanding to be taken.

A tremor of unimaginable pleasure shot through her when his hot tongue stroked one distended tip and then the other. In turn he laved, then sucked one sensitive breast and then the other, causing shudders of desire to ripple throughout her being—all the while, he murmured gentle words of loving—telling her how beautiful she was—how much he wanted her—what he wanted to do to her.

Reese was caught in a vortex of yearning. She felt weak and at the same time powerful, knowing that she was able to awaken such passion in this man who kept such a tight rein on his emotions. And she was humbled by that knowledge.

The wall came down, brick by brick. Reese was pulling them away, dismantling his impenetrable wall with each breath she took, each outcry of his name. He wanted to stop her before she discovered the direct pathway to his heart, but she was too close, her hold over him too secure. He could not have detered her path if he'd tried. And deep inside he realized he didn't have the strength to withstand her entry into his soul.

"Not here," he rasped gathering her trembling body close to him, willing her to become a part of him, drawing on his last bit of self-control. "Not like this." He stared into her glowing eyes—eyes that held so many unspoken questions.

He lifted her, letting her body slide down the length of his. "I know the perfect place," he whispered against her mouth, taking one last kiss. He took her hand, snatched her purse from the table and led her out of the house, back to the parked car. He glanced at her just before they pulled away. "I want our first time to be the only time you'll ever remember with any man. Once I let you into my heart, Reese, there's no turning back. You'll be mine. I promise you that." His eyes raced over her face. "Are you sure this is what you want?"

She moved toward him, her hand reaching out to caress his face, stroking away the final vestiges of worry from his countenance. "Yes," she whispered. "You are what I want."

He leaned closer, taking her chin in his palm and pulling her toward him. His mouth covered hers in a long, mind-shattering kiss. Slowly he eased away. "Then that's what you'll have."

Maxwell put the car in gear, backed out of the driveway, and headed toward the docks.

"They just pulled off," the man in the dark sedan said into his radio.

"Keep a safe distance. And don't lose them," came the reply.

"Yes sir."

"Keep me posted."

Chapter 10

"Do I at least get a hint this time about where we're going?" Reese quizzed, wiggling down in her seat.

"I'm going to take you to someplace beautiful, sultry, and romantic," Maxwell teased, planting a kiss on Reese's forehead. "The stars will be our canopy, the hot night our blanket, ancient ruins that have withstood the test of time will be our beginning."

"It doesn't sound real," she said wistfully, shutting her eyes and smiling at the images.

"It's very real. I will tell you this. It's across the water and we'll be there in about an hour. Now just sit back and relax. I promise it'll be worth the ride."

On the short drive to the open-air trolley, Max stole furtive glances in Reese's direction, intermittently holding her hand then bringing it gently to his lips. He knew there was no turning back now, he'd crossed the last line of his defense. He'd stated his intentions and she'd capitulated. Part of him still clung to the security of elusiveness. Yet the part that needed to be cared for—accepted—loved totally—fought the winning battle.

When she looked at him, as she was doing now, as if he were the only man in the world, all of his doubts and reservations blew away with the tropical breeze around them.

"I know it's going to be wonderful, Max," she whispered as if reading his thoughts. "It seems as if a part of me wanted what is sure to come the moment I saw you." She moved over and rested her head on his shoulder. "I'm putting my trust, my heart on the line and in your hands. Trust me with yours."

Maxwell looked down into her eyes that sparkled up at him with so much hope, so much faith. He smiled, gently kissed her lips and turned his attentions back to the road.

As promised, the drive to the trolley was short, accented by the beautiful scenery of San Diego's countryside. Maxwell smoothly donned the role of tour guide, pointing out sites of interest. "That's Horton Plaza to our right," he indicated with a thrust of his chin. "Every store that's worth its logo is in there… As a matter of fact…" He turned off the main highway, cut around traffic, and pulled into the plaza's huge parking lot. "We have a stop to make before we get on the trolley," Maxwell announced, bringing the Corvette to a squealing halt.

"Max. For heaven's sake, what now?" Reese asked, giggling as he rounded the car and helped her out.

He pulled her long, lush body fully against him, briefly sampling the sweetness of her thoroughly kissed lips. "I don't think you have everything you're going to need in that little purse of yours," he said in a husky undertone. Reese's heartbeat accelerated when she witnessed the fire dance in his eyes.

"Is that right?" she countered, looking boldly up at him. "What did you have in mind?"

"Anything your heart desires, baby." His fingers ran along her jawline, causing her to shiver with need. "Something soft, something sheer, something for the water, the nightlife, and then—nothing at all." His mouth curved upward in a devilish grin.

Reese put her hand in his and smiled wickedly. "Let the shopping begin."

They both laughed like two young lovers and headed off toward the stores.

Maxwell had insisted on paying for everything. Loaded down with shopping bags, straw hats, dark glasses, and an array of baseball caps, they stuffed their joint purchases in the trunk and sped off toward the trolley in downtown San Diego, laughing, kissing and holding hands all the way. By the time they arrived, parked and unloaded their packages, the last passenger was boarding. Racing like mad down the street, they hopped aboard and headed off toward the Mexican border only to hop a taxi into Tijuana. Reese was sure this was their final destination, until Maxwell announced that they needed a water taxi to cross the bay. Totally perplexed, Reese followed, this time not bothering to ask where they were going. It was apparent that Maxwell was a man of few words and many secrets. Whatever he wanted her to know he'd tell her, and the hell with anything else.

The water taxi pulled to a stop some fifteen minutes later. Maxwell stepped out and helped Reese to her feet. The bags followed. "We're really here this time," Maxwell grinned, seeing the look of skepticism on her face. "I swear," he added, holding up his hand.

"That remains to be seen," she answered, doubtful. Reese took the opportunity to look around and realized that she was actually on an island. "Can you please tell me where we are?"

Maxwell put his arm around her shoulder. "We're on Coronado Island across the bay from Tijuana, Mexico."

Reese blinked back her astonishment. When Maxwell Knight did something, it was no holds barred. She wondered what else he had up his short sleeves.

"When I said I was going to make our time together memorable, that's exactly what I meant. Now, come on. We have to check in."

Reese was too awestruck to respond, so she put her faith in this man who had her head spinning.

Reese slowly spun around in the room they'd share together. Her heart filled with joy and wonder. It was straight out of the movies. High archways, in lieu of doors, led from one open-aired room to another. The whitewashed stucco walls, flower-filled balconies, huge four-poster bed, and hardwood floors made her sigh with delight. She felt as if she'd been transported to another time and place. Any minute she expected Clint Eastwood to step onto the scene. It was no wonder that Hotel del Coronado was deemed a historic site on the tiny island. From the balcony, she could see the large sand dunes covered with brilliant colored flowers and the slow-walking, hand-holding couples who strolled along the white, sandy beach and dusty roads. Vendors peddling their wares overflowed onto the street, against a backdrop of houses built into the mountainside.

Even though the hotel, built in the early 1900s, maintained its aesthetic look, it also boasted ultra-modern facilities. The bathroom was right out of *Architectural Digest* with gold-plated faucets, a Jacuzzi, his and her sinks, and a stall shower.

"This is absolutely fabulous, Max," she murmured. She

shook her head, at a loss for words. She looked up at him from beneath dark lashes. "You did all of this for me?"

"For us," he corrected, crossing the room to meet her halfway. "Because no matter what happens between us Reese, we've started building memories. From the first moment we met." His smile was slow and seductive as he tapped his index finger against her temple. He slid his arms around her slender waist and pulled her close. He lowered his head to drop a soft kiss on her lips. "And I have no intention of letting you forget any moment that we share." He took a deep breath. "Since it's still early, why don't we take a quick tour before everyone pulls in their tents for siesta?"

Reese grinned. "Sounds perfect." She held up a finger and spun away. "Let me just grab my hat," she said, snatching up the wide-brimmed hat and setting it jauntily on her head. She slipped her dark glasses on and posed, pulling her glasses down to the bridge of her nose with one hand, and fisting the other on a jutting hip. "Ready when you are sailor," she said in a Mae West affectation.

Together they wandered in and out of small, quaint shops, inhaled the beach-washed air, ate tacos and washed them down with margaritas. Maxwell haggled with each and every vendor, just for the fun of it, Reese realized—tickled by his un-Maxwell-Knight-like behavior. Here was a man who could be romantic, charming, fun, full of mischief, extravagance, and mystery all rolled up into one. What had she gotten herself into with this man who defied explanation? Away from the office, he was a completely different man. He wasn't some impenetrable force. She looked up at his profile while he pointed out yet another place for them to traipse. If anything, she thought, he was a very vulnerable man who longed to share a part of himself with that special someone.

* * *

The blazing summer sun was at its highest point in the sky. When they reemerged from their room donned in bathing suits, it was still a balmy eighty degrees with the warm sea air blowing off of the beach.

Maxwell had challenged Reese to a race on Jet Skis, and of course Reese never backed down from a challenge—whether she knew how to Jet Ski or not! She figured she'd seen enough on television. So what could be so hard?

Drenched and waterlogged from the amount of water she'd ingested, Reese threw up the white flag and herself across the warm sand.

"You win," she puffed, draping her arm across her eyes.

Maxwell stood over her chuckling. "Are you all right?" He laughed.

Reese removed her arm and squinted up at him. She sucked her teeth, rolled her eyes, and continued to suffer in silence.

Maxwell reached down and grabbed her arm, pulling her to her feet. "I have just the thing to make you feel better."

"What now?" she grumbled, "deep-sea diving?"

Maxwell roared with laughter pulling her snugly against him. "There is fish involved. But we won't have to get it ourselves."

"Small blessings.

"Come on, let's get changed into something more appropriate."

"Where did you learn to Jet Ski?" Reese asked, toweling off her hair.

Maxwell crossed the room and opened the closet door in search of an outfit. "When I was about eighteen my father was stationed on one of the bases in Los Angeles. I spent tons of time on the beach that summer. I got better when I went to Nassau. It's a favorite pastime over there."

Reese wrapped her damp body and wet bathing suit in a towel and plopped down on the bed. "You've done so many wonderful things. Traveling around the world with your parents did have its merits."

Maxwell shrugged. "I suppose. In terms of expanding my horizons," he said sarcastically, "I guess it did. But family life was pretty null and void."

"What about your stepmother? What did she do?"

"Tried unsuccessfully to make a life for me and my father." He shook his head. "We were both so busy trying to get my father's attention until we pretty much ignored each other. When she wasn't redecorating one of the many homes we lived in, she was tending to our needs." He sighed. "Looking back now, I realize how hard it must have been for her. Unfortunately, growing up I didn't see and didn't care. By the time I was old enough to 'get it' we were practically strangers. I had withdrawn into the solitary world of computers and she withdrew into her books, and volunteer organizations."

"What about now?"

He shrugged again. "I call, she calls, we exchange cards on all the appropriate occasions." He turned away, memories of his lonely childhood washing over him.

"What is your relationship with your father?"

"Humph." He chuckled mirthlessly. "My father, big-time special forces agent… What can I say about James Knight? The bottom line is, he is a man who is dedicated to one thing and one thing alone, the United States government—no matter what the cost. He's a hard-line military man with a military man mentality. There's no room in his life for sentimentalities, second guessing, or anyone who doesn't understand."

Reese shook her head sadly. "I thought I always had it rough," she commented wryly. "My aunt Celeste treated me as if I had the plague or something. I know she felt trapped with having to raise me. But I could never understand her resentment of me. She always treated me as if my existence was somehow responsible for my family's death. As if by not remembering I was denigrating their memory. I would have thought that she would have loved me, if for no other reason than I was her sister's daughter—the only connection left of her family." Her voice broke. "But she never did."

"So you retreated into a world of writing?" Maxwell interjected. "As I escaped into the world of computers."

She nodded. "Yes. That and an insatiable desire to find answers, the truth in every story I wrote. Like that would somehow validate my life," she continued in a wistful tone.

"What a pair we are," he said, trying to make light of the situation.

Reese abruptly got up and came to stand in front of him. She looked up into his stern face. "I'd say we make a great pair. We're survivors. We have strength of character. We know what it feels like to need to be cared about and wanting to give that caring in return tenfold." She smoothed her hand across his cheek. "No matter what happens in this relationship, we'll be richer for it. I just know that."

Maxwell touched her lips lightly with his. "Is that your writer's instinct talking again?"

"No," she grinned. "Woman's intuition."

Reese had changed into the sea-green gauze dress that Maxwell had specifically chosen for her. He said it did enchanting things for her eyes and flawless chocolate-brown complexion. She'd twisted her hair atop her head, leaving wispy tendrils draping around her face and neck. Her only jewelry was gold studs and a single gold bangle that she wore on her left wrist.

Maxwell selected a soft cotton shirt of cinnamon with

matching slacks, set off by a lizard belt and coordinating sandals, the earthy colors accenting his smooth bronze tones. Reese was shocked, yet pleasantly pleased to see a tiny, twinkling diamond stud in his left ear. Maxwell was full of surprises.

As they walked hand in hand toward the restaurant, Maxwell realized how light of spirit he felt. It had been so long since he'd just enjoyed without reservation—time spent with a woman for the pure pleasure of it. If he and Reese made love he was sure it would be wonderful. But even if they didn't, these magical moments would always remain in his heart. What would life be like to have Reese Delaware in it every day?

The tangy aroma of Mexican food swirled around the restaurant. Fajitas sizzled and popped on table tops, the scent of green peppers, onions and steamed tomatoes were enough to make your mouth water. Sautéed and grilled fish permeated the air. And margaritas and tequilas flowed as readily as running water.

The tiny restaurant was filled to capacity. Every red and white checkered table was occupied with couples or groups reveling in the evening, tapping their hands and feet to the strumming of guitar players who serenaded the audience.

"This is marvelous," Reese said, taking in the atmosphere. She turned her smiling gaze on Maxwell. Her eyes glowed with happiness.

"I'm glad you like it. The food here is fabulous."

"Even if it wasn't, I'd still have a great time." She laughed. "Being an investigative journalist has its merits," she admitted halfheartedly. "Unfortunately, when you travel, you're so intent on getting a story you rarely have the time to forge relationships or enjoy the ambiance of the places you visit. This is like a trip to heaven. I'll never forget it. And I want to thank you for it."

"I have to admit, I was being a bit selfish when I came up with this brilliant scheme." He grinned. "I needed to get away, probably just as much as you did. And—" he reached across the table and clasped her hand in his "—I wanted to spend some time with you, away from the office, away from the things that have shaped us into what the world sees. I wanted to find out what kind of woman you were, not how good you were at your job."

"And?" she probed gently, her heart racing.

"So far, pretty lady," he said roughly, stroking his finger along her nose, "things are looking damned good."

After dinner, they strolled along the white sandy beach, letting the warm, lapping waves rush across their bare feet. A crescent moon hung at that old precarious angle, illuminating the picture-perfect sky to a backdrop of countless, twinkling stars.

Reese's ankle-length dress blew sensuously around her long bare legs, molding the near-sheer dress to her voluptuous body. Maxwell was totally taken with her unadulterated beauty. She was a vision to behold and for now, she was his.

"Let's go upstairs," Maxwell said, in an urgent whisper, turning her to face him.

Reese's eyes swam across his face, taking in the hunger in his eyes, feeling the heat fan out from his body and surround her. She felt the hardness of him pulse with need against the juncture of her thighs and she felt suddenly weak and powerful in the same breath.

She reached up and cupped his face in her hand. "Yes," she whispered with the same fervid urgency. "Yes."

Reese stood facing him, the romantically haunting moonlight, streaming in from the arched window, cast an ethereal glow around their silhouettes.

Maxwell stepped closer to her, his hand grazed each of her shoulders, trailing down her smooth arms until he captured her hands. "You tell me when to stop," he said, shuddering at the thought that she might resist his ardent advances.

"Never," she whispered in response.

He eased his caress back up her arms until he reached her shoulders. Slowly, he eased the straps down until the dress was only held up by the tips of her rounded breasts. He moved closer and tilted her face up to his with the tip of his finger.

The meeting of their lips was languescent, tentative, coming together for the very first time on this awakening new level of awareness in their budding relationship. The fire between them began as a single, tiny flame fanned by the gusty wind of their longing for each other, building to a roaring inferno as their bodies melded one onto the other, discovering the textures, contours, swells and valleys of one another.

Soft and groaning murmurs both whispered and cried out spoke of their need to be filled and cocooned. Bare and beautiful to each other under the moonlit night, they came together as man and woman.

Pillowed on the downy softness of their mating bed, Reese clung to Maxwell, raising her hips to meet and allow for his entry into her soul.

Maxwell's vise-like fingers held her steady. "No," he moaned, "slow, take me slow, just a little bit at a time," he uttered hot in her ear. Reese acquiesced, succumbing to his erotic command.

His descent was painstakingly deliberate, filling her by infinitesimal degrees until she swore she would scream from the denial of total fulfillment. And then, he was there, all of him—filling, lengthening, and expanding the walls of her dewy cavern. He released her then, giving her full access to him, allowing her to meet his ebbs and flows with undulations of her own.

Together they found a new beginning, alerting nature to their arrival with each beat of their hearts. Heat surrounded and engulfed them and they played upon each other, fanning and intermittently cooling the flames at their leisure—because they would take their time, knowing that this first time between them could never be recaptured. "Make it last" was their signature song and the words in their hearts as they reached for the pinnacle of completion, allowing the sweet splendor of their ardor to transport them beyond the spectrum of any world they'd ever known.

Reese gave all of herself to him as she had with no other man. She totally opened to him like a budding bloom flourishing under the ministrations of his tender nurturing. He was so right, she realized through the haze of her passion. She was his now and for as long as time allowed. He put his brand on her as surely as if burned into her heart with a searing iron.

Maxwell released the final embers of his doubts as they poured from him, flowing outward to be washed away, absorbed, and shared by this woman who had metamorphosed his world. Her tender fingers danced and caressed his body. Her lips played a sultry tune against his mouth. Her body became one with his, and he knew that the final explosion that they jointly shared could never be matched by another. His heart ached with joy and surrender when the last drop of his mortality was withdrawn and unified with hers.

"You are a wondrous gift, Reese," Maxwell murmured against her neck as he held her tightly against his body. "I'll always treasure this time we've had together."

Reese's heart tripped with an unspoken fear. "You sound

as if this will be the first and last time," she said, adjusting her body to withstand his weight.

He breathed a heavy sigh. "It may be. No one knows what tomorrow will bring. I can't make you any promises Reese. I haven't reached that point yet. I thought you understood that." His eyes roamed over her face before he pressed his lips to her mouth.

She felt a constriction in her heart that radiated outward to her limbs, immobilizing her. "Memories," she whispered. "We're building memories." She placed her hands around his face. "But what if I want more, Max? What then? Will you deny me what we both know is inevitable?"

"If it is to be Reese, then it will. And nothing in heaven or on earth will stop it. But for now, let's just enjoy what we have without strings, without promises of some rose-colored future. I know what I feel for you is more potent than anything I've ever experienced with any woman. There's no doubt in my mind about that. But before I can be all the things that you need—that you deserve—I have to be right with myself. And now I know that I'm not. Will I ever be? Only time will tell. It's up to you to decide if you want to be a part of the process."

Reese swallowed down her hurt and eased out from beneath him. Pushing her hair away from her face she sat on the edge of the bed, pressing her palms down into the mattress. "What did she do to you Max?" she asked softly.

Maxwell turned over to lie on his back. He stared sightlessly up at the ceiling, slipping his hands beneath his head. "Everything and nothing."

"Victoria is part of the reason why you've erected this emotional wall, Maxwell. Isn't it about time you took it down? Talk to me, please." She angled her body to face him.

Maxwell shut his eyes as the painful, humiliating images

replayed. Reese was sure he'd elected not to respond when suddenly, he began to speak in slow, halting tones.

Reese felt every nuance of his hurt as he poured out the story of him and Victoria Davenport from the moment they'd met until the day he walked in on her and her boss.

"I guess I could have dealt with her infidelity if only it would have ended there." He shook his head. "But her betrayal went even farther. All along, I trusted her like a fool in love. I shared every detail of my new design for an internet program. The next thing I knew, every newspaper in the English-speaking world was heralding the Air Force's latest technological computer innovation, which of course, was using my methodology. Somehow they got wind of our relationship as well as my work, and of course the general consensus was that I was trying to gain information from a government worker to augment my own work. Victoria never said a word to the contrary. And what could have been a crowning glory in my career, became hers." He laughed a harsh, self-deprecating laugh. "Victoria Davenport became an instant superstar and I was the one who 'attempted' to ride on her coattails. It took years for me to regain any sense of respect in the industry."

"Max." She reached out to him and he pushed her hand away.

"I don't need you to feel sorry for me, or impart words of solace and wisdom." He turned his face away. "All I want is for you to understand me, Reese. Understand my reservations, my unwillingness to open up—even to you," he added turning to face her. "I've dealt with losses all of my life—part of my heritage, my stature, my ability to totally commit to someone. I don't intend to lose everything ever again." He closed his eyes. "If that means shutting down and only depending on— me—the one person I can trust, then so be it."

"In other words, you intend to live the rest of your life in this self-imposed vacuum—only taking in what you need for the moment and not letting anything out? You don't strike me as the type of man that would capitulate to circumstances beyond his control." She lay beside him and turned on her side. "I don't care what you say, Maxwell Knight. I was here with you when our worlds collided. That wasn't just good sex and you know it. That's what's scaring the hell out of you. I don't give up easily. My life is a testament to that. Now that I've found you, I have no intentions of letting you shut me out." She leaned down and placed a solid kiss on his parted lips. "So get used to it. I can understand your reluctance. I can even accept it. But only for now. I'm in for the long haul. And you'll find a way to deal with it."

A slow smile of relief washed over his face. Her words were exactly what he needed to hear. He needed to know that she would accept him with his shortcomings and his doubts no matter what. "Is that right, Ms. Delaware?" he taunted, pulling her atop him. "Well how about if we start with trying to get our worlds to collide again…"

"I think that's a perfect beginning," she answered, raising her hips to welcome him back.

"Looks like they're in for the night sir," the agent said, speaking into his car phone.

Keep your eyes and ears open," came the response. "And keep me posted."

Chapter 11

Reese awoke several hours later. Blinking her eyes against the blackness, she focused on Maxwell's sleeping form. Gently she extricated herself from his hold and tiptoed to the bureau to retrieve her purse. In the frenzy of her day, she'd completely forgotten about Lynnette. She took a peek at the digital clock. It was nearly 2:00 a.m.

"Better late than never," she muttered to herself. Quietly she took the bedside phone and dialed the hotel. Moments later, a sleepy Lynnette answered.

"Girl, I am so sorry," she whispered.

"Where are you?" Lynnette mumbled, rubbing the sleep out of her eyes. "I was worried and didn't have a clue as to where to look for you."

"I have so much to tell you. But the main thing is I'm fine. Better than fine." She paused. "I'm with Max."

"What!"

"We're on Coronado Island. I'll be back in the morning. We'll talk then, I promise."

"Damn, girl. Now I'll never get back to sleep wondering what he's like."

Reese giggled. "I'll just say this...words escape me."

"Ooh, chile, can't wait. You enjoy yourself. And I mean that. See you tomorrow."

"'Night." Reese hung up and tiptoed back to bed, curling up beside Max and fell into a peaceful sleep filled with Technicolor images of her extraordinary day.

As much as she knew they had to return to the real world, Reese dreaded its inevitability. On the ride back she was uncharacteristically quiet.

"What's wrong, Reese?" Maxwell asked as they pulled up in front of her hotel. "You haven't been yourself since we left the island."

"The past twenty-four hours have been like a fairy tale, Max. I'm just reluctant to let it go." She looked down at her hands instead of at him. "I guess, what I'm saying is that I'm afraid we'll drift back to the tension-filled relationship we had...before...yesterday."

"Listen, baby, believe me, I've had the same feelings. But the reality is, life goes on. You have a job to do and so do I. We can't let what happens between us on a personal level interfere with that."

She breathed deeply. "The rational, workaholic side of me understands that." She turned to him, her eyes filled with uncertainty. "It's the rest of me that won't cooperate." She gave him a lopsided grin.

Max leaned over and kissed her gently on the lips. "This can't be the same woman who told me to 'deal with it,'" he teased. "We're just gonna take this thing one day at a time. Okay?"

She nodded in assent.

"Now let's get you upstairs so you can relay your adventures to your friend," he said giving her a sly grin. "Just make sure you tell her I was kidnapped and seduced under duress."

Reese's eyes widened in shock. Her mouth opened to deny his statement, but all she could do was laugh with joy.

Maxwell took Reese to her door, saw that she was safely inside, and turned to leave. "I'll be at the office for the rest of the day," he said when he approached the door. "You can reach me there if you need me for anything."

"I'm going to try to work on the article today. I seem to have fallen behind," she said coyly.

"I can't imagine how that could have happened," he returned, chucking her under the chin. "I'd better check on Carmen, too. She's probably worried out of her mind. Or more likely she's probably rubbing her hands together in glee. I'm sure she's put two and two together by now and got us as the end result," he chuckled.

Reese covered her mouth in horror. She'd forgotten all about Carmen. "How will I ever face her?"

"You're a resourceful woman. You'll think of something. See you later."

"Promise?"

"We'll see. Get to work." He turned and strode out of the door.

Reese closed the door behind him and emitted a heavenly sigh. Then without further ado, she dashed for the phone and dialed Lynnette's room.

"Sounds like you're in deep, girl," Lynnette said over a greasy cheeseburger. "What are you going to do?"

"There's not much I can do. I'm falling for the guy, Lynn."

"But you've interviewed hundreds of eligible men over the years. You've never resorted to jumping into bed with them just to get a story and then falling for them on top of it—or on the bottom—depending on your preference."

Reese's amber eyes snapped with outrage. "And it's not what I'm doing now," she hissed. "Don't you get it, Lynn? This isn't about a way to get a story."

"You're really serious, aren't you?" she asked in wonder.

"Yes, I am. I thought you knew that."

Lynnette swallowed. "Hey, girl, I'm sorry. I just thought it was one of those 'things' when we talked on the phone. But what about ethics? I mean you are out here to do a job. What if this got out? What would it do to your credibility?"

"I know. So that's why it can't. Our relationship—such as it is—is not fodder for a story angle. I can't let how I feel about him cloud my objectivity on this story."

Lynnette waited a beat. "You said your relationship 'such as it is.' What aren't you telling me?"

Reese took a breath and looked away. "Max has been hurt before. I mean really hurt and he's leery about any sort of commitment. He wants us to just take it one day at a time with no strings or promises."

"And you…?"

Reese looked into her friend's eyes. "I want more," she confessed. "I want it all."

"And what if he's never ready? Can you handle it?"

Reese pursed her lips. "I don't have any other choice, now do I?"

"Know you, girlfriend, you'll think of something."

Maxwell tried to concentrate on the designs that rested in front of him, but his thoughts kept drifting back to his day and night with Reese. She was under his skin. There was no denying it. Sure, he could let the relationship ride until it was time for her to return to Chicago. But then what? If he did decide to pursue a full-fledged relationship with her, what about the distance that separated them? Would she be willing to pull up stakes to be with him? Would he be willing to relocate? Or would he find himself in another long-distance relationship—one that ultimately spelled trouble?

He shook his head in frustration. He was getting way ahead of himself. So, he'd slept with her, so she'd made him feel whole, so he'd realized there was an emptiness that she filled. Where was it all going? He'd felt this way before and it had brought nothing but heartache. Reese isn't Victoria, his conscience warned. She deserved a chance and so did he.

The ringing of his intercom intruded on his swirling thoughts.

"Yes, Carmen," he answered, depressing the flashing button.

"Ms. Davenport is on line one," she said with a distinct note of disdain in her voice.

"Thanks." He paused, debating whether he should take the call. "I'll take it," he said finally. He pressed the steady red light on the dial. "What can I do for you, Victoria?"

"Hello, Max," she said hesitantly. "I'm going back to D.C. this afternoon. I was hoping we could meet, before I left."

"For what? It's a little too late for you to get any inside information. The chip is already in production."

"I deserved that."

"To say the least."

"Listen, Max, I can't undo what I did to you. I don't expect you to ever forgive me, but at least give me an opportunity to tell my side. If we ever meant anything to each other at least give me this one chance."

For three long years he'd wanted to know what had made this woman that he thought he loved turn on him. More times than he cared to count, he'd picked up the phone to dial her number and then didn't. He'd spent sleepless nights trying to figure out how he could have been such a fool. He'd avoided the answers for years. Maybe it was time that he finally put this part of his life to rest.

"What do you have to say?"

Victoria let out an audible sigh of relief. "Can we meet somewhere? My plane leaves at five."

"…things were really crazy for me back then, Max. I know I was never truly candid about my life but it was spinning out of control." Victoria looked deep into his penetrating gaze. "You were my anchor."

"That doesn't explain or excuse anything, Vicky."

"I know that. Please, just listen. I was up for promotion. A big one and my mother was dying. Her treatments and care were costing me a small fortune. She'd exhausted her medical coverage."

"I'm sorry. I didn't know."

"Somehow, Air Force intelligence got wind of our relationship and the work that you were doing. They convinced me that if I could get them inside information on your new design it would be well worth it for me." She looked away. "My back was against the wall." Her voice broke. "I know what I did was wrong, Max. But I couldn't see any other way out."

"I suppose sleeping with the enemy was also part of the deal," he bit out.

She lowered her eyes and nodded her head in shame.

"You could have told me. You could have trusted me. I would have given you anything, Victoria—anything." His heart constricted in his chest with the memories.

She swallowed. "I know that—now. All I could think of at the time was my mother and what she needed. Other than you, she was all I had." It was on the tip of her tongue to tell him about Reese, her half sister, about the life she was excluded from.

Maxwell shook his head. "So now I understand. You had a reason." He looked into her pleading green eyes. "But it doesn't change anything, Vicky. It never will. It's too late."

"I don't expect you to take me back, or blindly accept what I've said. I know I made a shambles of your life and I would do anything to make that up to you." She paused. "I was only hoping that the truth would be a start."

"A start of what?" he asked, his eyes narrowing dangerously.

"A start of the healing, Max," she said, sincerity ringing in the crystal clarity of her voice. "I know you. Remember? I took your trust and your love and crushed it. And by knowing you, I know what that would have done to you. Please, don't let what happened between us tarnish any happiness that you might find."

"Since when did you become the concerned citizen?"

"When I ran into you the other night with that woman, I envied her. I envied the very idea that anyone would experience with you the joy I've known. But what bothered me most of all was the notion that you may never be willing to give that part of you again. And that would be the greatest loss. I don't want to be the reason." She let out a breath and shook her head in wonder. "I can't believe I'm even saying this to you. I spent nights praying that you'd never find anyone else. That one day we'd find our way back to each other. That you'd forgive me. But…I did what I did. And if the same circumstances were to arise, I'd do it again…and again. That's who I am, Max." She smiled a sad, lonely smile. "And you know it as well as I do."

Maxwell looked at her, really looked at her and he knew she was right. Victoria Davenport was finally a part of his life that he could close the book on.

He reached across the table and covered her hand with his. Victoria felt the tears of regret burn her eyes. "We can't go back, Vicky. We both know that. But we can go forward—from here. I don't know if I can ever truly forgive you, but at least I can begin to understand."

"I just don't want you to hate me, Max. I couldn't bear that."

"I don't hate you. I stopped hating you a long time ago. Maybe now, I can start liking you and finally accept you for who you are and not what I imagine you to be."

She sniffed back her tears and smiled. "So…tell me about this lucky lady that you have goo-goo eyes over."

"He's in the restaurant with Davenport," the agent said into the microphone.

"We know she's headed back here. I'll have one of the team pick her up at Dulles."

"Yes, sir."

"I'm going to head over to Max's office. I need to interview a few more of the employees before they quit for the day. I plan to really dig into this article tonight," Reese said as she and Lynnette walked down the palm-lined street together.

"Do you have time for a blitz shopping spree before you head off to the drudgery of work? I was able to get in contact with Quincy's publicist and I have an appointment for tomorrow afternoon. I've got to look fly!"

"You go, girl. You didn't tell me you got the assignment."

"How could I? Between the stars in your eyes and love notes in your voice I couldn't get a word in edgewise."

Reese playfully pushed her aside. "Very funny."

"Well do you?"

Reese checked her watch. "All right. You have one hour

and then I've got to get across town or this whole day will have been a bust."

"Charge!" Lynnette giggled.

An hour and a half later, totally worn out, Reese pulled up in a cab in front of Maxwell's offices. Just as she stepped out of the cab, movement caught her attention in the corner of her eye.

There was Max, with one arm around Victoria Davenport's waist, the other carrying a designer garment bag, squiring her into his Corvette.

Reese stood still as stone as she watched them drive away.

Chapter 12

A multitude of explanations poured through her mind as she rode the elevator to the executive floor. But none of them eased the hurt that carved out a corner of her heart.

She'd listened to him tell of his betrayal by that woman. She'd empathized with his anguish. Yet there he was, live and in living color, smiling at her, holding her as if she were the dearest being in the world. Was it all lies?

"Reese," Carmen greeted, nearly bumping into her in the corridor. "Max is gone for the day. I wasn't expecting you," she said with a knowing smile.

"There's a lot of that going around," she replied in a monotone.

Carmen gave her a curious look. "Are you all right? You seem—distracted."

Reese gathered her wits about her. "I'm just fine, Carmen. And you're just the person I wanted to see. Do you have a

few minutes? I need to get some additional background
information on Mr. Knight."

After dropping Victoria off at the airport, Maxwell took
the two-hour drive out to his home in San Diego. He needed
some quiet time to gather his thoughts and absorb what Vicky
had told him.

Mixing himself a light drink, he stepped out onto the deck,
watching the rays of the setting sun span across the bay as
he leaned across the railing. Victoria was a complex woman.
There was no denying that. Yet even with all that she revealed,
he still felt in his gut that there was something she wasn't
telling. But he couldn't put his finger on it. He took a sip of
his drink.

He could believe the part about her mother. He could
even believe the part that she felt she had no other choice.
What he had a hard time swallowing was her concern for
his happiness. Victoria had never been one to be interested
in another person's happiness for as long as he'd known her.
Had she changed that much in the three years? He sighed.
Perhaps their breakup had affected her as well. At least in
some small way. He wanted to believe that she wished him
well and wanted the best for him without reservation.

He might be able to forgive her. But he wouldn't forget,
nor would he find it in his heart to trust her no matter how
sincere she portrayed herself to be. Her interest in Reese, in
her background, and the standing of their relationship piqued
his suspicions.

Victoria never asked a question or opened the door to a
conversation without a reason. Then again, maybe it was time
for him to put the past behind him once and for all. Whatever
Victoria's motives were for doing anything was none of his
concern. What he had to deal with now was his spiraling
feelings for Reese and where it would lead him.

Now that many of his unanswered questions had finally been answered, perhaps he could begin to really live again and open his heart to the gifts that Reese wanted to give.

Reese sat across from Carmen taking notes as Carmen spoke.

"Did you know Max before he opened his offices?"

"No. I met him at a conference in Washington, shortly after my husband died. My husband, Carlos, was also a computer engineer. I'd worked with him on several projects and was familiar with Max's name in the industry. I attended the conference to hear him speak. When I had an opportunity to talk with him in private to tell him how much Carlos had admired his work, he told me about his goal to open his own offices. He offered me a job right on the spot," she smiled, reminiscing the moment.

"Everything that I've heard about Max always points back to his work, his brilliance in the electronic field. But what about Maxwell Knight the man? And please—be candid. I want to make him as rounded as possible for the article and you seem to know him best," she coaxed.

"Maxwell is a very private person. It's rare that he discusses his private life," she said, looking away.

"But I get a sense that if anyone knows that side of him it's you," she smiled encouragingly. "As a matter of fact, while we were out to dinner the other night, we ran into an old friend of his." She pretended to look at her notes. "A Victoria Davenport. Max seemed a bit reluctant to speak about her. Perhaps you could shed some light on their relationship."

Carmen looked at her for a long moment, debating on how much she should say. In her heart she strongly felt that Reese was the perfect woman for her Max. The very idea that Victoria Davenport had been in contact with him again made her skin itch. If Reese was to have the slightest chance in winning Max's heart she needed to know what she was up against.

"She nearly destroyed him," she said finally. "Both personally and professionally. They met about five years ago at the same conference I spoke of earlier. I knew she was trouble from the moment I set eyes on her…"

Reese listened with her heart in her hand, hoping that Carmen's story would match what Max had revealed to her.

"…Maxwell is the type of man who puts his heart and soul into everything he touches. That included Victoria. And when she turned on him, he was never the same. The light seemed to die in his eyes. He turned inside of himself and devoted his every waking moment to his work to the exclusion of everything and everyone." She looked across at Reese. "It wasn't until recently that I've seen the old sparkle back in his eyes," she stated, giving Reese a pointed look. "Give him time," she added sagely. "He'll come around."

Reese hid her obvious attempt at gleaning information about Maxwell and Victoria behind a wall of questions of which she already had the answers. "What is the general feeling around the office about the company's status in the industry?" she parried.

Carmen smiled in understanding. "Everyone is thrilled that Maxwell has been able to direct the company to this level in such a short space of time. It's a testament to his brilliance as a businessman as well as an engineer."

"Can you tell me a little bit about his family? What was his life like before he became 'boy wonder'?"

It was after eleven o'clock when Victoria's plane finally touched down in D.C. All she wanted to do was go home and regroup. Her meeting with Max had been more stressful than she'd anticipated. She thought that, for the most part, she was over him. But she wasn't. The time that she'd spent with him only rekindled the smoldering embers of their relationship. She'd messed up big time. And she knew there was no chance in getting him back. When she'd said that she envied Reese, it was true, more so than she'd ever be able to admit. But what was also true was that she did want him to find happiness. If it happened to be with her half sister, there wasn't much she could do about that. Revealing their kinship would change nothing. She loved him enough to finally let him go—whether he ever believed it or not.

Walking slowly through the terminal, her thoughts were focused on her life and where it would take her. She didn't see the Special Forces agent until he was right next to her, clasping her elbow.

"Come with me, Ms. Davenport, the general would like to speak with you. There's a car outside waiting to take us to Chevy Chase."

Not again, she prayed silently. Not again.

On the far side of the terminal a second agent walked casually to a pay phone and dialed the designated number. The phone was answered on the first ring.

"Yes."

"Davenport was just picked up at the airport."

"Keep her close. I'm sure they're bringing her in."

James Knight hung up the phone. He leaned back in his seat. "What will you try to do to my son this time?" he asked aloud.

"Have a seat, Victoria. Make yourself comfortable," said General Murphy. "I do apologize for getting you out so late, but we have pressing matters to discuss."

Victoria took a seat and folded her hands in front of her. It had been over three years since she'd been in these rooms bartering with the devil. She looked around. Nothing had changed. "Why am I here, Uncle Frank? I would have thought I paid my dues in full by now."

Murphy gave her a sardonic smile. "Interest, my dear. Interest." He turned away from her and took a seat. "You've been in contact with Knight again, Vicky, after being given specific instructions to stay away from him—for good. Why?"

Victoria swallowed. They'd been following her. What else did they know about her life? "We had things to discuss," she said in a tight voice.

"It's my business to know what things."

"Believe me, *general,* our conversation had nothing to do with anything that would interest you."

He leaned forward, his cool green eyes burning through her. "Everything you do interests me. The only reason why you've reached the level that you have in the Force is because of my benevolence! And don't you ever forget it," he seethed. When he looked at Victoria Davenport he could see the face of her mother as surely as if she stood in front of him. Guilt and something much deeper twisted into a painful knot in his belly. He reached into his pocket, extracted a packet of antacids, and popped two in his mouth.

He was one of two people who knew of Victoria's unsavory beginnings. He and Victoria's mother. For a man of Hamilton Delaware's stature, that type of scandal would have ruined his career. They'd been the closest of friends since their early days in training. They were brothers at heart, even though their race denied it. And Murphy had sworn he'd help keep his secret, even though it tore at his heart to do so. Hamilton was totally unaware of just how much they shared. They would have still been friends if Hamilton hadn't discovered the experiments that the Force was running, with Frank Murphy as head of operations. Hamilton decided to turn his findings over to the Senate. Frank's career would have been over. He'd worked too hard. He couldn't allow that to happen. Hamilton had betrayed him. He betrayed their friendship and all that he'd done on Hamilton's behalf. He couldn't let him get away with that. Yet even after it was over, he never broke his promise to maintain Hamilton's secret. He kept the money flowing into the accounts Hamilton had set up for Victoria as well as Reese.

He blinked back the memories and focused on Victoria. She was a casualty of internal warfare. She and her half sister. What was done was necessary. There was no turning back. And he couldn't let family ties interfere with what he had to do.

"I want to know everything you discussed with Maxwell Knight. And I want to know how much information Reese Delaware has about his life."

James paced the small space that he used as his office. He didn't like what was happening. The fact that the general had taken Victoria in was reason to believe that the general was getting leery. And when he did, people were eliminated. Victoria had probably been working with him all along. But why did she suddenly go to see Max after all this time? He was sure it had something to do with the interview.

They couldn't take a chance on approaching Reese for fear that any reappearance of the military in her life would trigger her memory. That was the last thing they needed.

He lit a cigarette and watched the smoke trail upward and cloud the room. So much could have been different if only Hamilton had elected not to take his entire family to the hearings that morning. Things would have been different if there were no communications breakdown that day. He shut his eyes against the images.

There was nothing he could do about the past. All he could do was try to protect his son. He knew he'd never been much of a father, but he did what was necessary for the life he led. And Max must never find out, especially now.

A soft tap on the door interrupted his musings.

Claudia stepped into the room. "Aren't you coming to bed, James? It's almost one o'clock in the morning."

James smiled absently. "I'll be up in a minute."

Claudia crossed the room to stand in front of him. She looked up into her husband's eyes. "What is it James? Something's wrong. I've known it for days."

He searched her smooth cocoa face. This woman, his wife, had stood by him unquestioningly for thirty-five years. She withstood the humiliation that he brought on their home. She cared for and nurtured a son that was not hers. She endured a loveless marriage and never flinched, never once complained.

His heart filled with regret—for all the things he could have been to his wife and his son and he wasn't. There wasn't enough time in his life to make up for what he hadn't done.

Slowly he put his arm around her slender shoulders and pulled her gently against his hard-packed frame. "Oh, Claudia," he hummed against her soft auburn curls. "I wish I knew where to begin. There's such a long bridge between us and it's my fault." He shook his head woefully. "I don't even know how to get back across—to you."

"I'm here to cross it with you, James. If you'll only let me." She reached up and cupped his beardless cheeks. "I've always been here. Meet me halfway?"

James looked down into her eyes, so full of hope and expectation. Just as they'd looked thirty-five years ago…

"Claudia, you know the kind of life I live." He sat down on the bench and stared down at his hands. Claudia took the small space next to him, her clean fresh scent wrapping around him.

"James. I love you and I know you love me. That's what's

important. I know that your devotion to the service is important to you also. I can live with that, but not without you. We can work it out."

He turned to her and when he did, the magic in her eyes made him believe that anything was possible. "I'm only twenty-one years old. You're barely nineteen, your parents will have a fit."

"I don't want to spend the rest of my life with my parents, James. I want to spend it with you." She pressed her warm lips to his. "They'll just have to understand."

James heaved a sigh. "You know I joined the Special Forces unit."

Claudia nodded and took his hand.

"That means I'm going to be traveling a lot. We're going to spend a lot of time away from each other. There will be aspects of my assignments that I'll never be able to discuss with you. We may even have to move around..."

She put her finger to his lips to still him. "Shh. I know, sweetheart. I know. And I can deal with it, so long as you can."

"You're sure?"

She smiled, her heart ready to burst with joy. "Yes, James, I'm sure."

He took her in his arms. "Then I guess I'd better have a talk with your parents. I'm scheduled to be shipped out to the Philippines within the next six months. You think you can pull a wedding together in that amount of time?" he grinned.

Claudia whooped with joy and wrapped her arms around his neck, planting countless kisses across his face. "I'll make you happy, James, I swear I will," she cried, burying her face against his chest. "I'll make a home for us and our family no matter where we are. Just meet me halfway..."

"Come on sweetheart, let's go to bed. We'll talk in the

morning," James said, pushing back the memories. He switched of the light and walked toward the door. "It's about time you understood everything. I owe you that much." He put his arm around his wife and walked with her upstairs.

Claudia sat across from her husband at the breakfast table. For the past thirty-five years of their marriage, she'd believed that she knew her husband, even if she didn't always understand him. Looking at him now and trying to comprehend the enormity of what he'd revealed, she realized she didn't know this man at all or of what he was capable.

"How could you have lived with this for the past fifteen years, James?" she asked, bewilderment stretching across her smooth features. "What about Maxwell, now that he's… involved with this Reese Delaware? Where does that leave him—you?"

James placed his elbows on the table and braced his chin with his fists. "I don't know Claudia. I just know that I have to protect him. Frank Murphy will do whatever is necessary to ensure that what happened that day and all that went before it and since, is never discovered."

Claudia jumped up from the table. "Then you have to go to your superiors, his superiors, and tell them." Her heart raced with fear.

"Don't be naive, Claudia," he spouted. "Who would believe me? I would disappear faster than I could get the words out. Do you honestly believe the United States government would readily admit to what they'd done for three decades to their own troops?" He hung his head and shook it in defeat. "Hamilton Delaware thought he could make a difference…" his voice drifted off.

Claudia wrapped her hands around her waist as a shiver ran up her spine. "In other words, we're at their mercy?"

"Pretty much."

"What about Max?"

"I debated with myself all night about what to do. There's no way I can tell him anything. I've had Larry trailing him. He's been keeping me informed of everything that's been going on. But he needs to be warned about Victoria."

"And what about that poor girl, Reese? What about her?"

Chapter 13

Carmen had just sat down at her desk when Maxwell strode in.

"Good morning, Carmen," he greeted a smile brightening his warm bronze features. "How are you today?"

Carmen raised an inquisitive brow. "Just fine and *you?*"

"Couldn't be better. Is Reese around yet?"

"No," she said slowly. "She came in yesterday, but she didn't mention if or when she'd be here today."

Maxwell frowned. "She was here yesterday?"

"Yes. For about two hours, late in the afternoon."

"Hmm. I see. No. I don't see. What was she doing here? She told me... I mean, I thought she would have been at the hotel working on the article."

"She said she needed some background information on you. We talked for a long time," she added coyly.

He braced his palms against her desk and leaned forward. His dark eyes narrowed in suspicion. "What exactly did you tell her?"

Carmen avoided his steady stare. "I started off by telling her what a wonderful man you are," she said, paving the way for the fallout.

He arched an eyebrow. "And?"

"And…well…she asked me some questions about…"

"About what?"

"About Victoria Davenport," she blurted out. "And I told her what a witch that woman was and that she had nothing to worry about, you were through with her." She folded her arms beneath her ample bosom in defiance.

Maxwell lowered his head and began to chuckle. He looked up at Carmen. "You're a real piece of work, Carmen. I have to give you that." He moved away from her desk, stopped and turned back with a soft smile on his face. "Thanks. She needed to hear that from someone other than me."

He hadn't been at his desk for more than five minutes, when the intercom buzzed.

"Yes, Carmen?"

"Max. Your father is on line one."

"My father?"

"Yes."

"T…thanks. I'll take it." He couldn't remember the last time his father had called him at the office, and to track him to L.A. immediately had him worrying. Something had to be wrong. His father was never one for chitchat.

He pressed the steady red light. "Dad? How are you?"

"I'm fine, son."

Claudia stood close, stroking his back, encouraging him to go on.

"I know this can't be a social call, so tell me what's wrong. Is it mom? Did something happen?"

"Your mother is fine. That's not the reason for the call…"

* * *

Maxwell sat at his desk, staring at the panorama outside his window. His gut instinct told him to stay clear of Victoria and, fool that he was, he let his emotions overrule his head once again. She came to see him for one reason and one reason alone, to find out what she could about Reese. But why? Why was Air Force intelligence interested in Reese Delaware, a woman with no past to speak of?

His father had cleverly avoided any mention of Reese, but it was clear to him, based on Victoria's questions, that it was her only reason for seeing him. There was nothing else they'd discussed that would be of interest to anyone.

His suspicions and his fears mounted. Reese was a target for something and he felt certain it had to do with the past she'd forgotten. But there was no way he could protect her if neither of them knew what was sealed behind the closed doors of her memory.

Reese barely slept the night before. Her dreams were plagued by the dark images and muted voices of her past. But now, for the first time, she could remember fragments of her dream.

She tried to concentrate on putting her thoughts down on paper, but she couldn't stay focused. Everything kept coming back to visions of her walking out of her house and seeing a figure near her family's car. She couldn't make out the face. But the frightening thing was that when she did try to force an image, the face was always Maxwell's.

"That's ridiculous," she said aloud, getting up from the couch. "If what I'm seeing has any validity, Maxwell couldn't have been more than seventeen or eighteen at the time."

Her head began to pound, and she knew by the symptoms that it was the onset of one of those mind-searing headaches. She went into the bathroom and took a pill.

"What could Max have to do with the deaths of my family? Nothing. Absolutely nothing. You're grasping at straws, and you're talking to yourself."

The phone rang. She picked up the phone in the bedroom. "Hello?"

"Hey, girl, it's me Lynn. My interview with 'Q' was slammin'! The man is gorgeous. You hear me—gorgeous!"

"Better than he looks on those videos?"

"Trust me, pictures and film do the man no justice whatsoever. I think I've died and gone to heaven."

"That's all good, Lynn, but did you get a story, or just get your panties twisted in a knot?"

"I should be so lucky," she said drolly. "Yeah, I got the interview. But I'm too pumped up to even think about writing. I thought I'd drop in and we could talk. I'm heading out tomorrow."

"Sure, come on up. There are some things I need to run by you anyway."

"Everything okay?"

"Not really, but we'll talk when you get here."

"Sure. See you in a few."

Victoria's nerves were strung to the breaking point. Her uncle was crystal clear about his instructions. *"If you value your job, you won't breathe a word of this meeting to Maxwell Knight. I expect to hear from you immediately if you hear from him and if he relays any information about Reese Delaware you are to contact me no matter what time of day or night."*

She rubbed her hands together as she carved a trail in the cream-colored carpet of her bedroom. Her slender body, sheathed in a bold red rayon suit, cut a brilliant figure against the cool tones of the opulent room. She should have been in her office more than an hour earlier. She was working on refining the tracking systems in the fighter jet's computer systems. The deadline for completion was barreling down on her, but she had to make a call and her office was already tapped. She couldn't be sure about her apartment, but she wasn't taking any chances.

Snatching up her purse, she headed outside. The instant she stepped out of doors she felt as if she were under a microscope. She had no idea who was watching or from where. But she knew they were out there. Waiting.

Taking her usual route to work, she continued to take furtive glances in the rearview mirror. At the first gas station she pulled in and up to a vacant gas pump. Casually she looked around and seeing nothing untoward, she went straight for the pay phone.

Dialing Maxwell's office number she thought of all the reasons why she shouldn't. But the reason why she should overruled. If he would only listen to her, this might be her one way to make up for all the damage she'd done in the past.

The phone rang twice before it was picked up.

"M.K. Enterprises. Good morning."

"Good morning. I'd like to speak with Mr. Knight please."

The hairs on the back of Carmen's neck bristled at the sound of Victoria's voice.

"I'm sorry, Mr. Knight is busy. I'll have to take a message."

"Please, Carmen. It's me, Victoria. I need to speak with Max. It's urgent."

"I'm sorry, Ms. Davenport," she replied curtly. "He's busy."

"Would you at least try?"

Carmen sighed heavily into the phone. "Hold, please." She buzzed Max and was immediately informed that she was not to put any calls through from Victoria no matter what she said. "And don't bother to take any messages," he added.

"I'm sorry, Ms. Davenport. Mr. Knight informed me not to put any of your calls through. Good day." Carmen broke the connection, thoroughly pleased.

"But Carmen… You don't…" The dial tone hummed in her ear.

Dejected, Victoria hung up the phone, looked around, and got back into her car. She had to find a way to reach Max. She pulled out into the right lane of traffic and headed toward her office. But why should she? It was obvious that Max didn't want to have anything to do with her. She choked back a laugh. What would make her think that he'd forgive and forget that easily? She'd deluded herself into thinking that she'd made some headway with him. But he'd left her believing that they could start over as friends. He'd even kissed her goodbye at the airport.

Her smooth peaches-and-cream face contorted into a mask of anger. She flipped her strawberry blond hair over her shoulder with a toss of her head. Her dazzling green eyes narrowed in fury. The old bitter jealousy stirred within her. *Reese.* Who else could have convinced him to stay away from her? She could almost laugh to think that Reese might feel threatened by her reappearance in Max's life. If she helped Max, she might inadvertently help Reese. And there was no earthly reason why she should do that. Reese had never been more than a constant thorn in her side since the day her aunt Celeste informed her of her half sister's existence.

Victoria was about ten years old on the spring afternoon that her aunt Celeste had come to her home in Norfolk to visit. Celeste came every month to visit her niece and Victoria always looked forward to spending time with her exquisite aunt who always brought her a toy, a game, or a beautiful outfit from D.C. She always told her wonderful stories about the capital city and the famous political faces that she saw on the street.

"Why can't I come and visit you sometime, auntie?" Victoria asked as they strolled along the tree-lined streets toward the park. She looked up at her aunt's face which vaguely resembled her own.

"I told you, sweetheart, auntie travels a great deal for the government. I very rarely stay in one place very long. That's why I always come to see you."

Victoria looked down at her polished patent leather shoes. "But why doesn't my daddy come and see me? Mommy won't tell me. Will you tell me?" The only constant male figure she had in her life was her uncle Frank, her mother Faith's older brother. But his visits, too, were rare. His pressure-filled life in the Air Force kept him away. She longed to have a father like her friends in school boasted about.

Celeste bent down and pulled Victoria into the comfort of her arms. "Oh, sweetheart, your daddy would come more often if he could. But he's so busy. That doesn't mean he doesn't love you, Vicky. He does."

"Why can't I go and see him sometime? I'm not too busy." Water brimmed in her green eyes.

Celeste took a deep breath. "Come over here, sweetheart. Let's sit down. There are some things…that I need to explain to you."

Victoria took a seat on the park bench and looked expectantly up into her aunt's eyes.

"You're getting to be a big girl now and you're a smart girl." Celeste brushed the strands of reddish blond hair away from her face. "Now I just want you to listen. Your daddy has another family who he lives with." She took a breath. "And you have a half sister. Her name is Reese. And she's twelve years old."

Victoria's eyes lit up with delight. "Really?" she squealed. "Can I go and see her?"

Celeste took Victoria's hands in hers. "No, darling, I'm afraid not. They don't know anything about you and they must never know. Vicky, your daddy is married to Reese's mother. Her name is Sharlene. She's my sister. And even though he loves your mommy very much he can't be married to both of them. Your daddy loved your mommy so much that they made you. You are very special, Victoria. You are a gift to your mommy and daddy." She searched for words. "So special that they want to just keep you to themselves. They don't want to share you with anyone else."

"I'm special?"

"Yes, darling, very special."

"I can't tell anyone?"

"No. Never. You are the special secret in your mommy and daddy's life."

The "special secret," Victoria thought, the rage brewing in her, singeing the corners of her control. She turned into the parking lot and pulled into her reserved space, her breathing expelled in rapid, panting breaths. For several moments, she gripped the steering wheel with such force that her palms began to sting. She shut her eyes and swallowed down the bitter pill of her pain.

Reese and Lynnette sat curled up on Reese's couch sipping glasses of iced tea.

"So how are the headaches and the nightmares?" Lynnette asked.

Reese shrugged. "They come and go. Unfortunately, a lot more frequently than I'd like." She stared, momentarily, down into her glass. "Lynn," she began slowly, "when I woke up this morning, I…I think I remembered something." She looked across at her friend with uncertainty swimming in her eyes.

Lynnette sat up straighter in her seat. "What—what was it? Did you see anything?"

Reese swallowed and closed her eyes, bringing the images to mind. "All I remember is that I see this young girl, which I get a sense is me. But it's dark and I'm walking down some sort of path with a bag in my hand. When I look ahead, I see a shadow, or a figure, kneeling by a car. I think it's a man. I feel as though he turns and looks at me, but I can't quite make out his face. I see myself opening my mouth, but no words are coming out. The figure, or shadow, turns away and then I can't see anything."

Reese expelled a long, shaky breath. "That's what I remember." She opened her eyes to look at Lynnette.

Lynnette frowned. "I don't know what to make of it, Reese. Did you call your doctor?"

Reese shook her head. "I haven't been in touch with any of 'those' doctors in a while. They'd probably just prescribe something and send me on my way," she said, sarcasm dripping in her voice.

Reese uncurled her legs and put her feet on the floor. "The one thing that sort of scared me was that every time I tried to focus in on the face, I kept getting a picture of Max."

Lynnette jerked her head back in response. "Max? That's weird. It's probably just transference. Maybe you just have him on your mind."

Reese sighed, not totally convinced. She knew it meant something, she just didn't know what. Then again, Lynn was probably right. She was the one who had a second degree in psychology.

"Speaking of Max. You haven't spoken of him since I got here. What's up?"

Reluctantly, Reese explained about the scene she'd

witnessed the previous afternoon between Maxwell and Victoria and her "interview" with Carmen.

Lynnette slapped her thigh and laughed. "Girl, you sure know how to use your investigative skills to your advantage."

Reese bit back a laugh and looked away.

"So why haven't you called him?"

Reese shrugged. "Maybe I just don't want to hear whatever lie he's bound to tell me."

"Why are you so sure he's going to lie?"

"You didn't see them, Lynn. I did." Her eyes flashed. "Sure, Carmen may think it's over and Max may even 'say' it's over. But it sure as hell didn't look like it to me."

Lynnette pursed her lips and stared at her friend good and hard. "When was the last time things looked like how they really were? Wake up, girl, and call that man. At least give him the benefit of the doubt. Anything could have been happening."

"Yeah, that's what I'm afraid of."

Lynnette pointed an accusing finger. "Afraid, that's the magic word. You'd prefer to walk around afraid of what you've only conjured up in your own head, rather than putting your fears aside and finding out the real deal? Is that what you're telling me? At the absolute worst, you'll find out that Maxwell Knight is a real dog and you'd be far better served devoting your time and attention to someone worthy. Or, you'll discover that what you saw, wasn't what you thought it was and that Max is just as crazy about you as you are about him." Lynnette folded her arms beneath her small breasts and concluded her monologue.

"Well thank you, Ann Landers."

They both burst out laughing.

"Seriously, Reese, give the man a break. From everything

you told me, he seems to be honest." She pushed her designer glasses further up her slender nose.

Reese sighed. "I suppose you're right."

"Of course I am."

Maxwell continued to work on his new software design without success. His thoughts wouldn't stay focused. They kept drifting back to the early-morning phone call from Victoria. She had some nerve trying to contact him. What could she possibly have to say at this point?

He tossed his mechanical pencil to the side and got up from his seat. His jaw clenched as he paced his office. He shoved his hands into his pockets. Where was Reese? Why hadn't she come into the office?

He turned toward the phone, intent on calling her at the hotel, when his intercom buzzed.

"Yes, Carmen?"

"Reese is on line two."

"Thanks." A slow smile spread across his face as he depressed the red light on the phone.

"I thought you were an early riser," he said in greeting.

"Oh, I've been up for quite a while. I've been working... and thinking."

His guard went up. "I take it you've made some progress... in both areas?"

"You could say that," she countered, pacing her words.

"Do you have something on your mind that you want to get off, Reese?"

"As a matter of fact I do. Let's start with Victoria Davenport."

Chapter 14

Larry Templeton sat parked directly across the street from Maxwell's office. He had the perfect spot for seeing everything that came in and out of the building without appearing to do so. So far everything looked fine. If Murphy had anyone out there, they were damned good.

He took a sip of his coffee and resumed his watch. Life was so strange, he thought. He'd spent most of his life watching and waiting for the perfect moment—waiting for the signal. When he joined the Air Force, he always dreamed of being a fighter pilot like the ones he'd seen on television and in the movies while growing up. He would have never imagined that his skill with high-powered rifles would have led him to the Special Forces unit as a sharpshooter.

He shook his head in wonder and in sadness. He never thought much of his uncanny marksmanship. It was expected from every red-blooded male in his household, which included five brothers. Hunting was their livelihood, and any man that couldn't shoot the eyes right out of their prey, couldn't eat. That was his dad's rule from the time each of them was old enough to hold a gun.

For the most part, he was proud of his career. There was only that one blotch—one error—one fatal mistake that had nearly ruined everything he'd worked for. He'd spent the last fifteen years paying penance for something over which he had no control. He still had nightmares. If only he hadn't dropped his radio and knocked out communications, things would be so different—he would have known. If only the little girl hadn't walked out into the yard that night. If only... But they were following orders. They were trained to follow orders no matter what.

Larry shook his head, sweeping away the damning memories. And now, the entire scenario had come full circle. The descendants had taken the places of their predecessors. He couldn't let anything go wrong. Not this time. James was depending on him, just as he had fifteen years ago. He'd allowed James to take the heat for him then. Not again. He wouldn't let him down.

Larry resumed his watch.

Claudia stared into the bubbly dishwater, mindlessly holding a plate in her hand as she listened to her husband. Her heart ached.

"You've been a good wife, Claudia. Better than I deserved." James shook his head in regret. "I allowed my work to consume me, consume us. I wouldn't let myself be a husband to you or a father to my son."

She turned away from the sink, dried her hands, and sat down at the table. Her warm brown eyes swept over her husband's face. "James, we all make choices in this life. I could have chosen to leave. But I didn't. When I took those wedding vows thirty-five years ago, I meant it when I said 'for better, for worst…until death do us part.' I can't blame you for the direction our marriage went in. I was one of the players. I allowed just as much as you did. I didn't fight for you, James, the way I should have. I didn't demand what was mine, which was your love and respect. I allowed you to use me as a doormat. Can I blame you for walking over me?

"Instead I withdrew into a world of books and social clubs. I shut you out and left Max to fend for himself. Sure I kept a beautiful house, and prepared delicious meals, never complained, and always kept a smile on my face. But my heart, James, was breaking into minuscule pieces day by day and I didn't know what to do about it."

He reached across the table and took her hand.

"I didn't have any real friends. At least no one that I could trust with my deepest feelings and fears. Growing up as an only child, you learn to just deal with things on your own. So I did." She gave him a wavering smile. "Or at least I thought I did. I couldn't go to my parents and let them know the trouble our marriage was in." She looked briefly away. "Not after…Maxwell." James's stomach knotted, seeing her hurt. "I needed you to love me so much that I was willing to put up with anything, in the hope that one day you would—that you'd forget about—Suki and love me the way—" her voice broke "—you once did." Hot tears rolled unchecked down her cheeks.

"Oh, God, Claudia." He came around the table and gathered her in his arms. His own tears mixing with hers. "Please, don't…"

Vehemently she shook her head. "No, James. It's been too long. I need to say this. You need to hear this. That morning, when I was out in the garden all I could think about was how long you'd been away in Japan—nearly eighteen months." She smiled wistfully and wiped her tears away. "I had the last letter you wrote to me in my apron pocket, telling me how much you missed me and you'd be home in six months. I was so busy thinking of all the things we could do together when you returned, I almost didn't hear the front doorbell."

James moved back to his seat as Claudia stood, her eyes transfixed on a place he could never be.

"I remember it was so hot. I was sweating like crazy and I'd just wiped my forehead with a muddy glove and had dirt streaked across my head." She smiled at the memory. "I tossed my gloves on the grass and dashed through the house, thinking it was probably the mailman. I pulled the door open…"

A young, strikingly beautiful Japanese girl stood on the doorstep. She couldn't have been more than eighteen, Claudia guessed. But all she could think about at the moment was her extraordinary ink-black hair that looked as if it must be two feet long. She had it braided and wrapped, layer upon layer atop her head. Claudia, self-consciously, touched her own hair that was damp and matted to her head. The girl had a flawless bronze complexion, devoid of any makeup and the most incredible eyes Claudia had ever seen. And she couldn't for the life of her imagine why this girl-woman was on her doorstep and carrying what looked to be a baby no less.

The girl gave a short bow and Claudia had the overwhelming desire to bow back. "Ah, hello, good afternoon. I am Sukihara. I beg your pardon for trouble, but I come from long way to bring baby to you."

"What? What are you talking about?"

"You are wife of James Knight?"

Claudia's heart began to race with dread. Her answer got caught in her throat. She nodded.

Suki extended her bundle toward Claudia. "This James's son."

Claudia shook her head. She knew it was hot, because sweat was pouring from every crevice of her body. That had to be the reason why she suddenly felt lightheaded. This woman, whoever she was, was lying. She was crazy. "Get away from me with your lies!" She started to shut the door, but the girl pushed the baby forward.

"No, please, you must listen. I cannot take care of this baby. I not live the life of a mother. You must take him. He will make a wonderful son. He is your husband's blood." Suki pushed the light blanket away from the baby's face and Claudia stared down in stunned disbelief at James's features.

With his eyes closed, he could be a miniature of her husband, with the wide, sweeping brows, high cheekbones, and cleft chin. He had his mother's beautiful complexion and silken hair.

Surely this was some bizarre mistake. Some miserable joke someone was playing on her. Claudia shut her eyes and ran a hand across her face. She opened her eyes. They were still there—this woman and the baby. It wasn't a joke, or an apparition. She took several deep breaths, looked down at the baby who'd begun to fret from the incredible heat. Finally reason took hold.

Claudia stepped aside. "Please—come inside."

"W…where did you meet my husband?" Claudia asked as she poured them both tall glasses of iced tea.

Suki smiled in remembrance. "I meet James almost two years ago. He and friend Larry came to where I work."

"Work? You don't look old enough to work."

Suki giggled behind her hand. "I have been working since I was fifteen."

"How…how old are you now?"

"Nineteen," she answered proudly.

"Where is it that you work?"

"I work for Ichitaro. She pay for this trip to America to bring baby. She is the proprietress of the teahouse…"

"Teahouse?"

"Yes," Suki smiled. "It is where the gentlemen come to be entertained. I am a geisha in training," she added with pride. "Ichitaro say I will make wonderful geisha and does not want to lose me. One day I will own my own teahouse and be very successful like Ichitaro."

A whorehouse. Dear Lord she's a prostitute. "My… husband met you at this…this teahouse?"

"Yes."

Claudia straightened her spine and jutted her chin. "Then how do you know this baby belongs to my husband?" she demanded.

Suki lowered her brilliant black eyes, focusing on the tiny baby suckling at her breast. "James…first man for me." She looked up and met Claudia's painstricken eyes. "That's how I know." She nodded her head sadly. "That's how I know…"

Claudia turned away from the window, from the garden that bloomed with brilliant life and faced her husband. "I never thought I'd ever get over the betrayal, the anger, the humiliation I felt. How could I go on? How could I face my family, my friends? I wanted to die. But I couldn't because she'd left that baby for me to take care of. It was so ironic," she added sadly, "that we could never have children and here I was raising some other woman's son. A child that you gave her but were never able to give me." Her voice grew in strength. "But I did go on. Because I wasn't going to let this come between us. I convinced myself that in a moment of weakness and loneliness, you and she…" She swallowed back the thought, recrossed the room and sat back down.

"Claudia, I never wanted to hurt you. When I met Suki, I was young and vulnerable. She was exotic, different. I thought I was in love. But it was separate from what we had. That was another life. You were my life."

"But you kept going back to her."

He looked at her with wide-eyed surprise.

"You think I didn't know? I knew." She looked down at her hands. "She wrote to me for the first year after she left Max. Oh yes, I have letters from Suki, too." She paused for effect. "She would tell me whenever you came to visit, how long you'd stay and how well you looked. She always asked about Max and was he growing to be as handsome as his father. But she always reassured me that these were two different lives that you led—and that I shouldn't worry. Life with her was a fantasy, because that was what she did, make men's fantasies come true. I was your real life, the one you would come back to."

James took her hands. "I did come back, Claudia. I know I made a shambles of your life. Because of me we had to pack up and move just to give some sort of legitimacy to Maxwell's life before he got old enough to ask questions or listen to the gossip from the neighbors." He shook his head in remorse. "And then the lies began. But what else could I do? How could I tell my son I was already married when he was born?"

Claudia took a deep breath. "There's nothing to do now but go forward, James. We've weathered many storms together. I too closed myself off from being the mother Maxwell needed. I have making up to do as well." She reached for her husband's hand. Her eyes pleaded with him. "This time, we'll do it together."

James pulled his wife to him, burying his face in her pillow-soft hair. "Oh, Claudia, can you ever find it in your heart to forgive me for all of the pain I've caused you?"

"I forgave a long time ago, sweetheart. It's time that you forgave yourself."

Chapter 15

"If you want to talk, Reese, I'd rather do it in person. I'll be there in twenty minutes."

"I don't recall your asking to come here," she tossed out, the excitement of seeing him bubbling through her veins.

Max grinned. "Consider the question asked and answered, Ms. Delaware. I'll be there shortly." He hung up before she had a chance to respond.

Reese hung up the phone, turned to Lynnette and giggled. "He's on his way."

"Of course he is. What did you expect?" Lynnette got up from the couch. "I'm only staying long enough to meet tall, dark, and handsome and then I'm out of here. But—if the two of you decide to take another one of your secret trips, please say goodbye before you go. My flight is at 7:00 a.m. tomorrow and I won't see you until whenever you get back in the States."

"I promise. And you're right. I don't expect we'll be back

in less than a month. Max said he has three separate facilities in Tokyo to visit."

"That's going to be so exciting, Reese. I swear I envy you. Not only do you get to travel with the man of your 'current' dreams, you get to visit probably one of the most mystical places on the planet."

Reese smiled. "That's what I thought," she chuckled. "But according to Max, Japan is just like any other bustling country only more crowded." She shook her head. "But I have a strong feeling there are a lot of answers in Japan. Answers that will give me the pieces of the puzzle I need to put Maxwell Knight completely together. The article is beginning to take on shape, but it's still all surface. I've battled with myself to keep my personal feelings out of it. I want to probe beneath the surface and immerse myself in all the aspects that make him the man he is. There's so much of him tied to Japan, and he hasn't found a way to totally deal with it. I know when he finally comes to grips with that part of his reality, he'll be whole. Maybe finding some of the answers about his mother and his Japanese heritage is what he needs. Everyone needs to know their roots and from where they came so they'll know where they're going."

"If anyone can find answers, it's you, Reese. It never ceases to amaze me how you are always able to turn up the most elusive pieces of information and tie it all together."

She sighed heavily. "I'm always searching, Lynn. I guess by digging up other family trees, I'm secretly hoping to reclaim my own roots."

"It'll all come together, Reese. For you and for Max." She stared pensively at her friend. "Whatever it is that's happening between you is acting as a catalyst to your memory. Both of you were brought together for a reason, to somehow help each other. Maybe he to help unlock you memory and you to help unlock his past. Don't fight it," she urged. "It may be the only way either of you will be whole."

I sure hope you're right, girlfriend. Want a refill on your tea?"

"Sounds good." She handed Reese her empty glass, just as the doorbell rang.

Both women looked wide-eyed at each other.

"Behave," Reese warned, pointing a finger in Lynnette's direction, while heading for the door. She took a quick look through the peephole and her heart did a hard knock. She looked over her shoulder and mouthed "it's him." Lynnette gave her the thumbs-up sign.

Slowly she opened the door and tried to look totally casual and aloof with one hand on her hip and her full mouth pinched as if she'd just tasted something sour.

"I'm glad to see you, too," Maxwell greeted, seeing straight through her. He stepped up to her, slipped his arm around her waist, and took what he'd been savoring on the entire ride to the hotel.

The instant Maxwell's hot, wet lips took hers, Reese forgot all about Lynn, the fact that she was supposed to be upset about Victoria, and anything else that didn't have to do with how Maxwell Knight was making her feel right at that moment.

He moaned against her mouth, while flicking his tongue across her lips. "I missed you, baby. I didn't think sleeping alone was going to be so hard. We're going…"

Movement over her shoulder caught his eye. Slowly he stepped back, giving Reese her footing. She looked curiously up at him, wondering why he'd stopped the erotic assault on her body. *Lynnette.* Reese spun around, and if she had been as fair as Lynn, she would have turned beet red with embarrassment. Fortunately, her deep chocolate complexion protected her. But she felt the fire burning under her skin nonetheless.

Lynnette stood across the room, with one hand propped beneath her chin, supported by her arm that crossed her waist. Dropping both hands to her sides, a slow smile spread across her face. In long-legged strides she crossed the room, her eyes like radar on Maxwell.

"You are obviously Maxwell Knight," she said, placing one kiss on his right cheek and then his left. "Otherwise, my friend here has a lot of explaining to do. If you haven't guessed by now, I'm Lynnette Campbell and I'm on my way out of the door." She brushed by Maxwell who grinned with unabashed astonishment.

"Pleasure," he mumbled to the departing figure.

"Believe me, it was all mine." She gave him a seductive wink and a smile. "Call me, Reese," Lynnette tossed out over her shoulder. She stepped onto the elevator with a wave and was gone.

Maxwell shook his head and began to laugh until he was doubled over with water squeezing out of his eyes. He stumbled over to the couch and plopped down on it, rubbing his eyes with the back of his hand. "Whew, your friend is a real winner. You should have warned me."

Reese fell into the spot next to him. "Believe me, you can't be warned about Lynnette. She defies explanation," she chuckled.

"That she does." He angled his body toward her and slid his arm along the back of the couch. "I understand you have some business you want to discuss with me." He let his fingers trail along the back of her neck while he spoke. "Sounded very important."

Reese opened her mouth to speak, but Maxwell put a finger to her lips. "Before you get started nailing me to the cross, I just want to say this one thing in my own defense. Victoria

Davenport means nothing to me. We met yesterday to finally settle some unfinished business—verbally—over lunch." He pursed his lips and lowered his gaze. "She finally explained a few things…that…I needed to know, and that was good, but it ended there. I took her to the airport and she's back in Virginia." He looked into her eyes and tilted up her chin with the tip of his finger. "Listen to me Reese, I've crossed some serious lines with you. I'm still trying to deal with that reality." He ran a hand across his hair. "I'm not the kind of man that goes backward—no matter what the incentive. When a relationship is over for me, it's over. I don't know what the future will hold for you and me, but I'm not going to be looking behind me to find out. If you want me to trust you with my thoughts, my feelings, and my heart—" he tapped his chest "—then you have to trust me equally."

Reese swallowed back the swell of emotion that lodged in her throat. "What I can promise you, Maxwell Knight, is that I will always try," she whispered.

He brushed a thumb across her lips. "I can't ask for any more than that, Reese." He leaned over and tenderly touched his lips to hers, taking in the soft texture of her lips before entering the sweet warmth of her mouth. His tongue dueled expertly with hers, advancing—retreating—giving—taking. He slid his hand down her spine, pulling her as close to him as space would allow. He felt the fullness of her unbound breasts press against his chest and the shock wave shot straight to his hardening penis. "What I will ask for," he whispered urgently, "is that you give yourself to me again—all of you." His hands stoked the embers that flickered within her into flames. "Will you do that for me, Reese?" He pressed a hot kiss along the tender side of her neck, running his tongue along its length. "Will you?"

Reese pressed herself closer, winding her slender fingers through his hair, down the side of his jaw, across his wide chest to meet the tiny white buttons that became unfastened beneath her fingertips. She pushed aside the fabric of the gray pin-striped shirt, exposing the soft nest of smooth black hair that partially covered the muscled bronze chest. Bending low, she laved one distended brown nipple and then the other.

A shudder raced through him. Maxwell's eyes squeezed shut.

"I'll try," Reese whispered softly, taking his hand to pull him to his feet. "Let me get started inside." She led him toward the bedroom and Max kicked the door shut behind them.

They lay nestled together bathed in the afterglow of their lovemaking. Maxwell caressed Reese's back, contemplating whether or not to tell her of his conversation with his father as he placed featherlike kisses along her face. He didn't want to frighten her, and maybe this whole thing would blow over once they were in Tokyo. But gut instinct told him otherwise.

Victoria was working with General Murphy, a man to be feared under the simplest of circumstances. His father had also informed him that his friend Larry Templeton was assigned to keep an eye on things and that Max should stay as close to Reese as possible to make Larry's job a bit easier. Staying close to Reese was not the problem, it was the reason why.

"Reese," he began softly.

"Hmm?" Reese opened her eyes and looked into his. "What is it?"

"I got a call from my father today…" Maxwell went on to explain how his father found out about Victoria and his concern about her being taken to Chevy Chase, leaving out the part about Larry Templeton.

"You seem to be the key, Reese," he concluded. "For whatever reason. My father didn't go into details but I suspect

it has to do with his connections to the Special Forces unit."
He paused. "Reese, what did your father do—before the
accident?"

Reese swallowed. "According to my aunt Celeste he worked
for the Air Force, too. I thought I told you that. He was on the
investigative unit, if I remember correctly. Why?"

"Somehow, your father and General Murphy are all tied up
in something together. Something that he feels you'll discover
by interviewing me." He shook his head. "I can't imagine
what it could be. I was just a kid when they would have known
each other. And even though my father didn't come right out
and say it, I believe he's involved in some way as well."

Reese sat up in the bed. "But what does Victoria have to
do with all of this?"

"I don't know." He lay back and stared up at the ceiling.
"When we talked, she asked a lot of questions about you. At
first, I just felt it was natural curiosity. But now...I'm not so
sure."

"I certainly couldn't give anyone any information. I don't
even remember who I was beyond fifteen years ago."

"That's just it. Everything keeps pointing back to that
time. And you may be the only one who knows. Now your
connection to me is posing a threat to someone."

"Max, you're scaring me."

He pulled her into his arms, burying her face against his
chest. "I don't mean to, sweetheart. I'm sure it's nothing. My
father is so accustomed to everyone having ulterior motives
for everything, he's probably overreacting. I mean Victoria
does work for the Air Force. There could have been a million
reasons why she went to Chevy Chase."

Reese mulled over what Maxwell said, and tried to put
it in perspective. He was probably right. His father was just
overreacting. But what if he wasn't? Maybe it wasn't really

Max who they were concerned about, but more what he could or could not reveal about his own father.

"Let's not worry about it," Max said. "I just want to enjoy our time together. The next few weeks are going to be really hectic."

Reese nodded, trying to dispel the effects of Maxwell's revelations and her own shaky conclusions.

"How's the article coming?"

"It's coming along," she replied absently. "I still have to work on getting it in shape and getting the feel that I want. Everyone I talked with has been so helpful. That makes things a lot easier."

"You do have a way of getting folks to cooperate," he teased, pinching her lightly on the behind.

"Very funny," she laughed slapping his hand away. "Max," she hedged. "I think I remembered something. I was talking with Lynnette about it just before you came over."

He turned on his side and propped up on his elbow. "Do you want to tell me about it?"

She took a long breath before detailing the remnants of her dream.

"That could mean anything, Reese."

"I know," she said with resignation. "I could have been remembering something from anytime in my past." She sighed. "The only part that upset me was that when I tried to put a face to the figure by the car, I kept seeing you."

He chuckled deep in his throat. "So you're seeing me in your dreams now, huh?"

"I'm serious, Max. It really bothered me. Lynn said it was probably transference, or something."

"She's probably right," he said, kissing her solidly on the lips. "Don't let it get to you. The harder you try to make sense of it the more difficult it will be. Did you write it down?" He gently began to massage her engorged breasts.

"As soon as I woke up," she said, shuddering from the sensations rippling through her.

"Good. And how about the headaches?" he crooned.

"I felt the onset of one this morning," she hissed between her teeth, as his touch became more demanding. "But I nipped it in the bud."

"When we get to Tokyo—" he took a hardened nipple in his mouth, then released it "—I want to take you to this place where they teach *Tai chi*. It's an excellent form of relaxation." His hand slipped between the juncture of her thighs, parting the tangle of black hair to make a path to the already wet cavern. "It will do wonders for the stress and headaches. And maybe you can stop taking the medication."

Reese rolled her hips and spread her trembling thighs to give him better access. "I'll try anything," she moaned softly.

"But in the meantime," he said in a husky whisper, pulling her on top to straddle him, "maybe this will help."

Inch by delicious inch she felt him fill her. Yet he held her immobile with a steely grip until he reached full entry before letting her take the lead. And as they began to move together in unison, the shadows that stalked them soon became incinerated in the heat of their passion.

"Well, it's pretty obvious that we're not going to get any work done wrapped up in each other's arms." Maxwell yawned, tweaking Reese on the nose.

"I thought I was working," she taunted, giving him a sly grin.

Maxwell chuckled heartily. "You're right about that one. But what I meant was work-work—the bread and butter kind." He untangled his legs from the twisted sheets and sat on the edge of the bed. He gazed at her reposed figure from over his shoulder.

"Why don't I help you pack your things?"

Reese slowly turned her head in his direction and frowned. "What are you talking about now? We don't leave for Japan for another week."

"I know that. I just thought you'd like to stay with me at the house in San Diego until we left."

Reese sat up and pulled the sheet with her. Her husky voice lowered as she angled her chin upward. "Are you asking me to move in with you, Mr. Knight?"

Maxwell turned completely around and stretched out on the bed until his chin rested on her knees. He looked up at her. "That's exactly what I'm asking." He stroked her thighs. "Temporarily, of course."

She pursed her lips and gave him a sidelong glance. "Of course." She looked at his face of innocence for a few moments. "The question is, why?"

Maxwell straightened. "Always the investigator," he said trying to sidestep the question. "Why can't I just want you to?" He began to pick up his discarded clothes.

"You're not the type of man who just 'does' anything. If you want me to 'temporarily' move into your house, you must have a reason, and I can't imagine that great sex is it."

"Would it be so hard to believe that I just want you with me, Reese?" He turned to face her. "Maybe I don't want to tiptoe in and out of hotel rooms. Maybe I just want to spend enough time with you to see where this thing with us is going." He sat back down on the edge of the bed and took a long breath. His eyes narrowed in question. "Do I really come across as someone who has no feelings, that is so unreachable?"

Reese caressed his jaw and searched the depths of his dark eyes that sought answers. "Max, you've held yourself in abeyance for so long that even when people are close—when I'm close, I can still feel the resistance—something invisible holding you back and keeping me out." She gently pressed her lips to his. "That doesn't mean that you're a man who doesn't feel. If anything, sweetheart, it shows me you're a man who feels too much. Way down deep in his soul. And he takes those feelings to heart. And sometimes, he just doesn't know how to share them because he's been dealing with them by himself for so long."

Maxwell pressed his forehead against hers and braced her bare shoulders. Then he looked into her eyes. "Maybe—we can start sharing some of them together." His jaw clenched. "What do you say about that?"

Her soft-spoken answer caressed his racing heart. "I say let's start packing. I want to reach home before it gets dark."

Reese and Maxwell spent the drive out to his house in San Diego singing old songs over the blast of the radio, nibbling on nacho chips and slurping sodas from the can like two teenagers. By the time they arrived, bubbling with laughter and newfound joy, the sun was setting majestically over the bay.

Maxwell slipped one arm around Reese's waist and carried her bags in the other hand. Stepping across the threshold he dropped the bags and swept her into his arms, lifting her off of her feet. "I have certain rules of the house." He began nipping on her lip. "First, in order to conserve water, all bathing and showering must be done jointly." Reese began to laugh. "Second, that guest-room thing is out. I don't expect to turn over in the middle of the night and find an empty space. Third, I expect you to take me whenever and wherever the mood hits you, as I will you," he added, nuzzling her neck. "And fourth, you can scream and holler my name in ecstasy as much as you want—our closest neighbors are miles way."

Reese punched him hard in the arm and scurried away, her ankle-length gauze skirt spinning around her legs. "Well, all I have to say is, you're going to have to work really hard to make me holler."

Before he could reach out and snatch her, Reese was off and running up the stairs with Maxwell hot on her heels.

Larry Templeton sat back in his car and dialed James's number. "Looks like they're in for the night."

"Don't let anyone near that house."

Chapter 16

Frank Murphy walked reverently across the grassy well-tended field. It was so peaceful here, he thought, moving around the headstones and up the small incline to his sister Faith's final resting place. It was here that he could come and think and talk with his sister about the things that troubled his heart and weighed down his spirit.

He removed his hat, his close-cropped dark blond hair streaked with gray, and chest full of medals glistened in the sunlight. He knelt down beside Faith's headstone and brushed away the leaves and dried flowers, placing a fresh bunch in its place.

"I know it's been a while, sis, but you're always in my thoughts." He paused measuring his words. "Things are not good, Faith. I feel everything coming apart around me." He chuckled disheartenedly and briefly shut his green eye. "My past is coming back to haunt me, as you said it would. But back then I didn't see any other way out. As much as Hamilton meant to me, I couldn't let him destroy my career." He sighed. "But now, looking back, I wish I'd done things differently. Maybe I could have reasoned with him. But he was so hellbent on seeing justice done, he was blind to anything else. I was given a job to do. I was following orders. He should have understood that. Chemical testing on our own men has been going on for decades. They did it in Korea and Vietnam and it continued in Desert Storm." He ran a hand across his weary face. "And now his daughter is interviewing James's son." He shook his head at the absolute irony of it all. "How long will it be before the trail leads back? We were able to cover up the 'accident.' But this…" He sighed heavily. "Victoria went to see Maxwell after all these years. We worked hard to dismantle that relationship, and I'll still do whatever is necessary to see to it that it never happens again." He looked ahead watching a family place flowers on a headstone.

"I don't think I can ever thank you enough for caring for Victoria all of those years. You were as close to a mother as she'd ever have. I know how much having children meant to you and how devastated you both were to find out that you couldn't have children of your own before John died. And I'll move heaven and earth, Faith, to ensure that Victoria keeps that memory of you as her mother. It was the one thing I could do for Hamilton and it's a final trust I'll never betray."

He sat back on his haunches and looked out onto the horizon. A soft breeze blew around him carrying the sweet scent of flowers and fresh cut grass. "I still think about Celeste, Faith. How different would things have been if I'd convinced her that we could be happy together? But her heart was always with Hamilton even after he married her sister, Sharlene. I've tried to stay away from her, Faith, to put her in the back of my mind. But I can't. When you love someone you want to share your life, your hopes and your fears with them. I guess that's what brought me to her house this morning. She's not well, Faith, and the thought that I'll soon lose her too is tearing me apart. I was able to handle loving her from afar. But not to be able to ever see her or hear her voice again… Now the painful irony is, she's at the end of her life, but she handed me a ticket to a new one." He shook his head as the sting of tears burned his eyes, slowly spilling over his dark lashes. "What…what am I going to do, Faith?" His voice broke as his body shook with sobs. "What am I going to do?"

Celeste moved slowly through the airy house, opening windows and pulling aside the curtains. She felt better today than she had in a while. The pain was bearable. Absently, she pressed her hand to her stomach. The doctors said the growth on her ovaries was inoperable, but perhaps it could be controlled with chemotherapy. She'd laughed at that then. Being a nurse, she knew what that did to a person. Often the treatment was worse than the cure. She'd opted to live out the rest of her life the best she could.

Turning away, she walked into the kitchen and poured herself a glass of lemonade and took it out to the enclosed patio. The patio was her personal haven, a place that she often retreated to when she needed to think. With the surprise visit earlier in the day from Frank, these few moments of reflection were just what she needed.

Birds sang melodiously in the trees, the sun shone brilliantly in the sky, all a testament to the wonders of nature. She pulled the long yellow-and-white-striped lounge chair closer to the front of the patio to get the greatest benefits of the sun and the breeze. Stretching out, she allowed the warmth of the sun to soak into her tired bones.

Placing the glass on the ground beside her, she leaned back and closed her eyes. Images of the handsome Frank Murphy as he looked that morning standing on her doorstep filled her vision. Her heartbeat picked up its pace at the memory. He still had the ability to make her feel weak in the knees, even after all of these years.

"I know I should have called first, Celeste," he'd said in greeting, "but I just needed to see you. Do you mind if I come in?"

Celeste stepped aside. "Please. Come in." She followed him into the house, thankful that she'd dressed in a bright yellow sundress and had put on some makeup to cover the dark circles beneath her eyes.

Frank stopped in the center of the living room and turned toward her holding his hat in his hands. She could see his struggle to hide the shock of her looking so thin.

"Can I get you something?" she asked nervously, rubbing her hands—which had suddenly become cold—together.

"No. Nothing thanks. May I sit down?"

"Of course. I'm sorry." She patted her soft curls and crossed the room, taking a seat opposite him. "What brings you out here, Frank?"

He folded his hands in front of him and leaned forward, resting his forearms on his thighs. "I know it's been a long time for us, Celeste. And I know you made a decision a long time ago that I've tried to live by." He swallowed and shrugged in confusion. "Maybe it's old age, maybe it's loneliness." He shook his head. "I just know that I've been doing a lot of soul searching these last few weeks—looking at my life—the choices that I've made and the things I've done." He looked up. "I know I'm not making any sense. But…what we had Celeste…I never forgot. I can't forget…"

"Frank, please…"

"No. Hear me out, Celeste." He averted his gaze then looked directly into her pleading hazel eyes. "I know you chose Hamilton over me even though he could never love you the way I did. I thought it would kill me when you became pregnant with his child." Celeste shut her eyes and lowered her head as the painful memories consumed her.

"But I made myself go on, Celeste. I had to. And all of these years I kept the secret and my promise to the both of you. I wanted to hate you. I wanted to hate him. But I couldn't. Instead I took my pain out in every other way that I could—through power and manipulation. For a moment, I was happy when he was killed. I thought that maybe you would come to me then. But you never did."

He stood up and began to pace the room, moving backward and forward through time. "And when Victoria was born and looked so much like you as she grew older, I wanted her to be my own daughter—our daughter. But that was never to be."

Unknown to him the prevarication of his words slammed against her, making her wince. Would she ever be able to tell him the truth, even now—that she envied her sister Sharlene so desperately that she'd been willing to take and claim what was never hers—if only to have whatever Sharlene had? As if that would somehow make her Sharlene's equal, worthy of love.

But how much time did she really have? It wasn't fair to Victoria for Celeste to go to her grave with a lie that she'd constructed to assuage her wounded heart.

Slowly, Celeste rose, her large eyes filled with years of pain and deceit. "Why don't we take a walk outside, Frank?"

More than two hours later, Frank returned to his car, his mind and heart still spinning from the revelations. His sturdy body felt as if it had been ravaged in battle. All these years he'd never known. He sat down in the car and turned his gaze toward Celeste's home. How could she have done this—deprived him—deprived them all?

His emotions struggled to consume him. They vacillated between rage and a pain so deep he could not find the words to describe it. And yet he still loved her—after all she'd done. She was a woman who needed love more than anyone he'd ever met. She measured her worth by what her sister had. It was not until today that he fully understood the magnitude of her resentment for her sister Sharlene, which stretched back to their days as young girls. But Celeste never outgrew the sibling rivalry between her and her younger sister. Instead, it bloomed, and grew like the cancer that now pecked away at her life.

Frank was visiting his buddy, Hamilton, when he spotted Celeste across the crowded grounds of the George Washington University campus. She was so beautiful in an almost effervescent way, he realized, his heart knocking hard against his chest. He poked Hamilton in the side and angled his square chin in Celeste's direction. "Who's that?"

Hamilton gradually looked up and in the direction Frank indicated. "What about her?" he asked with caution, a slight edge to his tone. "That's my lady's older sister, Celeste. Why?" Hamilton's dark eyes drilled into his friend's green ones.

Frank gave a little shrug. "Why don't you introduce me?"

"Why should I? It can't go anywhere, Murphy, and you know it. So why stress yourself?"

Frank stared at him belligerently. "Because I'm white?"

"Yeah, pretty much. You may not have a problem with it, but plenty of others will, including her folks. You may be a liberated northern boy, and all that good stuff about crossing the color lines is not a problem for you, but this is still the fifties, man. Down South fifties. Whether you want to believe it or not, blacks and whites still don't mix in most of this 'liberated' country of ours."

"If you won't introduce me, then I guess I'll just introduce myself," Frank replied, totally ignoring Hamilton. He pushed himself up off of the grass and began a slow stroll across the sloping hill.

"You're asking for trouble, Murphy," he yelled to Frank's retreating back.

And trouble was exactly what Frank Murphy got, from the instant Celeste Winston turned around and stared at him with those incredible hazel eyes. His heart was hers for the taking.

He'd never felt so quickly, or so intensely about anyone as he had about Celeste Winston in the short months that they went from discreet friends to secret lovers. He knew it was a forbidden love—a love frowned upon by society. Maybe that was the incendiary device that fueled their clandestine passion. All he knew for certain was that he couldn't stop himself if he'd tried.

Foolishly he'd believed they could surmount the obstacles. What he could never defeat, however, was Hamilton Delaware and the hold he had over Celeste's heart, or the obsession she had in besting her sister.

Frank put the car in gear and mindlessly pulled away, looking back only once. All he'd ever coveted in this life was now a possibility. Celeste had handed to him the key to a dream he'd lost forever. Within his grasp was an opportunity to make some atonement for the deaths and destruction of which he'd been a part. But what awaited him on the other side of the door, should he dare to open it? If he dared, he'd have more reason than ever to keep Reese from uncovering his past.

Reese puttered around in the spacious kitchen, pretending to fix something edible for breakfast. "Can't go wrong with toast," she mumbled, looking over her shoulder for any signs of Maxwell. She popped two pieces of whole wheat bread in the toaster and depressed the lever.

Smiling and rubbing her palms together as if she'd accomplished a great feat, she pulled open the refrigerator door and took out the container of apple juice. Moving easily around the center island she retrieved two glasses from the overhead cabinets and placed them on the counter at the precise moment the rather burned toast ejected.

"What are you burning in here?" Max grumbled, turning up his nose as he entered the kitchen. He took a quick glance at the toast in Reese's hand and the total look of dismay, overlaid with disgust on her face, and he burst out laughing. "Please tell me you can boil water," he howled.

She slammed the two damning objects on the counter, pieces of burnt bread scattering across its top. Whirling away, her silk kimono fanning around her, she stomped toward the door, her humiliation complete.

"Hey, hold your horses," Maxwell chuckled, biting down the last of his laughter. He grabbed her arm just as she attempted to whiz by him. He spun her stiff body around until it lined up perfectly with his. Merriment danced in the depths of his onyx eyes and it took all Reese had to maintain her irate front and not laugh instead.

He ran his finger along the bridge of her nose. "I'm sorry?" he asked more than stated. She gave him a good punch in the chest, or at least the best she could do under such close circumstances. He kissed her forehead. "Why don't I fix breakfast and you just relax and look beautiful?"

"Don't patronize me," she huffed, pushing away from him. "I just never really learned to cook. My aunt Celeste refused to have me in the kitchen. I had no sisters or brothers or other relatives to learn from." She shrugged. "When I finally moved out on my own, my life was so fast-paced I didn't have the time or the inclination to learn. Take-out is my middle name."

Maxwell bit down yet another chuckle. "That's understandable," he said off the cuff. He inhaled deeply and let out a long breath. "We'll just have to remedy that situation. Instead of hitting the town restaurants, we'll whip up our own meals." His smile was slow and warm and it touched another corner of her heart. This man would never stop surprising her. "Starting with breakfast, 'cause I'm starved. Especially after the workout you gave me this morning," he said, flashing her a leer.

Maxwell was patient to a fault and as many times as he wanted to shake his head in disbelief at her lack of culinary skills, he kept his own counsel, encouraging her all along the way.

By the time they were finished preparing a breakfast of hash browns, western omelets, corn muffins and herbal tea, his once spotless kitchen was a disaster area. But Reese was so pleased with the outcome, her pleasure erased any thoughts of the big cleanup.

Maxwell took his last mouthful of the delicious fare. "That wasn't so bad," he commented.

"It was actually fun," she grinned. "Now if I can just remember everything…"

He chuckled. "You will," he assured. "It just takes practice—and patience."

She gazed at him with a newfound awakening. "Something that you seem to have plenty of with some to spare. I really appreciate that."

He winked. "See, I'm not such a bad guy after all." He leaned back in his seat and patted his full stomach. "And just to prove that point, I'm going to help you clean up the kitchen."

With the dishes finished and the kitchen returned to its immaculate state, Reese and Maxwell walked out onto the deck. Maxwell sat along the railing, his arms crossing his hard body. Reese opted for a seat on the lounge chair. She lay back and closed her eyes against the brilliant sun.

He'd thought long and hard about telling her of his father's suspicions. Watching her now, having been with her in the most intimate of ways, opening up to her—he knew he couldn't lose her and telling her might just make her run all the way back to Chicago.

Yet not to tell her that she might be in jeopardy was only serving his own purposes. He couldn't keep her sequestered out here forever.

"Reese," he whispered, reluctant to mar this peaceful moment.

Slowly she opened her eyes and squinted up at him. Her pulse picked up an extra beat when she saw the strain etched across his face. She bolted up in her seat.

"Max…what is it? Don't look at me like that."

He kneeled down next to where she sat and took her hands in his. He looked down at their hands, then into the depths of her questioning amber eyes. "You already know that for some reason, Reese, there are people in very high places who don't want you digging into my past." He swallowed. "And apparently they'll do whatever is necessary to keep you from finding out whatever it is they don't want you to know." He took a breath. "I had more than the reason I gave you for asking you to come out here with me."

Her eyes widened in alarm. "What's the reason, Max?" she asked with hesitation.

He let out a short breath. "My father felt it best if we stayed together," he paused, reluctant to continue when he saw the flash of fire in her eyes. Her mouth tightened into a thin line. "It would be easier for Larry to keep an eye on things if we were…"

She held up her hand to stop him. "I don't want to hear

anymore." She threw her legs over the side of the chair and stood up, nearly knocking Maxwell down in the process.

"Reese, listen…" He reached for her arm. She pulled away so violently the lightweight chair turned over on its side.

"Go straight to hell, Max," she spat, her anger causing her to tremble. "All the while you were whispering sweet nothings, that's just what it was…nothing!" Her voice sounded strangled as she fought back tears of despair. She leaned dangerously forward, hands on hips with her neck rolling in time to her condemnation. "You're just following orders. What makes you any different from Daddy, who you claim you can't understand?" she retorted with venom.

Maxwell felt as if he'd been blindsided. How could she think so little of him—even now—after what they'd shared, after what he'd given of himself? His response was hollow. "If that's what you think of me, Reese, then this relationship isn't worth the time it took to drive down here. If I didn't give a damn about you, do you really think it would matter to me where you were? Do you really, deep down in your heart—" he poked her in the chest and she recoiled "—believe that I went through all of this—" he waved his hands expansively "—just for a few days and nights of rolling in the hay?" His voice lowered to a grumble. "If that's all I wanted, there are more women than I care to count that would have been more than willing to warm my bed." He lowered his gaze and shook his head. "You really don't get it, do you?" With that he brushed past her and strode through the house and up the stairs.

The door to the upstairs bedroom thudded so loudly, Reese jumped out of the daze she was in. She spun toward the sliding glass door, her eyes winding up the spiral staircase. Without further hesitation she followed in Maxwell's wake.

Maxwell stalked the four corners of his bedroom. Hurt wouldn't adequately describe how he felt at the moment.

Disappointment moved in the right direction and even that wasn't sufficient. Maybe he should have told her that part of the reason for them being together was for her own protection—and he'd do whatever was necessary to keep her safe.

Abruptly, he halted his pacing and paused for a moment in front of the window. He braced his palms against the window frame and stared, unseeing onto the horizon. She had every right to be upset, even to doubt him, he rationalized. He, of all people, should know about mistrust and deceit. He swung toward the door just as it opened.

Her eyes were two large pools, drawing him into their bottomless depth. His heart knocked in his chest, a combination of anticipation mixed with an inkling of fear.

Reese stepped into the room. She closed the door silently behind her and pressed her spine against it—hesitating—unsure of what it was she saw in his gaze.

Maxwell clenched his jaw and crossed the room in—what appeared to Reese—slow motion. He kept coming until the barest whisper separated them. She held her breath as his invariable gaze bore down into hers.

He lowered his head. His kiss was tentative, treading lightly, slowly seductive. She wanted more.

Reese wound her long, bare arms around his neck. Reaching up on tiptoe she pulled him closer. "I'm sorry," she murmured against his hot mouth.

"*I'm* sorry. I should have told you everything," he groaned against her neck, trailing kisses along its length. "I wanted—needed to protect you." He pulled back and searched her face. "Can you understand that, baby? I'm not going to let anything happen to you."

"I can't remember the last time anyone cared enough about me…" her words caught in her throat. Shimmering pools floated in her eyes.

Maxwell crushed her lush body solidly against his. "Until now," he whispered finishing her sentence.

She hugged him tighter. "But I'm a big girl, Max," she uttered against his chest. "I need to know what I'm dealing with just as much as you do. I've spent the better part of my life in the dark. Please." She looked up at him. Her eyes implored him. "Don't you do that to me, too."

Chapter 17

Maxwell slowly pulled out of the comfort of Reese's embrace. He crossed the room and sat down on the small sofa in front of the bay window. Looking across the room to where Reese stood—waiting—he held out his hand to her.

A tentative smile quivered around the corners of her mouth as she came to meet him. She took his outstretched hand and brought it to her lips, before lowering herself to the floor to sit at his feet.

"I don't know quite where to begin," he started in a hushed, halting voice. "I've been going over everything my father said to me on the phone, but more importantly, what he didn't say."

Reese curled closer, pressing her head against his thigh. "I've thought about it, too," she said. She looked up at him gauging the look of caution in his eyes. "I don't think the problem is with us, but with our fathers, Max."

With great reluctance, colored with relief, he nodded

in agreement. "Somehow, there's a connection and they—someone—doesn't want you to find out what it is." He paused and took a long breath. "And I don't know if I want to find out, either. And yet—" he looked down into her upturned face "—finding the answers may be the only way either of us will ever be free."

Hadn't Lynnette said almost the same thing? Reese reflected thoughtfully. "So what are we going to do?" she asked.

"We," he began, standing up and pulling her to her feet, "are going to use your investigative skills, and I'm going to use all the resources in my power to find out whatever it is we're not supposed to know."

Reese smiled openly and released a long held breath. "Now you're talkin'." She grinned.

Together they went back downstairs and out onto the deck.

Maxwell hopped up on the rail and sat down. Reese took her place on the lounge chair.

"I was thinking I would put a call in to Lynnette when she returns to Chicago and see if she could tap into the computers for some background information," Reese said.

Maxwell nodded. "That may work. My only concern is involving anyone unnecessarily. Is there any way that you could get the information yourself with the computers at my offices?"

Reese pursed her lips. "If there is a way to link up with the mainframe at my office in Chicago it might work," she said, slowly thinking out the possibilities.

"I'll give R.J. a call. He'll get you a terminal set up in the morning. I'll make the connections myself. Is that all you'll need?"

"I'll still have to give Lynn a call. She'll be back in the

office tomorrow. She can get me the access codes for the hook-up."

"Great. But—is she going to ask a ton of questions?"

Reese laughed quietly. "I'm sure she will. But I won't give anything away."

"Just remember, the less said the better." His voice grew serious. "I don't know how desperately they want whatever it is to stay hidden or what lengths they'll go through…" His unspoken words hung in the air between them, his meaning clear.

For several moments they sat in silence, shrouded in their private thoughts.

"Let's go for a walk," Reese said suddenly. "I'd like to see the beach."

Maxwell jumped down from his perch. "And I'd be honored to be your guide," he grinned.

They strolled along the beach for several hours, talking quietly at times, at others simply enjoying the pleasure of each other's company and the beauty of the landscape. By the time they returned to Maxwell's house, the sun was beginning its descent. Never once did they realize that they were being watched.

"I'm getting hungry," Maxwell announced when they'd returned to the lower level. "Why don't you and I fix something and take it out on the deck?"

Reese flashed him a cynical look. "Are you sure you want me to participate?" she asked with a half grin. "Breakfast is one thing, dinner is something else entirely."

Maxwell chuckled. "Practice makes perfect." He crossed the expansive kitchen and began opening cabinets, pulling out an assortment of ingredients. Then it was on to the refrigerator where he removed four pieces of red snapper from plastic bags and the mixings for a salad.

He gave Reese patient instructions for preparing a Caesar salad along with a homemade dressing. After cleaning and seasoning the fish, he said, "Let's grill the fish outside. It gives them an unbelievable taste." He piled the fish in a Pyrex dish and covered it. "I'll take this. Just bring out the salad and the bottle of wine from the fridge and we can get this party started."

Maxwell got the grill going, while Reese adjusted the volume on the sound system. She dashed back inside and got the dishes, silverware, dinner napkins and glasses. In short order, the aroma of grilled fish mixed with the sounds of Anita Baker's throaty love ballad "Giving You the Best."

Reese sat down in what had become her favorite seat with a long sigh of contentment.

"Everything should be ready in a few minutes," Maxwell announced, taking a sip from his glass of wine.

"Smells heavenly."

"Compliments to the chef." He smiled, saluting her with his glass.

Reese grinned. "I had plenty of help."

"Before it's all over you'll be wheelin' and dealin' all by yourself." He stuck a fork into the fish and turned them over one by one.

Reese pulled herself up from her reclining position and began putting the salad into the bowls and sprinkling the garnish on each.

"Soup's on," Maxwell announced. "Pass me your plate."

"This is absolutely incredible," Reese sighed rolling her eyes to the heavens, while savoring the succulent taste of their dinner.

"I knew you'd like it. Now you can add grilled snapper to your repertoire."

Reese eased her plate aside and took the last sip from her

glass of wine. "We've avoided talking about what we're going to do for the entire evening," she began without preamble. "I still get the feeling that you're not telling me something."

Slowly Maxwell shook his head and chuckled softly. "You're beginning to know me just a little too well for my taste."

"And you're avoiding the inevitable," she challenged. She leaned back on the recliner, crossed her long, bare legs and stared—waiting.

Maxwell was quiet for several moments, attempting to pull his fleeting thoughts into perspective. To give voice to his suspicions would cast a pall of doubt over his own father and maybe his mother. Was he willing to do that? But not to explore every option would leave them both vulnerable to the unknown.

He took a long, thoughtful breath. "I've been doing a lot of thinking since the phone call from my father. And at first I didn't think much about the dream you said you remembered." He looked off across the horizon, his bronze skin glistening from the iridescent glow of the full moon. "I tried to figure why you would see my face in your dream."

"You look a great deal like your father," she stated more than asked.

Maxwell nodded slowly, looking at her with pain in his eyes.

"Do you have a picture of him?"

"No."

"What is it that you're thinking, Max?"

"I don't want to think anything," he snapped.

"Then let's leave it at that—for the moment."

Maxwell crossed his long legs at the ankle. "There's something else."

Her heartbeat picked up its pace.

"Something major happened when I was about seventeen,"

he said, his thoughts rushing backward. "We were living in Maryland, my father was on some assignment and then suddenly, we packed up and moved to Los Angeles. Usually when we moved, we had months of notice." He shook his head. "But not that time. My father never explained anything. But I could feel the tension in the household and I remember my mother being very upset about the upheaval. She'd never seemed to mind before."

Reese's investigative instincts went into full gear. "Do you recall any specific incidents during that time? Did your father ever mention anything he may have been working on?"

"I just remember the phone ringing constantly, at odd hours, and my father talking in a hushed voice, which wasn't like him at all."

"That could have been any number of things," she offered, seeing the strained look on his face.

"I suppose." He breathed heavily. "We could spend forever trying to guess this thing out. There isn't much more we can do until you get what ever information you can from the computers."

"You're right," she said with a soft smile, trying to sound light. She stood up and stepped up to him, placing a tender kiss on his lips. "Whatever happens, Max, we're in this together. Please remember that."

He pulled her into his arms, breathing in her essence. "I will," he whispered, even as the seeds of doubt burrowed their way beneath his skin.

Reese stretched out next to Maxwell, incredibly satisfied from their hours of lovemaking. Hypnotized, she watched the rise and fall of his chest. She curled her leg between his and draped her arm across his chest, the steady beat of his heart lulling her to sleep.

It began slowly at first, the vision clouded and murky,

the shapes—shapeless and dark. Then bit by bit the voices became clearer, the images sharper.

The shouting woke her from her sleep and she watched herself tiptoe out of her bed and into the hall. Silently, she crossed the hallway and knelt at the top of the stairs, listening in fear to the violent argument ensuing between her mother and father.

"How could you, Hamilton?" Sharlene screamed. "My own sister!"

"Sharlene, listen to me," Hamilton shouted above his wife's tirade. "It was only that one time…"

"One time," she cried incredulously. "How many times does it take to be an adulterer? Does one time absolve you of something—you bastard! I want you out of here—now—tonight."

"Sharlene you're being unreasonable. You know I can't do that. I won't do that. This is my home, too. We can work this out. What about Reese?"

"You should have thought about your daughter before you decided to jump in bed with my sister."

Reese's stomach did a somersault. Her father and her aunt Celeste—in bed? She jumped suddenly and stifled a cry of alarm when she heard the sound of dishes and glasses breaking below.

"Sharlene—please—sweetheart, I love you. I made a mistake."

"Get out!" Another dish was hurled against the wall.

And then Reese heard her mother's sobs. They began softly then built until they were a keening wail of agony. She didn't realize that she, too, was crying until she felt the tears trickle onto her hands that were clenched into fists on her lap. Without thinking she ran to her room and grabbed her knapsack, and stuffed a change of clothes into the bag. She was going to make her aunt tell her the truth. She would bring her aunt Celeste to the house and all of the lies would go away.

Her parents were still arguing when she ran down the stairs and out onto the lawn, unnoticed by them. That's when she saw the man leaning down by her father's car. She stopped in her tracks. He turned and look at her.

Maxwell was pulled out of his sleep by the thrashing next to him. He sat straight up in the bed and turned toward Reese who was twisting, turning and moaning unintelligible sounds.

"Reese. Baby, wake up. You're having a nightmare." His heart lurched seeing the torture that she was obviously enduring. Her nude body was covered in a thin sheen of perspiration. "Reese, please." He grabbed her shoulders and shook her.

Reese's eyes flew open. A scream hung soundlessly on her lips as she stared into the eyes of the man who killed her family.

Chapter 18

Maxwell gathered Reese's trembling body tightly against his. His own racing heart matching hers beat for beat. "Shh. It's all right. It's over, baby. It's over." Gently, he rocked her back and forth.

"My head," she said weakly, the pain in her temples building in intensity. Tears squeezed from her eyes. "My head," she whispered again.

"Okay. Just relax. Take it easy. We'll make it all right. I promise. Lean against me." He adjusted his position allowing Reese to lean her back against his chest. "That's it. Now close your eyes and breathe deeply through your mouth just like we did it before."

With infinite tenderness he began the ritual of massaging her temples, while evoking soothing images of beaches, sailing ships and soft summer breezes. By degrees he felt the tension in her body begin to relent. The trembling had ceased.

We'd like to send you two free books to introduce you to Kimani™ Romance books. These novels feature strong, sexy women, and African-American heroes that are charming, loving and true. Our authors fill each page with exceptional dialogue, exciting plot twists, and enough sizzling romance to keep you riveted until the very end!

KIMANI ROMANCE...LOVE'S ULTIMATE DESTINATION

Your two books have a combined cover price of $12.50, but are yours **FREE!**

We'll even send you two wonderful surprise gifts. You can't lose!

THE EDITOR'S "THANK YOU" FREE GIFTS INCLUDE:

➤ Two Kimani™ Romance Novels
➤ Two exciting surprise gifts

YES! I have placed my Editor's "thank you" Free Gifts seal in the space provided at right. Please send me 2 FREE books, and my 2 FREE Mystery Gifts. I understand that I am under no obligation to purchase anything further, as explained on the back of this card.

PLACE
FREE GIFTS
SEAL
HERE

About how many NEW paperback fiction books have you purchased in the past 3 months?

❏ 0-2   ❏ 3-6   ❏ 7 or more

FDCD   FDCP   FDCZ

168/368 XDL

Please Print

FIRST NAME

LAST NAME

ADDRESS

APT.#   CITY

STATE/PROV.   ZIP/POSTAL CODE

Thank You!

If offer card is missing write to: The Reader Service, P.O. Box 1867, Buffalo, NY 14240-1867 or visit www.ReaderService.com

BUSINESS REPLY MAIL

FIRST-CLASS MAIL   PERMIT NO. 717   BUFFALO, NY

POSTAGE WILL BE PAID BY ADDRESSEE

THE READER SERVICE

PO BOX 1867

BUFFALO NY 14240-9952

NO POSTAGE
NECESSARY
IF MAILED
IN THE
UNITED STATES

Her rapid breathing was slowing to near normal. He continued the soft pressure with his thumbs against the pain.

He placed a featherlike kiss against her brow. "That's it, just relax," he crooned. He continued his ministrations until he heard her soft sigh.

"It's gone," she whispered. Her eyes fluttered open, trying to focus. She struggled to a sitting position, resting her head on her bent knees.

Maxwell massaged her shoulders. "Are you sure you're all right?"

She nodded.

"Do you want to talk about it? Do you remember anything?"

Reese swallowed, desperately wanting the memories to return from whence they came. "Unfortunately, I do," she said slowly, twisting her body to face him. His heart thudded with trepidation.

Maxwell listened with a mounting sense of foreboding as Reese painstakingly recounted her nightmare. The implications of her dream went much deeper than the scenes depicted. A young girl had overheard her father accused of infidelity with her mother's sister. She'd seen a man who apparently looked like him near the family car the night before they were killed. How did it all tie in together? And what role, if any, did his father play?

"Reese," he said softly, moments after she'd finished. "What date—was the accident?" He held his breath, waiting for the answer that he possibly didn't want to hear.

"June 28, 1995," she answered in a monotone, the one memory forever etched in her mind.

Maxwell's pulse began to race. Two days later, his family had left their home in Maryland and moved to the West Coast. Coincidence? His fear of the worst mounted, but he kept his own counsel.

"Come on, let's try to get some sleep." He eased her down on the bed and drew the sheet up her body. "We have a busy day ahead of us tomorrow."

Too tired and drained to do more, Reese merely nodded in agreement. All she wanted to do was sleep. And as she drifted off to a dreamless slumber, curled in the protectiveness of Max's arms, she finally understood her aunt Celeste's resentment of her. The realization carved out a painful place in her heart. A silent tear of regret slipped down her cheek.

The drive the following morning back into Los Angeles was done in relative silence. Images of Reese's past continued to haunt her in the light of day. Could she truly rely on what she'd dreamed? she repeatedly asked herself. Did she want to remember so desperately that she'd begun to fabricate the missing pieces of her past? She sighed deeply and looked to Maxwell from the corner of her eyes. She didn't want to believe that his father had anything to do with the deaths of her parents. The thought chilled her to the marrow of her bones. Where would that leave them?

"I've been trying to avoid thinking about all the things you said last night," Maxwell began, as if reading her thoughts. "The idea that my father may be involved in some way—" he hesitated, then turned briefly toward her "—I just don't want to believe that." He shook his head in denial. "I can't believe that."

"But why was he there, Max? Why, the very night before my parents were killed and half my life was erased, was he near the car?"

"You're not even sure it was my father," he snapped in defense, even as his own thoughts traveled in the same dangerous direction. "It could have been anyone," he added with less conviction.

Reese slowly shook her head, a part of her certitude

weakening. She knew he was right; how could she be sure?
Yet, a part of her, a deep instinct, told her that she was right
on target, and she also understood that an invisible line had
been drawn between her and Maxwell.

"I'll get R.J. to come over and get you set up," Maxwell
said offhandedly when they arrived at his office. "Carmen
will set you up with an office space so you can have some
privacy." He finally looked at her and his stomach knotted.
"Is there anything else you think you'll need?"

"No," she said softly. "That sounds like everything."

"Good. I have two meetings to attend and some loose ends
to tie up today." He paused, purposely avoiding her steady
gaze. "I'll probably be unavailable for the rest of the day."

Reese raised her chin. "No problem, Max. I'm sure I'll
have plenty to keep me busy," she added, her tone of challenge
unmistakable.

"I'll walk you over to R.J.'s office and get the ball rolling,"
he offered, his voice losing its hard edge for the first time
since they'd left San Diego. Reese's tummy curled with
remembered warmth as she picked up her pace to match his
long-legged stride.

Maxwell stopped abruptly outside R.J.'s office door.
He turned toward Reese, a combination of apology and
confusion swimming in his dark almond-shaped eyes. He
lowered his gaze then looked directly at her. "Listen, about
this morning…I'm sorry." He took a breath and shook his
head. "I just don't know if I'm ready to handle whatever it
is that you may find out, Reese." His low timbre seemed
to shudder with the emotions that raged a war within him.
"It's almost like taking sides." He swallowed and clasped her
shoulders, wanting instead to take her in his arms and push
the world away. "My father and I may have never been close,
but…I still don't want to believe the worst. I feel disloyal, as

if by helping you uncover whatever this is, I'll be turning on him…my own family. I'm not sure how to deal with that." His gaze narrowed. "Can you understand that?"

Reese didn't care who was looking or what they thought when she reached out and stroked away the lines of worry from his forehead, letting her hand trail down his smooth bronze cheek. "Of course, I understand," she uttered softly. "Do you think last night has been easy for me? I've been going through the same torture as you. I've asked all the what-ifs." She moved closer to him, needing to be near him. "But we don't know anything for sure. At least not yet. I don't want this to come between us, Max. But I also have to be realistic. It might." She pushed down the pain of that realization.

"And then what?" he asked looking deep into her eyes.

"We'll have to deal with it then. If what we have is worth fighting for, this will certainly be the test."

Maxwell gave her a half-baked smile and his heart suddenly filled with an emotion so intense it left him momentarily without words. Even now, with all the unknown factors that lay ahead of them, she was still willing to give them a chance. She really cared—about him—about them. He felt his chest tighten. "It is worth fighting for, Reese," he said slowly. "If I never realized it before, I realize it now."

A slow smile of pure joy spread across her dark chocolate face. She squeezed his hand, took a quick look up and down the corridor, then put a soft kiss on his lips, just as R.J. opened his office door. They sprung quickly apart.

"Hey, folks," he said in greeting, giving them a sly look and a grin. "Good to see you again, Reese."

"You, too." Reese smiled. "We still need to make time to talk before I leave."

"You name the time." He smiled expansively. "Comin' or goin'?" R.J. asked, turning his attention to Maxwell.

"Actually we were coming to see you," Maxwell

answered, briskly pulling himself together. "Did you get my message?"

"Sure did. I can get Reese set up in about twenty minutes. Did you get office space?"

"Not yet."

"Reese is free to use my office. You know I'm heading to San Francisco for a few days? I wanted to get up there and back before you left for Tokyo."

Maxwell tapped his head with the heel of his palm. "I'd completely forgotten. Listen, R.J. I can take care of this myself. I'll make all of the connections and you get yourself together for the trip."

"It's no problem," he assured, needing to see just what it was Reese was attempting to do.

Maxwell clapped him heartily on the back. "Don't worry about it, man. You have enough to deal with for the moment." And the more he considered it, the more he realized he shouldn't involve R.J. unnecessarily. He'd been so accustomed to R.J. taking care of situations at the L.A. offices, it was just second nature to secure his assistance. But prudence told him to follow the same advice he'd given Reese less than twenty-four hours earlier. "But I think I will take you up on your offer for the use of your space."

"Mi casa es su casa," he chuckled, opening the door and waving them through. "Just make yourself at home Reese," R.J. instructed as she walked in and took a look around at the orderly office. "I won't be back until the day after tomorrow, so it's all yours."

She turned toward R.J. and smiled. "I'll keep it just the way it is," she promised.

Maxwell checked his watch. "Maybe this would be a good time for you two to get better acquainted," he offered. "I have a meeting in a half hour that I need to prepare for." He looked to Reese.

"Fine with me," she replied. "Do you have a few minutes, R.J.?"

"What man in his right mind would turn down a few minutes with you?" He grinned.

"Watch him," Maxwell warned solicitously, pointing a finger at R.J. "He's not as innocent as he makes himself out to be."

Reese laughed. "I think I can handle myself."

"See you in the conference room, buddy. And thanks."

"Don't mention it."

Maxwell closed the office door behind him and R.J. moved to his seat behind the desk, while Reese took out her tape recorder and notebook, placing them both on the austere desk.

R.J. leaned back and watched Reese from beneath hooded lids. He folded his arms across his flat belly and waited.

Reese flipped open her notebook to the page where she'd jotted down some information on R.J. She crossed her long legs, depressed the record button and began her interview. She was surprised to discover that R.J. had had his own company before starting with M.K. Enterprises. Unfortunately his company had folded just as Max's doors were opening. Maxwell had been more than happy to bring R.J. and his expertise on board and immediately had him head up operations on the West Coast when the offices opened. Yet, even with all of the high praises that R.J. sung about Maxwell, there was something in his look and intonation that bespoke something else.

On more than one occasion, R.J. had referred to Maxwell as being lucky, being in the right place at the right time. Only once, almost as an afterthought did he mention Max's talent or his vision. He focused on his own contributions to the expansion of the company and how important *he* was to M.K. Enterprises and to Maxwell. Reese found it all very curious and a bit disturbing. There was an almost grudging resentment beneath the accolades.

Reese looked up from her notetaking and gave R.J. a pinched smile. "Well, I think that just about does it, R.J." She snapped her notebook closed and turned off the tape recorder. "I really appreciate your time."

R.J. stood up. "It was my pleasure. It's about time Max got his due."

Reese tried to read the expression behind the statement, but all she saw was the open face of a rather handsome, middle-aged man. She cleared her throat. "I know you have to get ready for the meeting as well." She hitched her thumb over her shoulder. "I'll just go and see Carmen for a few minutes. And thanks again, R.J. You've been a big help." She extended her hand which he shook.

"Anytime."

R.J. waited a few moments after Reese left and closed the door. Slowly he turned in his swivel seat and checked the wall clock. Phillip Hart should be in his office at *Visions*. He dialed the Chicago number from memory. Phillip picked up his private line on the third ring.

"Hart," he boomed into the phone.

"I just had a little one-on-one with your crackerjack reporter."

"And?"

"She doesn't have a clue about the company going public."

"It doesn't matter, we do. I intend to make a lot of money out of this. Her article is just icing on the cake. If she's on schedule like she usually is, it gives me just enough time to get it out before the company hits the market."

"I don't know if I like this, Phillip. People do big jail time for inside trading. If this thing blows up, I'm the one going down."

"You should have thought of that when you ran up a one hundred and fifty thousand gambling bill." Phillip laughed uproariously. "You did your part by giving me the information so I could squeeze the Board. If anyone takes a fall it will be Ms. 'Hotpants' Delaware. She won't even know what hit her."

Chapter 19

Since the meeting with her uncle, Victoria had been on edge. She'd had to force herself to concentrate on her work, force herself to concentrate on her lukewarm office romance, concentrate on just getting up in the morning.

For the past week, she'd done a great deal of reflecting on her life and the choices she'd made. Much of what she found herself embroiled in now, she'd brought on herself years ago. She could have decided to do the right thing and tell her uncle to just go to hell when he asked her to choose between her relationship with Maxwell and her entire future with the Air Force. Sure she'd gotten plenty out of the deal as a result. She had enough money to make her mother's last days beyond comfortable. She moved to the top of her profession with no one to rival her. But she'd lost so much more.

"Yes, Victoria Davenport, you have it all," she said with resignation, staring at her reflection, her look pensive. "A stellar career, a beautiful home, more money than you could ever spend, even a man to warm your bed at night when you need him." She laughed, a hollow sound. "But *you* have no one. No one to love you, or for you to love in return."

Victoria turned away from the damning reflection and picked up her purse. She squared her shoulders and walked toward the door. Today, the lies and deceit would end. She refused to spend the rest of her life indebted and under the thumb of a man who should care about her as a human being, not as a pawn in his game of life. Whatever happened from this moment forward would be of her own choosing.

She looked quickly around her, opened the door to her car and slipped in. She took one final look at her reflection in the rearview mirror. The light of determination sparkled in her green eyes and she knew she was making the right decision.

Victoria put the car in gear, backed out of her driveway, turned right, and headed in the direction of her uncle Frank's headquarters in Chevy Chase.

Frank Murphy sat behind his desk, his large tanned hands clasped beneath his chin. Since his visit with Celeste, he'd been unable to come to terms with her revelations and what the full implications were. For twenty-six years he'd been lied to, he'd been betrayed by his closest friend and the woman he loved. For the same twenty-six years he vented his hurt and frustration on the one person who didn't deserve it.

His stomach knotted with guilt. Yet, even now he wasn't sure how to make things right or if he ever could. So many people had been hurt by a lie that began so long ago. He took a deep, sobering breath simultaneously with the knocking on his office door.

"Yes, come in."

"Excuse me, sir, Ms. Davenport is here to see you."

Frank's heart knocked hard in his chest. So much had changed since the last time he'd seen her. He paused. "Send her in. And I don't want to be disturbed."

"Yes, sir."

The moment Victoria stepped across the threshold, they both sensed that something was dramatically different between them—that this moment was the turning point in their relationship.

Victoria walked across the room and took a seat opposite Frank. "There are some things we need to discuss, Uncle Frank, and they have nothing to do with Maxwell Knight," she qualified.

Frank looked at Victoria, really looked at her, through different eyes. Eyes of awakening and maybe even a sense of hope. He gave her a short smile of acquiescence and nodded. "I've been thinking the same thing, Victoria," he said in a tone so gentle it was totally unfamiliar, even to his own ears.

His tense expression seemed to soften to Victoria and the realization was disturbing. She had the unsettling sensation that he looked at her as if he really cared. But, of course, that was impossible. Her Uncle Frank didn't care about anyone or anything unless he could get something out of it. And knowing that, made his revelation that much more unfathomable.

Victoria tried to contain the shudders that rippled up and down her spine. Eyes of disbelief stared at those almost identical, in color, to her own. She gazed down at her trembling hands, turning them over as though unsure of their use.

Frank reached across the desk to touch her and Victoria leaped back, turning over the chair in the process. Her heart raced and her pulse roared like a raging tide in her ears.

"Don't touch me," she hissed. "Don't you dare touch me." She pointed a finger off accusation at him. "You're nothing but a filthy liar. You'd do anything to hurt me." Her voice rose, bordering on hysteria. "How can you expect me to believe you?"

"Victoria, please—you've got to believe me." He came around his desk. Victoria backed away, stumbling over the upturned chair. "I've been deceived as well." His voice pleaded with her to understand. "All these years, I never knew…"

Victoria snatched up her bag and spun away, unshed tears glimmering in her eyes. "I won't listen to you anymore." She flung open the door and ran down the corridor.

Frank ran as far as the door. "Victoria!"

She kept running even as several office doors opened and the curious poked their heads out at the commotion.

"It's all right, everyone," Frank assured, waving them away. "My niece," he shrugged in explanation.

He returned to his office, shutting the door quietly behind him. For several moments he leaned against it, listening to his heavy breathing, reliving the turmoil of the past hour with Victoria.

He took a long, calming breath, then crossed the room to his desk and picked up the phone, dialing the number from memory.

The phone was answered on the third ring.

"Hello?"

"It's me, Frank. Victoria was just here. I told her—everything."

"Oh, my God."

"I think she's on her way to see you."

"What can I say to her, Frank?"

"The truth. Finally the truth. She deserves that. We all

do." Before hanging up the phone he added gently, "I'm here if you need me."

Celeste stood rooted to the spot, the phone clutched against her breasts. She closed her eyes, and silently prayed she'd find the strength and the words to confront what lay ahead.

Victoria drove with a blind vengeance through the streets of Frederick, barely missing cars and darting pedestrians. Her thoughts were out of control. Her whole life had been a lie—one big grotesque lie. And the people whom she should have been able to trust, were the perpetrators of the lie. She felt as if her world were slipping from beneath her feet.

Even with all she'd been told, it was still too impossible to comprehend. Her thoughts were so disjointed she was unable to put the pieces of this bizarre and twisted puzzle together. How deep did Frank's and Celeste's betrayal truly go? Did it begin and end with the lie of her birth or was there even more that she was still unaware of?

Celeste, her aunt, her… She shook her head and swatted away the tears that streamed down her face with the back of her hand, streaking black mascara across her cheeks. She would make Celeste Winston tell her the truth if she had to wring it out of her frail body.

Celeste nearly leaped out of her skin when the bell, compounded with the banging on the front door, shattered the silence of the house.

With deliberation, she pushed herself up from the recliner and crossed the room to the front door. Her hand hovered, with uncertainty, over the knob. The bell pealed again, seeming to shimmer down her spine like an icy finger. Briefly she shut her eyes before pulling the door open.

Her breath caught in her throat when she gazed upon the devastation etched across Victoria's pale face.

"Tell me it isn't true!" Victoria cried in a tortured voice, her body trembling with each breath she took. "Tell me that you aren't my mother! Tell me that Frank Murphy is not my father!"

Chapter 20

Reese went back to Maxwell's office after her interview with R.J., hoping to catch him before his meeting, but he was gone. She strolled across the office toward the window.

Looking beyond the smoggy horizon, she was filled with a sense of unease. There was something not quite right about R.J., but she couldn't put her finger on it.

She shook her head and turned away, wrapping her arms around her body as she retraced her steps to the other side. It was probably her imagination, she concluded, taking a seat and crossing her long legs. With everything else that was going on, she was getting paranoid, seeing skeletons in every closet.

Turning her left wrist, she checked her watch. It was 11:30 a.m. in Chicago. Lynnette should be in her office by now, if she wasn't out on an assignment. She could kick herself for not calling her friend before she left, but Reese was confident that once she got Lynnette talking everything would be fine.

She dug in her bag, plucked out her calling card, and called the Chicago office.

"Lynn. Hi, it's me."

Lynnette sucked her teeth long and hard. "Humph, you were supposed to call me. What happened? You get yourself a little bit and forget all about your friends," she retorted, struggling to contain her mirth.

"Very funny. You know better than that, girl. We've been friends for too long. You know I would never let a little good stuff come between us," she chuckled. "I would have called—if I could have," she added, her last words full of sexual innuendo.

"You need to stop," Lynnette laughed "Anyway, whatsup? I know you didn't call just to apologize."

"You're absolutely right. But, I can't discuss it on this line."

Lynnette sat up a bit straighter. "What's going on, Reese?"

Lynnette could be a major asset if Reese was totally candid with her. But on the other hand, Max was right about involving as few people as possible.

"I need your help. But you have to call me from a pay phone and it will be even better if you use one outside of the building."

"Listen, I like all the cloak and dagger stuff, just as much as the next guy, but you're making my neck hair tingle."

"Lynn, just do it—please."

"All right, all right. What's the number out there?" Lynnette jotted down the number on an index card and stuck it in her purse. "I'll take an early lunch and call you in about fifteen minutes."

"Thanks, Lynn." Reese sighed in relief. "I'll be waiting for your call." She hung up the phone just as Maxwell stepped through the door.

"Hi, I didn't expect to find you here." He walked across the office and dropped an armload of files on his desk, missing the troubling look on Reese's face. He sat down and briefly shut his eyes, rolling his neck simultaneously. When he opened them, Reese was staring at him. He sat straight up in his chair.

"What's wrong?"

Reese looked away, then turned the full force of her amber eyes on Maxwell. "How well do you know R.J.?"

Maxwell's eyes narrowed. "Why?"

"I have my reasons for asking, Max."

"Then why don't you start by telling me your reasons for asking." He leaned forward and clasped his hands in front of him, his movements now unnoticeable.

"I talked with R.J. for almost an hour and I don't like the feeling I walked away with, Max." She crossed her slender wrists over her knees. Her voice was gentle but decisive. "I've been an investigative journalist for the past eight years. Those years of dealing with all kinds of people, good, bad and indifferent, have taught me what to listen for, how to separate what I hear from what a person is really saying. I think I'm a pretty damned good judge of character."

"And?" he interjected impatiently.

"And, R.J. means you no good."

Maxwell instantly pushed away from his desk and stood, his dark eyes like thunderclouds. "First my father, now R.J.," he growled. "Who next?"

"Listen to me," she demanded, her own voice taking on a steely edge. "R.J. seems to be under the impression that he's the force behind M.K. Enterprises and you were just 'lucky,' as he put it."

"What!"

Reese nodded. "I began to feel that he's extremely jealous of you, Max. So much so that it borders on resentment."

Maxwell shook his head in disbelief. "R.J.? I've known him for years. I just can't…"

"Believe it," she finished for him. "Are there any plans in the works that I should know about?"

He slanted his almond eyes in her direction. His guard went up. "What do you mean?"

"Is there anything going on that R.J. could…" she searched for the right word "…sabotage?"

His thoughts went immediately to the impending move to the stock market. Everyone on the upper management staff knew the necessity of keeping that information under wraps until the right time. Any deviation from that would ruin everything as well as the person who divulged the information. However, the financial windfall from inside trading was enough to tempt a saint. But R.J.…no, impossible.

"There's nothing going on of any significance," he lied. The less she knew the better. If anyone got wind that a reporter knew beforehand about M.K. Enterprise's plans…well, he didn't want to think about the ramifications, or what it would do to Reese's career.

"Fine," she conceded. Slowly she rose from her seat. Just be careful," she said gently. "I don't like the feeling I got, Max. And I'm very rarely wrong."

"There's a first time for everything," he said with a half smile. "Even your reporter's instinct and your feminine intuition can have a bad day."

"At the same time?" she tossed back with a self-assured grin. "Highly unlikely."

Max chuckled. "Touché. In the meantime, Sherlock, where are you going to work?"

"I'd prefer to use your office since you'll be in meetings all day. And I'm expecting a call from Lynnette shortly. She'll get me access to the files at the office and I'll see what I can come up with."

"Then let me get you set up."

She followed him to the alcove that contained an elaborate computer system built into the wall. Within moments he'd connected her laptop to his office system.

"You're all set." He flicked his wrist and checked his watch. He crossed the room, grabbed a stack of folders and placed a quick kiss on her lips. He cupped her chin in his palm. "And if I stand here a moment longer looking into those beautiful eyes of yours, I'll be late for my next meeting. I should see you in about an hour."

She tugged the front of his shirt and pulled him close. "Can't wait," she breathed in a husky whisper.

"You keep looking at me like that and neither of us will get anything done." This time his kiss was long, wet and hot, sending waves of current charging through her body. "Stay out of trouble," he said, his voice low and entreating, before turning and walking out of the door.

Reese stood still for several moments, taking long deep breaths, hoping to shake the erotic sensations that Max had aroused within her. "You got it bad, girl," she chuckled. "And it sure is good!"

She turned way from the door and moved across the room. Pulling notes from her briefcase she sat, waiting for Lynnette's phone call.

Maxwell strode down the corridor, his thoughts were on anything but the meeting ahead. He took then exhaled a long breath. Since Reese's arrival into his life, so much had changed. This was the first time in a very long while that he'd allowed vulnerability to creep into his life and find a haven. For years he'd prided himself on his ability to keep his feelings, his needs, his fears and his doubts tucked neatly away where no one would find them.

He turned down the corridor and stopped in front of

the elevator. He simply stared at the doors until the low conversation between a pair of technicians, en route to the lab, prompted him to press the up button.

Reese was slowly beginning to uncover all of the layers, strip by strip. How soon would his soul be bared to her? What would she see? Would she see the dark, secret fear that he'd lived with all of his life? Would she run or would she stay? And better yet, what would he do if she chose either?

Here in the States, he'd learned to deal with who he was, what others thought him to be. He shook his head slowly as the elevator made its ascent. Tokyo would be different. It always was. The slow burn built in his belly.

The light tap on the office door caught Reese right in mid-stroke. She swiveled away from the computer to face the door, just as Carmen stuck her head in.

Reese's face brightened. "Hi, Carmen. Maxwell left for that meeting already," she offered.

"Oh, yes I know. There's a call for you on line two. I wasn't sure if you'd answer the intercom if I buzzed."

"Oh…thank you. I should have told you I was expecting a call."

"No problem," Carmen smiled, slipping back out.

Reese crossed the room and pressed the flashing light on the phone.

"Lynn?"

"Who else? Now what's going on?"

"First, you've got to promise not to ask any questions." Reese heard the quick intake of breath that was the preamble to a Lynnette monologue. She rushed on not giving her a chance to interject. "Second, you are not to mention this to anyone. Third, I need you to get me access to our mainframe library. I'm pretty much set up here."

"What are you involved in, Reese?" she pressed, completely ignoring the first directive.

Reese smiled. "Let's just say that this story is taking on bigger dimensions than I anticipated. And that's all I can say for now. But," she added, "I promise to tell you as much as I can when I get back to Chicago."

"Believe me, I'm gonna hold you to that." She took a breath. "All right. Stay put. I should have you connected within the hour."

"Thanks, Lynn."

"And Reese…"

"Yes?"

"Be careful, girl."

Reese instinctively knew that those few simple words said so much more, a true testament to their friendship.

"I will. I promise."

Chapter 21

Celeste's heart hammered painfully in her chest as she stared immobilized by the intensity that radiated outward from Victoria's stricken face. Accusation, outrage and a palpable agony raced like a torrential rain across her features.

Finally, Celeste found her voice. "Come in, Victoria," she said quietly, stepping aside to let her brush past.

With slow deliberation, Celeste followed Victoria into the living room. Victoria swung around to confront her, her eyes blazing and red-rimmed.

"Why don't we sit down?" Celeste offered, struggling to contain the tremors that scuttled up and down her body.

For a moment, Victoria was taken aback by the fragility of Celeste, but her own concerns were so consuming she immediately cast the observation aside. "I'd rather stand," she spewed.

Celeste pressed her lips together and nodded. She took a

seat in her recliner and folded her hands in front of her, almost in prayer.

"Are you going to answer me?" Victoria demanded, pacing the floor, her strawberry blond hair fanning out around her.

Countless explanations tumbled through Celeste's mind at once. Reasons. Excuses. She knew in that instant that she had it within her power to change the course of so many lives, but nothing could reverse what had been done. No words. No acts of attrition. She stood precariously on the precipice of indecision.

"Answer me! Is what Uncle—" her vehemence momentarily faltered "—Frank said true?"

Celeste pushed down the last of her doubts. She looked directly into Victoria's green eyes. "No," she stated, clear and emphatic.

Victoria seemed to crumble before her eyes as she dropped, as if in slow motion, into the nearest seat. She sucked on her bottom lip to keep it from trembling, but she couldn't stop her hands from shaking. She balled them into fists on her lap.

Through tear-filled eyes of confusion she looked across the short space at her aunt. "Why?" she croaked. "Why would he tell me something like that? Why?"

Celeste took a long breath. "Your Uncle Frank is a very bitter and lonely man," she began, gulping down the bile of her lie. "He wanted to hurt me through you, for not loving him." She paused, then looked off toward the window. "It all started a very long time ago…"

Reese paced the office waiting for Maxwell's return. Running through her veins was a combination of excitement and dread of the unknown. She'd always felt that rush of adrenaline whenever she was on the threshold of uncovering new information. It was like food for her soul.

Ever since she began putting the pieces of her life back

together, after her parents' deaths, she'd been obsessed about the truth. For the past fifteen years there remained a hidden part of her that believed there was so much more to what happened to her parents than the reports and what her aunt grudgingly told her.

Aunt Celeste. If any piece of her nightmare held any validity, it would explain why her aunt resented her so much. She was in love with her father, and from the few pictures she'd seen of her mother, Sharlene, Reese could have been her twin.

Reese shook her head and sighed heavily, crossing the room to stare out of the window. Miles of gently swaying palms greeted her. It was curious to her that her mother and her aunt didn't resemble each other in the least. On all counts, they were direct opposites; from height to disposition to complexion. Night and day, she mused reflectively. She'd never thought too much about the disparities until that moment. Everyone knew the African-American race had been diluted with so many other ethnicities that there were all types of deviations, even within the same family. It was quite possible for two dark-skinned parents to give birth to a high-yellow child with light eyes. Those were some of the nuances that made the African-American people so unique, the gamut of the hues they encompassed.

Yet, knowing these things did not quite settle the stirrings of something deeper within her. Every gut instinct told her it was more than just a color thing between her mother and her aunt. But not knowing her grandparents, she'd never questioned the dissimilarities between the two striking women. At least, she ruminated ruefully, if she did ever ask, she didn't remember the answer.

However, the big question remained. If what she saw in her dream were true parts of her past, what reason could Celeste ever have for engaging in an affair with her sister's husband? And what kind of man did that make her father?

She blew out a breath and crossed her arms beneath her breasts. "Pure speculation, dear girl," she muttered. "You are a journalist—with integrity. You deal with facts, not speculation."

"Don't tell me this assignment has got you talking to yourself," Maxwell chuckled as he entered the room.

Reese jumped at the sound of Maxwell's voice. She spun around and caught the gleam in his eyes and the smile that danced around his full mouth. He moved soundlessly across the room in fluid long-legged strides. "Did I hear you mumbling something about speculation?" he asked nearing his desk. He pushed some papers aside, removed a file and looked at Reese.

"We had this conversation before, Mr. Knight." She sauntered forward and pressed her palms on the desktop.

The corner of his mouth inched upward in a grin. He leaned so close that air could barely pass between them. His voice dropped an octave as he inhaled her scent. "And what conversation was that?"

Her husky voice matched the beat of his. "The one where I told you not to sneak up on people." She threaded her finger through the opening between the buttons on his shirt, brushing it across the smooth hairs on his chest.

Max instantly felt his stomach muscles tighten, his groin throb. It seemed his libido always went into overdrive whenever he was in Reese's airspace. He'd never been so affected by any other woman. And inside he knew it wasn't just about sex. It was so much more than that. Reese made him feel like just a man when he was with her, inside her. She accepted him as he was, not as a trophy, something exotic to show off to friends, not something to conquer because he appeared so unattainable. She listened, saw what was in his heart, what fueled him and still she understood, opening up to him her own fears and misgivings. Those things, most of all, were what turned him on. The combination was erotic and so very sensual. Which made making love with Reese Delaware an almost spiritual experience. Just thinking about the passion she evoked in him pushed him to the brink of his limits time and time again. Like now.

Her fingers released one button, then another and brushed their tips across his hardened nipples. Maxwell felt his erection surge against the fabric of his pants.

He groaned deep in his throat, as a flash of white heat whipped through his body. "Now Reese, what if I did…" He slid his hand into the open V of her suit jacket and cupped her breast. Reese expelled a shuddering moan of both surprise and pleasure. "…This to you?" he finished.

Reese took his chin in her palm, pulling him closer. Her lips pressed against his, challenging him to deny her entry. Maxwell willingly succumbed, welcoming the sweetness of her teasing tongue.

Slowly, she eased away. Hot passion sweltered in her eyes. She covered the hand that caressed her breast with her own, applying gentle pressure. "I would say," she uttered in a silken whisper, "that someone had better lock the door."

Maxwell muttered an unintelligible expletive as he pulled himself away to lock the door. Returning quickly to her, he pressed the intercom and buzzed Carmen.

"Yes, Max?"

"Hold all of my calls, Carmen," he said, his gaze never leaving Reese's face. He clicked off before Carmen could respond.

"Now where were we before precaution stepped in?"

"Right about here," Reese taunted, placing his hands on her thighs.

Maxwell chuckled. "Good a place as any." Slowly he

pushed her skirt up to her hips all the while wondering how he would deal with all of the paraphernalia that women wore beneath their clothes. Suddenly, his eyes widened in surprise. He looked at Reese and she had the wickedest look he'd ever seen gleaming in her amber eyes.

Nothing but garters and no panties greeted his exploring fingers. His heart raced. "Damn," he whispered, sealing his hungry mouth to hers.

Victoria left Celeste's home more disturbed than ever. The lies carouseled in her mind. The deceit ran so deep, she was certain she'd never know the whole truth. Who was she to believe, her uncle who'd always manipulated her life, or her aunt who'd been the only one who'd cared about her all these years?

Slowly, Victoria drove through the streets of Frederick, trying to make sense of the past few hours. If only she had someone to talk with, to help her sift through the mire of her life. But she had no one. At least no one whom she could trust implicitly. What a sad testament to her life, she mused with resignation. What would it have been like to grow up with a sister—to have someone to share your adventures with, giggle with in the dark of night?

She released a shaky breath. "I guess I'll never know." Then her green eyes narrowed in thought and a picture perfect image of Reese and Maxwell, entwined together, emerged before her with Technicolor intensity. Her stomach twisted into the hard knot of resentment that had been planted years ago. It strangled her with its vines of jealousy. She would have to find a way to rectify the wrongs that had been done to her.

Lynnette stepped out of the phone booth and off of the curb, her thoughts focused on the tasks ahead. What in the world had Reese gotten herself involved in? This whole thing with her and Maxwell Knight was blowing up big time. And it gave her a very bad feeling. She couldn't shake the notion that Reese was in way too deep. It was already obvious that she'd totally lost her objectivity. And that never led to anything but trouble for any journalist, even one as seasoned as Reese.

But she'd promised to help her sister-friend and she would. Lynnette grinned as she planned her strategy. First she'd just sweet talk that cute technician in the computer room and…

The driver saw her the instant she stepped off of the curb, stepped on the accelerator, and headed straight for her.

"Woman, you are just incredible," Maxwell breathed against the cords of Reese's neck. He chuckled lightly, easing her legs from around his waist. "I don't believe we just did that."

Reese grinned and shielded her eyes behind long, dark lashes. All the while that Max was making love with her on the edge of his desk, she kept thinking over and over again how much she'd changed since she'd met him. Max brought out something in her that no one else had ever been able to do. Sure, she'd had relationships before, but none that touched her in the secret place that Max had uncovered.

"Max," she uttered, pressing her head against his chest. She slid her arms around his waist and eased closer, comforted by the beat of his heart.

"Hmm?" he mumbled, touching his lips to her hair.

For several moments she was silent, contemplating the veracity of what was in her heart. She wasn't sure at what point it happened, or even how, but she'd fallen in love with Max. Head over heels, irrevocably in love. Yet she understood that her feelings were not returned. Maxwell had made himself perfectly clear from the beginning. He had no desire to establish any sense of permanency, or develop emotional attachments that he believed he was ill equipped to handle. Her head understood, but her heart could not. And now she found herself in the precarious position of not only having become sexually involved with a client, but falling in love with him to boot. And even though the words churned and bubbled in her throat like a volcano waiting to erupt, she knew she could never tell him.

"You haven't fallen asleep on me, have you?" Maxwell teased, hugging her just a little tighter.

"No," she whispered, "I...I was just thinking that you're the first man I've ever told about...my memory. I mean, other than the doctors." She raised her head and looked up at him, only to find him staring down into her eyes. The softest smile framed his expressive mouth.

"And what does that mean for you?" he probed gently.

"I trust you."

Her simple statement touched him as nothing else she'd ever said and his heart filled with a joy that had been missing until her. "And I won't do anything to jeopardize that trust. I promise you that, Reese."

"Neither will I."

Maxwell's warm eyes grazed lovingly across her face, still unable to believe just how good he felt in her presence. He felt the walls tumble around him brick by brick, day by day. And for the first time, he wasn't afraid of what she would find. Slowly he lowered his head, brushing his lips across hers, in a kiss so soft, so light, that Reese thought her heart would break from the pureness of it.

With great reluctance he pulled away. His smile was teasing. "In the meantime, uh, I think..." His thick brows rose up and down.

"Yeah." She grinned. "I think we'd better pull ourselves together."

Maxwell chuckled deep in his throat. "And I thought we were pulled together."

"Very funny." Reese slapped him playfully on the arm and adjusted her skirt.

"You first," he instructed, pointing to his private bath.

While Reese waited for Maxwell to finish up it dawned on her that she had not heard from Lynnette.

"What's that look all about?" Maxwell asked, stepping back into the office and straightening his tie.

"I was expecting a call from Lynnette." She checked her watch. "Nearly an hour ago," she added, frowning.

Maxwell continued to prepare for his next meeting while he talked. "She probably just got tied up. She *is* at work you know. I'm sure you'll hear from her soon." He moved quickly from behind his desk, covered the short space that separated them and stood in front of her. He tipped up her chin with the pad of his finger. "Don't look so worried. She'll call." He pecked her on the lips. "I've got to run. I'll see you in about an hour and then we can get out of here."

Reese nodded absently and wondered what could be keeping Lynnette.

Chapter 22

"Have you heard anything from Max?" Claudia asked.

"No. I haven't." James heaved a long breath and pushed himself away from the table. "But I don't expect to. Larry is keeping an eye on things for me." He turned, slung his hands in his pants pockets and unconsciously began to pace the room.

Claudia's senses were immediately heightened seeing her husband's telltale sign of worry.

"Even though Frank Murphy has been relatively quiet since our meeting," James began, "I still don't trust him. He's not above doing what he feels he must to get what he wants."

"Do you really think he would hurt Max?"

"If he thought that Max was a threat." He turned and faced his wife. "Yes."

Claudia swallowed and the old knot of guilt tightened in her stomach. She'd spent the better part of Max's life wishing him away. Wishing he'd never been born. Wishing that things could be different.

She'd tried to love him, be a mother to him, but between her own animosity and James's unwillingness to let her get close to Max, she'd never forged a relationship with him. She knew he was hurting, lonely and confused all of those years, but she couldn't help it. Every time she tried to reach out to him and he looked at her with those dark, exotic eyes, she'd see her husband in the arms of Sukihara.

Claudia squeezed her eyes shut. She now had an opportunity to make amends. If it wasn't too late. But the gnawing sensation that what they were dealing with went much deeper than what James was telling her, persisted. Her husband was involved in something that had changed the lives of too many people. She'd found a way to live with past deeds and even her own indiscretions. What was frightening was that those deeds had been resurrected and stood blocking their future.

"I have a meeting at Chevy Chase," James announced, pulling Claudia from her reverie.

Her heart beat a bit quicker. "What does he want now?"

James's jaw clenched. "He wouldn't say over the phone. Only that he expected me to be there."

Claudia busied herself with the dishes in the sink. "Have you gotten any word from Larry?" She kept her gaze focused on the suds.

"Nothing more than Reese seems to have moved in with Max while they're in California. They're staying at his house in San Diego."

"That's good though, isn't it?"

"It makes Larry's job easier," he responded noncommittal.

Claudia turned from the sink. "What aren't you telling me, James?"

He sidestepped the question. "If we get into a discussion about this, I'll be late for my meeting." He crossed the room and pecked her on the cheek. "I don't know how long I'll be gone," he tossed over his shoulder, walking out of the door.

Claudia nodded at the familiar refrain and also understanding that her husband had no intention of telling her anything further. For him, the subject was closed. She turned her attention back to the dishes, floated in the suds. She needed to talk with Larry.

Larry spotted one of Frank Murphy's men the moment the blue Chevy Nova pulled up in front of the building that housed Maxwell's offices. All of his senses shifted into gear. He peered intently at the figure shadowed behind the wheel.

Moments later, a tall athletically built man emerged with a small duffel bag in his hand. He leaned casually against the car as if waiting for someone or some signal. The man checked his watch and looked toward the revolving doors.

Larry reached for the lock on the car door, just as a throng of lunch-goers exited from the building. Larry jumped out of the car, but not before the unidentified man merged with the crowd. Larry quickly scanned the area as he tried to dodge the two-way traffic. The man was gone.

He pulled a cellular phone from his shirt pocket and punched in the number to Maxwell's office.

"M.K. Enterprises."

"Maxwell Knight," Larry barked into the phone, racing across the street and through the revolving doors.

"I'm sorry, he's in a meeting. May I…"

"Don't let anyone who's not an employee near him or Reese Delaware. Call security."

"What? Who is this?" Carmen demanded, her pulse beginning to race.

"Just do it!" Larry stabbed the button for the elevator to the executive floor, changed his mind and took the stairs. He had just as much reason as anyone for not wanting Reese Delaware to uncover the truth of fifteen years ago. But he would no longer be a party to anyone else getting hurt, even if it meant that his role would be revealed. He pushed those thoughts to the back of his mind and took the stairs two at a time.

Carmen's hands were shaking when the messenger appeared in front of her desk.

"Package for Mr. Knight," he said, pulling his cap lower on his brow.

Instinctively, Carmen signed for the package, subconsciously recognizing the uniform of the messenger service, even as her mind was on the disturbing phone call.

The messenger took his clipboard, turned and walked onto the elevator, just as Larry pushed through the stairwell door. He rushed toward Carmen's desk, his physical presence and tense look on his face, a frightening combination.

Unobtrusively, Carmen depressed the button, silently signaling for security. This was obviously the man the phone call was about.

"Has anyone…"

But before Larry could get the words out, two plainclothes security guards flanked him on either side.

"Problem, Ms. Lopez?" asked the guard to the right of Larry, casting him a hard stare.

"I just got a very strange call to be on the lookout for anyone asking for Mr. Knight." She pointed a finger of accusation at Larry. "Then he came charging in here like a madman."

"Okay, buddy," said the second guard, putting Larry's upper arm in a vise-like grip. "Let's see some identification."

"We're wasting time, dammit! I made that phone call."

"I.D. Now!" the security guard ordered.

"What's going on?"

The group of four turned in the direction of Maxwell's voice.

Carmen jumped up from her seat. "Mr. Knight..."

"Larry?" Maxwell moved quickly toward the group, his own fear building with every step. He kept his expression calm and unreadable, not daring to expose the sense of apprehension that was steadily building within him. It's all right, fellas," he said flashing a smile that took in everyone. "I know him."

"Are you sure, Mr. Knight?" Carmen queried not totally satisfied.

"It's fine, Carmen. Larry's a friend of my father." He put on his best smile, clasped Larry around the shoulder and ushered him away.

"Why don't we go in my office?"

"One of Murphy's men was here," Larry said in a low, urgent voice.

Maxwell felt his stomach muscles clench. "Maybe we should go in the conference room," he said, changing direction, remembering that Reese was in his office. There was no need to alarm her unnecessarily, or at least until he knew exactly what was happening.

Once behind closed doors, Maxwell spun on Larry. "This better be good," he bit out through his teeth. He stood splay-legged with his arms across his chest.

"I'm sure your father told you that Murphy would have someone watching you. We have no idea what his plans are, but we know he has no intention of you divulging any information to Reese Delaware about your father."

Maxwell methodically paced the room as he listened to Larry. "How in the hell can he prevent me from talking? And how would he even know if or when I told Reese anything? Besides the fact that I don't have anything to tell."

"They can't be sure about that. Since they haven't made any overt moves, my guess is that your office is probably bugged as well as your house."

The thought that someone may be listening or had listened to him and Reese made him feel physically ill. His nostrils flared in fury.

"I need to get into your house in San Diego and sweep it. This office, too."

Maxwell turned his dark eyes on Larry. He took in a long breath and expelled it as he pursed his lips and sat on the edge of the conference table. He braced his palms on the table's edge and focused totally on Larry Templeton. "Are you going to tell me what's really going on? What is it that I'm not supposed to tell? Don't you realize that I may inadvertently know something and wind up saying the wrong thing without realizing it? Then what's going to happen?"

Larry turned away from Maxwell. "I'm not free to discuss this with you, Maxwell, and you know that. And…"

Maxwell's deep voice dropped to a threatening low. "You walk in here and tell me that my office and my house may be bugged. You tell me that Frank Murphy will do just about anything to keep me from giving Reese information that I know nothing about, and you aren't free to discuss it! My father insisted I keep Reese close by—as a precaution, so that you could keep a watch over us. And you aren't free to discuss it!"

Larry raised his hands in a fending-off gesture. "Max, listen to me, it's best that you don't know. Believe that," he said with sincerity, thinking back to that fateful morning. He shook his head with regret. "It's best that you don't know." He moved toward Maxwell's taut frame. "My best suggestion is not to discuss anything with her that is even remotely related to your father."

Max nodded and leaned back against the table's edge.

"Will you let me check the office and the house now?"

"Do I have a choice?"

Larry shook his head. "I know you're a risk taker, Max. But this is a risk you want to avoid."

Maxwell inhaled and slowly stood. His body tensed with unspent anger. This was too close. The reality of seeing Larry brought the seriousness of their situation to the forefront. Sure he could play Mr. Macho and tell Larry to get lost. But he couldn't let his pride stand in the way of Reese's safety. Slowly he nodded in agreement.

Larry breathed a sigh of relief. "I'd better get started."

Maxwell moved toward the door and stopped. He turned toward Larry. "Don't let anything happen to her, Larry."

He'd been under orders fifteen years ago. He'd followed them and it had cost lives. Now was his opportunity to make restitution, if he had to put his own safety on the line, he would.

"I'll do everything in my power to see that the both of you stay safe." He put a firm hand on Maxwell's shoulder. "If you can leave early for Tokyo—" he paused "—I suggest that you do."

Maxwell looked at him for a long moment, then nodded.

With all the excitement of the past few moments, Carmen had completely forgotten about the package for Maxwell. She looked at the plain manila envelope now, picked it up and headed toward Maxwell's office.

Carmen tapped lightly on Maxwell's door, then stepped inside.

"Oh, hello, Reese. Isn't Max here?"

Reese looked up from her laptop and smiled vaguely. "No.

I haven't seen him since he left for his second meeting." She closed the cover to the machine and stood, stretching her tight muscles. "Is something wrong?" she asked, noting the odd expression on Carmen's usually even face.

"No," she responded with a slight shake of her head. "It's just that I saw him a few moments ago while I was covering the front desk, and I…well, never mind. I'll just leave this for him." She walked toward the desk and placed the envelope on top of a stack of folders. She turned to leave then stopped and faced Reese.

"Uh, Reese, has anyone, I mean anyone you don't know, been here or tried to reach you?"

Reese frowned and the rush of adrenaline began to pump through her veins, making her heartbeat quicken its pace. She moved closer to Carmen. This time, clearly seeing the look of distress which her expressive eyes failed to mask.

"Carmen, what on earth is wrong?" She placed a hand of encouragement on Carmen's shoulder, and instantly felt the slight tremors running through the petite body. "Sit down," Reese instructed, "and tell me what has you so rattled—and why someone would be looking for me."

Carmen did as she was asked, silently thankful that she could sit before her knees gave out. Reese took a seat opposite her.

Carmen breathed deeply and for a moment shut her eyes, remembering the urgent phone call, the man rushing in and Max claiming that he was a friend. None of that explained his near-frantic call. She shivered again.

"I'm sure it's nothing." Carmen flashed a smile that fell short of reaching her eyes.

"You're sure *what's* nothing?" Reese pressed, annoyance and agitation building by the minute.

Carmen patted Reese's folded hands. "Mr. Knight will handle everything. I'm sure it's all just a misunderstanding."

She stood to leave. "Sometimes I just overreact." She walked quickly toward the door. "I'm sorry if I upset you. It was totally inappropriate," she apologized.

"But Carmen…" Reese called out.

Carmen opened the door and stepped across the threshold, fighting down the urge to tell Reese what happened even as she closed the door behind her. She already knew that Max would have her head for opening her big mouth in the first place and upsetting Reese on top of it all. She inhaled a shaky breath. But Maxwell was like a son to her and she'd come to care about Reese. The very thought that something could happen to them sent another chill scurrying up her spine.

Reese was up pacing the floor, her look dark and pensive when Maxwell strolled in about twenty minutes later.

He plastered a big smile on his face as he approached her. He knew he had to get her out of there as soon as possible so that Larry could do his work. And he still had to keep her away from the house long enough for Larry to check it out as well. It would take at least twenty-four to thirty-six hours to change the flight and make hotel arrangements. And he had to have a plausible reason why they were nearly a week early.

"Hey, baby. What's with the long face? I thought you'd be happy to see me," he grinned. He closed the distance and kissed her lightly on her pouted lips.

"Have you see Carmen?" she tossed out almost as an accusation.

Maxwell frowned. What had Carmen gone and done now? "About a half hour ago. Why?"

"She was here not too long ago and we had the most curious, uninformative conversation I've ever been involved in." She stared at Max, looking for any reaction. As usual his expression remained nonplussed. But Reese already knew that meant nothing, Maxwell Knight was a master at masking his expressions.

He chortled lightly. "That sounds like Carmen."

"No, it doesn't" she retorted. "And you know it." She crossed her arms beneath her breasts. "What's going on? And don't give me the ole 'oh, it's nothing honey' routine," she cautioned.

"Well, if you must know," he began in a teasing tone. He put his arm around her stiff shoulders. "Our trip to Tokyo has been pushed up. We'll have to head out sometime tomorrow or at the latest the following morning. That's probably what has Carmen rattled. She's such an organized person, she hates distractions. She's had to work like a madwoman over the past hour to try and get the arrangements changed." He peered down into her speculative gaze and smiled. "Sorry for the short notice. But all of this happened within the last hour or so." At least that much was true.

Reese's body slowly began to relax, but she was still wary. There was obviously something that he wasn't telling. But she also knew that if Max had no intention of divulging anything, even the Chinese water torture couldn't make him talk.

She let out a long breath through her nose. "Fine. Don't talk," she huffed, wanting him to know that she was aware of the holes in his story. "What time is the flight?" she cocked her right brow and was pleased to see his calm facade slightly shift.

"The confirmations aren't all done, but I should know something by the end of the day. In the meantime," he hurried on, wanting to stave off any further questions. "I thought we could do some shopping, have a late dinner on the beach and then turn in. How does that sound?"

She tilted her head to the side. "It sounds like you're trying to put me off. But a short shopping spree and a romantic dinner may just soothe my wounded ego."

Maxwell tossed his head back and laughed, both at her quick repartee and in relief. At least he'd bought himself and Larry some time. "Great, let's get out of here."

Reese grabbed her purse and laptop, which Maxwell promptly relieved her of and opened the door.

"Oh," Reese stopped in midstep. "Carmen left a package for you. She put it on the desk."

Maxwell raised his brows and went to get the envelope. Slicing it open with a letter opener, he extracted the single sheet of paper and a chill shot through him.

While Maxwell kept Reese occupied, Larry returned to his car and retrieved his kit. On the elevator ride, he thought back to the events of the morning. He was losing his edge. Five years ago that guy would have never gotten past him. How could he have let him slip through? And where was he now?

The latter question disturbed him the most. If he made no contact with Maxwell or Reese, then why had he come?

The main thing for the moment was that both Max and Reese were safe. Security was on alert. And with any luck, this time tomorrow Max and Reese would be on their way to Tokyo.

He stepped off the elevator, checked with the security guard who had been forewarned of his return, and turned down the corridor, the guard in tow. Maxwell had promised he'd have her out of his office in fifteen minutes. Larry checked his watch. Max's time was up. They made the turn down the corridor to his office just as Maxwell and Reese emerged. Maxwell gave him a quick look and kept walking.

Reese looked over her shoulder as they continued down the hall. "Who was that?" she asked as he escorted her to the front desk. "I don't remember seeing him before."

"That's one of the part-time techs," he said offhandedly, switching the laptop from his right to left hand.

She gave him a suspicious look. "You could have introduced me."

"Sorry. I guess my mind is on this trip and just getting out of here." He gave her his best smile and was thankful that Carmen was missing from her desk. His nerves were ready to pop and he wasn't in the mood for any more of Carmen's questions. All he wanted to hear was that their travel arrangements had been taken care of.

"I wanted to say goodbye to Carmen," Reese said easing away from Maxwell's hold on her upper arm.

"She probably went out to lunch." He placed his palm at the small of her back and gently urged her forward. "You'll see her tomorrow."

Reese suddenly spun around and stopped dead in her tracks. Maxwell's skill of movement from years of martial arts training was the only thing that saved him from tumbling over the unmoveable woman.

Reese glared up at him. Her amber eyes snapping with annoyance. She planted her hands firmly on her hips. "Are you going to tell me what in the devil is going on around here?" she hissed through her teeth.

Maxwell's gaze swept the area around them. "This one time, Reese, I'm asking you... No—" he stepped closer and brought his face within a breath of hers "—I'm telling you to keep your writer's instinct and your woman's intuition out of the way."

Reese's head snapped back in a gesture of shock. She opened her mouth to lash back, but not before Maxwell issued his final directive.

"I'll tell you if and when the time is right and not a minute before. Now, let's go."

Now he'd gone and done it, she thought with growing ire.

She planted her feet firmly on the floor. Her scathing look screamed defiance. "I'm not going anywhere until you tell me what's going on. If I'm involved, I deserve to know what I'm dealing with. Now, either you're going to tell me or we're going to miss our flight because we'll be standing right in this hallway."

With every word she spoke, he knew she was right. But his male ego had kicked in and the instinct to protect his woman had taken over his thoughts. Just the idea of anything happening to her pushed him too close to the edge. But he also realized that Reese was the type of woman who knew how to take care of herself. And his leaping to her rescue like a knight in shining armor would not be appreciated unless she asked for his help. For a flashing moment, he wondered if Reese Delaware would ever truly need him.

Reese sensed his temporary acquiescence by the nearly imperceptible shift in his wide shoulders and the easing of the tiny lines around his luminous eyes.

Maxwell's gaze swept over her face and Reese was suddenly afraid, but poised for whatever he had to reveal.

Chapter 23

By the time Maxwell finished telling Reese all that transpired, she was trembling with outrage and a healthy dose of fear. Mechanically, she wound her arms around her body and pushed herself deeper into the plush leather of the Corvette's seat. She bit down on her bottom lip, deep in thought.

Maxwell peered at her from the corner of one eye while trying to keep the other on the road. "Are you all right?"

Reese, slowly nodded. "I wanted to know," she said in a distant voice. "Now I do." She chuckled mirthlessly. Then she angled her head in Maxwell's direction. Her right eyebrow lifted in an arrogant arch. "If they think I can be scared away from this story, they are sadly mistaken. This time they're messing with the wrong one."

Maxwell fought down the smile that bubbled around his mouth and tried to still the pride that made his heart fill full. He pulled the car to a stop at a quiet intersection and cut the engine. He removed his seat belt, eased closer to Reese and popped hers open as well. He cupped her face in his hands and drew her to him. He took her mouth in a long, slow, drugging kiss. Reese closed her eyes and succumbed to the rapture of his mouth.

With a long sigh, Maxwell eased away and found Reese looking into his eyes with the same fierce determination that initially drew him to her. And he knew there was nothing in heaven or in hell that would stop her from going after what she wanted.

"I'm only going to say this once," Maxwell began, his tone low and even. "You do whatever you need to do. Dig as far as you can dig. At first I wasn't sure I wanted to find out whatever this 'thing' is that no one wants uncovered." He clenched his jaw and continued. "But I want you to find out Reese, even if it somehow implicates my father. I need to know. My own past is somehow tied into it all. Who and what I am is a direct result of the type of man my father is, what he has done, and how he's lived his life. Maybe at the end of all of this I'll finally find the peace within myself that's eluded me all of these years."

Reese felt as well as heard the pain that punctuated his every word. His own sense of worth had always been linked to outward appearances and preconceived notions. He'd spent his life doing all he could to overcome the, not always, silent prejudices. He'd struggled to be just a man and accepted for the man he'd made of himself. Yet, even with all of his accomplishments, there were still those lingering doubts, those elusive threads of his heritage that remained out of his reach. And now, a father who was becoming as much of an enigma as the mysterious Sukihara. They'd both gone through life with so many parts of it missing. Somehow, they'd surmounted the obstacles. But the restlessness, the need to know was never out of their thoughts. She reached out and stroked his firm, smooth jaw.

He took her hand and stilled it, pressing it against his face. "I also want you to know this. I'll do everything in my power to help you. I'll put all of my resources at your disposal. And I will do whatever I must to protect you—at any cost. And you've got to accept that." He shook his head slowly. "On that issue I won't budge."

Reese's heart was pounding so loud and fast she swore it would leap out of her chest. Max's declaration of protection was as close as he'd come to truly expressing the depths of his feelings for her. Was there really a chance for them after this was all over? Or was the excitement of the whole process the juice that flowed between them? She didn't have the answers and maybe that scared her most of all.

"Can we at least agree on this one thing, Reese?"

A slow smile tugged the corners of her mouth. "It sounds like something I could live with," she replied, her voice a husky whisper, her smile in full bloom.

In that instant they both understood that "this thing" that pulsed between them had just reached another level. And as scary as that concept was to accept, they were willing to deal with it—together.

Everything hurt. When she tried to open her eyes, blinding pain shot through the sockets and ricocheted through her body. She fought down the nausea as a wave of pain engulfed her.

"I think she's coming around," came a soft voice that seemed to float to her.

Lynnette took a deep breath and slowly opened her eyes, blinking rapidly against the light and stark white walls. She was obviously still dreaming, she thought in a haze. That could be the only reason why everything was so blurry.

Then someone leaned very close and their face came into focus.

"I'm Doctor Moore, Ms. Campbell."

The deep resonance of his voice seemed to instantly soothe her. She blinked several more times, trying to make sense of what the man with the thick, black mustache was saying.

"You're in St. Luke's Hospital. You were in a car accident."

Then it all came back to her in little bits and pieces until the puzzle was complete. The last thing she remembered was talking to Reese on the pay phone and heading back to the office.

"Will I live?" Lynnette croaked, thinking of her deadlines, her Quincy article and her promise to Reese.

Dr. Moore fought down a smile. "I'm afraid so, Ms. Campbell. However, you do have a concussion, a fractured rib, an assortment of cuts and bruises and a hairline fracture of the tibia."

"The what?" she frowned.

He pointed toward her leg which was encased in plaster and suspended from what looked to Lynnette like a trapeze.

"Ugh," she groaned. "I've got to get out of here, doc. I have work to do. I'm on assignment. I…"

"Ms. Campbell," he interjected, "there's no possibility of you going anywhere anytime soon."

"You can't keep me here!"

Dr. Moore had had his share of troublesome patients over the years. He prided himself on his patience, and even temper. And he knew he'd have to use every bit of both with Ms. Lynnette Campbell.

He pursed his full lips and expelled a long breath. "Ms. Campbell," he began in his favorite doctor-patient voice, "if you can find a way to unhook your leg from traction, write out the prescription for the painkillers that you'll need, get yourself dressed and sign yourself out of this facility—" he paused and smiled broadly, displaying a deep dimple in his right cheek "—then you're free to leave."

Lynnette tried to sit up, changed her mind, and rolled her eyes instead, which immediately set off the drill team in her head. She briefly shut her eyes until the pain subsided. "Well," she huffed with great reluctance, "if I have no other choice." She opened her eyes and looked up at him, giving Adam Moore the full benefit of her dazzling smile. "I guess you should call me Lynnette."

Adam chuckled deep in his chest. "I'll have the nurse bring your medication." He turned to leave, then stopped and looked at her over his shoulder. "Lynnette."

She smiled as he neared the door. Then the enormity of her circumstances fully hit her. "Hey, doc, did they at least get the idiot that hit me?" she called out.

"Sorry," Adam admitted softly. "Hit-and-run."

Chapter 24

Reese's relative silence was blatantly evident during the first leg of the drive toward Maxwell's house in San Diego, he noted. There was no longer a reason to delay their arrival since he'd told her as much as he knew. Everything except what was in the note. The words came back to him now, rippling through him like a stone skimming over water. He pushed them aside.

"What's on your mind, Reese?" he asked. "It's not like you not to talk."

She took a long breath and turned her gaze away from him. "I know you said you wanted me to find the answers no matter what the costs." She turned to face his profile. "I'm not so much afraid of what I'll discover, but what will happen to us when I do."

He nodded in understanding, having asked himself the same question more times than he cared to admit. "I wish I had the answers. But I don't. All I can say is that we'll have to find a way to deal with it. If it's what we want."

Reese pressed her lips together in thought. "I know from experience how I've been viewed from the perspective of the person I've interviewed when I uncover elements of their lives that they'd prefer to keep under wraps."

"And?"

"Things invariably change. I become the bad guy. The one who was out to get them."

"So you think I'll feel the same way?"

Slowly she nodded. "You already came into this with preconceived notions. You thought the worst of me before we even met. And somehow I feel that because of the attraction between us you've put those feelings aside. But they're still there, just beneath the surface." Her soft amber eyes searched his face, silently praying that he would emphatically refute her statement.

"I've tried to put that out of my mind. I've tried to allow myself to be objective and I admit, getting involved with you provides no objectivity. But—" he paused, gauging his words "—you're right. Much of my ambivalence still remains. The difference is that I'm learning to trust again. And that trust began with you. I trust you to do the right thing—for everyone."

"I can't ask for more than that," she said.

"And neither can I."

They pulled into the driveway of Maxwell's home just as Larry stepped out of the front door. He walked up to the parked car and leaned down to meet Maxwell at eye level. Maxwell lowered the window. His gaze held the question.

Larry nodded. His dark brown eyes somber. "The house was loaded. No less than one in every room. Your office as well."

"Damn!" Maxwell slapped his hand against the steering

wheel. The horn blared causing Reese to jump. "How could they have gotten in? The house is alarmed and no one but staff can get beyond reception and into my office."

"At this point, there's nothing we can do about it. But from here on out, we take extra precautions. Understood?"

"Yeah."

"When are you two headed out?"

"I'm waiting on a call from Carmen. It'll either be tomorrow or the day after at the latest."

"Good. The sooner the better. I'll be making my arrangements as soon as I leave here. I'll be in Tokyo as soon as I can. In the meantime, we need a contingency plan in place."

"I'm way ahead of you. Chris is already in Tokyo. He's in a tournament. I plan to contact him tonight."

Larry smiled for the first time. "I can't think of anyone better." He patted Maxwell solidly on the shoulder. "Everything's going to work out," he assured. "You know, Max, we can put a quick end to this by just backing off from this interview. It would be safer for everyone."

"No way in hell," Reese spouted definitively. She'd sat by in silence listening to these two men decide on what was best without any input from her. That had to stop. "No one is going to scare me away from a story. There's obviously something that they want to keep hidden. Which gives me all the more reason to find out what it is."

Larry looked at her and saw the same determination in her eyes that had been in her father's the day he faced down Frank Murphy and told him he was going to the Senate SubCommittee with his findings—knowing full well the risks to himself and his career. His decision had ultimately sparked a series of events that still reverberated fifteen years later. His decision had cost him his life. Would Reese's decision cost her life as well? He didn't want to envision the possibility and blinked back the memories. "I'll be in touch." He turned, walked toward his car and drove away.

Reese pressed her hands to her face. "They're really serious, aren't they?" she asked from between her fingers.

"Yeah," Maxwell expelled. "They're serious." He popped the lock on the door. "Come on, let's go inside and get settled."

Maxwell slid his arm around Reese's waist as they walked toward the house, pulling her close to his side. He bent his head, speaking low in her ear, "Everything is going to be fine. I swear to you, I won't let anything happen to you."

Reese leaned into his embrace, struggling to ward off the pain in her head which had begun as a dull throb back at Maxwell's office. She thought she could fight it off, but she couldn't. Briefly she shut her eyes and missed a step.

Maxwell tightened his hold, steadying her. "Are you all right?"

She turned her amber gaze upward to meet his and he instantly knew she wasn't. His dark eyes narrowed in concern. "Why didn't you tell me?" He opened the door, swept her up his arms and proceeded up the stairs to the bedroom.

By the time Maxwell placed Reese on the bed she was moaning softly, squeezing her eyes shut to fight the pain.

He crossed the room in swift strides and turned the wand on the vertical blinds, blocking out the light.

Maxwell came to the bed and placed her head in the cushion of his lap. "Try to relax, baby," he cooed, placing his thumbs at her temples. He began the slow rotation, the gentle pressure, the soothing words that, had in the past, brought her relief. He worked with her for fifteen minutes.

Reese braced her body, anticipating the moment when freedom from pain would flow freely through her body. But it didn't come. Unbidden, tears of pain squeezed from her shut eyes. "I need m-my medicine," she moaned. "It's not working, Max. I can't s-stand it anymore."

"Where?"

"In the top drawer of t-the dresser," she mumbled.

Maxwell brought her the medicine and a glass of water. He lifted her head while she took the medication, then slowly eased her head back on the pillow. He knew from experience that the potent medication would soon begin to do its job. At all costs, Maxwell strove to stay away from any chemical substances which altered the way the body naturally worked. It was why he studied and mastered the art of *Tai chi*. He knew all too well the long-term effects of chemical dependency, having seen so many promising brothers and sisters fall by the wayside.

He gingerly sat on the edge of the bed, trying not to disturb her. Already, her breathing had slowed, the tight knit across her forehead was beginning to ease. Her eyes weren't squeezed shut, but merely closed. In this state between asleep and awake she would be more receptive to letting her mind flow freely. Perhaps she'd be able to give some clue as to what precipitated this attack.

"Reese," he called softly.

"Hmm?"

"Do you have any idea what brought on the pain?"

"No," she replied in a thready whisper. "Not really. It started at the office."

"Can you remember when, sweetheart—what was happening?"

"I—I think it started when Larry passed us in the hallway."

Maxwell let that piece of information settle. What reason could there be for Larry to act as a catalyst for her headache? What was his connection to Reese? What hidden part of her memory did he occupy? It was becoming apparent that the reasons for her headaches stemmed from people who entered her life that somehow resurrected memories of her forgotten past.

He placed a light kiss on her brow. "Try to get some rest," he said in a gentle whisper. "By the time you wake up, you'll be feeling better and we can talk some more over dinner."

Maxwell knew he had at least two hours before Reese would awaken. He headed downstairs and used the phone in the den.

After several false starts he was finally able to connect to Chris's room.

"Hey, man," Chris greeted. "You just caught me. I was on my way out. Don't tell me you're already in town."

"No. Not yet. But I'll be there sooner than scheduled."

Chris was instantly alert to the tension in Maxwell's voice. "What's up and what can I do to help?"

James made the return trip home after his meeting with Frank Murphy. He gripped the wheel to keep his hands from shaking.

Frank told him in no uncertain terms that if Maxwell continued to cooperate with Reese Delaware, he'd do whatever was necessary to stop him *and* her. James had one last chance to convince his son to back off. Frank also intimated that there'd been two warnings sent. James didn't want there to be a third.

He had to get in touch with Maxwell and convince him to give up this story.

No sooner had Maxwell hung up from speaking with Chris than his phone rang. Anticipating the caller to be Carmen, he was more than surprised to hear his father's voice.

"More problems?" he greeted, the disdain plain apparent

in his voice. "Larry's already been here, if that's why you're calling."

James took a steadying breath. "You've got to back off from this interview, Max. Now."

"The time for you to tell me what to do is long gone, Dad." His nostrils flared in anger. His voice dropped to a threatening low. "Unlike you, I'm my own man. The only orders I follow are the ones that I set up for myself. I don't know what your role in all of this is, but I won't be a party to helping you keep it a secret, directly or indirectly."

As James listened to his son's angry dismissal of him, he knew how right he was. He couldn't remember the last time he'd made an independent decision, and when he did, it resulted in the birth of his son and completely changed the very fabric of his marriage and nearly destroyed his wife. He knew he couldn't change the past. He only hoped that he could somehow make up for what he'd done by trying everything in his power to protect his son. A son whom he'd never forged a relationship with. A son who could not forgive him for that.

"There's more than just me to consider. I know you don't have much regard for our relationship. I know that I'm the last person who can tell you what to do. I'm not asking you to take my concerns into consideration." He paused, taking a short breath. "If you aren't concerned with your own safety, at least consider Reese's."

"Reese has made her decision, Dad. All I can do is stand by her."

James let out a long sigh, laden with sadness. "Just be careful, son."

Maxwell's heart pinched at the word *son*. For a brief instant his stand faltered. "I will be."

Chapter 25

The house was quiet. Claudia had apparently gone out, James concluded. Wearily he made his way down the short foyer to his den. He'd truly believed that he'd been given an opportunity to, somehow, be the father of Maxwell that he had not been for thirty-three years: protector—counselor—friend.

For several long moments, he sat in his favorite chair recalling the caustic, detached tone of his son. And, yes, he deserved it. He deserved the animosity, the isolation. James sighed with regret, pressing his fists against his temples.

Maxwell made it very clear that he was his own man, and faced with the unknown, he was still capable of taking care of himself. Even as the object of all of Max's ambivalence, James felt the surge of pride. His son was a better man than he'd ever hoped to be. Perhaps by some macabre twist of fate, his life as a slave to others' directives had in some way been responsible for Maxwell being just the opposite.

James pushed himself up from his chair and slowly stood.

There was no doubt that years in the service of his country had left its mark indelibly ingrained in him. But whether his son wanted to accept or believe it, his love for him was far greater than his obligation to his country. This one time he could not follow orders. Even at the risk of his career and possibly his own life, he would protect his son. Although he felt he would never be able to confess his role to Max, he would do everything in his power to see that he had the tools necessary to uncover the truth. It was time.

James reached for the phone and was just about to dial when he heard Claudia's soft voice in deep conversation. Surprised that she'd returned without him hearing her, he started to hang up until he caught the voice of the person on the other end. For the briefest instant, his heart seemed to freeze in his chest. *Larry Templeton.*

Victoria sat unmoving in the plush gray armchair in her bedroom. Her slender hands folded in her lap. A thin shaft of light peeked through the drawn pale pink drapes. For the past few hours she'd contemplated what she was about to do. She no longer had anything to lose, and she'd be damned if she let anyone else gain any more satisfaction in their life.

Her day had been filled with lies and deceit. She'd listened to the most outlandish story she'd ever heard. And then less than two hours later, her uncle's story was refuted. She was still at odds with what she'd been told. Both Celeste and Frank had reasons for misleading her.

She stared sightlessly across the room, her mind a jumble of tormented thoughts, her spirit raw and beaten. She sighed heavily. It didn't matter anymore, she decided. Today would be her day of retribution. Everyone who'd hurt her would pay. And then, finally, she would feel relief from the constant emptiness that had carved out a hole in her spirit. Soon it would be filled with revenge.

* * *

The pain was more intense now. Celeste winced as it sliced through her body. This was her penance. Her payment for all the hurt she'd caused. The lies she'd told. But she'd rather bear the pain than reveal what she'd done. To do so would shred the fabric of her existence. She squeezed her eyes shut and took long, shaky breaths until the agony subsided.

In measured steps, she climbed the stairs to her bedroom. With each footfall, the vibrations of the truth shot through her limbs, reverberating outward to her limbs.

With great effort, she made it across the mauve-colored carpet to her bed. She could have told Victoria the truth, she realized, laying her pain-racked body across the floral quilt. But to do so would have been to admit truths that were too painful. The truth of her own beginnings, the truth about her feelings for her sister Sharlene. The truth about her involvement with Hamilton and the truth about Victoria.

The truth would have imploded the very foundation upon which she'd built her life. The lie that she'd constructed so that she could live. It was the one entity that allowed her to go on day by day.

Celeste closed her eyes against the waning sunshine that slid across the room. The sheer chiffon curtains fanned soundlessly in and out of the open window. A sudden pang of remembrance made her heart race. This day was so similar to the afternoon that Hamilton was killed, and all of her hopes for a life with him died in a rubble of twisted metal. All that was left was Reese. Reese who was almost identical to her mother, Sharlene. The one who'd come into her perfect world and destroyed it.

A single hot tear trickled down her cheek. How different would things have been if Sharlene had never been born? She, Celeste, would have been the only one, the one whom her parents loved and cherished. After all, she was the one who'd lost everything and everyone. She'd put all of her childlike faith and hope into her new family, and they'd promised to love her.

But when Sharlene came along, everything changed. They forgot her. They forgot their promise. Sharlene became the little princess.

Celeste tried to remember the moment the resentment began.

If she thought about it hard enough, not only could she conjure up crystal-clear imagery, she could reincarnate the pull in her chest and the sinking sensation in her stomach.

It was Sharlene's fifth birthday. Celeste was eight. Their parents had gone all out to celebrate Sharlene's birthday.

The huge backyard was filled with brilliant colored balloons and matching streamers. There was a clown performing tricks for the innumerable neighborhood children and the brood of relatives. There was even a riding pony complete with a cowboy.

Sharlene wore a pink dress with a full skirt lifted by a crinoline slip and decorated with white satin ribbons, which matched those in her hair.

"My dress is so pretty," Sharlene announced, looking up at Celeste for confirmation. Her large dark eyes trailed up and down Celeste's body. "It's prettier than yours," she taunted.

"So what," Celeste snapped, pursing her slim pink lips and fluffing her Shirley Temple curls.

"My dress is prettier because I'm the princess. Daddy said so."

"You are not. I'm Daddy's princess. You're just a little black nothing," she spat. "I have the long straight hair and pretty skin. Everybody loves me the most."

Sharlene glared at her. Her large amber eyes shimmering with burning tears. "You don't even look like us," she tossed back, her voice wobbly with emotion.

"Sharlene, sweetheart," April Winston, her mother called.

"Come on over here, baby. There's someone I want you to meet," her father Paul added.

Her spirit buoyed by her father's endearment, Sharlene sniffed back her tears and skipped over to where her parents stood beneath the tree. Celeste followed close behind her.

The two girls positioned themselves on either side of their father. Celeste slipped her hand in his and grinned up at him.

Then suddenly Celeste felt as if the world had begun to move in slow motion and she was witnessing the entire scene through a clouded lens. The moment would be etched forever in her head.

She felt her father release her hand as he turned and picked up Sharlene, holding her proudly in his arms. The man, woman, and little boy who stood across from them smiled effusively while Paul made the introductions.

"This is her," Paul announced with pride. "Our little princess." He placed a kiss on Sharlene's cheek while April tightened the ribbons on Sharlene's two thick ponytails.

Sharlene grinned, unabashed at the love pouring from her parents, directed only at her.

Celeste felt herself slowly disappearing, separated from everyone by a thin mist of indifference. They were all talking and laughing at once. All the attention was directed at Sharlene. The noise was becoming deafening to Celeste. Her heart began to race erratically. Her skin grew clammy with perspiration. She tugged on her father's arm to gain his attention. When he looked down, she smiled up at him.

"Not now, Celeste. Why don't you go on over there and play with the children," he added, pointing to a cluster of frolicking, squealing boys and girls. "Go on now and be a good girl." Paul turned his attention back to the couple.

In her chest a rock settled, stifling her breathing. It seemed to push the air in her lungs upward, filling her throat and her eyes with a burning sensation. Through tear-filled eyes she looked up at her sister who was beaming in the adoration. It was at that moment that the seed of jealousy was firmly planted.

Over the years it grew, drawing in strength, threading its way through every fiber of Celeste's being. She dedicated herself to besting Sharlene at everything. In Celeste's mind, Sharlene had taken away and captured the love of the two most important people in her life. Celeste vowed to take away everything that would ever be important to Sharlene. Celeste had no intention of ever losing anything ever again. No matter what it took. And when opportunity presented itself she took it and the lie took root. How ironic it was, Celeste thought, that even the memory of Sharlene was lost to her own daughter.

Celeste opened her eyes, casting the memories backward into her subconscious. For a moment, twinges of guilt pricked at her heart. Perhaps there were innocent victims in all this: Victoria and Reese and even Frank. And at odd, melancholy moments she had flashes when she wanted to exorcise herself of her guilt. Like this morning with Victoria. The truth had hung on the corners of her mouth like cookie crumbs, but she swallowed them back and repeated the tale she'd told for so many years. It was all that she had left.

She knew she could never face Victoria with the truth. She realized that the moment the words of accusation spewed from Victoria's lips. She would never forgive her. Not now. Not after all of this time.

If there was anyone left in her life whom she was capable of loving and having it returned, it was Victoria. And when faced with the crucial possibility of losing that, she knew she could not bear it. She knew at the moment that their eyes met that whatever thoughts she'd had about finally revealing the truth about what she'd done, they were eradicated. She wouldn't lose Victoria's love.

As James descended the stairs, myriad thoughts raced through his head. *Larry and Claudia*. He didn't want to believe it. But they sounded so intimate, so personal, even though their conversation seemed innocent. It wasn't the chit-chatty tone of conversation shared between friends—especially friends of your husband. Rather it was the tone of two people who knew each other well.

How could this have happened? But even as he formulated the question, he knew the answer. He'd been responsible for opening the doorway long ago. For a moment he halted on the staircase and shut his eyes. He gripped the banister with all of his strength. Anger and outrage coursed through his solid body. He wanted to blame her somehow, to make it be her fault—Larry's fault.

He opened his eyes, his heart laden with remorse and acceptance. He had no one to blame but himself.

James entered the kitchen, just as Claudia was hanging up the phone, unaware of his presence. He took this moment to quietly observe his wife; the flutter of her hands as she patted a stray strand of hair in place; her thoughtful movements around the kitchen fixing, straightening, wiping down the counters making sure everything was just so. *Perfect*. The perfect illusion to what lay beneath.

He took a long, thoughtful breath and stepped into the kitchen. Claudia turned at his approach, the dolorous look that brimmed in her eyes told him all that he needed to know and suddenly, his heart lifted with hope.

His gaze held hers as he crossed the room. Claudia looked at him with wonder, almost an awakening.

James took her hand in his, before he spoke. "Sometimes

we find ourselves in situations that prompt us to make life-altering decisions," he began in deliberate, measured tones. "Some of us without thinking of the consequences, or the people that we may hurt as a result, make those decisions and take those chances." His voice broke with raw emotion as he continued. "Unfortunately, I was one who made a wrong decision a lifetime ago." He swallowed hard, his eyes running over her perfect, unlined face. "You had a choice, too."

Claudia shielded her eyes behind her long lashes, her heart racing in trepidation with each word that he spoke; afraid of what he would say, and more so of what he would only imply.

"When I picked up the phone a few minutes ago and heard you talking with Larry, I thought my world had finally come crashing down around me. I heard the same joy and lightness in your voice that at one time was reserved for only me."

"James, please, it's not…"

"Shh, please let me finish." He took a breath and squared his shoulders. "In those moments, I realized that I deserved whatever you and Larry had done. I gave you every reason and opportunity to find comfort in another man's arms."

With the pad of his thumb he wiped away the lone tear that trickled down Claudia's cheek. "I came down here to tell you that I didn't blame you, that I couldn't blame you, and that even though it would devastate me—" he swallowed back the knot of emotion that welled in his throat "—I would let you go."

The tears rolled freely down her face, her vision of James clouded by them. She clamped her lips together to imprison the sob that struggled to burst free.

James tenderly caressed her face, cupping her damp cheek in his palm. "But when I saw you just now, and you turned to me with a look that spoke acceptance, I knew in that instance that you would have never gone to Larry. What I saw in your eyes was the look of a woman who has accepted and lived within the foundation of her wedding vows for better or for worst, no matter what it may have cost her."

Claudia blinked back her tears and swallowed hard. She moved away from him and turned toward the sink, gripping the edge for support. "So many times I wanted to hurt you for what you'd done," she began, her voice trembling with emotion. "When you stayed in Japan and Larry was stationed here...we became close. He was the only one I could talk to." She turned to face him. "My family had cut me off. I had no real friends." She choked back a sob. "But Larry was always there and I think we grew to love each other in a way I'll always appreciate. He gave me strength, James, on those days when I thought I would go out of my mind with bitterness and hurt. On those days when Max would cry or need me, or the walls seemed to close in around me, he was there for me." She wiped away the fresh flow of tears and took a shaky breath.

"But we never crossed the line." She stared at her husband, searching for the entry to the depths of his soul. "And I've never regretted my decision."

Claudia stretched her arm to touch him, smoothing his hair with her hand and loving him with her eyes. She managed a small, quivering smile and a surge of relief like one he'd never known filled him with an exquisite joy.

Their hearts beat together in perfect synchronization as James pulled his wife into his arms.

Victoria pushed herself up from her seat and crossed the room to her night table. Opening the top drawer, she pulled out her business phone book and flipped to the W's.

The phone was answered on the second ring. "*Washington Post,* Stan Tilden speaking."

"Hi, Stan, this is Victoria Davenport."

Stan beamed, the story she'd fed him years ago had made his career. "Vikki, how are you? Long time. How's the computer business?"

"That's what I want to talk with you about, Stan," she replied in a soft Southern drawl. "I have some information I believe you'll be interested in."

Stan opened his appointment book. "I'm free this evening. Where can we meet?"

Chapter 26

Reese pulled herself up from the grip of sleep. She blinked several times to clear her vision. By the angle of the sun streaming in through the window, she surmised it must be close to 7:00 p.m.

She turned her head to peer at the digital clock on the bedside table. Her conclusion was confirmed: seven-fifteen. She yawned and stretched her long limbs. She'd been asleep for close to three hours. And thankfully her headache was gone. She yawned again.

With effort she sat up in bed and swung her legs over the side, her toes tickled by the copper-colored rug. Stretching her arms over her head, she drew in a deep breath and her nostrils were instantly filled with the aromas of something delicious. Her stomach growled in response.

Smiling, she ambled into the adjoining bathroom, splashed cool water on her face, brushed her teeth and ran a comb through her hair. Finished, she reentered the bedroom and selected a white T-shirt and a pair of salmon-colored shorts to change into.

Moments later she descended the spiral staircase and entered the kitchen to be greeted by the magnificent spectacle of Maxwell's bare chest.

"Hello, sleepyhead." He smiled in greeting. "How's that headache?"

"All gone, doc." She crossed the room and slipped her arms around his waist. "I feel like new." She pressed her head against his chest. "And I'm starved, I might add."

Maxwell's deep chuckle rumbled in his chest and she snuggled closer. "Now how did I know that?" he teased. "Well, m'lady, dinner will be served as soon as you set the table."

"Great," she enthused. "Inside or outside?" She moved toward the cupboard, removing dishes and glasses.

"It's still really nice out, and I'd love to share the sunset with you."

"Then outside it is." She placed the dishes, cups, silverware and serving bowls on a large tray and took everything out to the deck.

The warm evening breeze blew gently through the screening that encircled the deck. The sounds of Earl Klugh's "Balladina" filtered through the air.

Reese took another mouthwatering forkful of Max's creation of sautéed shrimp and diced chicken over a bed of herb-drenched pasta topped with the creamiest sauce she'd ever tasted. She closed her eyes in contentment. "Absolutely delicious," she cooed.

Maxwell leaned back in the redwood chair and crossed his hands over his taut stomach. For several moments, he simply stared at her, relishing the moment of peace and tranquillity. He wasn't sure what he would do if anything happened to her because of him. If only he could just take her away from all of this treachery and lies and betrayals, he would. But he also realized that Reese would fight him tooth and nail and then resent him for it in the end. As infuriating as she could be when she'd made up her mind, it was one of the many attributes that he admired in her. Maybe even loved, his conscience whispered, the now formalized thought jolting him.

He shook his head, scattering his thoughts, when the ringing of the phone intruded. "Be right back." He pushed open the sliding glass doors and stepped inside.

Hearing the phone ring reminded Reese that she still had not heard from Lynnette. That was so unlike her, Reese thought, her initial concern mounting. Perhaps she'd called Max's office after they'd left. But even so, she was certain that Carmen would have told Lynnette where she was.

"That was Carmen," Max said, stepping through the sliding doors. "Our flight is scheduled for tomorrow evening at six o'clock."

"Did she say anything about Lynnette?"

Maxwell shook his head. "No, she didn't."

Reese got up. "I'm going to call and see if I can reach her. I may be able to catch her at the office." She brushed past him and into the house.

Reese tapped her foot with impatience and growing anxiety listening to the phone ring. Lynnette's voice mail finally triggered. Immediately she bypassed the message by pressing 0 and was switched to the main line.

"*Visions Magazine.* May I help you?"

"Hi. This is Reese Delaware. I'm trying to reach Lynnette."

"Oh, Reese, I'm so glad you called. This is Diane," the receptionist said.

Reese's pulse raced as a wave of apprehension swept through her, "What is it, Diane?" she insisted.

"There's been an accident," Diane said as calmly as she could. "Lynnette's in the hospital. She was hit by a car."

A tiny gasp sputtered from Reese's lips. "Oh my God," she cried, fear of the worst rioting through her. "How bad—when?"

"It was earlier this morning around eleven. She'd gone out…"

Reese began to shake as the frightening image of Lynnette lying in the street took shape in her head. With a pang she realized that it must have happened when she'd gone out to call her. Guilt snatched her by the throat cutting off her air.

"…the doctors said she's stable and awake."

"Did they get the driver?" Reese asked in a tremulous voice.

"That's the worst part," Diane replied. "It was a hit-and-run."

Reese clenched her hand until her nails bit into her palm. "Give me the name of the hospital and the number," she said in a thick unsteady voice. "Please," she whispered as an afterthought.

"Hold on. I have it right here."

Reese took down the name and phone number fighting to steady her shaky hand. "Thank you, Diane." She hung up before Diane could reply.

"Everything okay?" Maxwell asked from behind her.

Reese spun around, an unspoken pain alive and glowing in her amber eyes. She seemed to be staring right through him Max thought, anxiety steadily winding its way through him.

"Reese, what is it?" He swiftly crossed the room and she flung herself into his arms.

"It's Lynn…" she cried, the tears now beginning to flow.

She began to shake and Max held her tighter. "She's been in a…car accident. A hit-and-run."

"Oh, Reese, I'm so sorry. How is she?"

Reese retold what Diane had said and all the while that she spoke, Maxwell knew without a doubt that it was no accident. The chilling words of the note he'd received earlier by the unidentified messenger played back in his mind.

"I've got to get to Chicago," Reese said suddenly, pulling away from his embrace. She swiped the back of her hand across her face streaking tears and mascara over her cheeks.

"No, Reese, you can't," Max said definitively, grabbing her upper arm to halt her progress.

But the steely tone of his voice would have been enough to stop her. She looked up at him, her eyes wide with uncertainty. "W-what is it Max? Tell me."

"Sit down, Reese." Her movements seemed to be guided by the sheer strength of his voice as she found her way to the nearest chair.

Maxwell stooped down in front of her until he was at eye level. He took both of her hands in his. "It was no accident, Reese," he began and tightened his grip when he felt her recoil. Holding on to her with his right hand, he removed the note with the other. "I got this earlier today." He handed her the note. "I'm pretty sure the messenger was sent by Frank Murphy."

He gently stroked her thigh as her eyes glided over the neatly typed words—*Your girlfriend is next*—which seemed to blur and dance before her eyes. Reese swallowed hard and crushed the thin sheet of paper in her fist. A sensation of intense sickness and desolation swept over her. She took several deep breaths until she felt strong enough to raise her head and meet Maxwell's gentle gaze. "What are we going to do, Max?" she asked over her choking, beating heart.

"You're going to call the hospital and find out about Lynnette. Then we're going to pack, try to get some rest, and catch our flight tomorrow. We'll be safe there. No one is expecting us to leave until next week. I spoke with Chris in Tokyo while you were asleep. He suggested that we stay in a hotel instead of my house."

Reese nodded numbly.

Maxwell reached up on the counter and handed her the phone. "Call Lynnette." He straightened. "I'll be upstairs if you need me."

Reese blinked away her apathy and began to dial the number to the hospital. After five unbearable minutes she was finally put through to Lynnette's room.

The sound of Lynnette's groggy voice was like a soothing balm to her soul.

"Lynn, oh Lynn, I was so worried. How are you?"

"I feel like I've been hit by a car," she said trying to make light of her circumstance. "But the doctor said I'll be fine," she continued in a raspy voice. "I'll be here for at least two weeks. And don't you even think about coming out here," she warned.

Reese breathed heavily in relief. At least she was all right. "What happened? How are you?"

In a slow, halting voice Lynn told Reese what had transpired and the extent of her injuries. "The one high point of this whole nasty business is that the doctor is gorgeous." She tried to laugh, but it stuck in her throat when a shard of pain shot through her head.

Reese heard the sharp intake of breath. "Lynn! Lynn! What is it?"

"I'm…okay. It's just this damned headache." She took a deep breath. "They gave me something for the pain. I guess it hasn't kicked in yet. It's just making me sleepy as all hell."

Reese gave in to a shaky smile. "You sound like yourself,"

she sniffed, fighting back tears of relief. "So it can't be that bad."

"That's what I keep tellin' myself," she replied over a yawn. "I'm sorry I couldn't get the information you needed."

Lynnette's statement brought to the forefront the real reason why she lay in a hospital bed. And the idea that she was the reason made her stomach knot in an unnamed fear. "I don't want you to worry about it. You just concentrate on getting well and out of there. And I promise you, all you have to do is say the word and I'll be on the next plane." Her throat tightened as she tried to fight back her tears. Even at the risk of her own safety, she would go to Lynnette the moment she asked. Maxwell would just have to understand.

"Don't you dare," she answered sleepily, dragging out her words. "Hmm, I think this…medicine…is finally beginning… to work." She yawned.

"I'll call you the moment I get settled."

"Mmm-hmm." She took a long slumberous breath, and Reese thought she'd dose off until Lynn's groggy voice came back across the line. "I don't think this was an accident sister-friend and neither do you. We're both too smart for that."

"Lynn I…"

"Don't worry about me, I'm in the best place I can be. But you, you be safe. Let that man of yours take care of you. Be safe, Reese," she cautioned in her final moments of clarity before sleep took over.

"I will," Reese promised on a thready whisper. "I will."

In the darkness of their shared bedroom, Reese curled next to Maxwell seeking the security and comfort that seemed to be steadily eluding her. She was frightened. More terrified than she'd ever been, even in the deepest grips of her nightmares. Her life and her actions were being dictated by people who would rather see her dead than let her get at the truth. They could even reach beyond her and hurt those close to her.

Sure, she could back off and turn her information over to the authorities, but she was never one to take the easy way out. And somewhere deep inside her soul, she knew that at the root of it all was the key to her past. Knowing that, she could never willingly hand over the pieces of her life for someone else to put together. She owed it to herself, and now she owed it to Lynnette.

"What are you thinking about?" Maxwell whispered in her ear. Gently, he stroked her hair in a rhythmic, soothing motion. His hands moved downward until they reached her neck. He began to unfurl the knots of tension that had found refuge in her neck and shoulders. Then he turned her on her stomach to afford her the greatest benefit of his ministrations.

Reese expelled an audible sigh of relief. "Everything," she murmured. "What's happened and what's ahead." She closed her eyes and propped her chin on her hands. "I just feel so helpless, like these unseen forces have taken control of my life. What's so ironic is that it seems to be the same circumstances that have dominated my life for the past fifteen years—the unknown—the dark corners. Just like I'm always primed for some hidden memory to spring to life, I'm primed for someone to take what little of me I have away."

"That won't happen, Reese. I promise that. You're not in this alone. It's about me, too. Do you think for one minute that I don't have the same doubts and fears? I do, sweetheart, ever since this whole mess began. Believe that. But I'm not going to let it paralyze me. I can't and neither can you. We're going to get to the bottom of this—together, me and you."

"I guess I just needed to hear you say that," she whispered. She turned over, looked into his eyes and cupped his face in her palms. "Because...for the first time in my life...I truly need someone." Her eyes misted over as they glided across his face. " I need you, Max," she uttered from the depths of her soul.

If he ever doubted her need for him, his doubts dissolved in her declaration and his heart filled with joy. "You have me, Reese. For as long as you want me." He held her tighter and he'd never loved her more than at that moment.

Yet even in the comforting security of Maxwell's arms, Reese could not fight of the demons that haunted her sleep.

Chapter 27

Reese awoke the following morning exhausted and spent. Maxwell hadn't fared much better, but insisted that Reese spend the early part of the day resting. He'd prepared an herbal tea to help her rest and she was finally in a peaceful sleep when he slipped from the bed.

For most of the night, Maxwell alternated between rocking her, massaging her, and talking to her, all while she tossed and turned throughout the night.

Maxwell prepared a light meal of several kinds of salads for Reese when she awoke, knowing she'd be hungry. He made some last-minute phone calls and checked with Carmen at the office. After a ten-minute debate, he'd finally convinced her not to take the trip with them. After hearing about what happened to Lynnette, he had no intention of letting anyone else be put at risk. He had enough to worry about without having to be concerned about Carmen's safety as well. She would meet them at the airport and bring his files that he'd need for his upcoming meetings. And that was as far as she was going.

While Reese slept, Maxwell sequestered himself in his den, going over his strategy for his negotiations with the Japanese contingent. His intention was to gain their support in expanding his manufacturing operations to Tokyo.

He knew it was a task that was far from easy. He not only had to combat the cultural barriers, but the ingrained prejudices that permeated the entire country.

Yes, he'd mastered the language, the customs, and adopted much of the culture. He'd learned the intricate art of negotiations and the genius of their financial and technological success. Japanese blood even ran in his veins. But he would always be an outsider, never a part of the powerful network that made the real decisions.

That was the barrier he had to crack if he were to ever gain a meaningful foothold for his enterprises in Japan. It had taken nearly a year of talks and trips back and forth across the globe to reach the point where the powers were willing to sit down and give real consideration to his proposal.

He knew the first few weeks would be a series of *machiai seiju*, or teahouse politics. No real decisions or business would be discussed for the first few days. And he must be prepared for every inevitability. He'd worked and planned too long and hard to blow it now.

He scrubbed his face with his hands to wipe away the weariness. He needed to be able to devote all of his energies to closing this deal. But the past few weeks had deterred his focus. He felt physically and emotionally drained. This was not the state of mind he needed to be in, and he had to make the transition before he met with the businessmen in Japan. What he needed to do was have a good workout in the dojo.

He exhaled heavily and squeezed his tired eyes shut.

He wished that Chris was there for him to kick around his thoughts and feelings. At least he'd see him soon enough. That would have to sustain him.

Since they would be arriving so early in Japan, he would at least have the opportunity to unwind and regroup. The change of environment would certainly do him and Reese a great deal of good.

Reese. Slowly he shook his head in wonder. From the moment she'd set foot in his office, his entire life had changed. He had changed.

All of the reasons he'd given himself for steering clear of relationships, he'd forgotten. Reese had made him forget. He'd allowed his heart to open and accept her in it. He opened doors to his life and let her in. And it felt good. And yes, he was in love with her—deeply and irrevocably in love with her. He was finally able to admit it to himself.

He smiled wistfully, envisioning her face. He was in love with her laughter, the sparkle in her eyes, her sexy voice, the way she walked, talked, made love with him. The way she looked at him and made him feel so very special.

He fully realized what he'd denied himself for so long, giving love to a woman who could love him back.

Maxwell's smooth bronze brow tightened. Could she love him? She'd said she needed him. And there was a time when he would have never thought she'd say that much. But need was a far cry from love.

He expelled a long breath and crossed the room to look out of the window. The soothing vision of the bay spanned out before him. The water lapped gently against the shoreline. Maxwell felt the tension that had coiled his spine and snaked up his neck, slowly being to wane.

He braced the window frame with his hands. Somewhere out there lay the answers to all of the questions. His eyes searched the horizon. But where?

"Hi."

Maxwell turned toward Reese's voice and he would have sworn that his heart stood still. She was a vision to behold. The near sheer peach lounging pajamas flowed around her slender body, giving the illusion that she floated across the room.

Standing with the light dancing behind her from the kitchen, he could discern every detail of her exquisite form. Her radiant chocolate-brown skin seemed to glow from some inner light, making her eyes sparkle with twinkling lights. Her thick hair tumbled in seductive disarray around her face.

Yes. This was the woman he wanted to wake up with, spend his nights and the rest of his life with. And when this whole sordid mess was over, he would tell her so.

Reese glided slowly toward him until she was inches away. And with every step, she struggled to conquer her involuntary reaction to that gentle loving look in his eyes. She couldn't allow herself to confuse his empathy for her with love. She was certain that it was sympathy she saw mirrored in those ebony eyes.

"Thank you…for last night," she uttered in a raw whisper, her throat still feeling the effects of hours of groaning and crying. "How bad was it?"

Maxwell traced her jaw with the tip of his finger. "Not too bad," he lied. The truth was, he'd been afraid for her. Even when she'd cried out and her eyes were wide open, she didn't seem to see him. Terror was in her eyes while she trembled and shook her head wildly.

"How are you feeling?" He eased her into his embrace, pulling her close. Shutting his eyes, he inhaled deeply of her erotic scent, filling himself with its nourishment.

"Better. I think." The corners of her expressive mouth struggled to form a smile.

"Do you remember anything?" he asked gently, stroking her hair.

She nodded against his chest, the images of her dreams brilliant in the light of day.

"I remember where I've seen Larry before," she murmured with a shiver of recollection. "He was the one who carried me away from the car before it burst into flames."

The silence lengthened between them, making her uncomfortable. Instead of feeling secure in his company, Reese felt suddenly anxious to escape from his disturbing presence.

Maxwell hadn't said a word since she told him of her dream. He seemed to have withdrawn somewhere deep inside of himself, shutting her out. Now she was angry at herself for having said anything at all. As much as he professed to want her to confide in him, he seemed unable or unwilling to accept what she told him. He acted the same way when she spoke of his father. Although she could understand his resistance, his reactions disappointed her.

They moved through the sprawling house as two separate entities, bringing their baggage to the car.

Reese stood on the passenger side of the car waiting for Maxwell to unlock the doors. She searched for some sign of emotion in his unreadable expression, made more difficult by the dark glasses he wore shielding his eyes. Added to that, she also knew that his face would reveal nothing of what he felt or thought, and she couldn't stand it another minute.

"Are you going to act like this for the entire time we're together, Max?" she suddenly spouted.

With his right hand he removed his sunglasses. His gaze flickered upward and settled on her face. He braced his arms across the roof of the car and looked at her for a long, silent moment. He seemed more pensive than angry or hurt, Reese realized when she made contact with his eyes.

"No," he answered simply. He blew out a long breath. "It's not you, Reese, or anything that you've said." He turned his gaze, momentarily, away then looked back at her. "It just seems that the more you remember, the more it points to my father's involvement and now Larry. I'm trying really hard to digest it all. To find out that Larry was on the scene the morning of your parents' deaths… It's just…"

"Too much to handle," she said, finishing his sentence.

He wasn't surprised to hear her words echo his thoughts. That seemed to happen a lot between them, as if they were connected on some higher level. "Yeah," he answered finally. "I'm just trying to process it all."

She looked at him, her soft amber eyes filled with compassion and understanding. "All I ask is that you talk to me, Max. Just tell me what you're thinking. I can't stand it when you shut me out. It's difficult for me, too."

His jaw flexed as he nodded. "Let's get out of here."

They drove for a solid twenty minutes without a word passing between them. Reese sat with her eyes glued to the winding tree-lined boulevards, her arms crossed tightly beneath her breasts like shields against the unknown. Intermittently, she stole furtive glances in Maxwell's direction and each time her own anxiety level escalated.

He was the personification of controlled energy; from the set of his square jaw to the pulse that beat at the base of his neck, the strong fingers that gripped the steering wheel like a vise, to the ingrained frown that furrowed his brow and narrowed his exotic onyx eyes. Yet, even with all that she could see, what he was feeling inside was omitted from his expression. One who did not know him would believe he was simply a man focused on arriving at an appointed destination.

So caught up was she in her analysis of his body language she flinched in surprise when he finally spoke.

"I've been thinking about everything you've told me, Reese, from the beginning." He paused gauging his words. "I no longer have any doubts that my father and now Larry were both somehow connected…to the death of your parents." He swallowed hard, the verbal acknowledgement of the truth like a bitter pill in his mouth. He risked taking a fleeting look at Reese.

She was biting on her bottom lip, her hands were clasped tightly in her lap, her eyes wavering between looking at him and the unwinding road as if afraid that to look directly at him would somehow validate what they both knew to be true.

The sorrow that he saw hovering in her amber eyes, he knew in no way reflected the depth of her pain or her inner turmoil.

His deep voice was low, controlled and decisive when he continued. "In accepting this, I also have to accept my own responsibility."

Her heart slammed against her chest and her head snapped in his direction. Her voice trembled with dread. "What are you saying?"

"When you began seeing the images in your dreams more clearly, and finally told me the date when the 'accident' happened, I remembered something. And I should have told you then. But I didn't want to believe it."

Reese pressed her lips together. "Tell me now," she gently urged.

"I always wondered about my father's late-night meetings with Larry and the hushed phone calls. I vaguely recall the news articles about your father and about the same time as the accident, reporters began hounding us and I never knew why other than I wasn't supposed to talk with them under any circumstances."

"And your distrust of reporters began," she said, her words giving credence to his emotions.

Slowly he nodded in agreement even as the memories grew clearer. "My mother and father seemed to constantly argue during that time, and then out of the blue we packed up and moved to California." He turned to look at her, marking the look of acceptance mixed with confusion on her face.

"What would the reporters want with your father?" she asked, caution outlining her words.

"Remember, my father works for the Special Forces unit of the Air Force. Your father, if I remember correctly, worked for Intelligence."

Reese nodded slowly. "And?" She held her breath, waiting for the painful answer that hung on her lips. But she would not speak the words. She needed him to say them. He needed to admit them. Otherwise her declaration of what she believed to be true would sound like another accusation.

"From the little I know of what my father did and does," he qualified, "his job is to infiltrate and remove any threats to the U.S. military—to the government. He's been thoroughly trained and is only called in for ultra-sensitive duty."

"There's so little that I know, and worse, can remember about my father," Reese said wistfully. "My aunt Celeste was always so reluctant to talk about him, and she wouldn't even speak my mother's name." She snorted in distaste. "Now I know why." Maxwell reached across the gearshift and squeezed her hand. "There was little or no written record of what happened," she continued, "and the Air Force has refused to tell me anything about him other than he served his country well."

"My belief is that your father discovered something he

wasn't supposed to and the wrong person found out and put a stop to it."

"My father, a threat to the government? Isn't that a stretch?"

"Is it? What else makes sense? That's my father's job, Reese. I never wanted to acknowledge the ugliness of his reality—but I can't ignore it any longer. And right now, my father's biggest challenge is what he believes to be his duty to his superiors and his duty as a father." His voice hitched with a modicum of emotion. "He's torn between me and them." He chuckled mirthlessly. "I suppose his big concession was getting Larry to look out for us."

"When Larry arrives in Tokyo, I'll confront him with what I know," she announced hotly, emotion overruling her journalistic sense.

Maxwell shook his head. "Not a good idea. The less anyone knows about your memory returning, the better."

Reese thought about it for a moment and nodded. "I guess you're right, especially since we don't know how deep this goes."

"Agreed."

When she tried to speak again, her voice wavered. "And whatever my father found out, Frank Murphy doesn't want resurrected at any cost," she said almost to herself. A slight shiver vibrated through her body. "What could my father have known that was so devastating people would kill to keep it quiet?"

"I don't know, baby. But I think it would be in our best interests to find out. That's our only edge."

"How?"

He turned to her, his gaze dark and direct. "That's your department. Go for it."

They drove for several more moments, each of them caught

in the vortex of their private thoughts, when suddenly Reese's husky voice filled the silence between them.

"My mother wasn't going to go with my father to the hearings that morning," she said in a faraway voice, as the images came into focus. "My father begged her. He said he needed her support. He promised that they would work things out between them. My mother was so hurt and angry about what she'd discovered about him and my aunt, she said she didn't want to be near him." Reese sighed heavily. "Somehow my father finally convinced her to go and she insisted that I go as well." Her voice cracked. "If only she hadn't…I would have…still had my mother." A single tear trickled down her cheek. She sniffed and wiped her eyes. "And my life.

"I'm so afraid, Max," she confessed, her breath coming in short panting gasps as she fought to forestall the tumult of tears.

Maxwell checked the rearview mirror and pulled over off the road. He unsnapped his seat belt and then hers. Gently, he gathered her in his arms and whispered soothing words of comfort in her ear. "It's all right, baby, get it all out. It's all right. I'm here."

"The more I remember…the more it hurts. It just hurts so bad. As long as I couldn't see their faces or recall their voices, I couldn't feel anything except…this inexplicable emptiness. And now, little by little, the emptiness is being filled with emotions that I haven't had to deal with." Her body shook with the force of her sobs, escalated by the gentleness of Maxwell's tender touch.

"I never mourned them, Max. I…never grieved because I didn't feel anything. I couldn't remember them. They were just two people who had died. Two faceless people who were supposed to mean something to me and they didn't. Oh, God," she cried, the agony of recollection impaling her heart.

At that moment, Maxwell's rage was so intense he felt that

he could take his two hands and wring the truth from his father. The thought that his own flesh and blood was responsible for the psychological and emotional agony and torment of the woman he loved went beyond his comprehension. He ached for her, mourned with her. He wanted to somehow absorb her pain, but he knew he could not. As painful as it was to watch, and experience, he knew that she needed this catharsis. All he could do was everything in his power to see to it that whomever was responsible was brought to their knees.

"I'm…sorry," Reese said weakly, easing away from his hold. "I…didn't mean to put all of that on you."

He wiped the tears away from her cheeks with his thumb, then swept back her hair from her face, tilting up her chin in the process.

"We're in this together. No matter that my father is involved. I know that I've said all this before, but there was still that part of me that fought not to believe it. Not anymore. I swear that to you."

Reese nodded and tried to smile. "We'll miss our flight if we keep sitting here," she sniffed, drawing back the last of her sorrow.

"The hell with the flight. My first concern is you. Are you all right?"

"I will be," she answered, her voice a bit stronger.

"That's what I want to hear." He put the car in gear and pulled back onto the highway. "Everything will work out and we'll get through this—together." And even as he uttered the words he thought of the hole in his own life and wondered if it, too, would ever be filled. Day by day, Reese was putting together the lost fragments of her life, which compelled him to take a look at his own. Her determination spurred him. Perhaps he would dare to do what he'd avoided for most of his life, find out what he could about the woman who was his natural mother. And maybe Reese would help him.

* * *

Maxwell kept Reese close by his side as they weaved around the throng of travelers at LAX airport. All of his senses were on alert to everything and everyone swirling around them. The airport would be the perfect location for an "accident" to happen.

He wrapped his arm tighter around Reese's waist as they approached the waiting area where they were to meet Carmen. His dark eyes continued to sweep the crowds—ever sharp and vigilant.

"If you squeeze me any tighter, you're going to cut off my circulation," Reese said lightly.

"Sorry," he mumbled keeping his eyes trained on the crowds, but he didn't slacken his hold. "There's Carmen on that bank of chairs," Maxwell said, angling his chin toward the left, before ushering Reese toward the waiting area.

Reese squinted in the general direction and couldn't discern Carmen from anyone else. She looked up at Maxwell in amazement.

Carmen rose from her seat as the duo approached. Her warm smile embraced them both.

Reese lowered her head and pecked Carmen's cheek. "Good to see you, Carmen."

"You, too, Reese. All ready for your trip?" she asked, noticing the slight redness in her eyes but opting not to mention it.

"As ready as I can be," Reese offered with a smile.

"I'm sure everything will be fine," Carmen replied sagely. A look of quiet understanding passed between the two women. Carmen turned toward Maxwell. "Everything you need is here," she said nodding toward the heavy leather briefcase that sat near her feet. "I put the mail in there as well."

Maxwell reached down and took the case with his initials

embossed in gold lettering across the front. "Thanks for everything, Carmen."

She smiled. "Be safe," she said, looking from one to the other, her soft brown eyes filled with concern.

Those were the same words Lynnette had spoken to her the night before from her hospital bed, Reese recalled. She suddenly felt chilled and knew it had nothing to do with the air-conditioning.

They were both settled in their seats with a dinner tray of sirloin steak, Caesar salad, and baked potato with sour cream and chives in front of them.

"Humph, I never knew they served this kind of food on airplanes," Reese mumbled over a piece of the succulent steak. The juice from the meat trickled over her lips which she licked away with a swipe of her tongue. "I'm used to peanuts and a half can of soda over ice."

Maxwell tossed his head back and laughed. "You've simply been in the wrong section of the plane," he teased.

"Very funny. But all of us working stiffs can't afford first class," she volleyed, adding a hard glare for good measure.

"Stick with me," he said, leaning over and placing a kiss on her forehead. "I'll have you spoiled rotten." His sensual smile did a slow dance up and down her body. "It's first class for you all the way."

"And don't you forget it," she grinned.

"I'm sure *you* won't let me."

Stan Tilden sat behind his desk at the *Washington Post* reviewing his notes and tapes from his interview with Victoria. He had no doubt that everything she'd said was true. In his ten years as a journalist, he'd learned that the United States government, the military in particular, was capable of anything. But this? He shook his head in amazement.

He would certainly have to corroborate what Victoria'd told him. There was no way he would go forward with the story otherwise. He also knew that no one would be willing to admit that the military paid one of its own to steal computer information and then tout it as their own. But that wasn't the meat of the story. It was the very idea that the stolen programming allowed the Air Force to advance their radar technology to such a degree that their successes in the Gulf War were inevitable. The designer of the program would experience wealth beyond his imagination if he were to be paid for what he'd created. And the military knew that.

He'd always envied those guys Woodward and Bernstein who blew open the "Watergate" scandal. He'd prayed for the same opportunity to put his own name in lights. His gut told him this was his chance.

He frowned, contemplating his options. He knew he had to be careful, the far-reaching ramifications...well, he didn't even want to think about it. But he had to start somewhere; and what better place than the source? *Frank Murphy.*

Chapter 28

Claudia sat on the couch next to her husband feeling momentarily secure beneath the weight of his arm draped across her shoulder. She struggled to remember the last time they'd really shared a quiet moment together.

The past few weeks had taken its toll on both of them. But for the first time in years she felt the burden of the emotions she'd carried lifted from her spirit. She knew it was far from over, and every instinct told her that there was much more that James had not revealed to her. And it was probably best that she didn't know. There were aspects of her husband's life that she could never and would never be made privy to.

"Claudia," James uttered softly, pulling her away from her musings. "I want you to be prepared."

Her heart knocked in her chest. "For what?"

"I can't stop Max from pursuing his course. He's determined and I don't blame him," he continued, staring off across the room. He shifted his position so that he could face her. "I haven't told you everything, Claudia, for your own protection. The less you know, the better. But when everything comes out, and I'm certain that it will, I'll probably spend the rest of my life behind bars. I want you to be there for Max. He's going to need you."

Claudia felt as if the world had suddenly shifted beneath her feet. A surge of heat shot through her, clouding her thoughts. Her stomach somersaulted and she felt sick. "No," she whispered in a tiny voice of denial, digging her nails into his muscled arm.

James cupped her smooth caramel-colored face in his hands, and his own heart constricted at seeing the well of tears rimming her eyes. "There's no way to avoid it." He stroked her soft brown curls.

"I can't lose you. Not now. There has to be something you can do, James. There has to be."

Slowly he shook his head. "I should have done it a long time ago, Claudia," he said with regret. "I should have said, no."

Victoria returned to her car after meeting with Stan Tilden from the *Post* with a new feeling of purpose. The dismal sense of hopelessness that had permeated her life had slowly begun to lift. She was taking charge of her life—such that it was.

She had been someone's pawn as far back as she could recall, bending and jumping to someone else's will. Everyone in her life had found a way to use her for their own personal goals, never caring how it would all affect her. The only person who'd allowed her to just be herself had been Maxwell, and she'd ruined that relationship by using him. How painfully ironic. But now she had the opportunity to make amends.

After the fallout from the *Post* article, perhaps Maxwell would see that she was trying to make things right and consider taking her back. Especially after he found out the truth about Reese. She had a momentary pang of guilt about how her recent act would affect Reese. But just as quickly, the unnatural feeling passed. She had no affinity to Reese Delaware, she told herself.

She slowed at the red light then made the right turn. Her next stop was her aunt Celeste's house. "Or is it mother?" she asked herself aloud, the vileness of the word burning her throat like bile. She threw her head back and began to laugh, the sound piercing, almost hysterical. Unbidden, tears mixed with the unleashed laughter and Victoria stepped harder on the accelerator.

The house was still. Shadows paraded across the floor with the play of waning light that peeked in through the blinds. The sheer curtains mated erotically with the breeze, fanning in and out in a slow, sensuous dance.

Then, the shrill ringing of the doorbell pierced the tomblike silence, slicing through Celeste like a jolt of electricity. Yet she couldn't seem to move.

Since her confrontation with Victoria she'd battled with her conscience as well as her physical pain. At moments, she didn't know which was more intense. Several times she'd picked up the phone to call Victoria—tell her the truth. But she didn't. She couldn't. The lie was so ingrained, so deeply rooted into her being, even she struggled to separate fact from fantasy.

The bell pealed again. Was it more insistent this time? she wondered idly. Whoever it was would get tired soon enough and go away, she rationalized. Besides, she couldn't imagine who would be coming to see her. She had no friends and her only family was Victoria.

She ran her index finger across the spot-free glass that covered Hamilton Delaware's photograph. He was so handsome, she sighed with a winsome smile. Tall and muscular with skin the color of milk chocolate. "Like Reese," she muttered, her irrational resentment evident in the venom of her tone. And Reese was a physical reincarnation of Sharlene, from the delicate bone structure to the lure of those damned amber eyes.

She frowned in confusion. How could everything have turned out so badly? She'd planned everything and it would have worked. She and Hamilton would have been together. If only…

The bell rang again, but this time the ringing was followed by what sounded like keys being inserted into the lock. Her spirits suddenly lifted. Victoria had come back.

Painfully, Celeste pulled herself up from her seat, and returned the framed photo to the nightstand in concert with the slamming of the front door.

By the time she reached the top of the landing, Victoria stared up at her from below. Celeste's smile of greeting was quickly erased when she saw the loathing floating in Victoria's green gaze.

"There are a few things I want to say to you, *Aunt* Celeste, or whoever you are. You can either stand there and I'll shout it loud enough for all your neighbors to hear, or you can come downstairs. Your choice."

Celeste took a deep, pain-filled breath and began her descent. She stopped two steps above where Victoria stood, gripping the banister for support. Celeste held her breath, fearing the worst while her heart banged out an unnatural rhythm in her chest.

Victoria lashed out at her in an icy high octave. "It doesn't matter anymore if what you and Frank told me is the truth or a lie. At first I thought it did. I needed to believe someone— something. But then I realized, *Celeste*," she spat the name, "that the only person I could believe in was myself. And for my entire life, at least until the past few hours, I've never been able to do that." She gave Celeste a long, cold look of contempt, edged with pity. Her voice grew calmer, but continued in the same chilling tone.

"I intend to rebuild by life, my own way. Maybe then I'll find some peace. But everyone who has ever hurt me, lied to me, used me, will pay. That much I can guarantee. And that includes you."

Victoria momentarily turned away and began to pace back and forth in front of the stairs. "I thought long and hard about what I could do that would remotely inflict the type of pain on you that you have on me. It was a struggle." She laughed, the sound haunting in its maliciousness. "What does she have that I can take and destroy?" She stopped her frenetic pacing and looked curiously up at Celeste as if half expecting a response. "And you know what I realized? You have nothing!" She threw her strawberry blond head back and laughed, so long and hard that Celeste began to tremble.

"Victoria, please…"

Victoria spun around, her pale face flushed with rage. "Shut up! Don't you say a word," she ordered pointing her finger at Celeste. Her icy green stare seemed to root Celeste to her spot on the staircase. "The only thing you have is me. I'm your only family, your only friend. The only one you've ever turned to. I suppose I should be grateful that you thought so much of me to include me in your perfect little world." Her eyes flashed. "But I'm not." She took several heaving breaths. "So, I decided I'd take myself away. Out of your life. Permanently. You'll never have to tell me another lie, you'll never have to pretend to care."

Celeste felt herself crumbling. She gripped the banister tighter. She opened her mouth but no words would come out.

"You'll never have to see my face again to remind you of everything you couldn't have. So now, Celeste, we're finally even. I have nothing and neither do you. My only consolation is that I have plans for the rest of my life and you've never had a life to plan."

With that she turned on her heel and slammed out of the door.

Frank stared at the phone. He could feel his pulse beat in his ears. How could the papers have ever known about the computer program? How could they have ever traced it back to him? A trickle of perspiration ran down the hollow of his spine. His mouth was dry. He needed water but his throat felt so tight he'd never be able to swallow. He wrung his hands together. He had to do something. But what? That bastard reporter had given him forty-eight hours to decide. Frank's green eyes searched frantically around the room as if some corner of his office held the answer to his dilemma. Why now, when everything else was caving in on him?

And then everything came together in one word... *Victoria.*

Maxwell looked over at Reese and smiled. She was fast asleep, curled up beneath her blanket. So far so good. He silently prayed that her nightmares would not pursue her across the skies.

Depressing the silver button on his left, he released his seat and let it slip back into a reclining position. He took his briefcase from between his feet and opened it searching for the mail that Carmen said she'd included. Sifting through the mail he sorted it into piles of "immediate attention" and "can wait." Near the bottom of the pile he pulled up a plain white envelope, postmarked the day before from Maryland. His pulse quickened with annoyance. The handwriting was all too familiar. He started to toss the letter that he knew was written by Victoria, but curiosity stopped him. He slit the envelope open and began scanning the letter-perfect scrawl.

Midway through the second paragraph, his stomach muscles tightened. A hot flush exploded in his head. He shook his head and reread the words because they couldn't be right. Yet there was a corner of his mind that knew every word was true. He began to feel sick as a wave of nausea tumbled in his gut.

Seemingly in slow motion he turned toward Reese's sleeping form and felt as if his world had come to a sudden end. How would he ever be able to hold her and love her again, knowing that doing so went against every iota of ethics that he possessed?

Chapter 29

Tokyo, Japan

Mioshi Tasaka looked up from the notes on his desk in response to the light that flickered over his office door indicating that his assistant, Namicho Ichibahn, requested entrance. It was a device he'd had installed at his offices and at home, to compensate for his loss of hearing. Or so everyone thought. Tasaka had learned years ago that what most considered to be disabilities could be used as *abilities* when implemented by the right people.

It all began some twenty years earlier when Mioshi Tasaka had what the doctors thought would be minor surgery. However, the simple tonsillectomy turned Tasaka, a poor but aspiring singer, into a very rich man. The slip of the young surgeon's scalpel had caused extensive damage to the throat. Tasaka's once rich basso, which had graced many concert halls in Tokyo, was never the same. Or so it was thought. One promising career was destroyed and a new one was born.

Seizing the opportunity, Tasaka hired the best attorney he could find. His lawsuit nearly brought the historic hospital to the brink of bankruptcy. However, being a benevolent man and an opportunist, Tasaka used his windfall to purchase 51 percent of the hospital's stock, making him its primary stockholder. He brought in friends and relatives to oversee and manage the facility, turning the hospital into a prosperous family business. That was the beginning of his empire.

Over the years, Tasaka built a reputation for being an astute businessman, knowing when to strike and how deep. He owned, or had a hand in, any and every enterprise throughout Japan that turned a profit. Politicians came to him for advice and no decisions were made without his approval. During the two decades of his reign, he'd amassed a fortune in land and building developments. But always with his eye toward the future, Tasaka entered the world of computer technology. Which was how Maxwell Knight's proposal had been brought to his attention.

"Come in please," he said in his nearly inaudible voice.

"*Sumimasen,* please, Tasaka-san. Should I make arrangements for dinner?" his personal assistant of five years inquired, giving a short bow of respect. Straightening to her full five-foot-three-inch height, the striking young woman stood patiently in front of Tasaka's black lacquer desk.

Although Tasaka had given his dinner instructions early in the day, he was prone to change his mind at a moment's notice, an idiosyncrasy that continued to baffle and infuriate his friends and adversaries. But it always gave Tasaka the upper hand and kept many at his beck and call. He thought it was quite amusing.

"They will remain the same," he said, his eyes slowly moving up from behind heavy lids to rest on his assistant's placid face. "Unless Knight-san changes his mind," he added in his hushed, practiced whisper. "Inform the others." Namicho bowed and left as discreetly as she had arrived.

Tasaka steepled his thick fingers in front of his nose, his heavy-lidded eyes appeared closed to the casual observer.

So the prodigal son had finally come home. Tasaka's lizard-like smile sent a chill through the air.

Maxwell and Reese arrived at Narita Airport some eleven and a half hours after take-off from LAX. Reese felt totally disoriented realizing that not only was it the next day, it was an additional four hours ahead.

"I don't see how people can do this." Reese yawned as they stood in front of the limousine waiting for Max's chauffeur and interpreter, Daisuke, to finish loading their luggage into the trunk. "The time difference is a killer." She slid her arm through the curve of his and immediately felt his muscles tighten. She frowned and looked up at him. "Max. What is it? You've barely said a word to me in hours. Are you worried about your meeting?"

Maxwell had been tormented by the implications of the note from Victoria—if it were true. And as much as he wanted to deny the things she'd said, he couldn't ignore the fact that she knew things that she would have no reason or way of knowing if it weren't true.

He looked down into her questioning gaze, and his stomach dipped. She already had so much to deal with. The last thing she needed at the moment was another trauma. Somehow he had to reach deep inside himself and come to terms with some moral and ethical decisions. The very nature of Victoria's claim precluded him from having any further intimate relationship with Reese. But how could he do that when her very existence fueled his soul? He would have to find a way to get beyond his ingrained convictions if their relationship was to survive. The injustice of it all left him bereft of any tangible emotion.

He gave her his most disarming smile and tweaked her nose, delighting in her giggles. "That's part of it," he admitted, glad for the out. "This is probably one of the biggest negotiations I've been involved in. Everything I say and do from here on out is crucial."

Her smile and the glow from her eyes warmed him from the inside out. "You've prepared yourself for this moment for the past year, Max. You've looked at everything from every angle. You've created a product that the world will clamor for. You'll get what you want out of this deal."

The left corner of his mouth turned up in a grin. "Thanks. I guess I needed a little stroking," he said sheepishly.

She tiptoed and planted a light kiss on his lips. We all do every now and then. Do you want to run your game plan by me?"

"Sure. Why not? We'll talk at the hotel. Even though I know that dinner tonight won't include business, I'd rather be prepared."

"Your bags are in the car, Knight-san," Daisuke said in perfect English, bowing as he opened the door.

Maxwell bowed in return and held Reese's elbow as she stepped into the lush leather interior of the Lincoln. Once they were seated, he instructed Daisuke in lilting Japanese.

Reese grinned, and whispered, "What did you just say? All I caught was Hyatt."

"I told him we're going to the Hyatt but he should wait because I have a meeting this evening and I'll need him to interpret for me."

Reese's milk-chocolate brow bunched in confusion. "But you speak fluent Japanese. Why do you need an interpreter?"

"To make my soon-to-be business associates more

comfortable. It also gives me an edge when they think I can't speak or understand the language." He winked conspiratorially.

Reese slowly shook her head. "Aren't you the clever one," she teased.

"I work hard at it."

Maxwell faced the full-length mirror shifting his burgundy silk patterned tie from left to right until it was perfectly centered. "I'm sorry I can't take you with me, sweetheart," he said, appraising his appearance.

"No problem." Reese came up behind him and ran her hands across his suited shoulders smoothing the charcoal-gray jacket in place. "I'll get some work done while you're gone, order room service and get our clothes organized."

He turned to face her and slid his arms around her waist. "Tomorrow I'll take you on a tour, and show you the locations I've selected for our sites."

"Well if this tour is anything like the one in L.A., I'd better forget about doing everything I've said and just go straight to bed!"

Maxwell tossed his head back and laughed. "That was because I didn't like you very much, or at least that's what I was trying to tell myself. I figured if I wore you out, you'd give up and go home."

"And look at all of the fun you would've missed if your diabolical little plan had worked."

"The best laid plans." He sighed, sarcastically.

Reese poked him in the chest. "Very funny."

Maxwell leaned down and kissed her cheek. "Gotta run." He moved toward the door.

Reese blinked in surprise then stepped back to let him pass. "A kiss on the cheek?"

"For now," he replied offhandedly, his unwritten rules of ethics rumbling to the surface.

"I hope it's not the start of something," she asked more than stated.

He turned to face her as he stood in the open doorway. "Of course not. I just have a lot on my mind at the moment." He knew his explanation sounded weak from the narrowing of Reese's eyes. "I'll see you in a few hours," he added quickly and strode down the corridor to the elevator.

Reese felt her stomach rise and fall as she watched him walk away. "Good luck," she said almost to herself. Mindlessly, she closed the door and stood there for several moments engaging in a mental retrospect of the past few hours. Maxwell had been acting strangely since midway through the flight. It was as if he were trying to put distance between them. He attributed his behavior to the meetings that faced him. But instinct told her it was more than that.

"What are you keeping from me this time, Max?"

Maxwell settled himself in the backseat of the limousine and stared, without seeing, out of the tinted window.

The teeming streets of Tokyo were awash with humanity, rushing in every direction and in stiff competition from a multitude of cars and jitneys. Maxwell saw none of this. His thoughts were focused on the letter from Victoria even as much as they should have been focused on his meeting with Tasaka. He knew he would have to tell Reese of Victoria's allegation. He'd already experienced her ire when he'd kept things from her.

Reflectively, he massaged his smooth chin. What would it all mean in the end? Perhaps he should try to verify Victoria's claim before he presented it to Reese.

He inhaled deeply and shut his eyes. For the moment, he would have to put that aspect of his life on hold. He could not risk being at anything but optimum when he sat down with Tasaka. If there were even the slightest bit of hesitation or uncertainty on his part, Tasaka would eat him alive.

For the balance of the twenty-minute trip, Maxwell employed the relaxation techniques of *Tai chi*. When he opened his eyes again, the car was pulling up in front of Tasaka Enterprises, the corporate headquarters for his multiple business endeavors.

The seven-story structure was a picture of high-tech tinted glass, chrome and steel. Maxwell's dark eyes traveled upward in concert with the outdoor elevator as it made its slow ascent. Light from the waning sun bounced off the steel support beams, giving the building the illusion of being illuminated from the heavens.

Maxwell alighted from the car, and stepped onto the street. "Ready?" he asked Daisuke, pushing through the revolving doors.

Mioshi heard the knock in concert with the flashing red light above the door. "Come in," he said in his hushed voice.

Namicho bobbed her head before speaking. "Maxwell Knight has arrived, Tasaka-san."

"Show him in."

Moments later Maxwell strode into the office and was momentarily taken aback by the stark similarities between his office in New York and Tasaka's. Maxwell's keen eyes quickly swept across the room assessing its contents.

The exquisitely appointed room spoke of wealth and taste. Tasaka surrounded himself with Japanese art and artifacts that adorned his walls and table tops. His desk, the obvious vocal point of the office, was a massive structure of black lacquer with winged corners rimmed in gold and jade. It remotely resembled the great Japanese sailing ships of long ago. Jade vases with matching bowls graced the credenza. Behind Mioshi, the metropolis of Tokyo spanned beyond him from the smoked floor-to-ceiling window. The paneled walls were soundproof, Maxwell knew. A man like Tasaka wouldn't have it any other way. Off to the far right of the office was the traditional low-level table surrounded by pillows. Inwardly, Maxwell smiled.

Mioshi Tasaka gingerly pushed himself up into a standing position, supporting his arthritic body by bracing his hands on the smooth finish of his black and jade lacquer desk.

"*Kon'nichiwa,* Tasaka-san," Maxwell said with a low bow as he stepped fully into the room.

Mioshi nodded in response, surprised by Maxwell's flawless delivery.

Maxwell turned toward his companion and dipped his upturned hand in Daisuke's direction "This is Daisuke Uchiyama. He will interpret for me." Daisuke bowed and repeated Maxwell's statement.

Aaah. So he does not know the language after all, Mioshi concluded, relaxing. Just a few choice phrases. Mioshi inclined his head and extended his hand toward the chairs that flanked his desk, never once extending his hand in greeting as was becoming common custom in Japan.

There was a time that handshaking was considered rude. But with westernization the practice was more commonplace. However, the fact that Mioshi held fast to this Japanese custom, in the midst of his westernization, gave Maxwell some of the psychological insight that he needed. He was certain that Mioshi expected that he would feel slighted and thrown off guard by what outwardly appeared to be blatant rudeness by American standards.

Maxwell took a seat to Mioshi's right, maintaining his ambiguous facade.

"Thank you for taking the time out of your busy schedule

to meet with me earlier than planned," Maxwell began.
Daisuke started to translate, when Mioshi halted him with
an up-raised palm.

In rapid Japanese he said, "I understand the English
language very well. I prefer not to speak it. Interpret please
for Knight-san."

Maxwell hid his amusement behind a guileless expression
as he listened to the translation that he already understood.
He nodded. So, it would certainly be a game of cat and mouse
throughout the negotiations, he surmised. Mioshi's tactic
was to keep him at a disadvantage. Now that he understood
the approach, he knew how to proceed. And even with that
understanding, he had the most eerie feeling of dealing with
a Japanese version of himself.

Reese's amber eyes darted back and forth between the
notes to her left and the screen of her laptop to her right.
Agile fingers tapped in rapid succession bringing the story
of Maxwell Knight to printed life.

So far she'd included quotes from dozens of people she'd
interviewed, interspersed with facts and figures about M.K.
Enterprises. Little by little, the elusive Maxwell Knight was
becoming three-dimensional. But Reese knew she needed
more, and she believed she'd find the missing pieces to the
M.K. puzzle here in Tokyo.

Much of what made him who he was rested in the part of
him that was Japanese. From his father and stepmother he'd
learned, to a degree, who he was as an African-American.
He'd experienced through societal prejudice what it was like
to be a black man in America. But the other half of who he
was, which he manifested through martial arts, mastering the
language, the culture, and the genius that make the Japanese
giants in technology, ran through his veins as well. But he
never had that other half to relate to.

Even knowing these things and living both lives, he never knew where he belonged. She imagined that's a dilemma that many biracial children faced. To embrace the culture of one parent was almost to negate that of the other. And even more difficult for those who never had the chance to make a choice and live in a society that remained bigoted about mixed-race children. Where do they belong? And Reese knew that Max compensated for the void in his life by becoming an overachiever, which allowed him to transcend culture and ethnicity but left him in his own purgatory.

Reese leaned back in her seat and squeezed the bridge of her nose between the tips of her fingers.

How would she find the words to express the complexities of Maxwell Knight—the man?

She saved her information and pressed the power button, shutting off the computer. With a flick of her finger she closed the lightweight top and pushed it toward the back of the desk.

Standing, she rotated her stiff shoulders and stretched her arms over her head, pushing her palms toward the ceiling, punctuating it all with a soft groan of relief. She walked out of the small alcove that she would use as her office and stepped down into the main living area of the suite.

Their living quarters for the next few weeks were actually two adjoining suites which occupied the Penthouse level of the Hyatt Regency. How Carmen was able to pull off such a coupe in that short space of time, was nothing short of a miracle, Reese marveled, running her hand through her hair.

Thinking about Carmen brought a smile to Reese's mouth along with remembering why they were in Japan weeks early.

Walking barefoot across the white-carpeted living room floor, she pushed open the polished oak sliding doors that led to the bedroom. Immediately upon entering the lavish rooms, decorated with eighteenth-century furnishings, her gaze fell upon the suitcase and travel bags.

Reese groaned, remembering her promise to Maxwell to put their things away. Pushing down her reluctance with a long breath, she padded across the vanilla-tinted room and began unpacking the suitcases and garment bags.

Rhythmically, she moved between the bed and the double closet. A half hour later, she'd finished putting away the last of Maxwell's shirts. Hands on hips, she slowly turned in a circle, surveying the room. She pursed her lips and shook her head. Max had carelessly tossed the jacket, slacks and shirt he'd worn earlier across the back of the armchair. She crossed the room in a huff and snatched up the discarded clothing, sucking her teeth in annoyance. He kept his home spotless. She hoped this wasn't an indication of how he intended to keep their hotel room.

She shook out the jacket as she approached the closet in search of one more hanger, when a half-folded letter fell out and floated to the floor at her feet.

Bending down from the knee, Reese picked up the paper intent on sticking it back in his pocket when the bold signature of *Victoria Davenport* caught and held her eye. Reese felt the pulse in her temple begin to throb. A swift surge jolted her stomach. Briefly she closed her eyes, the ethical part of her wanting to put the letter back, the female side needing to know its contents.

She swallowed hard as a hot flush of guilt pulsed through her veins. Taking the letter she sat down at the small desk. She stared at the pages, knowing that she had crossed the line of trust the instant she did not promptly return the letter when it had fallen.

The beat of her heart thudded wildly as if she were being pursued. Maybe she was—by her conscience, she thought as shaky fingers unfolded the sheets of soft pink paper.

Dear Max,
I know I'm the last person you want to hear from but
there are some things you should know about me and
about Reese.

When I was ten years old, my aunt Celeste came
to me and told me about a half sister. Her name was
Reese. We didn't share the same mother, but we did
share the same father, Hamilton Delaware.

I was so elated to learn that I had a family and was
eager to meet my sister. My aunt quickly informed me
that it could never happen. Although my father loved
me dearly, my existence would remain a secret. He had
no desire to leave his family or ruin it by announcing
that he had another daughter. I was devastated, and
I think that's when my resentment for Reese began. I
believed that she had it all. She was the golden child
and I was the black sheep—the unmentionable bastard
child of Hamilton Delaware.

I never had the opportunity to confront my father
before he died in the car accident. I went on with my
life and a part of me was almost happy that Reese no
longer had the family that I'd coveted.

It wasn't until several days ago that yet another
layer of my life was stripped away. Frank Murphy,
the man who I believed was my uncle is actually my
father, not Hamilton Delaware.

For the first time since she began reading, Reese allowed
herself to breathe. "Thank God," she whispered in a gush.
She squeezed her eyes shut in relief. But when she opened
them again, they fell on the words that were just as mind-
blowing.

Celeste Winston and Frank Murphy had a long-stand-
ing affair. Dear Celeste was also having an affair with

Hamilton Delaware, her sister's husband and Frank's best friend. I was the result of one of those liaisons. According to Frank, I am his daughter. But my dear mother was so obsessed with Hamilton that she convinced herself, Frank, Hamilton, and me, that I was Hamilton Delaware's daughter. Hamilton paid her every month to keep the secret, and Frank, being the love-struck fool that he was, made sure we were taken care of even after Hamilton's death.

When I confronted Celeste she denied it all. She said that Frank was just a bitter man who never forgave her for not loving him. That much may or may not be true. I could see lies in her eyes, hear them pouring from her lips, I just couldn't tell which ones. She was afraid that to reveal the truth to me would make me hate her for what she'd done and she would lose the one family member she had left. I realize that now, and that is how she will pay for what she has done to me.

Why am I telling you all of this? I asked myself the same question as I wrote each word, completed each line. Because, Max, in order for me to make restitution in my life, my slate has to be clean. Celeste will never tell Reese the truth. Frank hopes, for some reason, that she never regains her memory. I had hoped that this revelation would put a thorn in your relationship with Reese and bring you back to me. That you would be unable to see yourself in bed with your ex-lover's sister. But deep inside I know that being the man you are, you will find a way to reconcile it all if you care enough. And my gut instinct tells me that you do. Reese. Reese. So much centers around her. So much seems to depend on her. I envy her and feel sorry for her in the same breath.

*Do what you will with this information. But I
wanted you to know and hope that it would somehow
help to explain who and why I am.*

*I've gone to a friend at the Washington Post and
told them the truth about the computer program that
you designed and the Air Force claimed as their own.
Stan Tilden is very thorough. There's bound to be an
investigation. And perhaps Frank will finally pay for
the things he's done. It was him who paid me to get the
information. I've kept careful notes, tapes and deposit
slips. They're all in a safe deposit box in Washington.
Stan has the number.*

*I hope some good can come out of all this, Max. I
know I hurt you, but perhaps now that wrong can be
righted. It seems such a waste that I spent the better
part of my life resenting a woman who never knew I
existed and whose life was no better than mine. Hers
has been stolen by fate, mine by betrayal. All the best
to you Max.*
Victoria Davenport

A single tear threaded its way down Reese's arched cheek
falling on the ink-blue words, making them shimmer and
merge on the page. Her heart clenched, thudded, then settled
down to a steady rhythm.

Slowly she refolded the sheets of pink paper and returned
them to Max's jacket pocket.

A sister, and the possibility that it was Victoria… The idea
was so… Her thoughts were shattered by the ringing phone.
Reese quickly crossed the room and picked up the phone.

"Yes. Hello? Oh, yes, send him up." She wiped her
eyes, dashed in the bathroom and splashed cold water on
her face.

*   *   *

"Max told me a great deal about you," Chris Lewis, Max's friend said, taking a seat on the sofa. "I'm glad to finally meet you."

Reese smiled. "Thank you. I'm happy to say the same." She sat down opposite him on the love seat and crossed her long legs. "I'm hoping Max will be back shortly. He's been gone about three hours."

"Well, if every rumor I've ever heard about Mioshi Tasaka is true, he'll be a while." Chris grinned, flashing a pair of perfect dimples in his saffron-colored face, set off by startling gray eyes and dark brown close-cropped hair.

Reese chuckled and nodded. "Max told me you're in a tournament."

Chris nodded. "It's an international tournament to raise money for the hungry children around the world. Our next stop is Korea."

"Sounds wonderful and it's definitely needed. But it must be hectic, too."

"It can be, but I enjoy what I do, so it never seems like work."

"That's how it is for me when I'm on assignment," Reese said, feeling totally at ease with Chris. "It's truly a joy when you can find pleasure in your work."

"Absolutely."

"Can I order something from room service for you?"

"No. Thanks. As a matter of fact," he breathed, standing up, "I'm gonna shove off. I thought I'd catch Max. Just let him know I stopped by and I'll be in touch tomorrow."

Reese followed him to the door, taking note of the way his broad, muscular shoulders moved beneath his fitted gray knit shirt. Chris wasn't much taller than she. He must be just under six feet, she concluded. But he gave the illusion of height from his proud gait and long, fluid strides.

He turned toward her, framed by the doorway. He kissed her cheek. "Lock the door," he instructed softly, his meaning clear.

Her heart knocked against her chest as the reality of her situation rose to the surface. Reese bit down on her lip and nodded, swallowing down her fears.

With that, Chris headed off down the corridor to the elevator. Reese slowly pushed the door closed and turned both locks. She turned away and headed back toward the bedroom where she was faced once again with the issue of Victoria Davenport.

How long had Maxwell known? she wondered, sitting down on the edge of the bed. How did he feel about it and why hadn't he said anything to her? Or did he plan to?

The turning of the locks drew her attention away from the disturbing thoughts. Quickly she got up and was standing in the living area as Maxwell stepped through the doorway.

"Hi," he greeted and instantly knew that something was wrong from the lack of sparkle in her eyes and the stiff set of her shoulders.

Reese swallowed, looked down at her clenched hands then across at Max. "Tell me it won't make a difference between us," she whispered in a shaky voice. "I don't think I could stand it if it did."

She'd found the letter. Maxwell briefly shut his eyes and felt his heart surge and shift in his chest. Slowly he walked toward her and took her in his arms, holding her as tightly as humanly possible. He felt her body shudder and heave with the sobs she tried to contain. And he realized at that moment that he could not let anyone or anything come between them.

"We'll work it out, baby. I swear we will," he uttered in a ragged voice.

Chapter 30

Mioshi slowly stuck his arm out of the car door allowing Keno, his driver, to assist him to his feet. Rising to his full height Mioshi brushed the folds out of his pearl gray suit and looked up at the House of Tasaka. The elegant four-story establishment was regarded throughout the Tokyo elite as the most lavish of its kind. It was located in the central business district in Akasanka, the playground for the rich and influential. Everyone in Japan was aware that many of the behind-the-scenes political maneuvers and big business transactions took place right in the dining rooms of Tasaka.

Mioshi smiled. Even at this late hour, customers were still milling in and out, walking along the deck toward the water. Some of the most beautiful and talented geishas in all of Japan worked here. But none were more beautiful or artistically brilliant than his sister.

* * *

Maxwell held her until her sobs subsided into soft sniffles. "I'm sorry," she mumbled against his damp shirt. "I really didn't mean to fall apart like that."

He stroked her back in a soothing up and down motion. "I felt like doing the same thing when I read the letter."

Reese giggled softly and hiccuped. They both began to laugh, slowly at first until it built, spilling over to ease their souls.

"When will it all end, Max?" She wiped her eyes with the back of her hand.

"I wish I knew." He heaved a deep sigh, blowing out air through pursed lips. He shook his head in frustration. "It seems that every time we get over one hurdle, another is thrown at us." He sat down on the edge of the brocade couch, resting his forearms on his muscled thighs. He stared at the white carpeted floor as if by some miracle the answer rested in the layers of thick nylon and wool.

He looked up into her melancholy eyes and reached for her hands. "I didn't mean for you to find the letter. You didn't need to find out that way. Not like that." He squeezed her hands.

Her smile was tentative as she spoke. "Max, in the time that I've known you, I've come to understand, realize and accept certain things about you. One thing is irrefutable: you are not a careless man. Everything you do, every move you make is carefully thought out and planned. Your life is like a master chess game." Her gaze held no admonishment, it remained gentle yet contemplative. "You wanted me to find the letter, Max," she said, her throaty voice heavy with conviction when she saw his jaw clench in denial. "Maybe not intentionally, but you did. Since day one, you've had trouble telling me the things I needed to know." She removed her hands from his grasp and gently smoothed away the frown forming between his sleek black brows. "Your subconscious found a way to let you off the hook." She brushed her thumb across his lips.

His voice was tender, almost a murmur. "How did you get to know so much?"

Reese lowered her gaze and grinned. "I've been analyzed enough times to open my own office, remember? Besides, I've helped Lynnette with more psychology reports than I care to count. That's the only reason why I understand my own illness. What I suffer from is called repression. The doctors said it would take a strong stimulus, something related to the accident, to trigger my memory. They could never determine what that something was without traumatizing me further." She looked into his eyes. "Strangely enough it was you, because you look so much like your father. That began what's called the 'cascade effect,' which has resulted in the dreams and the return of the headaches." She laughed halfheartedly. "I should have gotten a psychology degree in abstentia."

Maxwell hugged her to him. "You're not angry?"

"I should be. But my biggest concern is how much of what Victoria said is true? It would explain so much. And the more I think about it, the more I realize that it must be true. My father had an affair with my mother's sister. Somehow, my mother found out. My God, Max, she found this out just before she died. Did she know about Victoria also? What must that have done to her if she died thinking that my father was Victoria's father as well?"

"You can't torture yourself with thoughts like that, Reese. The reality is, we may never know and even if we did, there's nothing that we can do to change it."

Slowly Reese nodded, silently agreeing to Max's logic. She frowned, sinking deep in thought. "Maybe the guy from the

Post is just the ammunition we need to get Frank Murphy off of our backs," she said suddenly.

Maxwell's eyes brightened. He sat up straighter. "If Murphy has his hands filled with an impending investigation about the computer chip theft, he may not be able to concentrate on us."

"It would certainly give me the time I need to get the rest of the information. I'm going to have to talk with my aunt, Victoria, Larry...and your father," she added gently.

"Do whatever you have to, Reese. You have my support and anything else that I can put at your disposal. You know that."

"Max," she said with steady awakening, "do you realize what all this will mean for your career when what the government did to you is uncovered? You're going to be a very wealthy man."

"I already have more money than I could ever spend. I wish that's all there was to it." He paused. "I'm just worried that Stan may never get to tell his story either."

She leaned forward, her eyes burning with passion. "Then we have to make sure that he does."

Mioshi entered the house and was immediately attended to by a young *maiko*—or geisha in training.

"Will you be having dinner tonight, Tasaka-san?" the *maiko* asked in a lilting voice, bowing as she spoke.

He patted her lightly on the shoulder. "Not tonight. I need to have a private room. Is there one available?" Mioshi had no need for a private room, he simply wanted to establish his importance by having one made available for him.

"Oh, yes. For you, of course, Tasaka-san." She smiled brightly and threaded her arm through his, leading him down the lavish sitting rooms that were occupied by the Tokyo elite.

All whom Mioshi encountered bowed in deference to him as he passed.

The *maiko* made light conversation, asking about his day and inquiring about his health.

In the entertainment room, about twenty men sat on huge silk patterned pillows watching an operatic performance by the geishas. In the center of the room, four geishas were engaged in a ceremonial dance accompanied by haunting music and song. Mioshi nodded in approval.

"Is my sister in her office?" he asked the *maiko*.

"Yes. She is reviewing the night's receipts, Tasaka-san."

"Then I will see her now. Tell her I am here."

"Right away." The *maiko* bowed and hurried off to find her mistress, leaving the soft scent of jasmine floating in her wake.

Mioshi decided to stand while he watched the performance, leaning on his cane of jade with the signature gold head of the dragon. Within moments his sister slid open the rice-paper door and stepped into the room.

She was just as stunning at fifty-one as she was thirty years ago when she'd become a full geisha. She had a regal bearing that rivaled the empress. Her skin, the color of pure honey, remained unlined and flawless. Her jet black hair, without a trace of gray, was fashioned in a single braid and wrapped intricately atop her head. This was the most powerful woman in Tokyo. In her ears had been whispered the secrets of the nation for nearly three decades. Even he sought out her wisdom and counsel.

She wore a full-length red and gold kimono with a lavish gold sash that cinched her tiny waist. Her petite feet encased in gold silk slippers moved soundlessly across the floor. She stood before him and bowed.

"Brother Mioshi," she said in greeting.

Mioshi bowed in return. "Sukihara."

* * *

"How did your meeting go with Tasaka?" Reese asked as she prepared for bed. She selected a soft yellow teddy from the dresser.

"Very interesting to say the least," Maxwell replied, unbuttoning his shirt. "It's strange," he said upon reflection, "but it was as if I knew him."

Reese turned toward him and squinted her eyes in confusion. "What do you mean?"

"It's hard to explain," he said struggling to find the right words. "He seems a lot like me."

Reese chuckled. "You're kidding."

"Not at all. Mioshi Tasaka plays by the same rules I do. He gives nothing away and has every intention of keeping me in the hot seat."

"Sounds like you're going to have your hands full," Reese added, sliding the teddy over her body.

"But there was something else, Reese," he said as the thoughts formalized in his mind. He sat down on the edge of the bed and pulled off his black Italian loafers. "I felt some sort of…" he frowned, "a kinship."

Reese crossed the room and sat down beside him. "I don't know what you mean."

Maxwell let out a long breath. "Neither do I," he admitted. "But I just felt something, some connection. I can't put my finger on it. I just felt that I knew him and what's more eerie, that he knew me. And not because of anything he'd read or had been told. It was in his eyes."

"What did you see?" she asked in a hushed voice of concern.

He turned to face her, his gaze unwavering. "Recognition."

"So brother, what is he like, my son?" Suki asked once they were behind closed doors.

Mioshi gingerly sat on the lounge chair of silk brocade, rested his cane against its ornate oak frame, and leaned back against the plush cushion before speaking. "Will you not even offer your only brother a cup of sake before we discuss your illegitimate son?" he asked in a clear voice, all traces of his feigned infirmity gone.

Sukihara smiled and nodded in compliance. She crossed the heavily carpeted room and took a tiny porcelain teacup from the bar and filled it with the powerful drink.

Mioshi thanked her, drank it down, and requested another. "Your son has grown to be a very formidable man," Mioshi finally said, setting the cup down on the table next to him. "He is quick, decisive and has a keen business sense. All good qualities."

"Is that all you saw?" she questioned, knowing that her brother was being intentionally evasive.

"What else was there to see?"

She cast him a long look from dark eyes identical to her son's. "Why must we play these ambiguous games, Mioshi? We save those skills for the conference room. You know well what I mean. I'm not interested in his business skills. If he did not have them, he would not have gotten this far."

Mioshi chuckled deep in his throat, mildly enjoying his sister's annoyance. "Oh, do you mean does he look like you— like one of us?"

"If you know that is what I mean, then you should answer," she stated in her mellifluent voice.

Mioshi smiled and took his cane, pushing himself to a standing position. "Perhaps you should see him for yourself to make that judgment."

"He is not to know who I am, Mioshi," she stated emphatically. She faced her brother with her hands folded in front of her.

"Do you think he will not find out once his company is

established here?" he challenged. "Then what will become of you and your liaison with the governor?" His smile was taunt.

Sukihara knew the moment that she'd been told of Maxwell's intention to set up operations in Tokyo, that her existence risked discovery. The governor had been her patron for more than twenty years. Although times in Japan had changed, he had not. Murayama Hosokawa was from the old school of thought. Japanese stayed with Japanese. Yes, geishas could entertain any man who was willing to pay for their services, but to indulge in an intimate relationship outside of your race was to disgrace yourself and your people. If Murayama were to discover that she'd been involved with James Knight, and had his son, he would withdraw his support and bring all the other politicians and businessmen with him. Even her brother's far-reaching influence would not be enough to stop Murayama's wrath. Her life as she knew it would come to an end, and this life was all that she had.

"Then you must not allow Maxwell to establish his business here," she said in finality.

"My dear sister, you do not instruct me on how to run my business affairs and I will do the same for you." He ambled slowly toward the door. "Your advice, however, is always welcome. And my advice to you *okasan* is to come to terms with your reality. Tomorrow night you will meet your son."

Suki spend a sleepless night fraught with dreams of imminent disaster. She was well past the age of starting over. Even though many "mothers"—or older retired geishas—lived out their lives in nunneries or serving as advisors to the new mistress, these were not options for Suki.

For twenty years, she'd worked hard at mastering her skills of music, song and dance. She was fluent in English, French and Spanish. She'd held court to some of the most notable men across the globe. She'd performed for cabinet members. Her keen ear and insight into world events had garnered her the trust and respect of politicians and businessmen alike. Her career and her fortune were rivaled by none. Discovery could erase all of that as if it never existed.

Weary, Suki opened her tired ebony eyes and looked out onto the red sun, rising majestically over the mountaintops. Levels of iridescent orange and gold light shimmered in a hazy pattern across the horizon. The signal of a new day. The day that she would meet her son.

Her heart beat a bit faster as the idea settled heavily in her stomach. Laboriously, she rose from the downy comfort of her futon, pulling a white silk robe over her nude body. Walking silently across the room to the window, she pulled aside the white gossamer curtains and looked at her world.

So much had changed since she'd come to this place as an eager but rebellious fifteen-year-old, she mused languidly...

Ichitaro, the mistress of the house, had immediately taken to the high-strung teenager and was determined to make her the quintessential geisha. She saw limitless promise in the hauntingly beautiful Sukihara, and she set out to teach her everything she knew. After all, Suki was her own patron's sister. And she would always do what she could to please Mioshi.

Suki was a brilliant student. She mastered her skills with ease and was a favorite among the *okyakusama*—or honored guests. Yet there seemed to be nothing that Ichitaro could do to contain Suki's willful ways. She was headstrong and determined to do things the way she thought was best, which was more with her heart than with her brilliant mind. Suki was a pure romantic at heart, a quality that was not befitting the lifestyle of a geisha. Geishas did not have the option of falling in love. But Sukihara did just that anyway. She fell in love with James Knight.

Suki brushed away a stray strand of her lustrous black hair, tucking it securely behind her ear. As the sun slowly began to infuse the earth with light, she, too, became filled with memories of the past…

Ichitaro had been furious to find out that Suki was pregnant. More furious to discover that she actually fancied herself in love with the black soldier. Suki was immediately sent away to have her baby. She could only return to her former life if the child were a girl. The stigma of being the child of a geisha, and thus illegitimate, is felt far more keenly by male than by female children, Ichitaro had explained.

The cultural style of maleness in Japan dictated female subservience, at least on the surface. The refined nuances of service in which geishas are trained are not meant for men. As a result, life is extremely hard on the egos of men who live within the geisha world.

The pampering of male egos, which is the cornerstone of geisha skills, does not extend to family. For males of geisha families, it is their mothers, sisters, daughters, or wives who are the leaders within that world in terms of actual work and socially recognized authority. This is probably the only place in Japanese society where the birth of a baby girl is more welcome than a boy.

When her son was born, Suki was torn between a mother's love and the life that she longed to live. If she kept her child, she could not hope to aspire to run her own establishment. She could not subject her son to life within her world. Male children reared in a geisha community grew up resentful and displayed their ambivalence to their lifestyle by being wayward and profligate.

Suki wanted more than that for her beautiful son. When she looked down into his dark, inquisitive eyes, she knew he was destined for great things, and in order for that to happen she would have to let him go. She could never hope to have a real life outside. No respectable Japanese man would love and marry her. What was she to do?

During her six-month absence from Ichitaro's house, she had not communicated with James and he was unaware that she'd borne him a son. Then one morning, Ichitaro came to visit her.

"It is time for you to return, Suki. The longer you stay with the child, the harder it will be to let him go."

"But what should I do, mother? I cannot just leave him."

From the sleeve of her kimono, Ichitaro removed a long, slim ivory-colored envelope. She handed it to Suki.

"What is this?"

"Open it."

Suki peeled open the envelope and removed the contents. Her dark sloping eyes widened in astonishment, then filled with tears. "Tickets to America? You are sending me away," she cried. "But what will I do? I know no one…"

"Hush. You are to take the baby to this James Knight's home. Give the baby to his wife."

Suki's skin heated with embarrassment.

"So you thought I did not know that your lover had a wife?" Sadly she shook her head. "Always the romantic, Sukihara. He will never leave his wife for you. You cannot adequately raise a boy child in our world. You have no other means of survival except with me. This is your only choice. You will give the woman her husband's son and you will return and go on with your life. You, above all the other *maiko,* have the potential to run your own establishment someday."

Suki lowered her gaze and knew that Ichitaro was right, even as her words broke her heart. "How did you know where to find his…wife?"

"My ears are always open. My friends are far and wide. My

reach even farther. That is how I know." She stepped closer to Suki and rested her hands on Suki's shoulders. "One day you, too, will have all that I have at your disposal."

And so Suki had done as she was instructed. She returned to Tokyo and devoted all of her energy and time into being what was expected of her, and became the most sought-after geisha in all of Tokyo.

Because of her notability, artistic skills, business acumen and extraordinary beauty, she'd come to the attention of Murayama Hosokawa, then a rising star in the Diet—the Japanese legislature. He had become her patron—or sole supporter and suitor. It was through and because of him that her own star continued to rise.

Sukihara closed the door to her past, cut off her letters of inquiry to Claudia and dedicated herself to her life, never again looking back.

She turned away from the window, her memories retreating as a dream upon first light. Now her past had returned to haunt her, and she was powerless to stop its pursuit.

Chapter 31

"My dinner meeting with Tasaka isn't until later this evening," Max said, stifling a yawn. He curled closer to Reese's warm body. "I wanted to take you on a tour." He kissed her behind her ear.

"Oh, I don't have to beg this time?" she teased, turning on her side to face him.

"Very funny. I figured I'd give you a break. I hate to see a beautiful woman beg." He grinned wickedly.

Reese pinched him hard on the behind until he yelped for mercy.

"Now that's what I call beggin'!" She leaped up out of the bed, scurried into the bathroom and slammed the door, barely escaping Maxwell's grasp.

"You've got to come out sometime," Max called out, gingerly rubbing his right cheek.

"Be a man. You got what you deserved," she taunted.

"I'll show you how much of a man I can be when you step

back out here, miss," he threatened in a voice full of sensual promise.

Reese snatched open the door, grabbed him by the elastic band on his silk boxers and pulled him into the bathroom. The depth of her voice reached down to his groin and caressed him to pulsating life. "Well now, Mr. Knight, let's just check out this man thang you were braggin' about." The hot coals, that were her eyes, raked over him.

The corner of Maxwell's mustached mouth curved up into a devilish grin. He pushed the door shut behind him. "That's the kind of challenge that makes a man do extraordinary things. And I have you to thank." His head lowered. His mouth covered and captured hers.

"How can people drive in this madness?" Reese asked mesmerized by the crush of humanity. "I can't believe this many people and this many cars can fit on any street. I've never seen anything like it."

Maxwell chuckled as Daisuke expertly maneuvered the car around pedestrians, cars, and trucks down the Ginza Yonchome crossing. "Just imagine, it's not even rush hour."

"Unbelievable." She gazed again out of the window, watching the fashions, which covered the gamut from ultraconservative designer suits to punk-rock outfits to traditional Japanese garb. The famous thoroughfare was so vast it was like crossing the intersection of the world. It was a mixture of New York City's west village, Washington, D.C.'s Georgetown and California's Rodeo Drive, all done with Japanese elegance. Rows of elegant restaurants, boutiques, and nightspots dotted both sides of the street. Incredible, Reese thought. "Ooh, Max, look." She pointed to a beautiful Japanese girl who looked to be no more than fifteen, dressed in full kimono, replete with face makeup and an elaborately styled black wig.

"Yeah, she's probably on her way to work."

"Dressed like that?" Reese peered closer and watched her progress. "She looks like those geishas I've seen in the movies, but she's too young."

"Not at all. Actually that's about the right age. She'd be called a *maiko*." He went on to explain the meaning and that most of the women who worked in the teahouses and restaurants lived elsewhere and commuted to work just like everyone else.

"Fascinating. I'd love to do a story on them one day. Most people are under the impression that geishas are no more than call girls."

"That's far from the truth. They receive professional training in music, song and dance and are well versed in the art of conversation. Traditionally, geishas were somewhat like indentured servants. Parents would turn their daughters over to the geisha house and the mistress would see to their room, clothing and training. Many of the geishas today are actually unionized."

"You're kidding."

"Nope." He grinned, enjoying her childlike wonder. "Although their numbers have dropped considerably since World War II, they're still going strong. Geishas are an integral part of Japanese life."

Reese let out a long breath. "You've certainly done your homework."

"It's all part of my life, too, Reese," he stated in a thoughtful tone.

She angled herself in the seat to better face him. "Do you ever wish you knew more about your real mother?"

He looked away and paused for a long moment as if weighing the question. He breathed heavily. "At times," he finally answered. "I guess more than just at times." A wistful smile overtook his calm features. "Whenever I imagine her, I see this beautiful, exotic woman who took my father's breath away." His short chuckle lacked humor. His mixed feelings about his mother were like old wounds that ached on a rainy day. Deep in his heart, he believed that knowing about her, that part of him that made him who he was, would somehow complete the picture, make him three-dimensional. And at the same time, he was afraid of knowing. Maybe there was some dreadful reason why his father refused to discuss her with him. "But maybe she wasn't like that at all," he ended like a little boy who'd discovered there was no Santa.

Reese reached out and clasped his hand in hers, understanding all too well what not knowing did to a person's sense of who they were. "Both of us seem to be on some sort of quest," she began with a hesitant smile. "Maybe it's time we both found the answers we've been looking for. I'd like to help you. If you'll let me."

From the moment the idea had taken shape in his thoughts, he'd wanted to ask for help. But she'd been so enmeshed in her own problems and constant disturbing revelations, he never believed that the opportunity would present itself, or that he would feel right asking her to take on any more. And now, here she was in the midst of her own turmoil, thinking of him. The sincere generosity of this woman touched his heart and drew him deeper under her spell.

"Are you sure this is something you want to do, Reese?"

Yes. I'm sure," she answered without hesitation, squeezing his hands to assure him.

A fleeting sensation of doubt darted through him. "All right."

For the next two hours they visited the locations that Maxwell had selected for his sites. Currently they were abandoned buildings in up-and-coming commercial areas.

"I think these locations will be perfect," Maxwell said after they'd left the last building.

"So do I, but it's going to take a lot of work. Those buildings will need a complete overhaul to bring them up to the standards of New York and L.A."

"I know. That's why I need the full cooperation of Tasaka. Without his blessing, nothing gets done. Besides the fact that I'll need Japanese technicians to work in the sites. We'll have to see eye to eye in order for it to work."

"I can't imagine why he wouldn't agree. Especially if it's going to provide employment as well."

"It's a funny thing about the Japanese way of thinking and doing business," he began, putting the pieces of his thoughts together. "Everything is a process, almost ritualistic in nature. Decisions are made as a group. No one person wants to take a position one way or the other for fear of being wrong. For the outsider trying to get in, you must convince the entire body."

"But I thought Tasaka made all of the decisions."

"He does. But he's going to be watching me to see if I can convince the others before he commits to anything."

"And they won't commit to anything because it's not in their nature to do so," she said, completing the thought.

"Exactly. No one will say anything specific. They'll dance all around the issue. The Japanese have mastered the art of ambiguity. They never really say what they mean. You must be able to interpret their meaning without putting them on the spot."

"So how do you win a situation like that?"

"That's the art of negotiating with them. They need to be able to see that I can be a team player; that I'm not here to tell them I can do things better; that I need them, not the other way around. They want to see the kind of person I am. That's why many business meetings are discussed over dinner and plenty of drinks outside the office."

Reese nodded slowly, understanding sinking in. "I have no doubts about your capabilities to charm anyone, Mr. Knight," she grinned, running the tip of her finger down the bridge of his nose.

"I just hope they feel the same way," he smiled.

Moments later he pulled the car to a stop in front of a beautiful restaurant with outdoor seating.

"We're here," Maxwell announced. He checked his watch. "Hopefully Chris arrived already and got our table. This place gets so crowded, that if you miss your reservation by a few minutes they'll give your table away."

Chris rose in greeting and gave Reese a light kiss on the cheek and embraced Max in a warm hug, which they followed up with an intricate handshake. Reese smiled at the ritual.

"You two look pretty happy," Chris commented, returning to his seat.

Reese turned to Maxwell and smiled, her face warm with memories of their morning interlude.

"We have reason to be," Maxwell offered, giving Reese a quick wink before turning to Chris. He held out the chair for Reese. "And we have plenty to talk about, buddy. How much time do you have?"

"I knew you would," he grinned. "So I left my afternoon open."

"Let's order first," Maxwell suggested, scanning the menu.

Reese picked up hers and immediately put it back down. Everything was in Japanese.

"Don't worry," Maxwell said, "I'll order you something delicious."

"As long as it's not raw," she exclaimed, screwing up her nose and setting off a round of laughter at the table.

Both Maxwell and Chris spoke rapid Japanese as they ordered their meal and Reese quietly observed the deference they were shown when the waiter realized they spoke the language. His attitude went from generally polite to total respect. Interesting, she thought. No matter where a black man seemed to go in the world, they are first judged by the color of their skin, no matter how well dressed, mannered, or spoken. At least here she'd seen levels of acceptance that did not automatically happen in the United States. That point was brought home when Maxwell and Chris's conversation broke into her thoughts.

"…that's one of the things I never have to complain about when I'm in Japan," Chris was saying.

"What don't you have to complain about?" Reese interrupted, catching up with the discussion.

"Me and Max were talking about all the times we got harassed in L.A. for no other reason than just because we were black men in the 'wrong' neighborhood."

"It's happened to me in New York, too," Maxwell added.

Reese's eyes widened in question. "What happened?" she asked, her reporter instincts switching into gear.

Maxwell leaned back in his seat, a dark, pensive look hardening his smooth bronze features. "It was a Saturday evening. I came into the office to get some work done." He pressed his lips together in thought. His eyes narrowed. "The building was relatively empty. I came down the elevator into the lobby and went out into the employee parking lot. I was walking to my car when two security guards came up on either side of me and pushed me up against the wall insisting that I looked just like the guy they'd been told had been breaking into offices.

"Every time I tried to tell them who I was, they didn't want to hear it. One of them said, 'Just shut up nigga, you better be glad we don't just take care of you ourselves.' They frisked me," he growled, the old anger and humiliation bubbling to the surface. "They started laughing while they frisked me, as if it was the funniest damned thing they'd ever done." His jaw flexed as he took a long breath.

Reese felt her stomach roil, her throat clench as she fought down her own outrage. She couldn't begin to imagine what Max must have felt like; what so many black men must feel every day of their lives.

"One of them finally flipped open my wallet and saw my ID. Their whole attitude changed in a hurry. They couldn't apologize fast or furious enough."

"What did you do? I hope you had them arrested for harassment!"

He snorted in disgust. "I reported them to the building security manager. I haven't seen them since. I was sent a formal letter of apology."

Reese expelled a long-winded breath and shook her head. "It's just so hard to believe. I mean I know I've reported on it. I've seen it on the news. Rodney King was a perfect example of 'don't believe your lyin' eyes.' I've just never known anyone who has personally experienced that kind of harassment."

"Believe me baby, I can testify. And I haven't even begun to tell you how many times me and Chris have been pulled over."

"Yeah," Chris echoed. "It ain't easy."

"That's why it's refreshing to come to Japan," Maxwell explained. "Even though you may not be Japanese, the Japanese culture is built on respect for everyone. They may not like you, they may not bring you home to Mama, but they respect you as human beings first and foremost."

Reese had to admit that what Maxwell said was true. Even though she was in a foreign country, she had been treated with the utmost courtesy.

"But enough of that," Chris said. "Bring me up to date on what's been going on."

Between Reese and Maxwell, they alternately explained about Lynnette's car accident, Victoria's letter, Frank Murphy, everything.

"That's a helluva lot of stuff going on. So what's the plan?"

"I think we need to use Stan Tilden to our advantage," Reese said. Max nodded in agreement.

"If we can get Tilden to put the pressure on Murphy, he won't have time to focus on us and maybe Reese can get to the bottom of it all."

"Why don't you just confront your father? He has to know something."

"Believe me, I've thought of that. But if my father does know anything, he'll never tell. And to be honest, man, I don't think he does know."

"Are you just saying that because he's your father?"

Slowly Maxwell shook his head in denial. "I'm not that naive. I know my father is involved in some major cover-up. That much is clear. But my gut tells me that he was just following orders. I can't imagine that Murphy would divulge that much to my father—to anyone."

"Then I guess we'll have to go with that," Chris conceded, not totally convinced. "So how do we get this Tilden guy?"

"That's Reese's thing. She'll make the contact, reporter to reporter."

"Journalist," she drawled.

Maxwell and Chris gave each other an "oh boy" look.

"What can I do?"

"I thought you'd never ask." Maxwell leaned forward. "I want you to keep an eye on my lady. I'm going to be doing a lot of running in the next few weeks, and Reese isn't always going to be able to be with me."

"No problem." He turned to Reese and winked. "I'll work my schedule around you guys."

"I haven't heard from Larry yet, so I don't know when he'll be getting in. But he'll be able to take up the slack when you have to break out."

"Got it. When do I start?"

"Tonight. I have a meeting with Tasaka."

"I'm beginning to feel like Whitney Houston in *The Bodyguard*."

"You look good enough," Maxwell said giving her a slow once-over. "But can ya sing?"

The trio broke out into a fit of much needed laughter.

"I'm parked around the corner," Chris said as they stepped out into the throng of human traffic. "I'll meet you guys back at the hotel."

Maxwell gave him a thumbs up and slid his arm around Reese's waist, before opening the car door for her.

"I like him even better than I did when we first met," Reese commented easing into the car. "You're lucky to have such a good friend."

"Believe me, I know. Chris and I go way back. We've been in each other's corner since day one."

"That's the way it is with me and Lynn. I guess we're just two lucky people."

The glow of her smile warmed him, and he realized that above all else, nothing was more true. Circumstance may have thrown them together. Danger united them. But what they felt for each other would surmount everything. Yes. They were lucky to have found each other, and even considering all that they had to deal with, he wouldn't have it any other way.

* * *

The trio returned to the suite and while Maxwell prepared for his meeting with Tasaka, Reese and Chris sat in the living room and got to know each other.

"How is your story going on our man?" Chris asked with a teasing smile, his gray eyes sparkling with curiosity. He leaned forward and rested his arms on his thighs.

"It's coming. A lot of facts and figures, some great quotes." She leaned back and sighed, running her hands through her hair.

"But?"

"I want to capture the essence of Maxwell Knight—the man. Anyone can write a story about the businessman. I want more," she concluded, her eyes and voice alight with the writer's passion that fueled her.

Chris lowered his gaze and smiled. "It would seem that would be easier…I mean…" He looked up at her and shrugged helplessly.

Reese gave him a long look and pursed her lips to the side to stifle a grin. "You mean because we have a…relationship… what I want should be easier to get?" She folded her arms in front of her.

"Yeah. Something like that."

"It may seem easier, Chris. But the reality is, it's more difficult. I have to work even harder not to interject my personal feelings." She took a deep breath. "Maxwell has so many layers, so many nuances to his personality it's difficult to see it all clearly, especially without putting a personal spin on it. Then compound that with all that's been going on and you can imagine what I'm up against."

"Whew. I see your point." He leaned back against the cushion of the couch and draped his arm along the top. "So, what are you going to do? How can you make it work?"

"Well, if I've found out nothing else about Max, I've

discovered that a great deal of who he is and what he's accomplished today has to do with how he feels about himself. And a lot of it is tied up in his Japanese heritage. He knows little or nothing about his mother and it's left this gaping hole in his life. He's done everything in his power to fill it by overachieving and being the best at everything he does."

"That's definitely true." He shook his head slowly in reflection and in admiration for her insight. "I've never known anyone who is more driven than Max. He's always been that way, even when we were undergrads together, here at the University of Tokyo. Max carries a lot around with him, Reese. And his mother does have a lot to do with it."

"I guess for him it's like being adopted," Reese said softly. "Even though you love your parents, you still want to find out where you came from."

"I wish I knew what to tell you."

Reese crossed her long legs. "I can't bring his mother back, but I can try to recreate her for him by digging up whatever I can find."

Chris raised his thick brows in skepticism. "That's going to be pretty hard to do. It's been over thirty years."

"I know and I don't have much time. Not to mention my own set of problems," she added derisively. She leaned forward, clasping her hands tightly in her lap, her smoky voice captivating him with its intensity. "I have to do this, Chris—for Max. I want to be able to give him this one thing."

Chris gave her a long appraising look. "I believe you can."

"Sorry I took so long," Max apologized, striding into the room and to the bar. "Can I fix you two anything?"

"Not me," Reese answered, leaning back.

"I'll take one of what you're having," Chris said.

Max fixed Chris's drink and joined the two on the couch.

"Ready for your meeting?" Chris asked, taking a sip from his drink.

Maxwell nodded. "As ready as I can be." He turned toward Reese. "Are you going to try to get in contact with Tilden today?"

"Yes. If I have my time and dates right, it's yesterday in the states about 9:00 a.m."

Max grinned. "Hey, you're getting good."

Reese smiled smugly. "I figured I'd wait until after ten, eastern time, and then give him a call."

"I'm curious. What makes you guys think this Tilden will help you?"

Reese spoke up. "He wants all that he can get for his story. That's just the nature of the business. I have information that I can feed him to fuel his interest in Frank Murphy."

"The harder this guy pounces on Murphy, the less time Murphy will have to concentrate on us," Maxwell added.

"I really need access to the Air Force's computer files. That's where the answers are," Reese stated, looking from one to the other. "It would have been extremely helpful if I'd gotten a look at our computers at the magazine. But…" Her stomach knotted and her thoughts flashed to Lynn. Reese pushed herself up from the couch. "If you guys will excuse me, I'm going to call and check on Lynn."

Briefly they stood as Reese walked from the room.

"You have yourself a special lady, Max. Don't screw it up."

"Thanks for the vote of confidence." He tossed down the remnants of his drink and set the empty glass on the marble coffee table. "Sometimes I feel like I have to pinch myself to make sure she's real—that we're real. I don't have any intentions of screwing up." The corner of his mouth curved upward. "I just want us to be able to get to the bottom of this mess so that we can put the pieces of our lives together and go on."

Maxwell stood and slipped his hands into his midnight blue pants pockets. His brow creased. "I know that whatever we discover is going to be devastating to a lot of people. I can't begin to imagine the impact on my own family, the military and mostly on Reese." He turned anxious eyes toward his friend. "I don't want this thing to destroy her—destroy us." Methodically he paced, his voice steady and even. "Day by day she's beginning to remember things and the shock of the revelations are traumatizing enough. When she puts it all together, I don't know what it'll do to her." His jaw worked in fear and frustration. "All I can try to do is keep her safe and be there for her when the nightmares and flashbacks take over and become our reality." His voice shattered with a barrage of untenable emotion, his eyes glistening as he continued. "She's the first woman in my life who has accepted me for who I am, and not tried to fit me into some mold or their own version of who I should be." His dark eyes narrowed as he formed the words. "She's helping me to see my own worth outside of business and the bedroom. I know I still have a long way to go, but I want to make sure Reese is there with me."

"If it's meant to be, she will," Chris assured, clasping Max on the shoulder. Chris took a deep breath before plunging into what he knew would be dangerous waters. "Listen, man, I don't mean to play devil's advocate—and I really dig Reese and all, but I think you need to back up and be a little more objective about her."

Maxwell turned glowering eyes on Chris, an undeniable warning layered his voice. "Don't go there, Chris," he growled, pointing a finger to ram home his point.

"I'm your friend, Max, and I always will be. So therefore it's my job to keep you in check. Reese seems like a wonderful woman. She's beautiful, intelligent and she seems to make you happy. But remember, she has an agenda and a truckload of her own problems. And heading the list is the fact that she's here to do a job." He walked slowly across the floor, ignoring the killing looks that Maxwell was throwing his way. Chris turned to face him. "I don't doubt for a minute that she cares a great deal for you. But as your friend, I don't ever want to see you hurt the way Victoria hurt you." Even though he saw Maxwell flinch, he continued. "Just take it slow, man, that's all I'm saying. When it's all over I want to see both of you come out of it in one piece."

"I know you mean well. And I appreciate your concern, but I know what I feel. This isn't another Victoria fiasco. I've been weighing the pros and cons for weeks. I've had my bout with uncertainty and misgivings, but the deck always stacks in her favor."

"I hear you. But you know I had to put it out there. Just don't let that 'whip appeal' get to you," he grinned.

"Yeah," Maxwell replied, smiling. "And just an FYI, I'm not whipped."

"Whatever you say, my man." Chris chuckled. "Whatever you say."

They looked at each other and couldn't stop the laughter that bubbled up from their guts. They both fell into a round of laughter clapping each other on the back, knowing that above all else they had each other's best interests at heart.

"You two are sure in a good mood," Reese said strolling back into the living room.

Both men turned in her direction, winked at each other, then turned on their dazzling smiles full blast.

Reese raised her brows suspiciously and planted her hands on her hips, giving them the once-over from the corner of her eyes. "Something's up."

"It's a guy thing," they said in unison. "You wouldn't

understand," and they immediately broke into another fit of laughter.

"Humph," she puffed, in mock offense. "Then it's probably insignificant," she declared with a dismissive wave of her hand. She stalked off toward the bar and fixed herself a glass of sparking water with a twist of lime over ice. Turning, she first pinned them with a look, then dropped into the spot next to Maxwell who was seated at the bar.

"Did you get through to Lynn?" Maxwell asked draping his arm across her shoulder.

She gently rotated her glass, letting the ice cubes chill her drink. She took a sip. "Yes," she said swallowing. "She sounds much better. She said her headache is easing up and the bumps and bruises don't feel half as bad as they did."

Maxwell released a sigh of relief. "That's good news. Did she say when she'd be getting out?"

"It'll still be a few weeks. But," she added with a grin, "she doesn't seem to mind. All she really wanted to talk about was her doctor. She almost sounded like she might invent some new ailment just to stay under his care a little longer."

"Sounds like a pretty interesting lady," Chris chuckled.

"Oh, that she is," Max rejoined. "Take it from one who knows."

Reese stood and eased Maxwell upward with a slight tug of his tie, while she made busywork of straightening out the red silk. "I wish I could go with you tonight," she whispered huskily, her tone full of invitation.

Maxwell's dark eyes began to smolder with growing desire. He stroked her cheek with the tip of his finger, causing a shiver to ripple through her. "I wish you could, too." He planted a hot, wet kiss on her glossy lips. "But Chris will stay and keep you company until I get back."

She lowered her voice so only he could hear. "Chris is real cute, but he's not you," she taunted.

He fought down the jolt that throbbed between his legs. He stepped closer and instantly felt the heat emanating from her body. "I'll make it up to you when I get back."

Reese's amber eyes sparkled like sherry. "I'm going to see that you do."

Chris loudly cleared his throat, and pretended to look embarrassed when they looked at him. "Oh, don't mind me," he drawled. "But if you don't get a move on, you'll be late. You know the traffic is murder."

"Yeah, you're right. Let me call down to Daisuke and let him know to bring the car around. Sorry, baby." He gave her a puppy-dog look and a peck on the cheek before dashing off to the phone in the bedroom.

Reese sighed wistfully and smiled. When she turned around she was slightly taken aback to see Chris staring at her. She looked quickly up and down her body thinking something was amiss. "What?"

"You really care about him don't you?"

"Yes, I do. Is that something you're worried about?" she challenged.

Chris pursed his lips, and gently rubbed his smooth chin with his ringless left hand. Briefly he glanced at the floor before his eyes connected with her steady gaze. For the barest moment, he was halted by the stunning picture she projected—a statuesque chocolate "Venus" with startling eyes the color of warm brandy—an erotic combination. He could easily see why his friend was so enamored with this woman. She walked a bit closer and Chris realized that she didn't merely walk from one spot to another she appeared to effortlessly glide to her destination, with a slow hypnotic sway to her hips. He swallowed hard when she stopped inches in front of him, her sensual scent wafting around him. Casually he backed away and took a perch on the edge of the arm of the couch. "Max is very important to me, Reese," he began slowly. "He's the brother I never had. I don't want to see him hurt again like he was with Victoria. He has enough to deal with." He held up his hand to stave off the firestorm he saw coming his way. "I'm not saying that you're like her in any way. All I'm asking is for you to be good to him and for him, and be honest with him and yourself about what it is you really want."

Reese bit back her stinging response when she fully observed the look of sincerity glowing in Chris's gray eyes. Pushing down her anger, she understood that he only wanted the best for his friend and she knew she'd do the same thing for Lynnette. Slowly her temper began to wane and was replaced by a budding respect.

She smiled beguilingly. "Does Maxwell realize what a good friend he has in you?"

Chris chuckled. "I keep trying to tell him."

She sighed. "Thanks for what you said. I mean, Max has told me all about Victoria and I know all of the reasons why he mistrusts journalists, but…" Her eyes implored him to understand. "I care about Max, Chris, more than I've even admitted to him. I would never do anything to hurt him."

"I'm glad to hear it." He extended his hand. "Friends?" He raised his thick brown brows.

"Friends."

Chapter 32

After more than an hour of haggling, cajoling, bargaining and strategizing, Reese came away from her conversation with Stan Tilden moderately confident. She'd finally convinced him that it would be in both of their interests to work together. She was surprised but happy to learn that he'd already put the squeeze on Frank Murphy about the software scandal. However, she revealed nothing at all about her involvement or anything related to Max's father. She wanted Stan to believe that getting to the bottom of the software scandal was what she needed for her piece in Maxwell's story. This way she and Max could still stay removed from Murphy since the pressure was being exerted from Stan. He would never guess their involvement.

Reese got up from the edge of the bed where she'd been sitting for the past hour. She arched her back and stretched her long arms over her head, then flexed her fingers—both hands being stiff from the nonstop use—one from holding the phone in a death grip and the other from writing pages of notes.

She picked up her notebook and scanned the hastily scrawled lines. One item stood out from the rest—Victoria Davenport's telephone number. Stan had given it to her, advising her that she should contact Victoria personally for any verification.

Reese's stomach did a slow dip when she contemplated dialing the number. What would she say? What would Victoria say? She inhaled deeply and flipped the notebook shut. She wasn't quite ready to deal with Victoria yet. In time.

Anxiety riddled her body like machine-gun fire. Suki stood shadowed in the window of the second floor watching the black limousine pull up in front of the building. Her heartbeat accelerated when the tall, elegantly dressed man stepped from the car. Her petite hand fluttered to her breasts. He was powerfully built, with the grace of a panther—intimidating. He moved with a fluidity of motion, giving the impression of one gliding effortlessly across a surface. When he walked it was with all of his weight centered in his lower stomach—*hara*—the place of power to the Japanese. She knew him instantly. Her son.

Maxwell and Daisuke were dutifully escorted through the finely furnished sitting and entertainment rooms to where they would dine with Tasaka and his entourage.

Maxwell's dark sweeping eyes roamed caressingly over the suits of Samurai regalia that hung on the walls, both threatening and humbling at the same time. Each suit of armor was encased in glass and stood out in stark relief against the white walls. Century-old antiques were boldly displayed throughout the rooms and every tabletop was touched off by pieces of jade and ivory or air-thin porcelain. It was plainly obvious that the owner of the house was extremely wealthy.

Men sat in groups or alone, conversing, eating and being pampered by the stunning array of beautiful geishas. Maxwell felt as if he'd stepped through a portal of time back to feudal Japan, as he witnesses the age-old scenes play out before him.

"Tasaka-san is expecting you," the *maiko* said, smiling brightly. "He is in the back room. Dinner will arrive shortly." The young woman stopped in front of a closed rice-paper door and slid it open.

All eyes turned in the direction of the newcomers. The *maiko* bowed and made the introductions.

Maxwell stepped forward bowing to the trio of men who flanked Tasaka. "This is Daisuke Uchiyama-san, gentlemen. He will interpret for me." Daisuke repeated what was said and there were nods of agreement all around.

"Please sit," Tasaka instructed in a husky, hushed whisper. The men took their places around the low wood table.

Then faster than they could blink a maid appeared from what seemed like nowhere with a tray laden with a platter of *Sashimi*—a striking presentation of extra thin slices of rosy raw tuna, pale sea bass, and halibut on a bed of shredded carrot and snowy daikon and accompanied by piquant wasabi paste—surrounded by steaming fresh vegetables. The first course of their meal was served with the first of many rounds of sake. Maxwell was quite aware of its potency and knew he had to keep his stomach full to offset the powerful effects of the rice wine.

During the initial hour of dining and drinking, no mention was made of Maxwell's reason for being there. He played along with the notion that he couldn't understand the language and laughed and nodded at all the appropriate places when cued by Daisuke.

To Maxwell's surprise and pleasure it was Tasaka who finally broached the subject of M.K. Enterprises. He methodically explained to his dining companions and business partners that Maxwell Knight was looking to set up his new headquarters in Tokyo. He also wanted to have Tasaka Industries' computer arm manufacture and distribute his new chip. There were nods of understanding all around mixed with deep-throat murmurs.

Maxwell kept a watchful eye on all four men to gauge their reactions, if any.

With Daisuke translating, Maxwell spoke. "I'd like to begin setting up operations within the next six months. I know that Tasaka Industries has some of the most talented computer engineers and programmers in the world. I want to see that my product is crafted by the best."

"What do we get out of it, Knight-san?" Tasaka asked in a near whisper. He eyed Maxwell speculatively.

"If we can come to an agreement, we would become partners. I would guarantee Tasaka Industries twenty percent of the company stock."

There was a flurry of excited, but muffled conversation as the men bent their heads and spoke rapidly among themselves.

Tasaka held up his hand and the room fell silent. He pinned his dark almond-shaped gaze on Maxwell. "I have done my homework on you Maxwell-san and your company is private. You are not on the boards, correct?"

Impatiently Maxwell held his tongue, while Daisuke translated.

"This is true, for now. Things will change rapidly within a matter of months." Maxwell's dark eyes merged and solidified with Tasaka's.

A thin smile moved slowly across Tasaka's month. *Doru* signs began flashing in his mind. A partnership with M.K.

Enterprises with a guaranteed share in its profits would make him wealthier than his wildest dreams. He had waited patiently for the opportunity to join forces with a thriving American business. The decline of Japanese business over the past three years had caused innumerable problems. Due to the recession, for the first time in modern history, layoffs were happening in earnest. Those fortunate enough to keep their jobs hadn't seen a raise in nearly five years. In an age where speed of information was paramount, whoever had a hand in the control of cyberspace on the Pacific continent, would garner millions. Tasaka had no delusions that he would not be an integral part of that process.

Tasaka took a long, slow sip of sake. Gingerly replaced the cup on the table and folded his hands in front of him. It seemed as if the room itself was holding its breath.

Maxwell was quite aware that Tasaka was banking on his impatient occidental nature to take over and push him to say too much or do the wrong thing, thereby giving Tasaka the upper hand. It was a common practice among clever Japanese to try and trap a *gaijin*—foreigner. However, Maxwell was very comfortable to play things out the Japanese way.

Tasaka finally broke the silence. "Your offer, Knight-san, sounds worth much consideration. How long will you be staying in Tokyo?"

Maxwell nodded following Daisuke's translation then faced Tasaka squarely. "As long as it will take to come to a mutually satisfying agreement. I can use my time here to research my roots," he said slowly, his eyes sweeping across the four men. "My mother, who I've never met, was Japanese." A ghost of a smile haloed Maxwell's lips.

Tasaka's lids lowered nearly obscuring his eyes. To the casual observer, one would think his eyes were completely closed. Maxwell knew better. He, himself, often slipped into the same transcendental state, a place deep inside of himself where he could be physically present but mentally removed, allowing him the peace of mind to make crucial decisions.

Finally Tasaka made eye contact with Maxwell. "We will speak again. Perhaps tomorrow?" he stated. "In the meantime, let me have one of these beautiful ladies escort us on a tour of this lovely establishment."

Maxwell waited for the unnecessary interpretation. "I'd like that very much," he responded in answer to both statements.

With the assistance of one of the *maiko* who had floated unobtrusively around them all evening, Tasaka rose to his feet. His entourage did the same, along with Maxwell and Daisuke.

The same *maiko,* who Maxwell learned was named Honniko, led them through the rooms, pointed out works of art and notable attendees, and explained the entertainment that was taking place in various locations.

The house was much larger than it appeared from the outside, Maxwell observed, impressed by the class and elegance that permeated every inch of the building.

"Who is the *hujin*—a lady responsible for running such an exquisite establishment?" Maxwell asked. "I would be remiss if I did not extend my appreciation for her talent and taste. She must be quite extraordinary."

"That she is," Tasaka murmured. He leaned close to Honniko and whispered in her ear. She bowed low and hurried away. "Why don't we sit over here?" Tasaka instructed, indicating an available entertainment area that boasted a rich emerald-green paisley couch and matching chairs, which formed a comma around the black marble table. Behind the serene setting the jalousied window gave a teasing view of the garden in full bloom.

Maxwell had barely seated himself when the most exquisite looking Japanese woman he'd ever seen appeared to float into the room. Although she was tiny in stature, her poised body language and dark searching eyes commanded respect. Even without an introduction, he knew this was the woman of the house.

She was dressed in the traditional double kimono, the top a brilliant burnt-orange silk, the color of the rising sun, the undergarment, only seen at the cuffs, was of the same material in the captivating shade of bronze that seemed to shimmer with the play of soft lighting in the room.

Maxwell rose as she moved soundlessly toward him and something vague but familiar took hold of him, gripping his stomach and accelerating his heart.

She bowed low before him and he reciprocated in like fashion.

"It is a pleasure to meet you Knight-san," she said in a perfect melodic English.

"The pleasure is mine. You have a magnificent establishment."

"Thank you. I hope you had a pleasant evening and all of your needs were met."

"They were, and I did. However, you have the advantage. You know my name, but I do not know yours." He smiled engagingly.

She stared directly into his eyes. "Sukihara Tasaka, Knight-san," she said softly, beating back the tremor in her voice.

Maxwell felt as if he'd been hit in the solar plexus. He looked from Sukihara to Mioshi and immediately made the connection. The family resemblance was unmistakable.

"My...mother's name was Sukihara," he said almost to himself, struggling to get his head back above water.

A shadow of a smile graced her rich mouth. "A very common name here in Japan."

Suki fought to maintain an aura of calm, but her skin tingled and her heart raced dangerously. She swore she would pass out. She inhaled deeply, wanting instead to gulp in all the air around her. This was her son, her baby whom she'd given away more than thirty years ago. Her large eyes began to burn with the resurgence of raw emotion that battled to claim her. She knew if she stood in that spot a moment longer, she would gather him in her arms and beg his forgiveness. He was more beautiful than she'd ever imagined, a perfect combination of the man she loved and herself.

For the briefest moment, Maxwell truly believed that she would embrace him. But, of course, it was inconceivable for a woman of her age and stature to make such a breach of etiquette. Yet he couldn't shake the sensation that she wanted to touch him, as he did her.

"Well," she breathed, "if everything is satisfactory, I hope you will excuse me as I must check on my other guests."

"Of…course," Maxwell said, trying to regain control of his spiraling feelings. "I hope we meet again."

Suki did not respond, but bowed instead and backed away. Then like a dream that vanishes upon awakening, she was gone.

Slowly Maxwell felt his breathing return to normal and the eerie feeling of familiarity loosened its hold.

Mioshi stood to the side and watched the entire scene unfold from beneath his hooded lids. Knowing his sister as well as he did, he knew that she was terribly shaken by the encounter. As cruel or painful as she may have believed the meeting to be, he knew it was necessary. They must all move beyond the past. Her patron, Murayama Hosokawa, would have to join everyone else in the present as well. Because he had every intention of solidifying this deal with his nephew as soon as possible. The alliance with M.K. Enterprises was what Tokyo needed, what he needed. And those fools who couldn't see that be damned. No one would stand in his way, not Murayama and not Suki.

Chapter 33

By the time Maxwell returned to the suite, it was fast approaching 3:00 a.m. After leaving the geisha house, he'd dismissed Daisuke for the night and had taken up residence behind the wheel. He drove around the crowded streets of Tokyo for hours, the flashing neon lights from the countless nightclubs and restaurants bounced off the tinted windows in rapid succession, like traveling through a prism.

Over and over again, he rewound his memory tape and replayed the meeting with Sukihara. He still could not shake the familiar feeling that ran through him like a current, even hours later. The sensation was similar to what he'd felt when he met Mioshi, only more potent. Then to discover that they were brother and sister only compounded his sense of unease.

Sukihara. She'd said it was a common Japanese name. Perhaps she was right. But that still did not explain the kinetic energy that flowed back and forth between them.

Suppose the unthinkable was true. Suppose Sukihara Tasaka was his mother—the most powerful and influential woman in Tokyo—and Mioshi Tasaka the *oyaban* of *oyaban* was his uncle.

Later that night as he pulled Reese's warmth closer to his body and whispered his unfathomable thoughts in the dark of night, a shudder ran through him.

Reese sat wordlessly on the opposite side of the small dining table, watching Maxwell spin his coffee cup around and around within the circle of the saucer. She took a sip of orange juice and waited. Watching the cup spin was almost hypnotic, but what was even more powerful was watching Max. His body was perfectly still. He appeared not to be breathing. His eyes remained focused on the cup, his only body part in motion was the tip of his index finger as he periodically set the cup spinning with a precise flick.

Although she knew and understood that this "side of him" was all part of Maxwell the man, adjusting to periods of total isolation from him was difficult to master. She also knew that if she spoke to him, right at that moment, or asked the most inane question, he would respond.

Instead, she removed her empty plate and glass from the table and returned them to the cart to be taken away. She slipped out of the room and went to take a shower.

As the water pounded and ran down her body, Reese went back over everything that Maxwell had told her about his meeting with Sukihara and the feelings that went along with it. Feelings were something she placed great stock in. She ran on feelings and instinct, and they very rarely failed her. And right now her feelings were telling her that there was a real reason for Maxwell to experience what he did when he met Mioshi and Sukihara.

Even though the idea that she was his deceased mother—in

the flesh—was far-fetched, nothing was beyond believing to her. They had both been lied to for so long there was no reason to believe that James Knight had been truthful to his son about his mother.

She turned off the water and slid the glass door open. Stepping onto the soft pale pink carpet, she grabbed a thick hotel towel and began wiping herself dry, secretly hoping that she could also wipe away the suspicions that were beginning to grow like weeds in an untended field.

Reese faced herself in the mirror and realized one thing— maybe she wouldn't have to look as far as she thought for Maxwell's mother. She smiled at her reflection, her amber eyes taking on the light of the chase. Now all she needed was a plan.

Suki stood still as stone as she waited for her brother to conclude his telephone conversation. She never came to his home unless it was to help with the entertainment of his guests, or if they needed the utmost privacy. Today's visit was due to the latter.

She'd barely slept for more than a few minutes at a time for the entire night. Her petite body was a mass of nerves and tightened muscles. She'd tossed and turned as visions of walls crumbling, flowers wilting and fire-breathing dragons destroying everything in their paths plagued her.

She awoke weak and trembling, realizing the truth behind the nightmarish images. Her world was about to change. All that she knew would disintegrate.

Mioshi cleared his throat, drawing Suki back from her dark thoughts.

"Sister, what brings you here today?" he asked in a clear bass.

"You know why I am here, Mioshi."

He looked at his sister for a long moment. "I cannot do

what you wish. The deal with your son must and will go through."

She stepped closer. "Why must it be with Maxwell? You could have your pick of American companies to unite with, Mioshi."

"That may be true. But what I and Japanese industry can gain from this endeavor cannot be had with another company. He has proposed the best offer. I intend to sign the contracts sealing the deal as soon as possible."

Suki momentarily turned away, her sense of right and honor warred with her sense of fear. Deep inside she knew her brother was right. A new Japanese-American conglomerate was exactly what her financially struggling country needed.

"Is there nothing I can do or say to change your mind?" she asked in a soft plea.

"Nothing."

She inhaled a shaky breath. Curtly she bowed her head, turned and walked out. On her ride home she contemplated her options. She had to find a way to keep Murayama from uncovering her secret.

When Suki arrived at home she was met at the door by Honniko.

"*Oyaban,* there is a woman, Reese Delaware, here to see you," she said. "I have had her wait in the front room."

Suki frowned. She knew no one by that name. "What does she want?"

"She would not say, only that she must speak with you."

She was not in the frame of mind to deal with anyone at the moment. But courtesy dictated that she speak with her visitor. To do otherwise would be the height of rudeness. "I'll see her shortly." Suki moved silently up the stairs to her room, and changed from her street clothing to a simpler single kimono of off-white raw silk. Moments later she entered the room in which Reese waited.

"Reese Delaware-san, I am Sukihara." She bowed in greeting and stepped into the room. "How may I be of service?"

Reese was instantly overcome by the regalness of this stunning, petite woman who magnetically drew her into the depths of her ink-black eyes. She stood up. "Ms. Tasaka, I'm a journalist doing a story on the modern geisha." She gave Suki her best "you can trust me" smile. "I understand that you would be the person to speak with. I hope you can help me."

Suki smiled thinly. "You honor me, Delaware-san. Why don't we sit. Can I offer you some refreshment—some tea perhaps?"

"No, thank you."

"Very well. Then let's begin."

For the next hour, Reese questioned her about the mystique and misconceptions of the geisha, easily lulling Suki into a sense of security. As she listened and took copious notes, she couldn't help but become fascinated by this woman.

Finally, Suki leaned back against the cushions of the settee and folded her hands demurely in front of her. "Was all of that helpful?" She smiled and her dark eyes sparkled.

"Actually," Reese began, leaning slightly forward, "I was wondering if you knew a man named James Knight. He was stationed here just about the time—" she flipped through her notes "—you began your training." She looked up and smiled encouragingly, but her smile soon faded. All the color seemed to have drained from Suki's face. Her nostrils flared slightly as if she were struggling for air, and her irises widened. "Are you all right?"

"Why do you ask me about this James…Knight?" she asked reaching deep inside her psyche for calm.

Reese pulled out her lie. "I interviewed him several months ago as part of my research. He said he'd met a woman named Sukihara while he was here. I just wondered…"

Abruptly Suki stood, cutting off Reese's explanation, propriety forgotten. "I'm sorry I can't help you further. I'll show you out." She turned toward the door.

Reese stood as well but wouldn't be put off, not when she saw the thin veil of veneer begin to crack.

"What do geishas do if they have children?" Reese probed, following Suki to the door. She saw the infinitesimal snap of her head and slight faltering in her precise step.

Suki spun around, her eyes glowing even darker, but her voice remained level. "If it is a girl, the child remains with the mother."

"What about boys?" Reese pressed.

Suki raised her chin a notch. "Sometimes they are sent away."

Her eyes locked with Reese's and she had the eerie sensation that Suki was begging her not to go farther. But Reese wouldn't let go, not when she was this close. "Do you have children, Ms. Tasaka?"

Suki swallowed. "No. I do not." She turned and continued toward the door, Reese close on her heels.

"I only asked because it's such a coincidence that Mr. Knight has a son and his mother is a Japanese woman named Sukihara."

Suki felt her heart begin to thunder in her chest. Her knees grew weak as a surge of heat flooded her body.

"Very interesting," Suki said, turning the knob and opening the door. She stood to the side to let Reese pass. "A coincidence, as you Americans say."

"I'm sure." Reese gave her a fleeting smile. "Thank you for all of your time and your help, Ms. Tasaka."

Suki bowed as Reese stepped out and into the sunshine.

* * *

Suki closed the door and shut her eyes. Her entire body trembled. James. Was his memory of her as crystal clear as hers was of him? She turned away and headed for the stairs. The woman was too close, and Suki sensed that somehow she knew the truth. And if she did, she would eventually get to Maxwell if she hadn't already. She felt the fissure snake its way along the veneer.

"How did it go?" Chris asked as Reese took her seat and fastened her belt. He nosed the car into the midday traffic. "You were in there a mighty long time."

"She's Max's mother all right."

"She admitted it?" Chris asked, astonishment raising the octave in his voice.

"Not in so many words." She twisted her puckered lips. "Well…not in any words at all, but she looked like someone stepped on her grave when I mentioned James Knight. She's one cool lady," she added with admiration. "I can see where Max gets it from."

"So now what?"

"Now the seed is planted. We'll just have to wait and see what grows."

Tokyo

Mioshi read the *Asahi Shimbun*—The Rising Sun newspaper—with a gleam in his eye and a smile of enormous pleasure on his lips, the very same article that was creating havoc on the other side of the globe.

Whenever his nephew's company entered the market, people would clamor for a piece of the pie. With a guaranteed 20 percent share, his stock would skyrocket virtually overnight.

If he had a moment's hesitation about consummating the deal, it was gone. He pressed the button on his intercom to signal for Namicho.

"Yes, Tasaka-san," Namicho responded.

"Try to reach Knight-san. Tell him I'd like to meet with him today, at his earliest convenience—here at my office," he whispered into the speaker.

"Right away, Tasaka-san."

Maryland

James went numb when he read the headline of the *Washington Post:* "Top Level Air Force Major Under Investigation." The story went on to explain that Frank Murphy, head of Air Force Intelligence, was under investigation for possible fraud. It further eluded to computer theft of a program originally designed and developed by Maxwell Knight, CEO of M.K. Enterprises in New York, and touted as Air Force technology. If the findings were proven true, the U.S. government could owe Maxwell Knight millions of dollars in reparations. Mr. Knight was out of the country and unavailable for comment.

The article also indicated that the information was obtained from an inside source who was part of the theft and cover-up. James folded the paper and dropped it on the table.

Claudia walked into the kitchen, her arms wrapped around a blue mesh laundry basket. She stopped short when she saw her husband staring at nothingness.

"James, what is it? What's wrong?" The basket landed on the floor with a thud. She hurried across the canary yellow linoleum to his side. "James." She pressed her hand to his chest, then followed his gaze to the newspaper on the tabletop. Her heartbeat quickened. A sense of dread filled her as she picked it up and read the front page.

Her soft brown eyes widened. "What does this mean for you, James—for us?" The paper fluttered from her fingers and fell to the floor.

James's jaw clenched. "It means that once they begin investigating Murphy, there will be no stopping them. And now that the *Post* has gotten a whiff of it, they'll be like a starving dog with a bone. It's only a matter of time before the whole Delaware incident is uncovered as well."

Claudia swallowed down the sour taste that rose from her belly and filled her mouth. "You've to go to them, James. Tell them what you know before they find out for themselves."

"There's still a chance they won't, Claudia," he answered working his bottom lip with his teeth.

Claudia heard the false note of hope in his voice. "How can you convince me of that, James, when you can't convince yourself?" She walked away, leaving her husband to stand alone with his conscience.

Frank Murphy read the headlines of the *Post* while sitting at his kitchen table. He knew it was coming. He'd been in meetings all week attempting to put plans into motion to control the damage.

Wracked with disbelief and despair, he wearily shook his head. His life, his career, was over. The government would not protect him once all of the facts were revealed. He would become the scapegoat, and anyone who was a part of it would go down with him. Maybe if he cooperated fully, the courts would be lenient.

He began to laugh, a slow laughter that built in volume and speed until tears welled in his eyes and fell unchecked across the light stubble on his cheeks.

Who could he turn to? He had no one. The woman he'd loved for so long was still obsessed by a dead man. His daughter, if she really was his daughter, wanted to have nothing to do with him. The Air Force was only days away from requesting his resignation. And what would become of him when they found out about Hamilton Delaware? His actions would never be sanctioned.

He covered his face with his hands as his shoulders heaved and shuddered with his silent tears.

Then an idea slowly began to take shape in his mind. His head came up, his green eyes sparkled. Yes, there was a way, he thought. A fragile sense of hope buoying his spirit. He hadn't accessed those files in years. But his codes were probably still active. Yes, it could work. He sat up straighter. Timing was essential. He had less than two days to save his life.

Tokyo

Maxwell steadily paced the carpeted floor as he listened to Reese describe her visit with Sukihara. If he'd been asked, at that moment, how he felt, there would have been no way he could have described the sensation that ran rampant within him.

It seemed as if a dark cloud had somehow engulfed him, taking away his light. Never before had he experienced such absolute emptiness. Even if he tried to deny what Reese said, he knew deep in his soul that she spoke the truth. His mother was alive. His father had lied to him all of his life. His mother denied his existence. Each fact repeated itself, reverberating in his head like a maniacal mantra. The hard knot that lodged in his throat pounded with a life of its own. He could feel the muscles of his heart constricting, threatening to explode from the pain.

Reese was struck by the outward calm that Max exuded. She knew that her revelations were emotionally devastating. Yet, he appeared as though he were listening to the weather report. The only clue to the emotions that raged within him was the darkening of his obsidian eyes and the slight flare of his nostrils.

"Is that all?" he asked in a hollow monotone. He turned to look at her, and for the first time Reese saw his eyes glisten with tears that he refused to shed. Her heart slammed against her chest, as a cry of despair rose to her throat and froze.

With slow, measured steps she came to him, her heart aching for him with every footfall. Their eyes met in an embrace of total understanding. She slipped her arms around his waist and tenderly pressed her head against his chest.

Maxwell's arms hung loosely at his sides. He shut his eyes and tilted his head toward the ceiling, taking silent shallow breaths. Unbidden, a shudder threaded through him and Reese pressed her warmth closer.

"It's all right," she whispered. "I'm here for you, Max. It's all right."

Unseen by Reese a single tear slid down his cheek in silent answer to the ones that flowed from hers.

Sukihara had sat unmoving in her room since the impromptu visit by Reese. For the past few hours she tried to figure a way out of her dilemma. Her only choice was to keep the truth from Murayama. But how?

Finally, she rose from her spot by the window. Wearily she rubbed her hand across her face. Deep in her heart she knew what the right thing was. But was she strong enough to choose it?

The life that she'd lived for more than thirty years was not the type of life that prepared you to do or be anything more than what she was—a geisha. She was still considered beautiful. But who, other than Murayama, would want her outside of "this life"? As it stood, their decades-old liaison was never discussed and most outside of the house considered it only a rumor.

She knew she could not delay the inevitable. Sooner rather than later she would have to come to terms with her fate.

Chris rang the doorbell and was met by a melancholy Reese.

"Did something happen?" he asked, his eyes darting from her to the interior of the suite. He crossed the threshold.

"I think he needs to talk," she said softly, indicating a reclining Maxwell with a tilt of her head. Unobtrusively she left the room.

Chris took off his jacket and dropped it on the chair by the door. Thoughtfully he approached Maxwell who seemed oblivious to his presence. But Chris knew better. Maxwell was always totally alert to everything in his space. Chris sat on the love seat, stretching his long denim-clad legs out in front of him. His thigh muscles bunched and rippled beneath the fabric.

"Let's talk about it, my *kyodai*."

Hearing the endearing Japanese term for *brother,* Maxwell was immediately reminded that what he and Chris shared was as strong if not stronger than any blood ties called family.

Slowly he lowered his lids, rose and his dark gaze met Chris's light one. He nodded, and like a cup overflowing, he poured out his story.

"You know at some point you're going to have to confront her. You have to confront her so that you can regain your inner peace and bring closure to this."

"I know. I plan to before we return to the States."

Chris reached across the space that separated them and heartily slapped Maxwell's rock-hard thigh.

A shadow of a smile flickered around Maxwell's mouth.

He gently rubbed the tip of his finger across the small scar on his eyebrow. *"Arigato gozaimashita, kyodai."*

"No thanks are necessary, *kyodai*." Chris smiled then blew out a long breath and stood. "Have you heard from Larry Templeton?"

"As a matter of fact he called this morning. I told him to forget about coming here. Everything is under control."

"Cool. But listen, will Reese be all right today? I have practice this afternoon for about three hours, maybe longer."

"No problem." He clapped him on the shoulder. "I plan to…" The ringing phone cut him off. "Excuse me." He crossed the room and picked up the phone that rested on a white marble and gold stand.

"Kon'nichiwa," he said into the mouthpiece. "Yes, of course. Three o'clock will be fine with me. *Arigato gozaimashita."*

He turned toward Chris, his dark almond-shaped eyes sparkling. "Things are happening faster than I expected."

"What things?" Reese asked entering the room and the conversation.

"That was Tasaka's secretary. He wants to meet with me today to close the deal."

Reese's amber eyes widened in delight. "Fantastic. That was quick."

"Tasaka must be getting old," Chris chuckled. "He's been notorious for dragging out negotiations to the limit. Or maybe he saw today's paper. Have either of you checked it out?"

They both shook their heads.

Chris retraced his steps to where he'd put his coat and extracted the paper.

Maxwell took it and read as he paced. His eyes raced over the article.

"Well, what does it say?" Reese asked, seeing that it was in Japanese.

Maxwell let out a sigh. "It seems as though the heat is on." He explained what was in the article.

"Whew. But I still don't see why this would push Tasaka into signing."

A slight shift of eyes passed between Maxwell and Chris. But not so slight that Reese didn't catch it.

"What?" she demanded. "I know there's something you're not telling me."

Maxwell swallowed. He knew that revealing this information could be potentially hazardous to his company if the information was leaked. Rapidly he tossed around the veracity of telling her. He did trust her. And he knew that she would never betray that trust.

"Sit down for a minute Reese." He put his hand on her shoulder and ushered her to a seat in the living room.

Walking the short distance she kept looking at him over her shoulder, trying to get a clue, to no avail.

Maxwell pulled up a chair and sat, leaning forward, bracing his arms on his thighs. "I haven't discussed this with you because it's very sensitive. If word of it got out before the right time it could be financially crippling for M.K. Enterprises." He paused a beat. "In ten days, the company is going public. We plan to hit the NYSE and NIKKEI simultaneously. A partnership between myself and Tasaka guarantees him twenty percent of the shares. He knows they will skyrocket because of the potential dollars arising out of the computer fraud. Not a word of this can be written anywhere until after the fact. The Federal Trade Commission doesn't take too kindly to inside trading."

Reese swallowed, digesting the implications. "Thank you for trusting me enough to tell me. I won't breathe a word."

"I know," he said with a smile. He patted her knee and

stood. "Now, if you two will excuse me, I want to pull my papers together for this meeting."

"I'm cutting out anyway," Chris announced, slipping into his coat. He gave Reese a light peck on the cheek, saluted Maxwell and headed out.

Reese angled her head in Maxwell's direction. "I'll work out here. I need to put in some major time on this article. So go ahead and do what you have to do."

Her low, throaty voice vibrated through him. What he really wanted to do was take her in the bedroom with him. Her casual cream knit top that subtly defined her breasts and the matching Lycra pants that outlined every nook and cranny of her lower body was enough to give him hot flashes. But he knew once they got started, they would never get anything done. So instead, he gave her a wink and set about his work.

The night lights of downtown Tokyo punctuated the sky with a multitude of vibrant colors. Bone weary, but mentally charged after three hours of talks with Tasaka and his associates, Maxwell was determined to make one last stop before returning to the hotel.

"Drop me off at Tasaka House, Daisuke, please. Then you can call it a night. I'll get a cab back to the hotel."

Chapter 34

Maxwell stood with his back to the door staring out onto the deck, watching the early-evening strollers meander along the walkway. What would he say? His stop here had been totally impromptu, and he had not had the opportunity to really think through his actions. He was running on pure emotion: anger, a sense of betrayal and a need to find out from his mother if he was ever loved.

"Knight-san," came the soft voice from behind him.

Maxwell spun around and eyes so much like his own connected and held. His insides tightened with anxiety then did a slow somersault before settling down. He bowed low. "Tasaka-san. Pardon me for just dropping in, but I needed to speak with you."

Sukihara's heart beat an almost unnatural rhythm as she gazed, once again, upon her son. Every fiber of her being warned her to avoid this moment, to make an excuse to

Honniko why she could not see him. But a power greater than rationale gripped her: a mother's undying love.

A part of her wanted him to leave and never come back so that she could return to the life she'd always known. But that other part of her knew that from this moment on, her life would never be the same again.

Ethereally she glided into the room, a tentative smile trembling around her rich red mouth. "Why don't we sit down, Knight-san. I'll send for some tea."

"I prefer to stand," he said in flawless Japanese. "And tea is not necessary. Thank you."

Sukihara hid her shock and pride behind a noncommittal mask. "As you wish." She, however, took a seat on the low bronze brocade couch. "How may I help you?"

"Perhaps with the truth," he began, his voice low and even, his gaze steady. "I'd like to know about you and my father. I'd like to know why I was told all of these years that you were dead. I'd like to know why you didn't want me."

"I think you are mistaken Knight-san. Why would I know these things you speak of?"

"All I want is the truth. Do you have any idea what life has been like for me, never knowing on what side of the fence I should stand, never fitting in the black world or the Japanese, always feeling that there was part of me that was missing? I think I deserve to know."

Suki rose and turned away, her conscience doing battle within her. To admit to the truth would ruin her; and would it really help him to know that she'd chosen a way of life over her own flesh and blood?

Slowly she turned back around and faced him and when she did she faced herself. She began in a low, halting voice as she took him back with her to where it all began. Nearly an hour later Suki concluded her story.

"This is all I have…my son. I know you may never forgive

me for the choice that I made, but at eighteen I believed there was no other way. Your father was already married. What was I to do?" She reached out to touch him, but halted, unsure of his reaction. "All I ever wanted for you was the best of everything. That would have never happened here. You have grown and prospered well."

He thought he would somehow feel better to finally hear her admit that she was his mother, that she'd given him up to pursue her life. But he didn't. All he felt was a different degree of loneliness.

"I know you may not think much of me, or the choices that I made. But…I…did it because…I loved you, Mioki."

Maxwell's head snapped in her direction.

"Yes, that was the name I'd given you when you were born."

Maxwell felt as if a dam had burst. Slowly the missing pieces of his life slipped into place like a Rubik's cube.

"Mother," he uttered in a ragged whisper.

"Son." She stretched her arms out to him and he walked into her embrace.

Inch by inch he felt the void begin to fill and he let himself become engulfed in its comforting warmth.

Sukihara was the first to break the tenuous contact. A soft smile lighted her lips. "I'm glad you came, Mioki. A great burden has been lifted from my spirit." She bent her head and slipped her hand inside her pocket, extracting a small, worn black-and-white photo. Almost reverently she handed it to him.

Maxwell stared down at the photo of his mother looking adoringly up at his father.

"I want you to have it so that you will always know that you were born out of a great love." She took a deep breath. "I need you to know this, because I must ask you a great favor."

Maxwell tore his gaze away from the photo and looked down into his mother's dark eyes. "Ask me."

"I must ask that you not…reveal our relationship."

Maxwell felt as if he'd been kicked in the stomach, all of the wind gushed out of him at once, but he did not speak. He couldn't.

"Murayama would never…"

"Please, don't say any more." Maxwell turned way and picked up his overcoat from the chair. His jaw flexed as he turned dark, dangerous eyes on her. "I suppose the lies will never end, will they…Mother?" With that he brushed past her and strode out the door, still clutching the photo in his fist.

"Oh, Max, I'm so sorry," Reese uttered, his pain reflected in her voice.

He turned away from her touch as if burned. "It doesn't matter," he responded in a deadly calm. "I found out what I wanted to know." He flashed her an unreadable look. "Thank you for all of your help. We're leaving on the next flight out. My business here is finished."

"Max. Don't do this."

"Don't do what?" he boomed, his voice jettisoning out of the monotone he'd maintained for the past hour.

"Blame me, because that's what you're doing."

"Your instincts are all wrong, Ms. Delaware." He spun away and strode off into the bedroom, slamming the door behind him.

Reese shut her eyes and tilted her head toward the ceiling. "We'll get past this," she whispered. "We will."

Releasing a weary breath, she opened her eyes, letting them sweep the room. Automatically she picked up Maxwell's overcoat to hang it up when she saw the tip of a photograph peeking out from his inside breast pocket. Sure that it must be the same photo he'd told her about, she pulled it out and stared at the unmistakable face of the man she'd seen the night before her parents were killed.

That night, in horrific clarity, the final pieces fell unrelentingly into place.

Chapter 35

Chicago/New York/Virginia

It took two days before they were able to get a return flight to New York. During those two days, Maxwell had completely shut Reese out. He refused to talk, saying that everything was fine. He wouldn't touch her even in the most platonic of manners. And inside, Reese felt like parts of her were slowly dying, like a plant without water. He had isolated her, and he couldn't have done more to hurt her if he'd cut out her heart.

He had withdrawn so far within himself that he was totally oblivious to what Reese was going through. From the moment she'd seen the picture her mind had been assailed with ragged images slowly taking shape. It got so bad that even when she was awake the images intruded like a heavy cloak dropped in front of her line of vision.

She was afraid to sleep, afraid to be awake. And she

realized that she was painfully alone. Neither of them seemed to be able to help the other. It was almost like a self-fulfilling prophecy. As much as they'd said they would not let whatever they found out come between them, no matter how devastating, they had. And that pain was more than she could endure.

Unknown to Max, Reese had made arrangements to take a connecting flight directly to Chicago from Kennedy Airport. She saw no point in dragging out the inevitable.

"I have a driver waiting. As soon as the bags come down we can go. I had my town house opened. You can stay there until you're ready to…go back to Chicago."

Reese raised her chin and stared directly into those eyes that had the power to make her weak with wanting. "I am ready to go, Max," she said in a steady voice that surprised her. "I'm catching my flight to Chicago in a half hour." She pulled her cream-colored cashmere coat tighter around her body from the sudden chill that tore through her.

How could he tell her how much he wanted her to stay, knowing that this time for them to pick up their lives would eventually come? He'd been a fool to think she'd give up her life and her home to make one with him. There were so many things he'd been struggling with over the past few days. He knew he'd been distant and difficult. He'd spurned her attempts of any type of comfort or affection, simply because he needed to prepare himself for this moment. He needed to reach inside of himself to find some sort of balance and while doing that, he couldn't take her on that trip as much as he wanted to. But he could have never imagined it would hurt this deeply. Yet he understood.

It seemed as if the lights went out in his eyes and for the barest moment she faltered, her resolve to leave him weakening, until he spoke.

"That's probably the best thing," he answered matter-offactly. "We both have a lot to do. It was presumptuous of me to make plans for you."

Reese pushed down the knot of pain that rose from the pit of her soul. "You're right." She gave him a tight smile and pulled her defenses around her like a wool blanket.

His bags came around on the carousel and he pulled them off. He turned toward her still form. She looked so vulnerable, so in need. But he must be mistaken. "Call me when you get in. Will you?"

"Yes," she said in a thready whisper.

He leaned down and placed a feather-light kiss on her lips, making her heart flutter with desire. Reluctantly he pulled away and silently prayed that she would change her mind.

"I guess I'd better get going or I'll miss my flight." She blinked, fighting back her tears. "Goodbye, Max," she uttered in a breathless whisper. She didn't wait for him to respond. To hear him say goodbye would destroy the last shred of her composure. Swiftly she turned and hurried across the terminal.

"Goodbye," he whispered as he watched her disappear into the crowd.

For the first two days back in her hometown, Reese merely existed—she didn't live. She moved through life and her day on autopilot, remembering to eat, sleep and bathe when necessary.

Painstakingly, she finished the article on Max. It was the most difficult piece she'd ever written. Bringing him to life on paper seemed to bring him closer, and still he was a lifetime away. Through tear-filled eyes she wrote her closing commentary:

For too many years, Maxwell Knight and all he represents has been cloaked in mystery. He was the man the world wanted to know about. Who was this "boy wonder" who wowed the electronic world with his genius and his vision? The answer is simple. Maxwell Knight is not some exotic blend of fact and imagination. He cannot leap tall buildings in a single bound. He does not horde a harem of beautiful women in his state-of-the-art homes. He does not wish that he was just Japanese or just African-American. He is your boy next door, who grew into a man with dreams. He is a man who took his dreams and made them a reality, never letting adversity take his dreams away. Maxwell Knight is a man.

With a heavy heart, she sent out the package by Federal Express, knowing that Phillip was holding space in this week's issue, and tried to put the past months behind her.

She'd been to see Lynnette on her first day home and they laughed, cried, and laughed some more. Yet, for the first time in all of the years they'd been friends, Reese was unable to share the depth of her pain. All she did share was that her memory had returned and the impact of it had buffeted her between moments of extreme anxiety, to levels of exhilaration, and then plunge her into a bottomless pit of despair.

"Yes," she'd called her doctor, she explained to Lynnette. She was informed that it was to be expected and she needed to be seen and medication prescribed. "No," she was not going back under the microscope and "no," she would not live under the haze of Prozac or whatever it was they were prescribing these days.

She'd promised to visit every day until Lynnette's release and she even met the handsome doctor Adam Moore. She could easily see why Lynnette was in no real rush to go home.

By day she tried to keep herself busy, reading, walking,

cleaning. When she lay in bed at night, that was when the hurt was so heavy it was like an anvil resting on her chest. Foolishly, she'd thought she could handle it when she'd talked to him like she promised. But hearing his voice only made it that much more difficult. A chasm had come between them. It was as if each of them were standing on a frozen river, too afraid to move toward each other for fear of plunging into the black, icy waters below. And after that first conversation, she knew it would be too difficult to talk with him again. Both of them were trapped in their own worlds, wallowing in their own pain and disillusionment.

She'd thought that when the day came that her memory returned, she'd feel whole. He believed that if he were ever to find out the truth about his mother, he would be whole. But the reality was, it didn't happen for either of them. They should be sharing their joys and their sorrows. But they never would, not until they were able to heal themselves first. They were each other's half.

And on the third day, when Reese awoke, that reality enveloped her and soothed her ragged soul. She had to find a way to heal herself and when she did, she would go to Max and they would finish the process together.

For the first time in what seemed like forever, Reese's spirits lifted. She finally knew what she had to do. She needed to talk to Victoria Davenport.

Reese could barely hear the phone ringing over the thudding of her heart. On the third ring she was on the brink of hanging up when she heard the soft, southern cadence of a very feminine voice.

"Hello?"

Reese swallowed down the last of her apprehension. "Hello…may I speak with Victoria Davenport, please?"

"Who's calling?" she asked, suspicion lacing her voice.

"Reese Delaware." Reese heard the short intake of breath, followed by silence.

Finally Victoria responded. "Well, I wasn't expecting to hear from you. Do you want a story for your magazine, too? It seems every newshound on the face of the earth has either called or is camped out on my doorstep," she babbled nervously. She ran a hand through her hair. "So, Ms. Delaware, what can I do for you?"

"I...read the letter."

Silence.

"It's all very hard to digest—" she pressed on "—but I want to know the truth as much as you do."

Victoria lowered herself onto the edge of her bed. She sucked on her bottom lip, willing herself not to cry. The moment she'd lived for—for years—had finally arrived and she was at a total loss as to what to say. She wanted to rant and rave. She wanted to tell Reese how isolated she'd been all her life, how she'd been so jealous of her and her life. But now that the opportunity had presented itself, all the hurt and jealousy seemed to have vanished.

"What do you want to do?" she asked, surprised by the calm in her voice.

"I...was hoping that we could...work together, Victoria. Somehow, I feel certain the real answers will be found if we can find out how my father..." she swallowed "...our father died."

Victoria expelled a breath of relief. Her full lips trembled as the unnatural sensation of kinship filled her. "I'd like to find out, too...Reese. How can I help?"

Reese smiled and blinked back her own tears of relief. "Can you gain access to the Air Force's computer system? I'd bet anything that the answers are buried in the files..."

Maxwell plunged into his work like an Olympic diver jumping from the high boards. He spent inhuman hours working out the mechanics of an elaborate encoding chip. He met daily with the Board of Directors and the broker Harlan Black, preparing for their market launch. He went to the gym at night, or ran for miles around Central Park. He swam, practiced his martial arts—anything to keep his mind from Reese. After their initial phone conversation, he realized that the strain was much too great. He couldn't remain miles away from her and not be able to touch her, hear her cry his name in ecstasy, to feel her writhe beneath him, listen to her laughter and her wisdom, feast on her chocolate-coated beauty. He needed more than just an occasional call, visits on holidays and long weekends. He thought she wanted that, too.

He pushed himself away from his drafting table and arched his back. He crossed the room and stood in front of the floor-to-ceiling window peering down below. He braced the maplewood window supports that ran vertically along the smoked glass.

Even knowing how much he wanted and needed Reese, he also knew that he would be no good to her now. He needed time to adjust, time to regain the equilibrium he'd lost after meeting his "dead" mother in the flesh. He needed to be on top of everything within his company, and within a phone call away from the broker once M.K. hit the boards. Sighing heavily, he turned away.

He had yet to contact his father and confront him with his thirty-three years of lies. He was just not ready to deal with or listen to his explanations. It was enough that he'd had to accept the fact that she was alive and preferred to keep their relationship a secret. He slung his hands in his pockets. He had not spoken to Tasaka about the issue, not wanting his uncle to "lose face" by having to discuss such a personal matter, which involved his sister.

When everything was up and running with M.K.

Enterprises and Tasaka Industries, and when he found a way to do away with the emotional baggage that plagued him, he would go to Reese. He would make her understand that without her, he was nothing; what he had or could ever acquire meant nothing—not if she weren't in his life. But first he must bring order and harmony back into his life in order to make one with her.

Victoria sat down behind her desk in the small room she used as her home office. Years ago, because of her seniority and wizardry with the Air Force's computer system, most of which she designed herself, she had her system at home linked to their mainframe at the communications center. She'd been the one to set up the codes for access to various areas. She maintained her high security clearance in the event that any one of the systems crashed she would be able to get in and get it operational.

These were the skills and the tools she was banking on now. Through a series of intricate maneuvers throughout the tangled web of classified and unclassified documents, defunct departments that existed only within the computer's memory, passwords that had to be overridden by a string of codes—and all to be done without alerting anyone that she'd broken every security dictum ever written—she arrived at the location she'd spent the past four hours attempting to reach.

Taking a long shuddering breath, she picked up the headphones from the desk, put them on. Through her built-in modem she dialed Reese in Chicago. Reese answered on the second ring.

"I'm in," she stated. "I'll begin to download the files now." Rapidly she keyed in a sequence of numbers and immediately files, notes, and minutes from meetings dating back more than fifteen years flashed on the screen in succession. "Sit back and relax, this is going to take some time. I need to scan the files to see what's in them. There's no point in transmitting unnecessary data."

Reese's heart began a rapid rhythm as the first page glided through the printer. "Here it comes," she said with a breathless catch in her throat.

They were both seeing the information virtually at the same time. As fast as it came up on screen it was printing.

"Oh, my God," they both gasped in unison, watching the damning words scroll across the screen and onto paper.

Frank Murphy keyed in his password and accessed his archival files. He'd been removed from duty, the day the *Post*'s article hit the stands. But there were still several security personnel who owed him favors.

Frank's breathing pumped in short staccato beats. This was the only chance he had to keep himself from possibly spending the rest of his life behind bars.

After several moments, the files he wanted were brought up. It had been years since he'd looked at them. Even now, years later, the guilt of what he'd been a part of assaulted him. Yes, his actions had been sanctioned by the government. He was merely a pawn in the chess game of life. But he'd also had choices. His choice was to follow orders and move up the ranks. He pressed Delete as the first completed file scrolled along the screen. The next one came up. Guilt stabbed him again, twisting the knife a bit deeper. He stared at the orders to "remove all obstacles." He swallowed hard. That obstacle had been Hamilton Delaware, his best friend—his nemesis. His eyes burned with the memories. Again he pressed the delete key. The rest of the files contained all of the names of the parties involved, what their assignments had been, who was in charge of each phase, and the names of the Air Force doctors who compiled the data. This page he printed. He might just need it for insurance. Then he pressed Delete.

* * *

"Something's going on, Reese," Victoria blurted into the headphone.

"What?" Reese's pulse raced. They'd been caught, was her first thought. She sat up straighter.

Victoria's fingers flew across the keyboard, trying to bring up and transmit the files. "The files are being deleted."

"How?"

"Someone is in the system, taking them out. Someone with high security clearance." She tapped out the send sequence. "Are the pages still coming through?"

Reese's eyes shot across to the printer. "Yes."

"I'm going to try something. These files are coming down faster than I can send them to you. There's no time to read them first. How much memory to you have on your hard drive?"

Reese must have been asked that question a dozen times and she always felt like an idiot for not knowing. But the fact was, she didn't. For the most part, she really didn't care. All she needed to be sure of was that when she pressed the power it came on and that her word processing program worked. "I don't know," she said lamely. "It's a Pentium," she added, hoping it would help.

"Good. It should work. I'm going to send the balance of the files to your hard drive. I'll tell you how to locate them later." Victoria started the transfer process and Reese could hear her machine click and hum as it took in the information. "We're almost there," Victoria said. "Four more files to go." And then her screen went blank as *deletion complete* flashed like a strobe light. "Dammit!"

"What happened?"

Victoria let out a long frustrated sigh. "I couldn't get the last two. I'm sorry."

"I'm sure we have plenty," Reese responded. "You did

everything you could. I know I couldn't have pulled this off without your help. Thank you, Victoria."

"My time for doing the right thing is long overdue, Reese," she said, forcing a weak laugh. She paused for a long moment. "Now that we know what happened, what are we going to do?"

"Are you sure that no one can find out who tapped into those files?"

"Positive. This line is scrambled. There's no way to track it."

"Good." She released a sigh of relief. "I think we both need to look over what we decided, to figure out what we should do. All I ever wanted was the truth. This isn't a vendetta against anyone, except the darkness that has enveloped the better part of my life." Her throat tightened as a crystal-clear image of her beautiful mother kissing her good-night snapped into view.

"We'll talk again in a few days," Victoria said.

"Sure."

"And Reese..."

"Yes?"

"Thank you."

Reese's brow crinkled. "Thank me...for what?"

"For giving me a chance. For trusting me."

"Hey, whatever happens, we're in this together. Okay?"

Vicky blinked away the water that clouded her green eyes. "Okay."

Frank pulled the printed sheets of paper from the machine, folded them and shoved them inside his jacket pocket. He patted his pocket, shut off his computer and the lights, and closed his office door softly behind him.

"...After the disastrous aftereffects of 'Agent Orange' during the Vietnam War, the world thought we'd learned our lesson," Reese said softly. "And to think that the testing of chemical warfare was resurrected and tested on our own men again is too reprehensible to comprehend."

Reese shut her eyes and tugged on her bottom lip with her teeth. "My father was killed, Lynn, simply because he found out and threatened to expose what was going on. My mother was an innocent bystander. They were on their way to the Senate hearings when they…were killed."

Lynn reached across the metal rail and squeezed Reese's hand. "It's all right, hon, let it out."

"I…I remember everything, Lynn. They were fighting the night before because my mother'd found out that Dad was having an affair with her sister. She told him to get out and he begged and pleaded with her. I got so upset and I didn't want to believe what my mom was saying about Aunt Celeste. My mother was saying that when Celeste brought her car back that afternoon, she broke down and told her everything, even the fact that they had a child together." Reese turned tear-filled eyes toward Lynn. "Oh, God, Lynn. My Mom was so hurt. She was hysterical."

Lynn pressed her lips together unable to find the words to console her friend, her own eyes filling with tears.

"I ran out of the house. I was going to get my aunt and make her tell me that everything was a lie. I ran down the path from the house to the street and just as I opened the gate, I saw a man getting up from crouching beneath the car. He turned when he heard my footsteps." She paused a beat. "It was Max's father. According to what Murphy's notes said, James Knight was assigned to put a tracking device on the car that could be detonated by remote control." She swallowed hard. "When I asked him what he was doing, he said he'd dropped his wallet and he hurried off. I didn't have time to think about it because my mother and father came running out when they realized I'd left."

"What in the world did they say to you?"

"The things parents usually say when their children hear them argue. They tried to tell me it was nothing that they couldn't work out and they wanted me to go back to bed. They apologized for upsetting me…and my mom…" Her voice cracked. "My mom hugged me. She hugged me so tight that, if I close my eyes real tight, Lynn, I can still smell the White Linen perfume she always wore." Her voice wobbled like a warped record. "My dad called me princess and kissed my cheek." Absently she rubbed the spot. "I know they were up for the better part of the night. I heard their voices every now and then.

"The next morning, my mom told me that she wanted me to ride with her into Washington. We would drop Dad off and she and I would spend the day together so that we could… talk." She choked back a sob and swatted the tears away. "We…we never had that talk, Lynn." Her eyes clouded over as she fixed her gaze on the past, reliving the final moments with her parents.

"My father was driving and my mother was sitting very still in the front seat. We were just approaching the Fourteenth Street Bridge when the car started swerving. He couldn't get it to stop and it just kept going faster and faster. I heard him yell that the brakes weren't working, or the steering. My mother started to scream. I unfastened my seat belt to grab them just before the car slammed into the embankment. I heard my father say to my mother, 'I love you, Sharlene.' Then I remember pain, squealing, horrid twisting sounds, tumbling and falling. When I opened my eyes, Larry Templeton was standing over me. He picked me up and ran with me to safety. Then I heard the explosion."

"Why was Larry there? Do you know?"

"According to the files he was the lookout. When the

car approached he was to detonate the explosion with a remote."

"But he never got to do that."

"No. He didn't. And if it hadn't been for him, I'd probably be dead, too."

"That still doesn't explain why the car went out of control."

"I know. And according to the files it says that everything went according to plan. Apparently, James Knight's and Larry Templeton's superiors gave them credit for a job well done."

Reese plucked a tissue from the box on Lynn's nightstand and blew her nose.

"You said your aunt had borrowed the car the day before. Right?"

Reese's gaze lighted on Lynn's still bruised face. The question immediately intrigued her. "Yes. And what are you getting at?"

"Do you think your aunt may have done something to the car before she returned it? I mean, from everything you've found out and even according to Victoria, your aunt was obsessive about your father. If she did do anything to the car, she probably figured that only your mother would get in it. Your father always had a car pick him up every day."

The chilling possibility of what Lynn implied clutched her by the throat. Without much conviction she shook her head in denial. "She wouldn't…would she…her own sister?"

Lynn's eyebrows rose in speculation. "People have done much worse for a lot less, Reese. You know they say, 'hell hath no fury like a woman scorned.' If your father let your aunt know he had no intention of leaving your mother, and he obviously wasn't claiming Victoria, maybe she reached her breaking point. Maybe she figured that once your mom… well…you know."

Reese nodded and let out a long shaky breath. "She'll never admit to that. And at this point, it can't be proven. If anything, the notes point to the Air Force."

"You need to deal with her, Reese, whether she admits to anything or not. She needs to know that you remember everything. I think she deserves it after the hell she's put you through for the last fifteen years." Lynn rolled her eyes.

Reese crossed her arms along the bed rail and lowered her head. She knew Lynn was right. Nothing short of confrontation would exorcise her pain. What she didn't know was how soon that confrontation would come.

Reese returned to her apartment, bone weary and mentally spent. Her body ached with fatigue and her mind was on overload. All she wanted to do was soak in a hot tub and crawl into bed, keeping the world and reality at bay for at least a week.

She stepped out of her shoes as she entered her foyer and slipped out of her coat. Almost blindly she followed the path to her bedroom and stripped. Out of the corner of her eye she saw the flashing red light of her answering machine. Her heart did a quick uptake as she hoped that it was a message from Max. She pressed the play button and Victoria's lilting southern drawl filled the room. Reese listened with growing alarm, her fatigue waning like an ebb tide. As soon as the message concluded she called the travel agency and arranged for her flight to Washington. Then she called Victoria.

"I'll be on the 8:00 a.m. flight into Dulles. Can you meet me? We'll go together."

Maxwell looked up from the paperwork strewn across his desk in response to the light knock on his office door. He pressed the balls of his forefinger and his thumb against his tired eyes and massaged them. "Come in."

"So tomorrow's the big day, eh, boss," R.J. said, stepping in and closing the door behind him.

"Yeah. Have a seat, man. I'm glad you could fly down. I wanted all senior management and board members to be here in New York."

"I wouldn't miss this for the world." He chuckled. "Anything you need me to take care of?"

"No. Not really. I'm just asking that everyone be in the office by 7:00 a.m. I want to be able to put my hands on any given person at any given time." He smiled.

"You look tired, Max. That pretty lady reporter keepin' you up at night?"

Maxwell held R.J.'s gaze, not a flicker of emotion was expressed on his face. "Not at all," he said simply. "She was just doing her job."

R.J.'s left eyebrow rose a fraction. "Oh. 'Nuff said." He made a show of checking his watch. "I'm going to be shoving off."

"What hotel are you checked in to?"

"The Hilton on Sixth."

Maxwell nodded. "Don't forget to turn in your receipts before you head back out to the coast," he ordered, pointing a playful finger at R.J.

"You know I won't." He chuckled. "See you in the morning."

Left alone, Maxwell leaned back in the swivel chair then spun it to face the window. The night sky had begun to fill with twinkling stars. From his vantage point, he could see beyond the towering buildings of the Manhattan skyline.

Tomorrow was his big day. A day when he could see beyond just tomorrow—into the future. Tomorrow he would lead his company into a whole new era. He should be flying high—soaring above the skyscrapers—adrenaline pumping, mind sharp and focused. Tomorrow he should be sharing his success with the woman he loved, and he knew that he would not. The thought caught and lodged in his chest. He never got to tell her he loved her.

Chapter 36

Reese's flight from Chicago's O'Hare Airport into Dulles was a half hour late in arriving. She spotted Victoria in a stunning magenta suit with matching purse and shoes anxiously pacing the waiting area as she rushed across the terminal. Suddenly, she stopped short when Victoria turned and saw her.

Since the last time they'd met, their relationship had altered dramatically. They'd gone from wary contenders to possible half sisters. How did she greet this woman; the woman who'd also slept with the man she loved; the woman who'd put her neck on the line to find the truth?

Reese took a short breath and continued across the black-and-white tiled floors. When she reached Victoria, she did what came natural—she wrapped her in an embrace.

For the first few seconds, Victoria was totally taken aback by the effusive greeting. But as Reese's genuine warmth enfolded her she felt her resistance melt, and without even realizing it she was returning the embrace—and it felt good.

Simultaneously, they both stepped back and looked at each other with new eyes and smiled.

"Hi," they spoke in unison.

"My car is in the lot. Do you have luggage?"

"No, just my carry-on."

"Good. We'll go straight to the hospital."

"Have you spoken to the doctors today?" Reese asked, sliding into the plush mint-green leather seats of Victoria's Mercedes Benz.

Victoria angled her head in Reese's direction as she pulled out of the parking space. "They don't think she'll make it through the night."

They arrived at George Washington University Center in fifteen minutes and were ushered directly to the Intensive Care unit and Celeste's room. The entire atmosphere had an eerie feeling of finality. The two nurses moved around the motionless patient in silence, checking equipment and vital signs. The only indication that there was life beneath the white sheets was the steady beep of the monitor.

Together they moved closer, bracing either side of the bed. The nurses gave them both smiles of sympathy and left the room.

Celeste looked to weigh no more than ninety pounds. The rate of her deterioration was heartwrenching. Looking down at her frail body, both Reese and Victoria cast aside their anger and resentment. This was not the place to air their individual grievances.

As if sensing their presence, Celeste slowly opened her eyes. She looked from one to the other and her eyes filled. "I'm glad you both came," she said in a thready whisper. "I know my time is short and I can't leave this earth without telling you both the truth..."

Maxwell activated the tie-line between himself and his broker Harlan Black and his counterpart in Japan. The opening bell on Wall Street would ring in five minutes.

"We're set for one hundred thousand shares. Twenty each at the bell," Harlan stated. "The figures are already running on the NIKKEI boards. That's bound to be good for us here. Okay, get ready partner, here's the opening bell. I'll check back with you shortly."

As Maxwell watched the stock figures scroll across his television mounted in the wall, he felt as if he'd been running the New York City Marathon. A surge of exhilaration raced through him when he saw M.K. Enterprises move across the screen. Within moments, shouts of joy could be heard throughout the floor. Although each member of M.K. Enterprises was guaranteed one share of common stock, no one except the chosen few knew when this momentous event would take place. There was simply a short memo left in each section the night before advising the staff to gather in the cafeteria at eight o'clock where the television was set and ready.

"Looking good, my friend," Harlan said, calling back as promised. "Ten thousand shares have already been sold and the floor has only been open for a half hour." He chuckled, thoroughly pleased. "I'll keep my eye on things and keep you posted."

"Thanks, Harlan."

"No problem. I only travel with the winners. I'll give you a call in a couple of hours."

"Sounds good." Maxwell disconnected the line. A sense of absolute elation filled him. His dreams were finally coming together.

He'd built M.K. Enterprises from scratch. When everything that he'd worked for nearly crumbled under the government's accusations, he'd pulled himself up, shook off the dust and brought his company into the twenty-first century.

Day by day, he'd begun to let go of the fragile hope that he would somehow reconcile with his mother. He started to let go of the pain inflicted upon him by the lies of his father and the denouncement by his mother. He knew in time the sting of those betrayals would recess to a dark place in his heart, and he would move on. Through determination he'd overcome every other obstacle in his life. He'd overcome that as well. He also knew that in time he would have to get over Reese and he understood that would be the most difficult obstacle he'd ever undertake.

His intercom buzzed, startling him out of his ruminating. He leaned across the desk and pressed the flashing red light.

"Yes, Carmen."

"Max, Mr. Black is on line two. He says it's urgent."

Maxwell snapped off and connected with Harlan. "Harlan what is it?"

"We've got a problem, boss."

Maxwell's pulse began to drum in his right temple. "What is it?"

"I've been watching the boards. There's been a lot of activity from a single company, P.H., Inc. I never heard of them and I can't find out anything about them. They've already purchased ten percent of your company's stock."

"What?" Maxwell sprung up from his seat.

"You heard me. Looks like you're going to be in for a fight. Somebody wants in big-time and has the capital to do it."

"But why would…" He never bothered to ask the question. He already knew the answer. Someone who knew about M.K.'s move into the market had leaked the information and the recipient of that information was going after his company.

His mind began to race. Or was it someone inside? But who? "Raise the price by five dollars per share."

"That's what I was hoping you'd say. Hang in there, buddy. It's going to be a long day." Harlan clicked off.

Maxwell stood in the center of his office taking long, deep breaths. This couldn't be happening. But Harlan had warned him and everyone connected with the move, that no one was to breathe a word. The threat of a hostile takeover was very real if the information about M.K. Enterprises was leaked too soon.

He ran a frustrated hand across his close-cropped ink-black hair. All he could do was wait. Maybe it was nothing—a fluke—a...

Carmen knocked and came in.

"Sorry Max, but I thought you'd want to see this." She handed him a copy of *Visions Magazine*. "It came out last night. I picked up a copy down in the lobby on my break a few minutes ago."

Maxwell stared down at his high-gloss image, which graced the cover, save for the lead title which read: "Maxwell Knight Electronics Icon: The Real Story." He felt a deep sinking sensation in the pit of his stomach as if he'd just plunged from the apex of a roller coaster.

"Thank you, Carmen. I'll take a look at it in a minute," he said, his calm voice masking the unease he felt but clearly indicating that he wanted to be alone.

"Yes, sir."

Carmen turned, and just as she was about to open the door Maxwell asked, "Have you read it?"

She bit her lower lip before answering. "Yes I did."

Maxwell nodded. Staring at the bold black letters that

represented his life, he found his way to his desk and sat down.

The story was filled with compassion and an insightfulness that reached way down in his soul and touched him. Reese had found a way to be both factual and passionate in bringing his story to the public. Slowly his anxiety began to wane. He read faster, and then his eyes widened in horror. There, for all the world to see was the announcement of his company entering the market.

The pulse in his temple pounded harder. The sudden heat of fury roared through his taut body. She'd betrayed him. She'd boldly betrayed the trust he'd placed in her. His eyes flew across the words. The article also included the company's financial position and enormous money-making potential.

A freight train of rage burst through his veins. He threw the magazine on the floor. How could she have done this? The article opened the door to any high-rolling company or individual to get the edge.

Suddenly his eyes narrowed in concentration. What was the name of the company Harlan mentioned? He wracked his brain trying to make the name come back. He rubbed a hand roughly across his face. P.H., Inc.!

He dashed to the phone and dialed Harlan's number. He answered on the first ring.

"Black here."

"Harlan, it's Max. Listen I think I know who's making the move. Phillip Hart of *Visions Magazine*."

"Well, Mr. Hart is still in the game. He just bought another five percent. That brings it to fifteen."

"Raise the price."

"I suggest that I set up an offshore account for you immediately. M.K. Enterprises can't buy chunks of its own stock, but we can set up countermeasures—your dummy company can. Then you simply transfer it back later or buy it back on the block."

"Do it."

"How much liquid capital do you have?"

"As much as it takes."

"I'm on it. I'll get back to you within the hour." He paused. "They just bought another five."

Maxwell's heart thundered. "Buy twenty shares immediately."

"Done."

Maxwell paced, his mind swirling with dangerous thoughts. She'd used him. Just like Victoria'd used him. How much did Hart pay her for the information? How much was it worth to her to turn what he thought they had into the possible ruination of everything he'd worked for?

She'd used her charms, her body, her ability to make him trust her against him. He knew he should have been cautious. He knew he should have listened to his instincts and kept his heart sealed. But he'd believed her lies. He'd fallen victim to her allure and now he was paying for it.

He turned hard, cold eyes on the skyscrapers that loomed toward the cloudless sky. He wouldn't let her win. He wouldn't start over again. And when he'd won the game, he would make sure that she paid for her betrayal.

Yet, even as the thought took shape in his mind, his heart was breaking in two.

Reese and Victoria listened in stunned silence as Celeste unraveled the most twisted story of jealousy and obsession.

She told them in macabre detail of how her hatred of Sharlene began and how from that day forward she'd vowed to take away everything that mattered to her.

"When she met and fell in love with Hamilton, I knew I had to have him. In the beginning, it was just to get back at her. But then, I fell in love with him. I wanted him to leave Sharlene, but he said he never would." Her light brown gaze fell on Victoria. "And then I got pregnant with you. I knew he would leave her then. But he said he wouldn't. I swore I would tell her if he didn't leave her. He told me he would continue to see me and take care of you if I promised never to say a word." She pressed her lips together as a wave of pain shot through her frail form. Breathless she continued, "I felt that if that was the only way I could keep him in my life, I would do as he asked."

"But...what about Frank? Is he really my father?" Victoria asked, her voice trembling with emotion.

Celeste shut her eyes. "Yes. I always knew he was. I was seeing them both." She swallowed. "Interracial relationships in the South weren't looked upon very favorably back then. We kept our relationship a secret, even though Frank wanted to come out in the open with it. When he found out I was pregnant, he was ecstatic, until I told him about Hamilton."

Reese looked away, unable to meet the pain in Victoria's green eyes.

"I wanted Hamilton so desperately that I maintained the lie. And he so wanted to keep it a secret that he asked his best friend, Frank, to help him." She shut her eyes, taking shallow breaths. "Frank loved me so much that he enlisted the help of his sister Faith. Between the three of them, they saw to it that my pregnancy was kept a secret. I was never close to Sharlene so when I moved away it was probably a relief to her. When I had you, Victoria, Faith adopted you and raised you as her own daughter. She was such a loving person and had desperately wanted children but was unable to have any."

"So you posed as my aunt."

"Yes."

Victoria turned way and moved toward the window. "How

could you have lived with yourself and your lies for so many years?" she demanded, her voice laced with an unbearable agony.

"There's more," she said in response.

Victoria spun around. "What more could you have possibly done?"

Reese felt a hot flush spread through her limbs. Would she admit the awful truth?

"There came a point when I couldn't live with it anymore." She paused and took a long breath. "The day before Sharlene and Hamilton died...I'd borrowed Sharlene's car..."

Reese and Victoria listened in horror as Celeste told in infinite detail how she'd cut the brake line and emptied the steering fluid just before returning the car. Her eyes clouded over. "I...never thought that Hamilton...would have gotten in the car. He'd...never driven it before."

"You were responsible for their deaths?" Victoria's voice escalated to a hysterical pitch. "You murdered them!"

A lead weight settled in the pit of Reese's stomach. It was true. Her aunt had murdered her parents. But with that awful reality also came a sense of relief. Even though Max's father had been sent to do the job along with Larry, they had nothing to do with the outcome. Maxwell needed to know that.

"I was responsible for maintaining a cycle of jealousy all these years. I recreated my and Sharlene's relationship between you and Reese. I let the jealously fester and grow. I relished the fact that you hated Reese so much, simply because she was a product of love between Hamilton and Sharlene."

"But why? Why, Celeste?" Reese pleaded. "Just because you and my mother had a childhood spat at a birthday party!"

"No. It was much deeper than that. Sharlene was not my real sister."

"What?" Reese and Victoria blurted in disbelief.

Intimate Betrayal

"Your grandfather, Reese, Paul Winston, was married before he married your grandmother April. He was married to my mother, Della. Della never married my father and I don't even know who he is or was. All I ever knew was Paul. I adored him. I was his special princess. When Della died and he married April, we were a family again. I was the center of their world until Sharlene was born.

"She was their natural child, born out of their love. Day by day I began to take a backseat to Sharlene. I suppose something inside of me snapped the day of the party. I believed that everything that was important to me—my parents—Sharlene had taken away. I was no one, nothing. I didn't belong. And a part of me died, the human part, and the first time I felt alive again was when I fell in love with Hamilton."

Hot tears of remorse so deep and pervasive that they shook her body, streamed from beneath Celeste's closed eyes. "The lies must end here. I can't leave this life with the weight of my guilt." She looked from one to the other. "I don't expect the two of you to ever forgive me for all that I've done. I can't forgive myself. My only hope is that somehow the two of you will find a way to be there for each other. You may not be bonded as blood relatives, but you are bound by the ties of family, something that I tried to destroy by my own sick sense of values. You have a father, Victoria, and I never let him be that for you. And because of what I did to him, he took his hurt and pain and turned it outward. He's going to need you in the months ahead. I hope you can find a way to be there for him. He doesn't deserve your animosity." She turned to Reese. "I know I took everything away from you and even enjoyed the fact that even your memory had been taken. I can never make that up to you. But I am so very sorry, Reese. So very sorry," she sobbed.

"I may never understand the depth of your hurt, Aunt

Celeste, or what you have done. But I do know that I cannot let it cripple me any longer. I have my memory back, Aunt Celeste. I…remember them. I remember my life. I have that to keep with me always. And maybe you did resent me and maybe you…could never truly love me. But you did care for me. I know that, deep in my heart. No one who didn't would have seen to it that I had the best doctors, the best school, clothes, an education that couldn't be rivaled. I may not have had your love, but you gave me everything else that you were capable of giving. For that I will always be grateful.

"As much as you may have believed yourself to be uncaring—beneath all of your pain was a heart." She reached out and squeezed Celeste's hand, blinking away her tears. Finally she was free. She felt as if she were on the highest mountaintop seeing the world through new eyes, breathing in the clean, crisp air that swept away the darkness that had captured her mind and spirit. She was finally free.

Victoria and Reese stood facing each other in the parking lot of the hospital; their eyes saying all the things that were in their hearts.

Victoria stretched out her hand and Reese placed hers in it, then pulled Victoria to her. The two beautiful women, one light, one dark, hugged and rocked each other, their tears mixing together and cleansing them.

Celeste had simply closed her eyes and passed away, leaving them both with the challenge of forging a new legacy for themselves.

Victoria stepped slightly back and sniffed, emitting a nervous laugh. "I…only knew what it felt like to have a sister for a very short time." She swallowed the knot in her throat. "I'm glad now that it was you."

Reese stroked away Victoria's tears. "It doesn't have to take blood to be sisters or family," she said softly. "It takes a common kind of love and respect." She smiled.

Victoria's brilliant green eyes sparked with joy. "That sounds real good." She knew from that moment forward that her life would move on. Looking at Reese, she realized that even though she would always have a place in her heart for Max, she could truly wish happiness for them both.

Victoria'd said that she would make all arrangements for her mother and Reese promised to return for the services in three days, sooner if Victoria needed her.

As the plane soared across the sky, all Reese could think about was getting home and calling Maxwell. She needed to hear his voice again. She needed to tell him that she didn't want to live without him, that he was the most important person in her life and she didn't want to waste any more time. She needed to tell him that she loved him.

Maxwell had tried unsuccessfully to contact Reese off and on all day. He wanted to hear her admit what she'd done. His inability to reach her only gave more credence to his belief that she'd betrayed him.

He'd had to fight off frantic calls from Mioshi, who threatened to break the contract if Maxwell couldn't find a way to stop the takeover.

By three o'clock P.H., Inc., had purchased 35 percent of M.K. Enterprise's stock. Harlan had set up the alternative account and had held P.H., Inc., off by buying 40 percent and transferring it to the new account offshore. It was costing Maxwell a fortune and as it stood now, he was out of liquid capital. If P.H., Inc., went for the big push, M.K. Enterprises would be ruined.

His phone rang and he snatched it off the cradle. "Yes," he barked into the phone.

"It's Harlan. Listen, there's just twenty percent of shares left. Hold on…five percent just got purchased. There's still fifteen. If P.H. buys it, they will be majority stockholders in your company. A hostile takeover will be inevitable. What do you want me to do?"

"Raise the price to fifty."

"I hope that does it. The increases haven't stopped them so far. I'll put it in pronto." He paused. "Are you a religious man, Max?"

"Why?"

"Because I think you'd better throw up a prayer or two." He clicked off.

Absently Maxwell hung up the phone and squeezed his eyes shut. For several moments he sat perfectly still in silent meditation, purging his mind and spirit of the corrosive energy that was poisoning him. The soft knock on the door brought him fully alert. He swiveled his chair in the direction of the door, just as Carmen came in.

"Max. I brought you something to eat," she said placing a tray on his desk. "You haven't had anything all day. It's nearly five. It's just a sandwich and a salad, but you need something," she insisted.

He gave her an empty smile. "Thanks, Carmen. Just leave it. I'll get to it." Food was the last thing on his mind.

Carmen eased alongside of him and placed her hand on his shoulder. "Everything will work out, Max. You've worked too hard for it to happen otherwise."

"Does the staff know what's gong on?"

"There's some buzzing but nothing substantial. I'm not sure most of them realize the implications."

He nodded his thanks. "Hopefully there won't be anything to alarm them about. So far everything is under control."

"And it will stay that way." She smiled. "Just have faith." She patted his shoulder in her motherly fashion and walked out.

No sooner was he alone again when the phone rang. He grabbed it on the second ring.

"Yes."

"It's over. The last fifteen percent was just purchased."

"Just don't tell me P.H., Inc., got it." Max heard the chuckle in Harlan's voice and the knot in his stomach eased.

"Then I won't."

Maxwell collapsed into his seat, threw his head back against the soft theater as a gush of relief burst from his lungs. "Do we know who bought it?"

"No. I could try to find out, but it won't be right away."

"Listen, you've done plenty," he congratulated. "And you know what, it doesn't matter as long as my company is safe."

"Sounds good to me. It's been a helluva day. I'm cutting out. I'll talk with you during the week. Congratulations on a fantastic initiation, my friend."

Maxwell chuckled. "Thanks, Harlan, for everything."

"It's my job."

It was after midnight when Reese dragged herself into her apartment. She couldn't even begin to put the events of the day together in her mind. Too much had happened. The enormity of the level of deceit was too much to handle. All she did know was that she needed to talk with Max and she wouldn't wait another minute.

Tossing her coat carelessly across the couch, she kicked off her shoes and carried them with her into the bedroom. She sat on the edge of the bed and stared at the phone. Taking a fortifying breath she picked up the phone and punched in Maxwell's home number. She bit down on her bottom lip while the phone rang.

"Hello," came Maxwell's groggy voice and Reese's aching heart filled with joy.

She swallowed hard. "Hi, Max. It's me, Reese."

Maxwell shot up in his bed, his heart hammering. His fatigue instantly vanished and was replaced with the rage that had simmered on slow burn all day.

"Reese." He snorted. "Your little plan didn't work. I saved my company."

She felt as if she'd been catapulted into the Twilight Zone. "W...what!" she sputtered, her heart beginning to race with fear. "What are you talking about?"

"Don't play the innocent waif, Reese. It doesn't become you," he spat. "You know what you did, and I, like a fool, trusted you with valuable company information. You sold it to the highest bidder. Tell me, Reese," he bit out in contempt, to mask his anguish, "how much did Phillip Hart pay you for the tip?"

Reese was so stunned by the accusation that she couldn't form the words to defend herself.

"Speechless? That's so unlike you," he taunted. "I guess you said everything you had to in your article."

Finally Reese found her voice. "I have no idea what you're talking about but if you think for one minute that I would sell you out, then you can just go straight to hell, Max! Never once did you give me the benefit of the doubt. Never once did you ask me anything!" she screamed in the mouthpiece. "You're so paranoid about yourself and your life you still think everyone is out to get you. Even me." Her voice lowered and she laughed sadly, because she refused to let him know that she was crying. "Everything between us meant nothing, Max. And do you know why? I'll tell you. Because you've learned nothing from all we've shared. And I feel sorry for you. I only hope that you'll find happiness with yourself because you're the only one who can tolerate you. Oh, and I thought you'd want to know, your father and Larry had nothing to do with my parents' deaths. Have a nice life, Max." She slammed the phone down so hard it toppled from the nightstand and crashed to the floor.

For several unbearable moments, she sat motionless on the bed. She was certain that at any moment torrents of tears would fall. But her pain was so deep, so complete that she was numb with the agony.

Two weeks had passed since Maxwell had spoken with Reese and every hour of the day of those two weeks, her condemnation rang in his head. Could he really have been so wrong? But fact was fact. The article was crystal clear and she wrote it. Yet she denied having betrayed him. The incongruity battled with his rational way of thinking.

Methodically he paced in front of his office window and realization finally struck him. He hadn't been thinking rationally. He hadn't since the day Reese Delaware walked into his life. Maybe it was about time that he did.

He crossed the room and dialed Harlan's number.

"Harlan Black."

"I need to run something by you."

"Shoot."

"Remember when I said I think I knew who P.H., Inc., was?"

"Yeah." Harlan adjusted his designer glasses and opened the two buttons on his midnight-blue Armani suit. He sat back, tapping a gold Cross pen on his desktop.

"An article was written in *Visions Magazine* the night before about our Wall Street move. How much bearing could that have had on what happened?"

Harlan didn't even have to think about it. "Not much if any at all. Perhaps for the last-minute shopper who wanted to try their hand at something new. There wasn't enough time between the article's release and the opening bell to mount the kind of attack we saw. Whoever P.H., Inc., is was knowledgeable long before then. They had time to check your financials, get background on you, your staff, your viability, make projections, meet with their members and a broker to plan. I can't see that happening overnight." He paused. "What I think you need to check, unfortunately, is your inside people. Whoever your enemy is, he or she is close. I would think it was someone who was promised something major in exchange for the information."

For the first time in two weeks, Maxwell began to breathe a little easier. The heaviness that had settled in his chest lightened. There was an enemy in his camp, and he was going to find out who it was.

Carmen knocked and came in carrying the dreaded accordion folder.

Maxwell groaned.

"I know you hate it, but it's the beginning of the month—bill time." She grinned wickedly.

"Thanks loads, Carmen," he dragged out sarcastically.

"My pleasure," she teased. Then on a more serious note she asked. "How are things going with your father?"

Maxwell exhaled a long sigh. "They're still investigating but it looks like they'll lessen the charges because he came forward. He will be dismissed from the Force, however, no matter what happens. Murphy's been indicted for his participation in the chemical warfare testing on the American soldiers and the attempt on the lives of the Delawares. But he's naming names. A lot of people are going down behind this. They gave Victoria immunity for cooperating."

"I'm so sorry, Max…about everything."

"I know, Carmen, and I appreciate it."

"Well, I'll be leaving shortly. If you need anything before I go, let me know."

"Sure thing."

Left alone his thoughts shifted back to his conversation

with Harlan. He had to find a way to discover who was behind the attempted sabotage of his company. Who had the most to gain? He immediately eliminated the Board Members. They'd stand to lose as much as he by a takeover. Moving mentally down the list of possible suspects he started with the managers and department heads. They were the only staff members who were privy, on a regular basis, to the financial reports.

He moved from behind his workstation and turned on his computer. Within moments he'd brought up the personnel files of the department heads at the three locations.

Hours later, his eyes burned with the strain of staring at the screen, and he was no closer to finding out anything than he had been when he started.

Frustrated, he shut off the machine and pushed away from the desk. "This is pointless!" he barked at no one. "I may never find out who did this or why." But the one thing that was becoming perfectly, painfully clear—it wasn't Reese, and he'd been a blind, arrogant idiot to believe that it was.

She was right, he thought. He hadn't learned anything. He'd let old hurts and mistrusts seep in and erode something beautiful. How could he ever hope to regain *her* trust? How could he ever hope to win her back?

He walked to his desk and picked up the folder, deciding to take the work home with him. At least it would keep his mind off of the fool he'd been. He took his pearl gray Versace jacket and slipped it over the pale pink shirt, tucking the folder securely under his arm. He switched off the light and the room was swallowed in darkness, just as his life had been since he'd pushed Reese out of it.

With a drink in his left hand, his calculator at his right, Maxwell methodically went over the bills. He'd successfully gotten through the myriad office-supply bills and signed the checks for payment. He was holding off the phone bills for last. It was the one job he hated most. With the countless phone lines, extensions, and fax numbers, sifting through the phone bills was equivalent to running the gauntlet.

The New York office was the easiest, so he started there first, making sure that all personal checks for long-distance calls were attached as Carmen had indicated.

One number was flagged several times with the Chicago exchange. His stomach did a little flip. It was the number to *Visions Magazine*. He remembered it because he'd had to contact Phillip Hart. He forced his eyes to continue down the page. Finally, he tallied up the New York bills and wrote the approval for payment. Then he moved on to the L.A. office bills, which were always a mess. He knew he had to go through each one with a fine-tooth comb, because Carmen refused to do it, saying that "cruel and unusual punishment" was not in her job description.

After about ten minutes, he realized that the same Chicago number was on the L.A. bills. He brushed it off at first, attributing the calls as being made by Reese. But something didn't sit right. He took a second look.

The phone line where the calls originated was not his office phone. He checked the directory just to be sure. Yes. It was R.J.'s private line. He frowned and looked away from the papers and figures in front of him, staring off at some unseen point across the room, his mind racing.

Maybe Reese called her office from there. She had been in R.J.'s office during her visit. His breathing deepened as he sought the elusive answer that fluttered in the back of his subconscious. Then it came to him. He checked the dates. March fourth. He and Reese hadn't arrived in L.A. until the twentieth.

His jaw clenched. His dark eyes narrowed as the harsh reality settled and took shape. But he had to be sure. He'd already been too quick to judge. He wouldn't make that same mistake twice.

Quickly he pushed away from the table and went to his files. He diligently maintained copies of all bills for three months, which he kept at home. Carmen kept all the originals for a year for audit and tax purposes. Bending down, he pulled open the small oak file cabinet that fit neatly beneath his computer station. He found the phone bill files and pulled them out, spreading the contents on the desk. He compared travel expenses, employee records, and vacation and company loan requests.

Page by page the hard truth slapped him, and a sick sensation rose from the pit of his stomach and burned his throat like acid.

The offices were abuzz for weeks after R.J. was terminated. The day that Maxwell fired him, he couldn't believe the things R.J. said to him. Reese had been right all along. R.J. was jealous of him and he felt that he was just as brilliant as Maxwell but was never given the chance. When his gambling debts became insurmountable, he found a way to kill two birds with one stone. Hart had promised him a top position with the company that he'd formed three years earlier. He'd been parlaying his money from the magazine, making wise investments, and had heavy backers. He also knew how to turn one dollar into a hundred, by loan sharking, which was how he'd gotten R.J. by the short hairs. They'd been gambling buddies since college. The difference between them was that Phillip Hart knew when to stop. Unfortunately, Hart would never get the opportunity to spend any of the money he'd made off of the stock market. All of his money would be going to pay lawyers. He was charged with extortion and his company was under investigation by the FTC.

Visions was being totally restructured and was under new management. Where did that leave Reese? Maxwell wondered.

* * *

Since her article on Maxwell had appeared, she'd been inundated with calls and letters from every newspaper and magazine across the country to do major features on the elusive elite. But her major concentration at the moment was her current project. She was commissioned by the *Washington Post* to do an exposé on the U.S. military and their involvement with chemical warfare testing. Her focus was the "code of honor" among the U.S. government forces, which compelled its members to perform and engage in heinous acts for the sake of a "code." As painful as it was to write, it was her way of paying homage to her parents, in the vague hope that their deaths would not have been in vain, while exposing the inner workings of a frightening system. There was already talk of a Pulitzer Prize for Journalism, but those accolades did not faze her. Her work had been a catalyst for so many things: the recovering of her memory, the uncovering of more than three decades of lies and betrayals, and the forging of a new and growing friendship with Victoria, whose help was immeasurable. And mostly it had been the starting point for the beginning of what could have been the one great love of her life. Instead, it was the albatross that had finally destroyed it. All of her genuine intentions to present to the world, a wonderful, complex human being, were obliterated by one simple sentence. Ironically, one that she did not write and that was only put there to turn the tables on her. She was expendable. What prize could ever compensate for all of that?

So, she continued to work, to accept assignments. In her work, she found the mindless solidity that helped to camouflage the deep despair of her loneliness.

She hadn't heard another word from Maxwell since that last fateful phone call, but she'd kept up with the trial of his father and Frank Murphy as it all became part of the saga that she was drawing out for all the world to see. But even as hurt and as devastated as she had been by Maxwell's unfounded accusations, she could not keep him far from her thoughts. The emptiness still pervaded her spirit. Her heart still ached during the long, lonely nights. And each morning when she arose, she wondered just how much longer the unbearable pain would last.

She uncurled her long, gray-sweatpant-clad legs and slid off the couch. Heading in the direction of her small lemon-yellow kitchen to fix a light snack, she was stopped midway by the ringing of her doorbell.

Sucking her teeth, she went to the door and checked the peephole. She groaned aloud when she saw the Federal Express agent. "Another assignment."

"Just a moment." She opened the door and signed for the package.

Closing the door behind her she flipped the thick envelope over to see who the sender was. She couldn't have been more surprised if it had come from the president himself. But absolute astonishment took hold when she opened the package and viewed the contents. In it, was a letter from Sukihara along with the transfer of fifteen percent of M.K. Enterprises stock from her to Reese. There was another sealed envelope addressed to Max, which according to the letter written to Reese, should be given to him when Reese thought the time was right. "When the time was right," she said in a soft faraway voice. "When will that ever be?"

Chapter 37

It had taken much longer than he'd wanted to settle his business and get operations up and running in Tokyo. Mioshi had assembled a top-notch team to open the site and Maxwell was confident that within the year the joint venture between his company and Mioshi's would show a solid profit.

Since R.J.'s termination, Maxwell had promoted Glen Hargrove to his position to run the L.A. offices. Everyone was thrilled for Glen and he couldn't have been happier over his promotion or his move to the sunny West Coast.

As hard as it was for him to deal with, he'd accepted the fact that his mother would never be a real part of his life. And with that understanding, although it hurt him, he had discovered something more important. He'd struggled hard, but he had begun to reestablish a relationship with his father and promised to stand by him through his ordeal. His mother, Claudia, he finally realized was the real backbone of the family. What she'd endured for the love of his father and family gave him a whole new level of respect and admiration and yes love for this woman who raised him. Through her, he forged a different outlook on what family really was. Family was made up of those people who loved you. His natural mother would always be family, because he knew that she did love him as best as she could, and with that knowledge came a sense of peace. He also realized that who you were could never be dictated by the color of your skin, the slant of your eyes, the texture of your hair, or the shape of your nose. Who you were was the person you made yourself to be, the decisions you made, the road you took. And with that knowledge he knew that his restless search for his identity had finally ended and that what he'd been looking for had been inside of him all along. And it was time that he put the rest of the pieces of his life in place.

It was impossible to control the erratic beat of his heart as he pulled up in front of the address that Carmen had given him. For several breathless moments he sat staring at the neat little town house. What if everything he'd hoped for crashed down around him? It had taken him this long to be right with himself so that he would be right for her with no doubts, no reservations. But what if he'd taken too long? What if she'd moved on with her life and no longer wanted him in it? Could he blame her if she did after the atrocious way he'd treated her? He didn't know how he would stand it if she turned him away. Then cool, calculated logic set in. He'd never find out sitting in his car.

Stepping out in a single fluid motion, Maxwell approached the house, his bronze-colored maxi-length raw silk trenchcoat fanning out around his matching suit.

Reese had just stepped out of the shower, when off in the distance she heard the tingle of her front doorbell. She pulled her pale peach terry cloth robe from off the hook behind the bathroom door and tied it loosely around her damp body, which was beginning to show the early budding signs of life. The bell rang again. She puffed her cheeks and blew an exasperated breath. She was going to strangle Lynnette. She'd told her less than twenty minutes ago she wouldn't be ready for another hour. Her appointment wasn't until two and it was barely ten thirty. She knew Lynn just wanted to pop by early so that she could regale her with more stories about her incredible Dr. Adam Moore.

Since Lynn's release from the hospital, they'd become a real hot item, and Lynn never grew weary of telling Reese just how wonderful he was. Although she was thrilled that her sister-friend had finally found true love, a part of her was jealous of her joy. It continually reinforced how desperately she missed Maxwell and how empty the rest of her life would be without him to share in their creation.

The bell rang again. "Just a minute!" She snatched a towel from the rack, briskly rubbed her soaking wet hair, then draped the towel around her shoulders. Padding barefoot, she dashed down the short hallway to the front door. On tiptoe she peered through the peephole and her stomach did a dizzying somersault. She turned away from the door, pressing her back to it for support while she covered her mouth to stifle the gasp that rushed from her throat.

Panic, fear and exhilaration swirled like a tornado within her. *Max. My God it's Max.* She was trembling so hard and her heart was beating so fast she had to pull on some secret source of strength just to get the locks open.

They faced each other for the first time in nearly three months, but time and space seemed to slip away, passing through and around them like morning mist, as their eyes and their spirits crossed the barriers they'd erected and met in the place that only true lovers dare to go, deep in the heart.

How could she have ever anticipated the sheer magnitude of the joy she felt at seeing him again? His familiar scent, so earthy and erotic enveloped her, seeped into her pores, stole her breath. Her dazzling amber eyes snaked across his face, remembering the fine scar across his eyebrow that he worried when deep in thought. She traced the outline of the body she'd never forget, then back up to settle on his eyes that still glowed with a savage inner fire. Instantaneously, she felt the unmistakable hot yearning begin its steady pulse as if it had been only yesterday and not nearly three months ago.

Maxwell felt his throat tighten as he fought to find the words to express his elation at seeing her again. His heart filled, his pulse pounded relentlessly in his temple. She was more beautiful than his imagination could have ever conjured. The same haunting allure of her eyes, the satin smoothness of her chocolate-brown skin, the way her pulse fluttered with excitement at the base of her throat, still held the magic to make him humble and weak with need in her presence. What was even more captivating was that she seemed to radiate with an inner glow that was almost surreal in its beauty.

Cautiously, he reached out, needing to make physical contact with her, know that she was finally real and no longer the floating image of his dreams. The tip of his finger brushed her cheek and he saw her shudder as her lids slid shut then slowly opened to look up at him. Her eyes shimmered and he saw the convulsive motion of her throat working up and down. His hand cupped her cheek and hers captured his—holding it tight.

He thought his heart would explode. "I…have a story I need to be told," he began, his voice low and threatening to break. "It's about a man who found a wonderful woman and he wasn't wise enough to listen to his heart, who needs to tell her how sorry he is for the hurt he's caused her. It's about a man who's tired of facing the world alone. It's about someone who had one of the greatest opportunities in his life—a woman who was willing to risk herself for him—who battled her own demons and was still willing to fight his…" He pressed his lips together fighting back a sob. His nostrils flared as he sucked in air, when he felt the hot trickle of Reese's tears run across his hand. "It's about a man who finally understands who he is and wants to spend the rest of his life sharing himself with that wonderful woman. It's about me, Reese, the man who never got the chance to say I love you…I love you…I love you."

In two short steps she was in his arms and felt for the first time in far too long that the world had finally settled beneath her feet. His arms locked around her and he buried his face against her wet hair, murmuring her name over and over again. She was home again. She was whole again. She heard his heart pound against her ear, in perfect rhythm with her own, and she knew nothing could ever be more right than this moment. She cried in earnest now, letting the tears wash away the bitterness, the pain, the loneliness so that there would only be room for the overwhelming love that she so desperately needed to give to him.

She angled her head back and cupped his face in her hands, staring deep into his magnificent coal-black eyes. Her full lips curved upward in that old seductive smile that he knew all too well. "I think I just may have some stories that need to be told as well," she murmured in that sultry voice that drove him crazy. Her eyes sparkled as she tugged him by the knot of his color-splashed tie. "Why don't we step inside and discuss it at *length?*" She grinned wickedly, and Maxwell threw his head back and laughed in joyous relief.

Before she knew what happened, he'd picked her up, stepped across the threshold, and kicked the door shut. His heated gaze scorched her face. "When you play with fire Ms. Delaware, you're liable to get burned," he taunted, instinctively finding his way to her bedroom.

Reese emitted a deep throaty laugh, remembering the first time he'd thrown down that gauntlet. "So, let the games begin." Without another word she gave the belt of her robe one good pull and the warm cotton garment fell open. She stretched her arms to him in welcome and he found *his* way back home.

Lynnette arrived about an hour later and rang the bell for a full ten minutes before she gave up and went to meet Adam for a late lunch. Maxwell and Reese didn't hear a thing except what their hearts and bodies sang to each other.

Epilogue

One Year Later

"Are you sure it's all right for the baby to fly?" Maxwell asked his wife for the millionth time.

Reese turned in her seat, pursed her lips, and narrowed her eyes. "I swear, if you ask me that question one more time, I'm gonna knock you right upside the head with Mikel's bottle."

Maxwell had to laugh, because the reality was, she would do it, right in front of all of these passengers. He settled back in his seat, keeping a cautious eye on his beautiful son. Every time he looked at him he still could not believe the pure awesomeness of his existence. He'd made a solemn vow to both Mikel and to Reese, as he stood in the delivery room and watched her bring him into the world, that with every breath he took he would always keep them in the forefront of his life, the choice that he made would always be his family first and foremost. If he made enough money to last him a lifetime, none of that could be more precious than his wife and son.

Reese took a sidelong peek at her handsome husband. The decision to make the trip to Tokyo had been a hard one for Max. She knew that. But she'd convinced him that the time to begin anew was with their son. She watched him now as he read again the letter from his mother, which Reese had decided to show him the day they'd brought Mikel home from the hospital.

My dear Mioki,

I am sure I will never be able to make up to your for the loss of our relationship. But I want to begin in some small way to mend the rift between us. I want you to know that I went to Murayama and told him the whole story. At first he turned me away as I expected, but he returned to me and told me that all of the years that we had been together I had brought him nothing but joy. He has asked me to marry him and I have accepted. I feel truly blessed, my son. I will start a new life very soon and I have you to thank—you and Reese. I have sent her something that I hope the both of you will use and pass down to children I hope you will one day have together. I was the one who bought the last fifteen percent of stock. But, of course, I do not need it. I have turned it over to Reese. She is a wise woman, my son. Do not let your pride turn her away. I hope that one day we will see each other again. Life is much too short to go through it carrying grudges and old hurts from the past. I hope that you will find a place in your heart for forgiveness and perhaps one day we shall see each other again. I love you, my son, Mioki.

Maxwell folded the letter and returned it to his breast pocket. He turned and looked at his wife who smiled knowingly. He took her hand in his and brought it to his lips. They were on a journey together, to heal broken hearts, join two cultures, share love, and begin a new legacy that would begin with their son Mikel.

A new beginning...

* * * * *

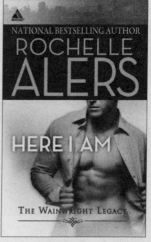

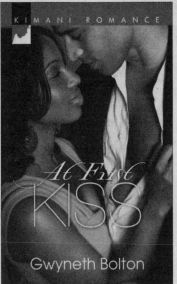

REQUEST YOUR FREE BOOKS!

2 FREE NOVELS
PLUS 2 **FREE GIFTS!**

KIMANI
ROMANCE ™

Love's ultimate destination!